HEADHUNTER

Also by Timothy Findley:

NOVELS
The Last of the Crazy People
The Butterfly Plague
The Wars
Famous Last Words
Not Wanted on the Voyage
The Telling of Lies

SHORT FICTION
Dinner Along the Amazon
Stones

PLAYS
Can You See Me Yet?
John A.—Himself
The Stillborn Lover

NON-FICTION
Inside Memory: Pages from a Writer's Workbook

HEADHUNTER

TIMOTHY FINDLEY

Crown Publishers, Inc. New York

All page references to Joseph Conrad's *Heart of Darkness* are taken from the 1974 edition published by Penguin Books.

Published by Crown Publishers, Inc., 201 East 50th Street, New York, New York 10022. Member of the Crown Publishing Group.

Random House, Inc. New York, Toronto, London, Sydney, Auckland

Originally published in Canada by HarperCollins Publishers Ltd in 1993.

CROWN is a trademark of Crown Publishers, Inc.

Manufactured in the United States of America

Library of Congress Cataloging-in-Publication Data

Findley, Timothy
Headhunter: a novel/by Timothy Findley.
1. Psychiatrists—Ontario—Toronto—Fiction. 2. Toronto (Ont.)—Fiction. I. Title.
PR9199.3.F52H4 1994
813'.54—dc20   93-50212

ISBN 0-517-59827-2

10 9 8 7 6 5 4 3 2 1

First U.S. Edition

This book is for R.E. Turner

*It makes all the difference
whether the doctor sees
himself as a part of the
drama, or cloaks himself
in his authority.*

C.G. Jung

There are great psychiatric institutions in Toronto, each of which offers excellent care and support to the mentally ill and their families. In part, this novel tells the story of what could happen if the wrong people wielded authority in such institutions. Both the story and its characters are fictional. Except for certain geographical, historical and architectural details, the portraits of the psychiatric centres in this novel are also fictional.

ACKNOWLEDGEMENTS

My thanks especially to Dr R.E. Turner, Dr Sylvain Houle and staff of the Clarke Institute of Psychiatry, Toronto; Dr Sam Malcolmson and staff of the Queen Street Mental Health Centre, Toronto; Diane Farris and staff of the Diane Farris Gallery, Vancouver; David Staines, University of Ottawa; Michael Peterman, Trent University; Ann Saddlemyer, University of Toronto; Marion Williams and her family circle; and, as ever, William Whitehead.

ONE

"...this also," said Marlow suddenly, *"has been one of the dark places of the earth."*

Joseph Conrad
Heart of Darkness

1

On a winter's day, while a blizzard raged through the streets of Toronto, Lilah Kemp inadvertently set Kurtz free from page 92 of *Heart of Darkness*. Horror-stricken, she tried to force him back between the covers. The escape took place at the Metropolitan Toronto Reference Library, where Lilah Kemp sat reading beside the rock pool. She had not even said *come forth*, but there Kurtz stood before her, framed by the woven jungle of cotton trees and vines that passed for botanic atmosphere.

"Get in," Lilah pleaded—whispering and holding out the book. But Kurtz ignored her and stepped away.

Lilah Kemp was a spiritualist of intense but undisciplined powers. She had once brought Teresa of Avila back into being and lost her on Yonge Street. The saint, in need of holy water, had stormed off into the Eaton Centre, thinking—because of its rising shape—she had found a cathedral. Worse things had happened. Jack the Ripper slipped from Lilah's grasp and killed two girls in Allan Gardens. Next, a woman named Rosalind Bailey got out through Lilah's mouth—which was not the usual path of flight—and gave birth to three deformed babies. Two of these were found in a plastic garbage bag on the grounds of the Queen Street Mental Health Centre. Both were dead. The third, in Rosalind Bailey's arms, was last seen boarding a bus for Buffalo, New York. Much was made of this on the television news and in all the papers. Lilah Kemp was named as next of kin, but Rosalind Bailey was never found. Now Kurtz was loose, in full possession of all his demons, and Lilah could not return him to the page.

She had not intended to call him forth. Her powers, she had thought, were dormant. She was sitting on one of those benches that broach the water's edge where the pool receives the waterfall. It was humid—almost equatorial—and Lilah had removed her winter coat. She had been reading *Heart of Darkness* since nine o'clock that morning—having begun her perusal of it in the newspaper room to the left of where she was currently sitting. She always felt safe in there because of the windows giving onto Collier Street. Moonmen wouldn't dare attack a person by a window. Not even during a blizzard. Windows were a godsend. They kept the visible world at bay.

No one minded Lilah. She had been coming to the Metro Library nearly every day since the Rosedale Public Library had burned to the ground and she had lost her job as its Chief Librarian. There were some, of course, who found her curious. The baby buggy didn't help. There wasn't any baby inside, but in spite of that, the buggy was her constant companion. It distressed her to leave it, as required, beyond the turnstiles in the lobby, but she accepted her separation from it without complaint.

Lilah was seen by many as eccentric, which she wasn't. Few detected the schizophrenic she was. Members of the Metro Library staff were used to the daily presence of any number of displaced persons who came in for warmth and safety from the street. Bag ladies, rubbies and dopers were tolerated to a degree. Moonmen and Leatherheads were not. In light of these others, Lilah Kemp and her baby buggy were worth little more than a tolerant smile. The incident with Kurtz, however, would change all that.

At roughly ten o'clock, and well into Marlow's journey up the Congo, Lilah had felt the need for some tropical atmosphere. This is when she had made her move from the newspaper room to the bench where she now sat, which gave her a view of concrete tiers and fretted light beyond the folds of the woven jungle. Pebbles flashed at her feet. She was lulled by words and water. In *Heart of Darkness*, Marlow had gone on foot in search of Kurtz. *I glanced*, she read, *casually into the little cabin. A light was burning within, but Mister Kurtz was not there...* Gone.

Lilah looked up.

The waterfall was making a noise she had not heard before—a roaring noise, like Niagara. A tall, pale man was staring at her. His hands were deep in his pockets and one of them withdrew a handkerchief with which he dabbed at his face. She recognized him at once, in spite of his dyed black hair—which might be a wig. It was Kurtz himself and he was watching her as if to see what she meant to do about his escape.

Lilah stood up. The roaring increased. Her head jerked back and she saw the roof above her begin to fall. *This mustn't happen here*, she was thinking. *I cannot bear to have it happen here...*

She forced herself to look at him. The effort was terrible. The power of his evocation left her quaking and her knees let go and she sat back down on the bench. "Don't," she said. But no one heard her.

Kurtz came forward—did he come through the water?—and stood beside her. She could smell him—the smell of old, dried paper was on him—and the smell of printer's ink and binding glue. He wore a pale grey suit, as pale and grey as his skin, and the shapes of his knees and elbows could be seen beneath the cloth. *Heart of Darkness* lay in Lilah's lap, open where Kurtz had been emancipated. She raised it up and snapped it shut in his face, as she might if trying to kill a fly. When she opened her eyes, he was buzzing still and wiping the palms of his hands with the handkerchief.

"Go back in!" she said to him. "They don't allow people out of books in here."

Kurtz merely smiled. "I don't believe we've met," he said.

"Don't try to charm your way into my good graces," said Lilah. "I know all about you."

Kurtz stepped away from her with what appeared to be genuine confusion. Perhaps he did not really know where he was. This had happened to others during their raisings. Some of Lilah's outcasts came a long way up through time and space to stand in her presence.

She was thinking of Otto, the arsonist, whose death had occurred in 1944. Otto, who burned books. The thought of him produced more panic.

"Return to your place!" she said to Kurtz.

Kurtz did not move.

Lilah stood up, meaning to force him somehow to be obedient. Perhaps if she used the book as a crucifix, the way an exorcist would.... She raised it over her head and held it out in his direction. Kurtz was startled enough to take a step backwards.

"IN THE NAME OF GOD," Lilah shouted, "GO BACK IN!"

Several people, laying down their books, stood up—alarmed. A bell rang. *Why? Was the building on fire?* Only a deaf man went on reading. Someone said: *oh!*

Kurtz moved further off.

Lilah's gaze wavered. Her heart raced. Her hands shook. She reached out to find support against a wooden truck of books. One of the books tumbled open. *Tropical Birds*. A parakeet was screaming. Lilah sagged. Another book fell. *Abraham Lincoln*. Shots rang out.

"Come back," she whispered. "Please."

But Kurtz was on his way. He turned and walked off. He was gone.

Lilah went after him through the pool. "Don't let him go!" she shouted. Aureoles of water splashed up around her. "Stop him before he reaches the street!"

No one could even begin to imagine what was happening. There was Lilah Kemp running after a man and shouting exhortations.

Kurtz went past, then, heading towards the exit onto Yonge Street. He was wearing, now, a tailored overcoat of soft grey wool and a Homburg—grey to the point almost of being silver. He also carried a briefcase. Black. He paid no attention whatever to Lilah. It was just as if she did not exist.

A blast of windy street noise greeted his departure. Feeling the draught, the deaf man looked up and spoke the required injunction: "be careful," he said. "It's a jungle out there."

Lilah watched as Kurtz was swept away.

*Yes...*she thought. *A jungle, now that Kurtz is in it.* Kurtz, the harbinger of darkness. Kurtz, the horror-meister. Kurtz, the headhunter.

2

The blessing of winter was that it reduced the number of deaths from sturnusemia. To date only fifty-five people in Toronto had died of it— less than in cities of greater size, but more than any other city in Canada. The deaths had reached their peak in July, when eight people died in one week. This had been during the height of the annual heat wave. Now, the coming spring—though some weeks away—was dreaded because of the expected influx of birds which carried the dis- ease—starlings, mostly—whose Latin tag had given the plague its name. Sparrows and pigeons were also identified as carriers, but none was so dangerous as the enormous flocks of starlings which settled in public parks and in the eaves of public buildings.

Early-warning alerts had already been posted—giant billboards spon- sored by the government, which showed a great, spring-naked tree whose branches were filled with birds. *IF YOU SEE THIS,* the billboard read, *REPORT IT AT ONCE TO THE NEAREST D-SQUAD.* The D-Squads (the *D* stood for death) would then cordon off the given area, moving in with tanker trucks and spraying equipment. Extermination procedures depended on weather conditions and the direction of the wind, but were otherwise swiftly accomplished. The D-Squads were so adept that within an hour or two of their arrival, the fires would be lit and the birds would be ash. This was upcoming. April would bring it. For now, the trademark yellow of the tankers was absent from the streets and the D-Squads' duties consisted mostly of going about from school to school, informing teachers and students of the dangers inherent in flocking birds.

Lilah Kemp had not yet encountered a victim of sturnusemia. The clos- est she had come to the disease had been at her bird-feeder, now illegal. But passing through the storm on the morning Kurtz escaped from *Heart of Darkness*, she came face to face with a victim whose telltale speckled skin gave him away. Looming up out of the blowing snow on Bloor Street West, a man of huge proportions passed her by with his clothing all undone.

"Wait!" Lilah cried. "You need help!"—but the wind erased her words. The man stumbled on and was gone. He seemed—though Lilah could not see his eyes—to be blind. His arms reached out and through the snow as if to locate some helpful landmark—a street lamp, perhaps, or a vendor's booth. His skin, all across his chest and forehead, was mottled—and his frame, while huge, was blue and wasted. Clearly, he should have been in hospital or under some restraint, but it well might be he had wandered out of safety in a demented state, or drugged.

Lilah turned back into the storm and pulled her tam-o'-shanter farther down towards her eyes. The wind made razor blades of the snow as it lashed against her face. She winced and spoke to the baby carriage. "Homeward bound," she said—and began again to push it forward.

So little was known and so much was rumoured about the plague, there was nothing with which it had not been credited. Lunacy, rape and murder had all been blamed on sturnusemia; loss of sight and hearing, impotence and miscarriage had also been named as side-effects. Two things were known for certain: in the latter stage of the illness, the victim's skin became speckled in much the same fashion as birds are speckled—and the brain was burned away by fever. Just as rats and their fleas had spread the bubonic plague, so birds and their lice—especially those on starlings—were said to be the universal carriers of sturnusemia—and thus, the terror of birds and the D-Squad extermination process.

Though the disease could be thwarted in its early stages with quarantine and massive doses of drugs, once the speckling began, death was certain to follow. Nothing known to science could prevent it. Clinics had been established and separate units in the hospitals had been set up—but a fail-safe procedure had not yet emerged. There was no panacea.

Lilah, however, was not afraid of sturnusemia. In this, she could count herself among the majority. Somehow, there seemed to be a secondary plague on the loose—one of non-belief. *This is not happening,* people said—*this is not plausible. We will wait for an acceptable explanation.* And yet, though no other explanation had been forthcoming, and even in spite of the mounting death toll, the population at large gave every indication of ignoring the threat of sturnusemia. This was not a unique reaction. In an earlier decade, the majority had turned away from the evidence of AIDS. Many were bored with what they claimed were *scare tactics.* Most were sceptical—others were incredulous. A very few believed—but neither belief nor incredulity prevented the disease from claiming its victims. It simply claimed them with increasing anonymity. The truth was, most eyes would open too late on a world without birds and a city under siege. But that was not now—that was later, much later, after Kurtz and after Lilah Kemp.

Lilah lived off the laneway that runs behind Lowther Avenue. She had rented a small apartment there in the days before her mind had given over, and what she called her *stipend* allowed her to remain there even after fire had forced her to give up her job as a librarian. Now almost forty, she had been thirty-five years old when she was *claimed*—the word she preferred to describe the onslaught of her condition.

Traces of Lilah's schizophrenia could be said to have appeared in earlier, younger behaviour—the emotional range of her enthusiasms—the mania for books—the abhorrence of darkness. But there had been no incidence of overt psychosis. She was seen in the past as a woman with fervid but disciplined inclinations. If she read all night, for instance, the following day was not given over to sleep. She was never late for work on a single occasion.

Lilah's seminars at the Rosedale Public Library—given on Thursday evenings—had been popular because, in the course of them, she imparted an evangelical passion for literature. In her decline, however, these passions had become so overstated she had more than once been laughed at. Her patrons no longer trusted her judgment and their seeming indifference caused her to wander from the given track of her notes. What began as a talk on *One Hundred Years of Solitude* would become a discourse on army ants, ponchos or madonnas. Lilah would lower her voice so that no one could hear what she said. One day, however, she broke all at once from her whispers and shouted out: *Heathcliff hath murdered sleep!* and the Thursday-night group sat frozen in terror. The seminars were cancelled and Lilah was advised to seek help. In time, she was committed to the Queen Street Mental Health Centre with a diagnosis of severe schizophrenia. But this was after her encounter with Otto, the arsonist, and the Rosedale Public Library had been burned to the ground.

Lilah now crossed over the snow with her baby carriage from east to west at the corner of Bloor and Avenue Road. For a moment, she paused at the windows of Edwards Books. Moonmen had recently staged a riot on the sidewalk here and one or two policemen had been thrown against the glass. Lilah stared in past the tape and the shatter patterns at what was on display. Art books and illustrated editions of children's classics. She dared not look too long at the latter, for fear of seeing the name of Walt Disney, whom she regarded as the patron saint of plagiarism. *Walt Disney's Alice in Wonderland*, indeed! It made her want to scream. Looking askance, she saw that John Dai Bowen had published another book of photographs—this one showing the Wylie girls on its cover.

The Wylie girls were well known to some—but John Dai Bowen's portrait of them was famous and known to everyone. It showed the sisters as they were today in a context with how they had been as children—posing as adults in the juxtaposition chosen by some other, anonymous photographer whose portrait of them hovered in the background. Three young girls and three grown women, lit with Bowen's trademark skill, the Wylies and their childhood ghosts were shown to be creatures of extraordinary beauty, seemingly aloof from one another—utterly aloof from strangers. Lilah had known them once—though she had been an outcast then, already moving in the shadow of her mother's scandal.

Lilah looked away.

She turned the buggy northward—passing Prince Arthur and Lowther avenues, cutting sideways through the falling snow when she came to Lapin Lanes. The plough had gone through before her earlier that morning, knocking all the garbage cans about while clearing the snow away. The baby buggy jumped and jangled. Its contents stirred.

Linton, I am sorry.

Lilah shut her eyes and pushed on down the lane to the gate for number 38-A. There, she came to the familiar smell of Mrs Akhami's cooking oil and opened her eyes. Mrs Akhami lived in the house directly across from the gate and her kitchen window looked out onto the laneway from beyond a high board fence. Lilah noted that, even in spite of the blizzard, several cats were huddled in anticipation of Mrs Akhami's generosity. Not that such generosity existed. Mrs Akhami did not believe in feeding cats—but she tortured them still with her tantalizing cuisine.

Lilah, walking backwards, dragged the baby buggy past the gate beneath the trellis and went along the walk. She administered the key one-handed and gave the door to her private world a push with her elbow.

Home.

The little hall lit up with warmth. The storm and its noise were shut away outside. Silence drew in where Lilah stood and she heard the mice in the walls give a welcoming cheer.

She sat in Hamlet's chair and drew off her tam-o'-shanter. Burgundy-coloured and dusted with snow. Her hand automatically went up to prevent her hair from escaping—a gesture that was known to anyone who encountered her more than once. Lilah Kemp had crazy hair. Parts of it wouldn't lie down at all and crept out from under her tam, no matter how firmly she pulled it down. Even when sprayed, the hair got right back up and stood there bouncing and waving at the mirror, leaning forward as if it wanted to see into Lilah's face or look into her ears. Her hair was more like a garden sprouting from her scalp than whatever other people had—the stuff they used to call *a woman's crowning glory*. Lilah's crowning glory was the tam-o'-shanter, pulled on every morning to keep her hair at bay.

House, she almost said aloud, *I have let Kurtz out into the world from Heart of Darkness—and I don't know where to find him...*

She rose from the chair and removed her gloves and her coat and threw them onto the floor. She turned then towards the baby carriage.

"You," she said, "must be tired unto death."

There was no reply.

Lilah bent down and pushed her canvas bags of books aside and reached in under the blankets.

There it was—safe and sound and warm in spite of its ride through the storm. *Wuthering Heights*—in blue.

She kissed it and held it up to her cheek.

"You must be exhausted," she said.

There was no reply.

Lilah went into her tiny kitchen after that and took a pill.

It is not every day that a person gets the chance to change the course of human affairs. It was not a sensation Lilah Kemp appreciated. She sat there very still and prayed that Kurtz would go away. But Lilah's prayers had a bad reputation. They were never answered.

3

Later that afternoon, in the reading room on the second floor of the Metro Library, a young man whose name was Calvin Davidson was clearing the tables of books and papers. This was his job—to throw unnecessary things away and return the books to their shelves.

Right at the centre of one of the tables, a number of books and periodicals had been left by that man with the dyed black hair. Calvin Davidson remembered him clearly because he had been the first person into the library that morning—and the first to whom Calvin had delivered books from the stacks. *The Will and the Way*—Knott's *Treatise on Sleep*—Folger's *Pharmacopoeia*—others. Calvin now placed them all in his cart and swept several pieces of scrunched-up paper into his portable garbage unit. Many scribblings—much, much waste. Calvin moved on.

Unnoticed beneath the wheels of his cart, an envelope had fallen from one of the books. It was a plain white legal-sized envelope of excellent quality and weight, densely packed with a number of pages of lined, folded paper. These, if Calvin Davidson had been inclined to look, were covered with the same fine script that had adorned the waste bits of paper where Folger's *Pharmacopoeia* had lain. Clearly printed on the back of the envelope was the name *Kurtz*. But there was no address and no other indication of identity.

Inside the envelope, Calvin might have read the words: *Towards Sleep—and Afterwards*. But he would not have understood this title, since sleep was not the true subject of the notes that were written there. These would not be understood by many, in fact, until the author had completed his present research. Which is what Rupert Kurtz had been doing in the Metropolitan Toronto Reference Library on the morning of March the 5th—a Monday—while it snowed.

4

By the middle of March, Olivia Wylie—married to Griffin Price—had still not told anyone she was pregnant. Nothing showed, but if her husband had paid attention, he would have known Olivia had failed to menstruate for three months. But men not greatly interested in sex lose track of such events in the lives of their women, unless it is drawn to their attention. PMS, for instance, meant nothing to Griffin Price. He had never heard of it—or had closed his imagination against it. *One of those feminine things a man doesn't want to know...*

Living in a separate bedroom—using a separate bathroom—Griffin was now approaching Olivia less and less because of his growing impotence—*one of those masculine things a woman doesn't want to know.* Olivia was not approaching Griffin at all. The Prices, in fact, were now merely living beneath the same roof and sharing the same social calendar. And the same foetus—though Griffin was not aware of this.

They were cordial to each other—loving *en passant*. They saluted each other in hallways and on the stairs. Griffin went off on his trips and Olivia continued teaching. She was increasingly paranoid about why he kept prompting her to do so. She was missing out on more and more journeys she had wanted all her life to make—and it seemed entirely possible this was why he was urging her to remain *one more year* at Branksome Hall. There had now been three *one more* pep-talks and, in the meantime, Griffin had romped off—ostensibly alone—to Austria, Bohemia, Poland and Romania. True, Olivia had made the summer journeys—but these offered none of the relief the others might have provided. Houston in July was not her idea of heaven.

Sometimes, Olivia found their situation amusing; most of the time it confounded her. Her dreams were bad. She never quite completely slept. The funny times were when she tried to imagine telling Griffin *we are going to have a baby.* These imagined conversations could not have been more gauche and awful if she had tried to write them for the movies. Other people came to mind to tell—her doctor, of course—her sister Peggy—one of the teachers at school. But, no. The telling had always been set aside. Olivia knew. The foetus knew. And that was the extent of it.

Consequently, one day in March, instead of going straight home from school the way she normally did, Olivia parked in front of number 39 South Drive—the Wylie family house. Branksome Hall, where she taught, was just around the corner. The Wylie house had once been Olivia's great safe place. Entering the past, she thought, could be the perfect way to get the present to stop. *And Mother would be the perfect accomplice.*

Number 39 South Drive had green shingled roofs that angled away from a central skylight over the stairs and this gave the house its charm. Also, its great tin gutters were set with ornate spillways and spouts: Chinese. Before Grandmother Wylie died, she was such a tremendous age her skin had yellowed and her eyes had narrowed. Olivia had thought she looked like the Empress of China. Old Mrs Wylie was carried everywhere, and this, plus the blue veil of cigarette smoke she hid behind, enhanced the imperial image. The house, with its swooping roofs and spouts, did the rest. It sat well back from the road beyond its lawns, in the shade of several weeping birch and willow trees. Its walk was made of brick and when they were children, Olivia's sister Amy had taken chalk and created the Yellow Brick Road to Oz. This transformation had not been popular. Grandmother Wylie took on the wrath of the Witch of the West and Amy was made to scrub away the chalk, brick by brick by brick.

At the rear of the house, the gardens fell away by terraces and wide stone steps to a damp ravine where there were pheasants, still—but no more songbirds. On spring nights and evenings, beginning just after sunset, the laughter of mating raccoons could be heard as far away as the screened-in porches, giving the effect of an unseen jungle down in the dark.

Olivia had spent every childhood Sunday afternoon in this house and this garden, always wearing an organdie dress and alternating pink and blue ribbons with Amy and Peggy from week to week, while her cousins—all boys—had come in neat scratchy suits that were always navy blue.

Sunday teas in the Wylie clan were a tradition unbroken until Grand-mother Wylie's death, when the last great tea was given in celebration.

Olivia's childhood had been lived at the very heart of Rosedale. South Drive was Rosedale's aorta. (Its vena cava was Crescent Road.) But the ebb and flow of its life was sluggish now—constrained and ill at ease. Newcomers—bearing gifts of money but none of taste—had come to buy the old houses, divide them up and rent them piecemeal back to the descendants of those who had been the original owners. The rents were exorbitant and sometimes smacked of a slap in the face—but that's what you got for being born out of time. Your name was often all you had—and the memory of place—and the absent shade of trees cut down in your exile. And of silent bird song. The D-Squads had been at work here, too.

In one sense, Olivia shared her sister Peggy's reverence for the past. One sense—but no other. She regretted the loss of beloved landmarks and people—the parks as they had been—the façades of houses now "improved"—the Rosedale Public Library, gone entirely—her father, Eustace Wylie; schoolteachers; dogs she had walked; neighbours. Others. But the past, in fact, had been a dreadful time—when everyone was lied to—much as they were lied to now, but then, for different rea-sons. In the past, you were lied to *for your own good*. Now, you were lied to for the good of others. Whoever these others might be.

Before she ventured to leave the safety of her car for the safety of the Wylie house that March afternoon, Olivia pensively finished her ciga-rette. It took her five minutes.

Every time you smoke one of those, you're killing me, you know.

The dialogue with the foetus had been going on since February 17th—the day Olivia first considered abortion.

Now, Olivia did not reply. As ever, she wavered on the brink of silence.

Eloise Wylie drank a bottle of Scotch a day. It rarely used to show till the evening came. But now, by late afternoon the effect was that of someone walking through a dream—coherent, comprehending, care-ful—but apt at any second to wake into panic. She had a live-in com-panion whose name was Nella Sutton. Nella sat in the kitchen playing solitaire and also drinking—but her drink was gin.

From time to time Eloise could not bear the loneliness of everyone's absence any longer and on these occasions Nella went up to her room, took off her blue smock, put on a dress (sometimes a hat), came back down and rang the doorbell. Eloise would go to the door, let her in and lead her, already talking, into the living-room where Nella would sit with her legs crossed, smoking Eloise's cigarettes, drinking Scotch instead of gin and listening while Eloise unburdened herself of all her troubles. At the end of these recitals, Nella would excuse herself, tell Mrs Wylie what a *nice time* she'd had and depart as she had come, through the front door. Then she would go around to the side door, let herself in—go upstairs— change into her smock and come down into the kitchen by way of the back stairs. Later, serving dinner—before she sat down—she might ask who had come to visit in the afternoon and Eloise would say: *someone you wouldn't know, Nell. Another perfect stranger.* They would then eat through the evening meal, play several hands of rummy and go to bed.

Olivia let herself in without a sound.

No one seemed to be about.

She stood in the hallway lit by the skylight, white in the mirror— wavering beyond the flowers. She wore her driving gloves and when she automatically lifted her hand to touch her hair, she wondered whose hand it was. The arm was lost in daffodils and irises. Obscured by ferns.

No one on the stairs and no one in the dining-room.

Through the arch, in the living-room, her grandmother's wing-back chair still sat in its corner. Waiting. If Lilah Kemp had been there, it would not have waited long. Grandmother Wylie was itching to come forth—but there was no one there to release her. Quite the opposite. There was an active campaign to keep her at bay.

"Mother?"

Smoke.

Olivia went in.

Eloise was seated on the piano bench with her back to the piano.

"I can't play any more," she said. "My hands don't want me to." Eloise turned sideways and touched the keys. One chord. A minor. "Schumann. You remember?"

"Yes. I remember very well," said Olivia.

This referred to the fiasco when Eloise had tried to master Schumann's *Scenes From Childhood* and failed. Aged sixty-two.

Eloise sighed and got up. She was wearing a handsome dress—her favourite shade of blue. No make-up. One piece of jewellery—a butterfly—and her hair had only recently been cut and restyled. It was swept back off her face—giving her a striking, hawklike appearance.

"If you're thinking of kissing me, don't," she said. "I don't want people touching me today." A mixture of alcohol and Estée Lauder drifted across the room.

Eloise walked in a more or less straight line to the sofa and sat down. Fell down. Taking advantage of the fact she'd ended up lying sideways, she pretended to plump up the pillows. Her bottle of Black and White and her glass were sitting on the coffee table. Also, a cigarette was burning—dangerously close to the edge of the ashtray.

"What do you want?" she asked.

"Just to see you."

"Hah!" said Eloise. "What do you *want*, Olivia?"

Olivia walked to the drinks table (more flowers—potted hyacinths) — got out a glass and poured herself some gin and vermouth.

"Don't tell me you've started drinking," said Eloise.

"Yes. Good heavens—why is everyone so surprised?"

"Olivia has always been Olivia—till now."

"Oh, come on."

"Well, she *has*." Eloise gave her a knowing look. "It's the company of teachers, that's what it is. I've always known that. Teachers are a drunken lot..." If Olivia had been a doctor, Eloise would have said that doctors were a drunken lot. Or garbage men or waitresses. "And Griffin? How is he?"

"Fine."

"Is he at home for a change?"

"Now, Mother..."

"Can't I ask you a question? Is he at home. Or off buying Europe?"

"He's in Prague."

"Yes—well. After all, it's for sale, now, isn't it."

"Griffin is doing well, Mother. Leave him alone."

Eloise put out the smouldering cigarette and lighted a new one. Her hands shook. "What *do* you want, Olivia?"

"Well...I was driving by. That's all."

Tell her.

No. Not yet.

Eloise looked at her daughter and put the cigarette lighter down. It almost fell off the table. She sat on the edge of the sofa, trying not to tremble. She wanted to fill her glass. Olivia could tell this—but Eloise was determined not to lift the bottle until Olivia looked away. Olivia thought how beautiful she was, with her powdered pallor and her white, white hair—and the eyes full of pain like someone condemned to death who won't admit she's afraid.

Olivia looked away and listened to the glass being filled. The room—the whole house—was full of forced flowers; beautiful but tenuous—straining forward on their stalks. Listeners—waiting. Perfect.

"I haven't heard," said Eloise, at last. "I haven't heard a word, if that's why you've come. So don't try to pump me. I haven't anything to say."

"What about?"

"Don't play games with me, Olivia. I haven't the patience. Everyone keeps waiting for me to explain. Well. I *can't*. How can I? They took her away—they put her in that dreadful place. What am I supposed to say?"

Amy—the youngest of the Wylie girls—had been arrested again for stealing food. Bird seed. Amy had now been arrested—but never charged—three times. She was known for her aberrant behaviour and was always referred to a doctor at The Parkin Institute of Psychiatric Research.

"She'll be all right, Mother. They only kept her there overnight." Olivia, in fact, had telephoned the Parkin that morning to check.

Eloise drank from her glass and stared at it dumbly—not unlike an animal hovering over its saucer of milk. "What am I supposed to say to people?" she said. *"She's mad—but she's mine?"* Eloise tried to laugh—but couldn't make it happen.

"It's no one else's business," said Olivia. "Pay no attention."

"I have to pay attention." Eloise tightened towards panic. "Someone has to say something. We can't just let it ride forever. Honestly—I get so frightened. I keep on thinking—what is wrong? What have we done? What are we paying for, all of us? For being born? For being us? Everyone else just sits there—smiling—placid—with their goddamn faces frozen. They haven't done anything. *They're* all right. It's me and you and Amy and Peggy who have to pay for this..."

"For what?"

"I don't know. Our blood? Our genes? I don't know." Eloise gulped from her glass and swallowed slowly. "People have no right to suddenly remove themselves from everybody else's life the way Amy has. With no explanation. Nothing. Madness is not an explanation, Olivia. Madness is... Maybe madness is just an accident. A gun that goes off by mistake. All her life, Amy has been firing at the sky. Aspirations. Isn't that what happened? You aim at the sky—and the bullet goes through your brain."

Olivia did not speak.

"After your father died we all knew why. We could all say—*yes, the War did that. He went away to war. It broke his spirit. And long, long after he came back to us—it killed him.* People understand that kind of thing. It's tragic—but you know what it means. *Look,* you can say—and you can even point to the map—*it happened right here. On a beach. In Normandy.* And the map is full of details—impossible landing sites— cliffs and gun emplacements. You can see what went wrong. Photographs will show you. You know what defeated him. Terror defeated him. Pity did it. All those dead young men. But where is there a map—where is there a photograph—something you can pinpoint for my daughter? For Amy. What impossible landing site? What gun emplacements? Where is Amy's map? Where is the photograph? Proof?"

Olivia still did not speak.

"I never used to be afraid," said Eloise. "I never, never, never used to be afraid. And now—I know that part of it is age—I'm over seventy. But the rest of it. Why should I be afraid of Amy—my own child? Of someone I love with all my heart?"

The afternoon began to wane. To darken. Neither of them turned on the lamps.

Finally, Eloise looked all around her and said: "it's beautiful, isn't it. Such a lovely house. I get up and go from room to room. I look at everything. And I think—that was a lovely table, wasn't it. Wasn't that a beautiful chair. Look at that vase—how wonderful it was." She sat absolutely still. "When am I talking about, Olivia? When was that time—and when was it over? I swear—I never felt it ending. But it did."

"You're alone too much," said Olivia.

"I want to be. Who is there left I want to see? Nella. My children. But you're the only one who ever comes here."

Children.

Olivia put down her glass. "Mother," she said, "we had a brother, didn't we? Who died before I was born?"

"Yes. Well. He died before *he* was born."

"But he did get *born*, didn't he?"

"Yes."

"Why did he die? An accident?"

"Why do you want to know all this? All of a sudden..."

Olivia lied. Partly. "Well, I was only thinking—you brought up the subject of children. Peggy—me—and Amy. Children. Just in general. And it reminded me..."

Tell her.

No.

"It reminded me—there are children who don't exist—who don't get born. Like my brother."

"He did get born."

"Yes. But..."

Tell her.

"He did get born, Olivia. The thing was—he didn't live."

"What happened?"

"They couldn't make him breathe."

"Was he called anything?"

"Of course not."

"Do you ever wonder...?"

"What?"

"What he might've been like. Don't you ever wonder? Who he might've been? When you think about him, what are you thinking...?"

"I don't think about him. Ever. Nothing sadder ever happened in my whole life. Except your father's long decline. I simply never think about him now—the baby. I wish you hadn't mentioned him."

"I'm sorry." Olivia got up. "But it isn't just idle curiosity. I really do want to know." She took her glass and went to get another drink. "Maybe it's all these deaths. AIDS. Sturnusemia. When anybody dies you think about the rest of the dead, I guess—stuff you don't think about when things are normal."

Eloise watched her and then looked away. "Things will never be normal again. Not in my life."

"You mustn't say that. Don't feel that. It isn't true..."

Olivia suddenly almost told her about the child—wanting to reassure her there was—or could be—a future. But Eloise cut her off.

"Damn you, Olivia, and all your questions. Why did you have to bring it up?" She filled her glass defiantly—right to the brim. "They didn't even bury him," she said. "He became a sort of specimen...or whatever it is they call that..." She looked at her drink. "A thing they looked at through glass. In a jar. Jar babies."

Dear God in heaven. Why did I make her remember this?

Because you want to know.

But I...

Listen. Nobody else is going to tell you this. So shut up. The foetus turned in its place. Olivia leaned back hard against the table.

Eloise said: "later on I thought: *well...I might as well have carried it for something*—seeing it might do someone some good. It hadn't any physical flaws, apparently. Perfectly formed."

It.

"When you were born—I hardly dared have you. But I did."

"I'm glad."

"Are you?"

Olivia did not answer that. She pretended it had not been said.

Eloise put her glass down and lighted another cigarette. The hawk-like profile was lit from behind, where the windows showed the garden under snow.

18

"Do you think your sister is permanently crazy?" she said. "Or just enduring another phase?"

"I don't know, Mother."

"All you want for your children is happiness. Nothing else. Nothing. And it's the only thing—apparently—we don't have the wherewithal to give."

Silence.

"Can you stay for dinner?" said Eloise. She seemed to mean this; it was not an idle invitation.

"No, Mother. I'm sorry. I'm taking advantage of Griffin's absence and having some people in for the evening."

"Oh? Who?"

"Fabiana Holbach. Warren Ellis. A few others. I'm not sure you know them. Fabiana is about to open a new exhibition at her gallery. I'm eager to hear about it."

"Isn't she Jimmy Holbach's wife?"

"Yes. She is, as a matter of fact."

"Whatever became of him?"

"He went off looking for something. No one knows what. And disappeared."

"Where?"

"Down in South America. The Amazon region."

"Disappeared?"

"Yes."

"Are there maps?"

Olivia looked at Eloise and was delighted to see that a smile had made an appearance.

"Goodbye, Mother."

"Goodbye, my dear."

"Do you want me to turn on some lamps? It's getting pretty dim in here."

"No. You can leave them. I like it this way. And Nella will come. She'll turn them on before it's completely dark."

"Good old Nella. Give her my love."

"I will. Come and kiss me. I've given up not wanting to be touched."

Olivia crossed the polished floor and the Persian carpet and bent in beside her mother and kissed her on the forehead. How beautiful her skin had become with age. Pale, translucent layers of powdered parchment—soft as if she had just been born.

"*Au revoir*," said Eloise. Her hand reached up and patted Olivia's arm. "Don't slam the door."

Olivia walked away then.

She did not look back.

The door made a *click*—but nothing more.

Olivia stood for a moment, perfectly still, on the porch. She took a deep breath of fresh air and drew on her driving gloves.

Jar babies.

Tell her. Go back and tell her.

No. It would kill her.

Better her than me, Olivia.

Olivia did not reply. Instead, she took another gulp of air and closed her eyes.

Are you going to buy me a jar, Olivia?

Please stop...

Olivia opened her eyes. She wondered if she was going to faint. Something was definitely wrong. A cramp began to grow inside her. Its shape was the shape of a sling. Something wet began to flow down her inner thigh on the left side.

No. Don't.

She stepped forward. The wetness spread.

She looked at the bricks below her.

Walk.

She made her way to the edge of the street—paused and crossed over—leaned on the car and fumbled the keys. She opened the door and slid inside.

Sitting behind the wheel, she waited while two girls in Branksome Hall uniforms approached along the sidewalk. They nodded. She could see them mouth her name: *Mrs Price.* She nodded back, hoping that what she produced was a smile.

She looked down.

Nothing. Still, she had to be sure. Rising slightly, she lifted her skirts until her hips were free of them. Her pantyhose were wet to just above the knee.

Not blood.

Not blood.

Cramp-urine. Nothing more.

She sat back, unaware she had been holding her breath. She exhaled with a great sigh.

You, she said. Are you still there?

Yes.

Olivia smiled.

Are you? said the voice.

Olivia laughed out loud. "Damn right I am!" she said.

She turned the key. The engine kicked over.

Pulling away from the curb, Olivia could not stop smiling. A vision had risen up in her mind of herself in the months ahead—billowing and burgeoning—the first of the Wylie women to wear a maternity dress since Eloise had carried Amy. And the only one of the Wylie girls who would ever complain of stretch marks. What a wonderful, crazy distinction!

Crazy?

Well—you know what I mean.

No. I don't.

Amen.

5

Lilah Kemp's apartment was, in fact, the servants' quarters and summer kitchen of number 38 Lowther Avenue. It could be reached by one of two ways—through the entrance in the yard beyond the lane, and through a door that opened into the kitchen proper of number 38. Oddly, the summer kitchen in Lilah's domain was a good deal larger than the one beyond the door. This was doubtless because it had also been where the servants ate and socialized. Lilah used this part of it as her sitting-room. Otherwise, there was a tiny bathroom and a bedroom of moderate size. A short dark passageway—which Lilah dreaded—ran between the kitchen and the turning that led to the entrance hall. The bedroom looked out into the yard, now covered with snow—and on its window-sills, as in the kitchen, Lilah grew African violets in ceramic pots—the only blooming plant she could find that abhorred direct sunlight.

Thirty-eight Lowther Avenue was owned by the University of Toronto and was leased to professors who came for varied periods of time from abroad. The current tenants were Professor and Mister Holland—Honey and Robert. Honey was a physicist and Robert wrote books which inevitably failed to get published.

The Hollands, who came from Southern Rhodesia (they refused to call it Zimbabwe) were white and vague and distant people who sat absolutely silent whenever they happened to be in the house together. They were condescendingly accepting of Lilah's presence beyond the walls of their kitchen and dining-room—but they rarely encountered her. The mice—which they slaughtered—were heard and seen more often than Lilah Kemp. The door between their premises was locked on both sides and Lilah had not yet enjoyed the privilege of being invited to pass through. *Best to lead separate lives,* Honey Holland had said, *would you not agree, my dear?*

Lilah had been leading a separate life for so long she could barely remember any other. Even in her days as Chief Librarian she had not been a social creature. Books were her centre, and from them she drew the majority of her companions. Neither had the distant past been greatly populated. Shy of strangers, whose lives had not been delineated on the page, Lilah had few—if any—people in her background who would have described her as anything but strangely aloof, excessively private and incomprehensible.

She had lived with her mother and father and sister, Joellen, in a large white house on Beaumont Road in upper Rosedale. It had been, while it lasted, a moneyed life of privilege and comfort. Also, a living hell. Her father had been abusive in the extreme—though none of the abuse was sexual. His verbal attacks were beyond imagining—and, even now, Lilah could recall the sound of his roaring voice—with its octave-climbing stridency and its terrifying volume. Its force had once driven her mother down the stairs in a terrible fall. Lilah always ran to hide—and her sister, who was the elder, had suffered for years from chronic anorexia as a result of his rantings. If you were skeletal, Joellen had reasoned—he would never find you. Both wife and daughters had been endlessly berated for *the horror of their sex*—for *not being men*—for *women's appalling stupidity and ineptitude*—for their *ugliness*, their *ignorance* and their *smell*. It had been Lilah's earliest ambition to kill him. Things do not work out as we would have them do. It was Lilah's mother who ended her life as the victim of murder. She had been a medium—*not a spiritualist, dear heart—never a spiritualist, dear heart—always a medium, dear heart...* Dear heart. Dear heart. Dear heart.

Her name had been Sarah Tudball, which was how she presented herself on her cards. By refusing her husband's name, she had the only victory she could claim against him. She had one unfortunate trait—for along with the talent to *raise the dead* (which is how she put it) she also passed on to Lilah her inability to control which dead were raised. On the other hand, she had also passed on the ability to raise up people from books—a talent that, before her daughter got it, was unique to Sarah Tudball. And this was how she met her death.

Across the street from the houses on Beaumont Road there runs a deep ravine—one of the many for which the city of Toronto is famous. Houses have since proliferated on the hillside there—but in Sarah's time, when Lilah was still a child, there was only one house on that side of the street. It sat on a sort of promontory at the far end. Otherwise, the hillsides were dark with trees and undergrowth—and there were vagrants there—and animals such as raccoons and skunks and foxes, rabbits, porcupines and many wild cats. Sarah often went down into this ravine or onto the hillside beneath the trees to conduct her business with the dead. Lilah was encouraged to go with her. But Lilah abhorred the dark—the condition in which she had been born—and dreaded the words: *come down with me, today, dear heart...*

Certainly, Lilah had not gone into the ravine the night that Sarah was killed. This happened when Lilah was ten—an event whose awful details she had failed to shed in all the years intervening. Every footfall—every broken twig—every ray of moonlight and the sound of every snuffling, scurrying beast was with her still, even though she had only watched that night from her bedroom window.

Sarah departed the house at eleven-thirty. The moon was shining. This was October 28th. She wore her best woollen coat and scarves and a pair of heavy boots. She carried a walking stick and a flashlight. On her head, she wore a tall, brown hat made of felt. In her pocket, there was a sandwich. She had been gone no more than half an hour when her screams and their echoes began to rise up through the mists—and they lasted a full five minutes. Several men and women went rushing to the hilltop and onto the Glen Road Bridge overlooking the ravine—but none went down to assist her. When the last of her cries had been issued, many birds flew up from the trees through the darkness, after which silence fell. It was only then that Lilah's father called the police.

Sarah was found with multiple bruises, and strangled with her scarves. Lilah never ceased to hear her crying—nor to find the words *dear heart* impossible to say.

What happened was this:

Sarah Tudball had gone forth to conjure Doctor Jekyll—but the man she had found was Mister Hyde.

<u>6</u>

Returning from Prague, Griffin Price's plane had landed first at Gander in Newfoundland and was now en route from St John's to Toronto. Night was falling and, with it, darkness was spreading out behind him. For a while the great white jet he rode in pursued the setting sun, but by seven o'clock the race was lost and the whole sky fell back into the moon's possession. Below him there was not a trace of cloud.

Griffin looked down at the Gulf of St Lawrence, wide as a land-locked sea—with nothing to show it was there but its flickering moonlit waves. No ships were visible, though once the world had flocked to its waters—African freighters and British liners, Russian whalers and South American cargo ships. No more. A ship was the rarest sight of all since the world had begun to fracture and to fragment, nation by nation. Commerce was now a faxed proposition—pursued by men with telephones, riding in aeroplanes.

The only other passenger up in first class was a man asleep with a lap-top computer on his knees. Griffin kept waiting for the thing to fall and smash its workings on the floor, but so far this had been avoided. The man was younger than Griffin—perhaps in his early or middle twenties—and a perfect innocent—at least, by appearances, while he slept. He was slight of build and dressed in the classic out-of-town business style—blue-striped shirt, grey wool suit, a St Andrew's tie—Griffin's old school, though he hadn't the slightest notion who the young man might be. Another pilgrim to the interior, no doubt—another explorer en route to the Pacific Rim; *Cathay. Go West, young man, for the Orient!* Farther—farther—always in motion, always pushing farther—never arriving—always on the lookout for a world already found...

Sept-Iles. Rimouski. Quebec.

The great river narrowed below them—shaped by islands, promontories, spits—dazzled by lights from the Citadel—frozen with black ice. How long ago—four, nearly five hundred years—they had come here from Europe, pushing inland. What would they think of it, now—Trois Rivières—Verchères—Varenne—Montreal? Little or nothing remained of what they had dreamed.

Griffin's own people—when?—had come this way—along the St Lawrence, deeper, farther into the interior. Dead by dozens—a whole clan of Welshmen—struck down by cholera, by lack of farming skills, by endless poverty. Not until Griffin's great-grandfather had there been a ray of hope—and that had been brief—a business that failed. But his grandfather, followed by his father, had pushed all the way to Toronto, where by dint of charm and killer instincts they had finally founded the sugar fortune from which Griffin Price now drew resources for his own enterprise.

The lake opened up below him—Ontario, marred by increasing clouds and darkness—the lights of Cornwall, Kingston and Belleville winking on and off through the snow. All at once, the aircraft dropped fifty feet—and the young man's lap-top flew up against the ceiling, where it opened like an egg and hatched its workings on the seat beside its owner.

Griffin looked over.

"Too bad," he said.

"Oh, that's all right," the young man replied. "I have another in my briefcase."

"Always be prepared, eh?"

"Why not?" The young man was smiling. "Everything you buy these days is shit. Nothing works. It all breaks. It's part of the plot."

Griffin said: "what plot?"

"The plot to force us all to buy things twice as often as we need to."

"Oh," said Griffin. "Yes. *That* plot." He tried to wave it off, but he felt a twinge of discomfort. If it was a plot, then he was part of it. "What," he said, "do you do with your life?"

"I'm a lawyer. A corporate lawyer—moving up."

"Oh, yes? And what venue?"

"I been in St John's all my life," the young man said, his accent having already betrayed him. "But I had enough of that. So I'm coming to Toronto, where I'm going to kiss ass."

"I beg your pardon?" It was not the language Griffin wondered at—but the ease with which the young man declared his intentions.

"We get one life," the lawyer said. "An' I mean to have it. Not to pussy-foot—not to bide time—not to wait on recognition. I got a talent and I'm going to make sure it gets the break it deserves. I'm not a fool. I know how it's done. You kiss ass, you suck cock, you get fucked. You *smile*. Success. *N'est-ce pas?* An' I can do it all in two official languages."

"Yes," said Griffin. "I dare say you can."

That was the end of their conversation. The steward came just then, and offered them one last drink before they landed. Below them, the city was blown about in wind and snow. It could not yet be seen—but it was there, and it was ready. On the journey inland—upstream, into the future—this was where the pilgrims paused to shed the past.

7

Lilah Kemp's talents as a spiritualist first showed their presence when she was five. Sitting out in the yard one day behind the house on Beaumont Road, she was reading *The Tale of Peter Rabbit* by Beatrix Potter.

It was a standard edition, about the size of an adult hand, and all the illustrations were in colour—except for the title page, which had a drawing of Peter done in black and white. Being precocious and seeking in books some safety from her father's abuse, Lilah had learned to read at the age of four. Peter Rabbit, his sisters and their cousins were her favourite companions and she rarely stirred from her room without one of their biographies in hand or in her pocket.

On the day in question, her father had been particularly abusive and Joellen had locked herself in the bathroom. While Sarah attempted to persuade her child to open the door, her husband went to find the axe. Knowing there was nothing the man would not do to exercise his authority, Sarah went downstairs—avoiding her husband's furious rummagings out in the garage—and propped a ladder against the west side of the house. She then persuaded little Joellen to *trust Mommy dear heart* and so, while her father was axing down the bathroom door, Joellen was escaping through the bathroom window.

As always, Lilah had fled—to a place, on this occasion, beneath the lilac trees—where she closed her ears and read her book.

She was so intent on Peter's company she had even managed to lose herself in his crisis with Mister McGregor, thus wiping out her own with her father. Peter had just gone round the end of a cucumber frame in his attempt to escape from the garden when there was Mister McGregor planting out cabbages.

Stop, thief! the farmer cried—and the chase was on, with Mister McGregor in pursuit of Peter, brandishing his hoe as Lilah's father was brandishing his axe.

Stop, thief! Stop!

Breathlessly, Lilah turned the page.

Peter, she read, *was most dreadfully frightened. He rushed all over the garden...*

Sarah, in the house, was shouting: "you can't! You shan't! I won't allow it!"

Lilah cringed.

At the bottom of the page, Peter lost his shoes—one amongst cabbages, one amongst potatoes...

And there they were.

Peter Rabbit's shoes, beneath the lilac tree, in the shadow of Lilah Kemp.

She set the book aside. *Page twenty-five*, she noted.

A rabbit was staring at her from the lawn.

Are you Mrs McGregor? he said, as one child might well say to another.

"No," said Lilah. "I'm Lily Kemp."

I've lost my shoes.

I know. I've got them right here.

Lilah failed to notice she had not spoken aloud.

May I have them back?

Oh, yes, said Lilah. Of course you may.

The rabbit dropped to all fours and, even in spite of his tight blue coat, he started towards her—*lippity-lippity*—crossing the grass.

Lilah held out the shoes. They were black and made of soft, pliant leather. She noted they were smaller by far than any shoes she had ever seen. Rabbit shoes, without a doubt.

Peter was now about a yard away. Lilah could smell him—sun-warmed and dusty. Just as she held out the shoes in his direction, a figure came crashing around the house—its axe held high.

There was a dreadful roar—a voice—and Peter ran.

The axe came thudding to the ground where he had been, but Lilah was nowhere near it. She, too, had fled—with the book and the shoes in her hands.

Now, two days after Kurtz had joined the ranks of Lilah's outcasts and escapees, she sat on her bed with Peter Rabbit's shoes in her lap. They were folded up in tissue paper and were normally kept in her handkerchief drawer or deep in her purse. The shoes were Lilah's talisman and, only when desperate, she got them out and spoke to them.

Dear shoes, she said through the channels between herself and anything spoken to in prayer, *I require some news of Kurtz. I have released him out of* Heart of Darkness. *He has disappeared and I am afraid. Kurtz, if he puts his mind to it, can destroy the world—and only I can prevent him. I have been chosen to be his Marlow—and must begin my journey—but I don't know where to start....*

She kissed the shoes and held them against her heart.

A voice said: *Queen Street West.*

What?

Queen Street West. It is time for you to take your medication.

"I don't want medication. I want Mister Kurtz!" This, Lilah said aloud.

Queen Street West. Medication. Now.

The voice was adamant.

Lilah wrapped the shoes in their paper and put them into her bag. She then went through to the hallway, were she put on her coat and scarves and retrieved the baby carriage from its corner. She put on her floppy galoshes—took up her tam-o'-shanter and gloves and dragged the buggy down the walk.

Queen Street ho!

And *medication ho!* to prevent what might happen next if she lost control—which, for others, could be the cause of mayhem.

8

Lilah's winter coat had been purchased at The Irish Shop on Bloor Street. She was partial to all things Irish, having got some Irish blood from her mother's forebears. It was prized. Lilah had made the journey to Dublin— a pilgrimage—while still a student. Standing there on O'Connell Street in the rain, she had heard the voices crying in the stones and had told her sister, Joellen: *I have stood in Dublin's tears.* She had gone there for three months of study under Nicholas Fagan at Trinity College.

Fagan, too, could "raise up persons from the page"—though he never left them stranded as Lilah did, among the living. Back they went and stayed between their covers until he called them forth again—in his role as teacher and critic. For Lilah, Nicholas Fagan's voice was the voice of English literature itself. He was her god—if such a thing was proper. No other living person commanded more of her respect.

Lilah was twenty-three when she made that journey, and since that time she had made no other. Her world was entirely where she was—and the insides of books. In the years since she had come home from Dublin, her walk through time had been more like a stumble. Her father went into a world entirely populated by men—the world of golf clubs and polo ponies at Palm Beach—where men could dine apart in segregated dining-rooms. The house on Beaumont Road was sold, and Lilah, together with Joellen, moved out of Rosedale into the city that surrounded it. Joellen chose Cabbagetown—Lilah chose the Annex. They saw very little of one another then—having their own lives to lead, and having their separate "conditions" to survive—anorexia and schizophrenia. Joellen, too, was somewhat ashamed of her sister's calling as a medium. The raising of the dead was "an embarrassment." Neither did it help that Lilah had chosen "a spinster's profession"—namely that of librarian. "Librarians all wear dreadful shoes and squint and actually *look* unmarried!"

Their mother had left them each a stipend—their father provided nothing. That was the burden of his parting words: *nothing—never—no.* Joellen took her stipend and bought a house. Lilah took hers and set a

28

portion of it aside for rent. The rest—some thousands—went for the books by which she lived. And her clothes from The Irish Shop. She made a point of taking care in her choice of shoes. She never squinted, unless she had lost her glasses. And she wore her mother's rings. A hand in rings is wedded in a stranger's eyes. She turned her back on Joellen and disappeared from her life.

Few expressions lit up Lilah's face, unless she was in the thrall of language and of literature. Her stipend, plus her salary, provided financial security—wealth but not riches. Friends—if she had them—remained offstage.

She was also—though no one was aware of this—a mother. The child, a boy, was named Linton. Born in early summer, he was weaned and independent by the time the autumn rolled around. Lilah—who had taken a leave of absence—returned to her post with a noticeable loss of weight—but no other sign of motherhood. The pregnancy itself had been camouflaged by oversize dresses and the fact that Linton had been so small.

On Thursday evenings, while she was giving her seminars, Lilah had paid a Portuguese woman who came to number 38-A Lapin Lanes and sat with Linton until his mother returned. The child was a pale, tiny baby who rarely raised his voice. One night—it was October—a storm shut down the city. Linton gave a cry in the dark and disappeared. He was one year and three months old. Not a trace of him had since been seen.

In distress, Lilah then had begun her decline—which deepened and grew as her seminar audience began its rebellion against her distracted behaviour. On the evening when she shouted: *Heathcliff hath murdered sleep!* Linton had been gone three weeks. Lilah came to the end of her tether—and that was when she fell into the mode of full-blown schizophrenia.

At the Queen Street Mental Health Centre where she had been committed, she was asked in an early interview to describe the events that had led to her downfall. She told about the child, of whom there was so little evidence in her possession—excepting a baby carriage. The psychiatrist assigned to her—whose name was Bagg—did not believe the child had ever existed. No men were known to inhabit Lilah's life.

Who, then, could be the father of the absent baby?

Heathcliff.

That was her answer. Heathcliff. And no other.

One of her nurses, having recognized the name, perused the pages of *Wuthering Heights* and there discovered the name of *Linton*. Heathcliff's son. Who perished.

9

Lilah had now been a patient at the Queen Street Mental Health Centre for three years. For the first of these, she was confined. She was diagnosed according to her raising of the dead and her conversations with literary characters and famous persons from the past. The hallucinatory aspects of her otherwise unique behaviour were a perfect match with the hallucinatory aspects of paranoid schizophrenia. Spiritualism, then, was just another disease. Like measles or the mumps. A medicated end to it could be arranged.

Lilah, kept under observation by Doctor Bagg, was subjected to methods considered to be advanced and innovative. He treated Lilah with bouts of forced confinement and massive doses of various neuroleptic drugs. The last of these—and the one she currently submitted to—was Modecate. The object of the confinement had been to separate Lilah from her "imaginary" companions. The drugs were meant to eliminate these companions altogether. Murder by milligrams.

In time, Doctor Bagg was satisfied that Lilah could safely live beyond the hospital's walls and she was discharged. There were conditions, of course. She must maintain her program of Modecate—and submit to regular check-ups.

When she was first discharged, Doctor Bagg had written in the Queen Street registry, *Lilah Kemp: residual schizophrenia.* It was a phrase Lilah hated. *It makes me sound as if I have little bits of something floating around inside. It makes me sound like the wide Sargasso Sea, where little fishes are eating me alive. It makes it sound as if Doctor Bagg has taken a hammer to my mind—like my father with his axe— and smashed it all to smithereens.*

Lilah could make up analogies by the dozen. It was one of the facilities she kept, in spite of her drugs. The main thing was that she hated Doctor Bagg, whom she dubbed *Bagg the Baleful.* He had, after all, deprived her of her world of wonders. He had tried to take away her powers. *No one understands what I have in here,* she said to her kitchen one day. *I am an open door through which the dead can come and go at will.*

One thing was clear. After her time at the Queen Street Mental Health Centre, Lilah Kemp could still summon forth. Her medication, however, made it more hazardous to do so. It was Lilah's theory, for instance, that Modecate had been the cause of the break for freedom made by Otto, the arsonist. That way, the Rosedale Library was burned down. That way, Lilah was returned—but briefly—to the Queen Street Mental Health Centre. That way, she lost her job.

The drug was meant to control paralogical thinking—and to curb delusions. But in Lilah's case, it merely incapacitated her ability to control her outcast's behaviour. If she had not been drugged, Rupert Kurtz might not have appeared. The trouble was, without her drugs, she could be forced to become a permanent resident of that part of Queen Street where they locked the doors. And that would be intolerable. That would be death.

So it was that Lilah Kemp turned up dutifully, pushing her baby buggy full of book-bags and *Wuthering Heights* into the Modecate Injection Clinic that March afternoon. Outside, the wind raged—a symbol for Lilah of someone else's "residual schizophrenia" blowing through the streets. She felt entirely fragmented.

Mavis Delaney, the injection nurse on duty, thought that Lilah looked the worse for wear and said so.

"It's just the wind," Lilah said. "I've fought it all the way from Bloor Street."

"Heavens!" said Mavis. "Didn't you take the subway and the street-car?"

"Subways are full of Moonmen," said Lilah. "Streetcars don't take baby buggies."

"Oh," said Mavis. "I see. Here you are, then." She rolled up Lilah's skirts, swabbed her thigh and administered a fortnight's dose of Modecate. Lilah was docile through this procedure and bit her lip. Delaney ticked her name off the list. "Why don't you go out into the Mall and have a cup of tea before you venture back to the street?" she said. "You look exhausted, to me. Are you sure you don't want medical attention?"

"Thank you," said Lilah. "I'll take the tea, but not the attention."

She bit back Kurtz's name as it began to rise. It wasn't wise to mention outcasts to someone like Mavis Delaney. The nurse was nice enough in some ways, but everyone who came here knew she was really a Queen Street spy. One false move and the orderlies appeared.

"Bye-bye," Lilah said—and trundled off.

The Mall, to which Mavis had referred, was a huge two-storeyed rotunda at the centre of the maze of hospital buildings. Closed-in walkways fed human traffic from all directions. There was a swimming pool off to one side where—so it was believed—recreation therapists drowned their charges. And a basketball court, where murderers were turned loose every day and allowed to kill one another. Out in the Mall itself, tables were provided for cannibals and other types of feeders to bring their cups of blood and paper plates of human entrails and to sit there feasting, day unto day, on one another. This, at any rate, was the description given by most who lived in the Mall.

Lilah brought her tea in its Styrofoam cup to a table where she could sit alone and she undid the buttons of her coat and sat with her back to the wall. Her hip was sore where the needle had gone in. The drug was shot deep into the muscle there and it made a knot. Not quite a cramp—but the next best thing.

Lilah was troubled. Kurtz was out there and Lilah Kemp was meant to be his Marlow. If only Peter Rabbit's shoes would tell her where Kurtz might be, she could then at least begin her journey up the Congo.

She rummaged in the baby carriage—pulling aside the book-bags and blankets, revealing *Wuthering Heights* and *Heart of Darkness*. Settling down, she opened the latter book at page 92—the dreaded departure point.

Sure enough, it still read the same: *Mister Kurtz was not there...*

Lilah read on. Marlow said he would have raised an outcry if he had believed his eyes. But he didn't. She read the words that Marlow used to describe how he felt—a perfect description of how she felt, herself. *Completely unnerved,* she read, *blank fright—pure terror—physical danger—something monstrous...odious had been thrust upon him...the possibility of a sudden onslaught and massacre...*

Lilah closed the book. It was bad enough that Kurtz had got out of it. She did not need confirmation of her fears. She had known Kurtz and Marlow now for many years and she knew what awaited Marlow at the end of his journey. The station where Kurtz had been agent, with its human heads stuck up on poles and its drugged inhabitants were not the half of it. Worse was to be revealed. The horror of what had been done in the name of civilization—the people enslaved—the slaughtered elephants—the sexual depravity—the blood sports with human victims.

Lilah glanced about the Mall. Someone was swimming in the glass-walled pool. The murderers were playing volleyball on the court. Several cannibals were feeding at the peripheral tables. No one paid her the slightest attention. She did not, so far as she could tell, exist. She opened her bag and fished out her talisman.

Some have rabbits' feet, she thought, *and some have rabbits' shoes.* She held them up like a compress against her forehead and closed her eyes. The Mall—all at once—filled up with sound—a cannonade of footsteps.

Leather soles and heels—three or four sets of them—marching. The sound of it was alarming.

Lilah opened her eyes and waited. She already knew who it was. A giant was coming.

Kurtz.

Lilah stood up.

He was marching like a general—Field Marshal Kurtz—with his aides and junior officers around him. They were not his own soldiers, of course. They were his enemies.

They've caught him! Lilah thought.

She took *Heart of Darkness* with her and started across the grey stone floor.

Kurtz saw Lilah coming and stopped in his tracks. The others fell back in a cluster. They were young. Interns, perhaps. There were six of them—one of them a woman. She wore, this woman, a navy blue suit and a large bow-tie.

Lilah raised the book above her head. "Here!" she cried, triumphantly. "This is where he belongs. Put him in here."

"Madame?" said one of the interns—pompous and pretentious. "Which of us do you want?"

"Him, of course," said Lilah—pointing the book at Kurtz. "He escaped from page 92."

The interns murmured and gave one another knowing glances. One of them took notes. The bravest of them, the woman, stepped forward and spoke to Lilah. "Surely you are mistaken," she said—in an even, condescending tone. "Doctor Kurtz has not escaped from anywhere."

"*Doctor* Kurtz!" Lilah was nonplussed. She shuffled two steps back.

Kurtz himself said nothing. He still wore the grey wool coat she had seen before and he carried the silver Homburg. The others entirely deferred to him; he was their leader—so it seemed.

Lilah was not the only person to have noted Kurtz's presence. Beyond the wall of glass—two teenage boys and a girl were holding hands at the edge of the swimming pool. All of them were bald and one of the boys wore a bathing suit that did not quite fit. It was somewhere down around his hips. The therapist came and stood behind him and pulled it up to his waist. She leaned in closer to tell him he should pull the drawstring tighter. The boy stood stiff and expressionless during this episode. He was staring at Kurtz through the grey-green glass. The reflections of the water gave his skin—already pale—an eerie colouring, not unlike the underside of a fish.

All three patients—for that is what they were—gave the appearance of being severely traumatized. Their bodies sagged, their heads hung forward and their legs, so it seemed, must be working very hard to hold them up. Only the boy who was staring at Kurtz resembled the living. The rest, Lilah thought, had been raised from the dead, and for a moment she wondered if she had been the cause of their presence.

Kurtz turned now and saw the boy. The boy was watching him intently. If his eyes had been lasers, his gaze would have burned a hole in the glass.

Beside the pool, the therapist was giving instructions. The boys and the girl were to jump into the water holding hands. The therapist would join them and was removing her oversized sweatshirt, revealing a one-piece bathing suit. She was trim and young and more like an Olympic athlete than a therapist. A whistle mounted on a wristband was raised to her mouth and even through the glass, the sound of it could be heard.

Two of the youngsters jumped into the pool. The therapist also jumped. But the boy impaling Kurtz with his stare did not. Instead he came around the pool at a pace that, however slow, was full of alarming energy. His bald head shot up as if in spasm, so that his chin stuck out towards Kurtz. Lilah could see that his hands were fisted. He came across the tiles relentlessly—his gaze never once leaving Kurtz.

Kurtz stepped back involuntarily, brushing his companions aside with his arm.

In the pool, the others had risen to the surface and were splashing spastically towards the shallow end. The therapist, too late, looked around for the missing boy and could not find him.

The boy himself had now reached the glass and his bathing suit fell down again—this time all the way to the tiles. He stepped from it, kicking it aside. His stare, Lilah thought, was terrifying. He was obviously obsessed with Kurtz and deeply disturbed. There were circles beneath his eyes and he looked as if he might not have slept for weeks. His mouth began to open, but nothing emerged. He seemed incapable of words. His hands went down towards his genitals and Kurtz immediately shouted—hoarsely—"stop him!"

Two of the interns ran towards the door leading to the pool. In the meantime, the naked boy had grasped his penis and was pulling at it frantically. It seemed, at first, like a manic form of masturbation—but in seconds it was clearly nothing of the sort. The boy was trying to tear his penis free of his groin and it began to spurt blood up against the glass.

The interns shouted: "locked! It's locked!" and began to pound at the door and to heave themselves against it.

Kurtz turned away. The sight before him was too alarming to be admitted. The woman in the bow tie also looked away in the opposite direction. Inside the pool room, the therapist had pulled her other charges from the water and was running—sliding and slipping—in the boy's direction.

Lilah put *Heart of Darkness*, open, against her face. "Stop!" she whispered. "Stop."

The boy had now begun to claw and tear at his scrotum. His mouth made screaming motions, but there was still no sound. The other two youngsters stood at the edge of the pool. They could be distinctly heard as they wailed in terror. The therapist reached the bleeding boy and threw herself at his back. She caught his arms at the elbows and tried to pinion them. He threw her off. For all the slightness of his build, his madness had lent him a formidable strength the woman could not contend with. She tried to pull him down by grabbing his legs, but he kicked her away. There was now so much blood it could not be told where it came from.

Suddenly, an orderly appeared with a table raised above his head.

"Stand aside!" he shouted.

Then he flung the table at the glass and stepped in over the shards towards the boy.

Kurtz turned back and watched. But that was all. One hand was jammed in a pocket—the other held the Homburg. Lilah lowered the book so it covered only her mouth.

The orderly—who was large and black and dressed in white—knelt down beside the boy and spoke to him. Lilah could not hear what he said. The boy was lying on his back and bleeding profusely. The therapist, holding a towel to her bloody nose, knelt opposite the orderly. One of the interns tiptoed in through the hole in the glass and found more towels and brought them to the boy. Then, with the therapist, he began to examine him. The ultimate damage—emasculation—had not been done, but the bleeding was extensive. One of the other interns went to bring assistance. Kurtz just stood and stared. Aloof.

The woman in the bow-tie had now recovered her wits and came back apologetically to Kurtz. "Are you all right?" she asked.

Lilah thought it was the strangest question she had ever heard.

Then the young woman said: "is he one of yours?"

And Kurtz said: "no."

"He certainly seemed to know who you were."

"Yes," said Kurtz. But that was all.

"What on earth do you think made him do it?"

Kurtz did not answer the question. Instead, he said: "you are McGreevey, is that correct?"

"Yes."

"You will learn in time, McGreevey, that self-mutilation is the weapon of the weak. It is petulance disguised as rage."

McGreevey did not reply.

Kurtz was looking down at the bloodied, silent boy, now wrapped in towels and being prepared for transport.

"This sort of thing is relatively rare," he said.

"I hope so," said McGreevey. She tried to laugh.

"As you have indicated, he appeared to be directing his act at me."

"Yes, sir."

Kurtz put both his hands and the Homburg behind his back and said: "I want you to understand this incident, McGreevey. I don't want it mis-interpreted."

"Of course not."

"Put it this way," said Kurtz. "I was not here."

There was a pause. McGreevey narrowed her eyes. Then she said: "yes, sir. You left before this happened."

Kurtz said: "good-day," and gave his dyed black hair a slow, flat swipe with his hand and put on the Homburg. Then he walked away.

Lilah watched him leaving with disbelief. When he was gone, she turned to McGreevey and said: "did that man just say he wasn't here?"

McGreevey pulled at the ends of her floppy bow-tie. "Which man?" she asked.

10

Half an hour later, Rupert Kurtz arrived at his destination on College Street. In the elevator, he rode to the top of the twenty-storey building and clicked along the marble hallway in his satisfying shoes to the office at the far end overlooking the city. Going through, he said to his secretary: "I want to be alone, Kilbride." In the inner sanctum, he went to his desk and sat there wearing his overcoat and hat. He perspired—but in that moment Kurtz would have perspired standing naked in a blizzard.

"Dear sweet heaven," he said aloud to the room. "Dear sweet Jesus Christ."

He closed his eyes and sat there desperate for twenty minutes before he rose and went into his private bathroom.

He removed his overcoat and flung it on a chair as he passed and also removed his hat. In the bathroom, he ran cold water over his wrists and took down a bottle of pills from the cabinet. Selecting two, he placed them on his tongue and swallowed. Then he counted slowly backwards from sixty, after which he felt himself begin to pass towards tranquillity. Looking in the mirror, he was satisfied he would survive.

"There," he said. "Done." And switched out the light.

On a marble panel outside his door, the name *T. Rupert Kurtz, M.D., F.R.C.P. (C.)* appeared above the following: *Director and Psychiatrist-in-Chief, The Parkin Institute of Psychiatric Research.*

In that same moment, Lilah Kemp was hearing the very same words at the information desk of the Queen Street Mental Health Centre.

Rupert Kurtz was God.

TWO

all your life you have been reading
of this, Catherine and Heathcliff crying out
beyond their own deaths
                    cats in the alley
dogs howling at the yellow hole in the sky

Catherine Hunter
Moon Poem for Z

Lilah felt disconnected—as if she were floating in water. A current pulled at her—an undertow, perhaps of Modecate. Her feet could not find the floor. She clung to the baby carriage, fearful of being swept away.

Beyond the hospital doors the wind was whipping up a fresh blur of snow. Nothing could be seen through this but the looming shapes of streetcars, reminding Lilah of submarines she had seen in films, moving through blizzards of air bubbles. Shaken by what she had witnessed beside the swimming pool and what she had consequently learned of Kurtz's identity, she went out into the storm.

What a blessing winter was. It gave you somewhere to hide. Lilah moved off the sidewalk onto the lawns. She had wrapped herself in extra scarves, one of them drawn up over her nose, and had pulled the tam-o'-shanter down around her ears. She now drew woollen mittens over her gloves and was about to head back onto the street when something fled through the snow at her feet.

Whatever it was, it was smaller than a dog. More like a cat—but not a cat. What could have survived such a storm? Not a squirrel, surely.

Lilah pursued it farther into the park—which was not a park but a strolling ground for the mad. Benches had been placed beneath the trees and, in summer, paths that were not now evident led the hospital residents from shade to shade in semi-privacy. Simplified, two dimensional statues had been erected there, and walk-through life-sized silhouettes with which to confirm your human shape. Games could be played with these. *Look at me! I've been cut from stone!* Now, in the snow, the silhouettes and the statues had the look of people caught off guard in the ice age—frozen in their tracks.

There was an old brick wall there, too—set deeper in the gardens—its bricks, once white, turned grey with age. This was a remnant of the nineteenth-century predecessor of the Queen Street Mental Health Centre, a place that had been called *The Lunatic Asylum.* Whatever animal it was that Lilah had followed had brought her to the wall as if on purpose.

It's a groundhog, said a voice. *Don't stare.*

Lilah looked up.

A figure loomed by the wall in blowing shawls and billowing skirts.

Is that you, Kemp? it said.

Lilah recognized Susanna Moodie—a companion from her own most recent incarceration at Queen Street. That had been after the fire at the Rosedale Library. Lilah had not been forced to stay for long in the wards, but long enough to take up Susanna Moodie as her confidante.

She said *hello* to her friend and asked her why she was standing out in the storm.

Groundhog here is pregnant and will soon deliver herself of a litter. We came here to look for food.

Oh dear. There won't be much food out here on a day like this.

I seem to remember someone who came to feed the squirrels. Peanuts and breadcrumbs. Anything like that in your buggy, Kemp?

I have a loaf of bread, but it's probably frozen by now.

Give her some. She's starving.

This, then, was not a groundhog from the spirit world.

Lilah fished around beneath the blankets and found the loaf of bread. Whole-grain country bread. Unsliced—no additives. Lilah tore off bits of it and threw them down in the snow.

The groundhog, looking up at her as it ate, had a face very like Susanna Moodie's—slightly bad-tempered, furrowed over the brow, a weatherbeaten red in colour—grey around the edges.

What's she doing here, anyway, in the middle of the city?

She lives here. Like I do.

But she's a groundhog.

Yes. Well—we cling to what we have, Kemp.

Lilah threw down more bread, torn into crusty pieces. The ground-hog ate voraciously. Her teeth were broken and yellow.

I thought you would have left this place by now, Susanna.

No, I'm stuck here same as you. Did you invoke me, Kemp?

I suppose I did. I'm sorry if it displeases you.

Susanna Moodie did not reply to this. She turned her attention from Lilah and concentrated on the groundhog whose feeding habits were a source of fascination to her.

Lilah had saved Susanna Moodie from the library fire.

Up to that moment, she had been contained in the books she had written: *Roughing It in the Bush* and *Life in the Clearings versus the*

Bush. Mrs Moodie had been considered, in her own time, as something of a blue-stocking—not the sort of person suited to pioneer life. But she had proved her critics wrong. Her books had come to be accepted as classics of their kind and had been read by every generation that succeeded her. In them, she had described her life as an immigrant of the 1830s, who came from England to what was then called Upper Canada.

Every new-world hardship that could be imagined had been visited on Susanna Moodie and consequently turned up on her pages. The temper of her tone was bitter—even contemptuous—but her wit had survived—and so had she. Blizzards and floods, insects and plagues tried their best to kill her, but she looked on them all with wonder and made them the cause of her endurance. *My love for Canada,* she had written, *was a feeling very nearly allied to that which the condemned criminal entertains for his cell.*

Lilah Kemp and Susanna Moodie had two things in common. Fire was their demon—and each could speak with spirits. Towards the end of her life, Mrs Moodie had summoned Queen Victoria, evoked from the body of a female patient in Toronto's Lunatic Asylum.

When Otto, the arsonist, put the torch to the Rosedale Library, Lilah had been the only member of the staff who was present. It had happened after hours on one of her Thursday-night seminars. A book called *Fahrenheit 451* had been the subject of discussion. Lilah had been intrigued by it. The author of the book, Ray Bradbury, had wanted to address the question of censorship in the time of McCarthy. To this end, he chose the theme of book-burning as a way of showing a world without words and a world without imagination. Fahrenheit 451 is the temperature at which books burn, and apparently Lilah—who was still attempting to recover from the loss of her son—had been caught up so completely in the story that she evoked Otto.

Otto, the arsonist, was not a character in Bradbury's novel. He had been the student whom Doctor Goebbels had chosen to ignite the piles of books when burning them had been the first Nazi gesture of contempt for German culture. Otto had considered the act a privilege and had torched the books with a sense of holy mission. How Lilah got him from the dead, she could not imagine. The next thing she knew, he was burning down her beloved library.

Before the firemen came, Lilah had saved a great many books, but there was no way she could save them all. Susanna Moodie had been among the last to be saved and the covers of her books had melted in Lilah's hands. This way, her hands were bandaged and useless to her throughout the early weeks of her internment in the Queen Street Mental Health Centre.

Susanna Moodie had gone with Lilah into the schizophrenic ward and was the cause of much trouble there. Lilah would speak to no one but Mrs Moodie, and Doctor Bagg had punished her severely for it—doubling her intake of drugs and separating her from the daily lives of her fellow patients. When Lilah had described herself as an *inmate*—and when she had used the words *incarceration* and *imprisoned* to describe her condition, Doctor Bagg had become extremely angry. *No one is imprisoned here!* he had shouted at her. But Lilah knew a lock when it was turned.

Mrs Moodie was a plain-faced woman whose body had borne many children—some of whom had died at birth but five of whom had lived. Once, in the dead of winter, she had saved them all from a burning house. Just as Lilah had been alone with her books when fire consumed the library, Mrs Moodie had been alone with her children when flames engulfed her home. Her way of saving them had been to wrap them round with blankets and place them each in a bureau drawer. She then dragged the drawers out into the snow and left them beneath the trees. This way, her children survived. She also saved her husband's flute. *Children and music, Kemp; that's what I got from the flames.*

Mrs Moodie had the habit of calling people by their last names. Perhaps, Lilah thought, it had been her way of fending off her attachment to them. Susanna had been fiercely independent and jealous of her status as an individual. She called her husband *Moodie*, just as she called Lilah *Kemp*.

Are you back here to stay? she asked by the wall that day in the storm.

Lilah told her what had happened. Kurtz meant nothing to Mrs Moodie. She had never heard of him.

Do you think he's heard of me? she asked.

I doubt it.

Well, he will hear of me if you come to harm.

He's dangerous.

Not to me.

Lilah smiled. Her friend from the other side—which is how Susanna Moodie described herself—had a fund of courage that Lilah knew she lacked herself. But the example of it was useful.

She threw down another portion of the loaf. The groundhog seized it and began to move away with it through the snow. She seemed, all at once, a forlorn and hopeless figure—incongruous in a landscape that included the looming shapes of the hospital buildings.

This whole field used to be filled with animals. Deer and raccoons and groundhogs. Rabbits. Now look at it! Covered with concrete.

Will she survive—the groundhog?

Did I?

Yes.

You'd best get on with it, then, if you want to do the same.

They said goodbye and the storm made a kind of whirlwind up against the wall. Susanna Moodie, not unlike the groundhog, climbed down under the earth and was gone. From her parting glance, Lilah took away the impression the groundhog and Susanna Moodie were sisters. Cousins, at least, in this new form of wilderness in which they found themselves. Dressed in matching grey and black and brown, they had the look of ancient relatives.

Lilah turned and made for home.

2

The Fabiana Gallery was on Cooper Street in the Annex. Number 45. Previously called *The Alton*, it had been a failing enterprise when Fabiana Holbach took on its future. This happened at a time when Fabiana herself was attempting to recover from another enterprise that had failed—her marriage to James Holbach. Holbach—as had been said at the time—*went off into the Amazon region*—where he disappeared.

Fabiana Holbach was no dilettante. The painter Francis Bacon had been the subject of her Ph.D. thesis. She had taste and daring where art was concerned—and a sense of adventure in lending her support to the young who were talented. Her stable of artists was considered to be among the most exciting in the country. Her money gave her the freedom—and what she called the *privilege*—of showing works that, under any other aegis, might not prevail. Having weathered the worst that a woman in love can endure, Fabiana was unafraid of censure or of scandal.

Cooper Street itself was a scandalous location. Number 45 had been, it so happened, a notorious brothel back in Edwardian times. Its notoriety stemmed from its clientele, among whom there had been a bishop of the church, a knighted captain of industry and a world-famous poet who stopped there while "passing through town." As things turned out, the poet did not emerge for a month. He had *fallen in love with a lady there*. Or so he put it. The fact was, the ladies of the house were nothing of the kind, but boys got up as fashion plates.

Across the road from the Fabiana Gallery, six Victorian mansions continued to stare down public reprobation from beyond admired and enviable gardens. Something rigid in their architecture denied all knowledge of what had gone on at number 45.

Cooper Street was one block long. To the west, it ended abruptly up against a wrought iron fence and, beyond the fence, a park full of chestnut trees and wooden benches. The east end of Cooper Street fed you back into the city via Avenue Road, known to many as *the ultimate address*. This was where, in tall red buildings, Fabiana Holbach and many of her clientele lived out their intricate private lives.

On the 18th of March, Kurtz looked into his appointment book near the end of the day and saw the notation: *Slade Exhibit/Fabiana's/7:00 P.M.* Then he glanced out the nearest window. His office overlooked both College Street to the south and, to the north, the St George campus of the University of Toronto. Now, the snows had given way to the year's first freezing rain, which had begun to fall around four o'clock from a yellow sky. Kurtz decided Slade and his paintings would have to wait for another, better day. He would phone Fabiana and tell her so.

Turning away from the window, he swivelled his tall leather chair until he could see his client of the hour. Kurtz never called his people *patients*. The word, he said, was demeaning. The client in question was sitting in the shadows, balanced neatly in his seat. His legs were crossed and his hands laid out, as if on display, on the arms of the chair. Kurtz always kept the lights at a deliberate density when a client was being interviewed. It was part of his technique, this thing he did with light. In the early stages, when Kurtz was probing for the source of the client's woes, he kept the lights down low in order to encourage confidence. In the dark—or very nearly in the dark—admissions will be made that would not, under brighter scrutiny, be forthcoming. The process was not unlike the rites of confession—where the pretence of anonymity encourages the supplicant to admit to his sins because it seems he is alone with God, and not with His priest.

When the Parkin Board of Governors had chosen Rupert Kurtz to be the Institute's Director and Psychiatrist-in-Chief, they had selected him from a field of contenders that included candidates whose names were known worldwide. Kurtz had received unanimous approbation. His credentials included teaching posts at Harvard and Johns Hopkins and in Zurich. His experimental work in chemotherapy for manic-depressives was widely admired and had garnered him both fellowships and influential followers. His theories concerning sensory deprivation and sleep therapy were revolutionary and, while they had caused some concern in certain quarters, they had been taken up and expanded in others. The fact that Kurtz was controversial was considered an asset so long as the controversies did not involve the courts. Kurtz's other great asset was his social poise. His success in the fund-raising aspects of his job had already made him a legendary figure. Other institutions feared him for these successes, monies for research being so notoriously hard to come by. Kurtz was the preferred psychiatrist at every social level—but he confined himself to his social peers. There was, of course, a reason for this—but what it was had not yet been fathomed.

The client waiting in the dimmed light was a plastic surgeon whose name was Maynard Berry. Berry's expertise was facial reconstruction—mostly having to do with burn victims. He also had a small clientele of men and women who took advantage of his talents for purely cosmetic reasons—but these constituted less than ten percent of his business.

Berry was married to his "masterpiece"—a woman who had come to him for corrective surgery following an automobile accident in which she had been burned. The extent of the facial damage was minimal—but Maynard Berry had seized the opportunity to perform a maximum alteration. The woman had bones that nature had failed to take advantage of—and by the time Berry's efforts were complete, she had become *the most beautiful woman in the world.* Or so he thought of her. She was his perfect gesture—the creation of an artist whose medium was flesh. Her name was Emma Roper and within a year of their meeting, they had been married. One child, Barbara, had been forthcoming but no others had been conceived. Emma's reproductive system failed. Adoption was considered—but rejected. Barbara was their own—and Barbara was enough. She was now almost twelve—and the Berry marriage had settled into a careful silence—becalmed.

Maynard Berry's presence in Kurtz's office was in response to a secret fear of fire. Its victims, whom he treated daily, had become his dream companions—the occupants of endless conflagrations—fires which no one could extinguish. He had been coming, now, to Kurtz for just three months.

Their session for the week was drawing to a close. The two men, long since on friendly terms, fell into a conversation on the subject of shared clients. One especially intrigued Kurtz—a man who had come to him through Berry's referral. Berry, at first, had agreed to perform some cosmetic surgery for this client—who gave his name as Adam Smith. The surgery had been minor—scar tissue replaced on the cheek-bones. An acid-damaged ear was given a new lobe. All of this had gone well and the man retired into anonymity. Six months later, however, he had returned requesting a restructured nose. This was not unusual in itself—but the man's life story and his attitude had altered and he now called himself Smith Jones—not Adam Smith-Jones, but simply Smith

Jones. His behaviour was sufficiently odd to suggest to Maynard Berry that his patient was more than a little paranoid—and might benefit from psychiatric assistance. *He seems to be going into hiding behind this new face of his for reasons not indicated in our first encounter,* Berry had told Kurtz.

Kurtz had sent Smith Jones to one of the Parkin psychiatrists whose expertise lay in the field of paranoia. This was a man named Purvis. The long and the short of it had been that Smith Jones gave up having a name altogether. Kurtz had then brought him under his own supervision. In practice, this was not unusual—but Doctor Purvis had been upset by what he saw as a "raid" on his clientele.

Today, Kurtz informed Maynard Berry that Smith Jones—now called X—had been hospitalized at the Parkin. He was downstairs right at that very moment under heavy sedation.

All this having been said, Kurtz promised to keep the surgeon up to date.

Berry glanced at his watch and stood up.

"Next week, then," said Kurtz, also getting to his feet. "Are you going to this opening of Fabiana's tonight?"

"The Julian Slade exhibit?"

"Yes."

"I thought I might. I'm not all that fond of Slade's work," said Berry, "but it's bound to be sensational—and I might as well go and see it for myself as read about it in the press. So much easier to turn up—look—and leave."

"And Emma? Will she be there?"

Berry was silent. He pretended not to have heard the question. Kurtz did not press it. He had the answer he wanted. Berry's silence signalled his marriage was still in the doldrums. It was not a subject broached in their discussions.

When the surgeon had departed, Kurtz went back to his desk and rummaged through the papers there. He had lost an envelope with some private musings in it, and he was eager to have it back. But it was nowhere to be found.

He crossed the room to the rheostat and adjusted the lights; nothing stark—but brighter than before. His grey wool suit fell over his figure in perfect lines as he moved. Even now, at the age of forty-seven, he had the weightless look of a thirty-year-old. He was pale—though not in a sickly sense. He was merely white. His hair was a different story. He dyed it black, disguising the grey that had begun to show when he was twenty-eight. He never walked in the sun. The overall effect of his appearance could be quite unnerving. It had been said of Rupert Kurtz that he wore the cadaver of someone who had died young.

Now he began to open and close the drawers of his desk. There was still no sign of the missing envelope. Perhaps he had misplaced it during his visit to Queen Street. He went there on a more or less regular basis as a consultant psychiatrist in the schizophrenia wards. Well, he concluded, it would either be there at Queen Street or at home. He was not a careless man. There would be a reasonable explanation.

He sat down then and made an attempt at order on the desk-top. Files—files—letters—letters—files. He often had other psychiatrists' files brought up for perusal. His given excuse for this was the need to keep tabs on how the Parkin Institute was functioning—what sort of progress was being made—the rates of success, et cetera. This was not, however, the true reason Kurtz kept an eye on the files. The fact was, he wanted to monitor who was being treated—why they were being treated—what sort of treatments were being administered. His deepest interest, as always, was in the foibles of the rich.

This file here, for instance. *P* for *Patient*—*A.P.* for *Austin Purvis*. Doctor Purvis was a nervy fellow—wound up and tense—a ticking bomb of a man. But a brilliant psychiatrist—with fascinating clients. Kurtz never tired of his files. Patient X had come from Purvis.

Kurtz drew the P-file in closer and lighted an elegant black cigarette. Beyond the windows, the freezing rain continued to fall as the afternoon rush hour built to a climax.

P.

Kurtz looked to see what the tab might reveal—but it was empty.

No name. No code. Nothing but the letter *P*. Perhaps the file itself would be more rewarding.

He flipped through the pages. Nothing—nothing—nothing. And then: *INSTIGATED BY PANIC CALL*—this in Austin's perfect letters—blocked in with a red marker—and dated. But the date had been covered over with white-out. Underneath, Austin had written the following—in plain black ink—using his fountain pen:

Call came from P. at 14:00 hrs. He was at M(etro) T(oronto) P(olice) H(ead) Q(uarters) Coll(ege) St(reet), brought there by two police officers, both male. No charges had been laid, P. having claimed he was a patient here and that I was his doctor. They allowed him one call, put through to me here.

Here was, presumably, the Parkin Institute. Certainly, the transcript that followed set down a session conducted in Doctor Purvis's office at the Parkin.

Kurtz gave the first page a cursory glance. It dealt with what had happened immediately after Purvis had arrived at the police station to rescue his patient:

AP: Why on earth did you get them to call me?

P(atient): It was the first thing that came into my mind. I thought it was rather clever, actually. The perfect alibi...

AP: What? That you're mad?

P: Well—give or take a little... (Laughter).

AP: It isn't funny. You aren't mad. We've established that—though, sometimes I think you'd like to be.

P: No. I wouldn't.

AP: We aren't going to argue about it. You realize, of course, you're in serious trouble.

P: No, I'm not. They haven't laid charges.

AP: Honestly. You astound me. Do you think, when I say you're in trouble, I mean with the police? Who was this person?

P: I don't know.

AP: You can't lie about this. Who was she?

P: I tell you, I don't know.

AP: Was she a prostitute?

P: Wearing a school uniform? You've got to be kidding!

AP: What school uniform?

P: How do I know? Something blue...

AP: Was she with friends? Or alone.

P: She was alone.

AP: Tell me honestly. Was it really an impulse—or were you sitting there waiting for her?

P: I'm not going to answer that.

AP: Then I can't help you.

P: But...what are you doing?

AP: I'm phoning the police.

P: Why?

AP: Because if you won't answer my questions—then you'll have to answer theirs.

P: (Shouting) But I haven't done anything! I only...

AP: Yes?

P: I talked to her.

AP: What about?

P: Oh, please. I can't...

AP: You were sitting in your car—and you offered her money. They saw that. They saw the money in your hand.

P: So? I wanted her to go to the store for me...

AP: Not funny...

P: Oh, for God's sake!

AP: Was it sex? (Pause) Was it sex?

P: It's not...it wasn't what you think. I'm so ashamed....

AP: Don't cry. It doesn't matter. Just tell me. (Pause) Come on, now...

P: (Unintelligible reply)

AP: Come on—I can't hear you.

P: I wanted to buy her panties.

Kurtz set the transcript aside. *Panties.* He wanted to laugh—but he didn't. Something prevented him—the urgency of Austin's questions. His persistence. Kurtz stubbed his cigarette and continued.

AP: Yes. Well... When you first came here it was underwear then, too, wasn't it. Ladies' underwear. Lingerie. They caught you in Creeds. Thank God it was Creeds. The only reason they didn't press charges was because they knew your wife.

P: I could make a joke here. I could make a very funny joke.

AP: Please—be serious...

P: I could make a very funny joke here about Creeds laying charges. Jesus fucking Christ! My fucking wife has spent a fucking fortune in fucking Creeds! Talk about fucking charges...!

Kurtz heard a distant clock—the one in the outer office—striking the half-hour. The sky beyond the windows had moved to the far end of twilight. The street lamps had come on and College Street was alive with homeward bound traffic.

He glanced at a few more sentences. The patient's kleptomania had moved from Creeds to K Mart—and, finally, to raids on the bureau drawers of his friends....

P: I got away with a lot of stuff at parties. You go to the bathroom—the bedrooms are right there—and there was something wonderful about knowing I had Fabiana Holbach's crotch-clutchers in my pocket while I sat at her dinner table....

Kurtz paused. *Fabiana's...*
He read on.

AP: Did you ever put them on?

P: Of course not! What the fuck kind of question is that? Put them on! I'm no trans-thing—whatever...

AP: Vestite.

P: Transvestite. Put them on! Jesus fucking Christ! All I want to do is have them in my hand, that's all.

AP: Why?

P: Because they...

AP: Yes? They what?

P: I got sick of the other, store-bought underwear. It was too impersonal, that's what it was. It didn't satisfy my curiosity any more.

AP: This girl today—this schoolgirl—how old would you say she was?

P: I don't now.

AP: Take a guess.

P: Thirteen. Maybe fourteen.

AP: Did she have noticeable breasts?

P: What? In a school uniform? You're crazy. Anyway—she wore a coat thing—a sort of raincoat, I guess.

AP: Was it open?

P: How do I know? Yes, it was. So what?

AP: Did she have breasts?

P: I've said no to that already. I'm not interested in her god-damn breasts. I don't give two fucks about tits. Tits are for dirty old men and dirty little boys.

AP: You think so?

P: Sure, I think so. Dirty old men and dirty little boys who...

AP: Who...? Who *what?*

P: Who can't get their fingers on pussy...

AP: I see. You mean—the way you can.

P: Sure I can. Tits? Who gives a shit?

Kurtz set the transcript aside and went over to the windows. He stood there, tall as he could make himself, looking down at the street below him where the rain rushed through the streaming lights of the evening traffic. Winter was being washed away and the city, seemingly, cleansed. Spring would soon enough begin and with its coming, the birds would return and the plague would take on new dimensions. But spring was more than that—it was life as well as death—and the promise of green.

This thought—of leaves, of burgeoning—excited Rupert Kurtz. This was the season of experiments—the time of new projects—a hunting season.

Below him, a car slewed sideways and knocked a pedestrian to the pavement. A crowd began to gather—all wearing Chinese hats, or so it seemed, crushed beneath their umbrellas. Fights broke out as Moonmen and Leatherheads tried to elbow their way to the front of the pack. *Has someone been hurt? Are they dead?*

Kurtz put the Purvis/Patient file in a drawer and gathered up the rest of his papers into his briefcase. He took his overcoat, his Homburg and his umbrella from their stand in the corner and turned out the lights. He had decided, after all, to attend the Slade Exhibit at Fabiana's Gallery. People would be gathered there, he knew, as they had gathered now in the street. *Has someone been hurt? Are they dead?* These were the hallmarks of Julian Slade's art. And then—there was Fabiana's pilfered underwear, lying crumpled in his mind. *Filched*—that was a good word. *Pilfered. Filched. Lifted. Fingered...*

"Good-night, Kilbride."

"Good-night, Doctor Kurtz."

The door swung open. He set his feet in their perfect shoes on the red marble path of the corridor and made his way to the burnished bank of elevator doors. Everyone he passed made a deprecating sound in the throat—a salute without words. Kurtz, not looking, said *good-evening—good-evening*—and went his way.

3

The name alone of Lapin Lanes had made it irresistible to Lilah Kemp. With Peter Rabbit's shoes in hand, she had gone all those years ago—how long had it been?—to inspect the premises of number 38-A. Someone from the university—a woman—had met her at the gate and, after showing her the yard, had taken her through the door into an instant haven. In summer, afternoon and evening sunlight slanted through the windows—filtered through maple leaves and the patterns of Virginia creeper growing on the fence. In winter, only the noonday sun shone into the yard, but this did not matter. The light itself—its quality—was enough to gaze upon—snow-reflected by day, lamp-infused by night.

That had been before the onslaught of schizophrenia and its distortions—before the shadows of trees had begun to crash in her path and the vines had begun to crawl through the windows to steal the food from her table. Then there had been the night when Heathcliff had come for her, wind-blown and rain-soaked, hoarse from his raging, all his black hair whipping his shoulders. Instantly, she had known who he was. His shape in the moonlight had arched above her, his skin the colour of pearl. Heathcliff, himself—no other. Every door and window had slammed against her banging fists. *Help!* And then he was gone— and every bone in her body, so it seemed, was bruised.

Then and thereafter, everything was changed. But Lilah, somehow, had weathered it and won. Even now, with Kurtz set free, she took heart in Lapin Lanes and the comfort of its rough perspective—set out between its high board fences—white and rutted—peopled with garbage cans and cats. *I'm coming home*, she would sing inside. *I'm coming home*, as soon as she turned the corner.

This day, under the freezing rain, she was doubly glad to have made the turn. At the Bedford end of the lane, there had been a skirmish involving Moonmen and Leatherheads. Lilah, as always, was traumatized by their appearance. They were so like the creatures in her dreams, and she could never be sure, in their presence, if she had been responsible for their appearance—the sheen of a Leatherhead ski-mask—a Moonman's silver fingers, coming out of the dark and reaching for her. *Did I do that?* she would say when she saw them. *Was I their transport?*

Even now she could hear the amplified voices of the Moonmen, roaring their battle songs at the end of the lane—and the Leatherheads banging the sidewalks with their baseball bats. *I wish it had been me,* Lilah thought, *that had brought them forth. That way, at least I might one day find out how to be rid of them for all our sakes.* As it was, like everyone else, she must live with the Moonmen and Leatherheads. They were as much a part of the moment as sturnusemia, D-Squads and dead birds.

Evening light had given way to lamplight and darkness. The cats were gathering by Mrs Akhami's gate and sitting on her fences. Lilah had some trouble with the baby carriage. Getting it through the freezing slush was not as easy as getting it through the snow. She thought of Susanna Moodie dragging out her bureau drawers of children onto the icy hill. *At least I don't have to do that...*

Mrs Akhami was cooking something she herself would have called temptatious in her peculiar and innovative English. Lilah counted the cats. Eight of them could be seen, though more were surely beyond the fence in Mrs Akhami's yard. The lanes were full of cats, but there were only occasional dogs. For whatever reason, dogs were disappearing from the city. Not all dogs—not dogs who lived in houses, safe in the aura of human need. Dogs were still a valuable source of protection—and people kept them for just that reason. But dogs that were wild and stray were rarely seen.

Lilah paused. Mrs Akhami's head and shoulders made brief appearances in her window as she moved about her second-storey kitchen. What could it be that smelled so delicious? Some sort of chicken dish—a curry, perhaps, though Lilah distinctly caught a hint of olive oil in the air. Olive oil, chicken, turmeric, coriander, saffron...

Lilah was hungry—almost as hungry as the cats—and she hung there with them, spellbound while Mrs Akhami wove her culinary magic with her spoons.

If only Marlow would come to Lilah out of *Heart of Darkness* the way the cats had come out of the dark to Mrs Akhami's fence. But nothing, so far, had drawn him—not his name, when she spoke it, and not the escape of Kurtz. Nor all the panic in the world. Marlow, it seemed, was locked between the covers of his book, where Conrad had put him, and nothing would induce him to come forth.

A dog began to bark nearby.

Lilah shaded her eyes against the rain and stared at the sky. Was there a moon?

How can there be. It's pouring rain.

And yet, there was a yellow cast to the clouds. Not the moon, but the city's lights shining upwards.

The dog went on barking.

Mrs Akhami's window was suddenly opened wide and an exaggerated draught of cooking smells flooded across the yard towards the lane.

"Stop that!" Mrs Akhami called to the dog. "Stop that!" And then a stream of invective in her native tongue.

Lilah felt betrayed. The silence into which Marlow might have stepped was shattered. She pushed the carriage through the gate and up along the walk. Out in the laneway, the dog that had been barking began to howl. But the moon—and Marlow—were reticent—and still refused to appear.

4

Every evening after work, Kurtz went home to his apartment in The Citadel on Avenue Road and changed his shirt and tie. This was part of his ritual of cleanliness. On some occasions, he also changed his underwear. He parked his car, a grey Impala, in the underground garage and rode up—silent, with his eyes closed—to the twenty-fifth floor. Kurtz was fond of the sensations this produced—the pull of gravity against his innards—the self-imposed disorientation.

The elevator glided to an almost imperceptible stop. A computerized voice announced *floor twenty-five* and the doors rolled back, giving Kurtz, his eyes now open, a view of dark mahogany walls and of crystal lamps. A mirror informed him the hallway was empty and he stepped out onto the thick pile carpet—royal blue with a burgundy border. He noted his shoes were grey with salt and slush. No matter. An attendant would come with a vacuum and remove all evidence that Kurtz had passed this way.

Reaching his own door, he gave the password into the voice-box and heard the bolt being withdrawn from within. His password this week was *ME*. On consecutive weeks he alternated this with *MYSELF* and *I*. It was easy to remember and impossible to duplicate. The system had to acknowledge the patterns of his own voice before it would activate the locks.

In twenty minutes, having washed his face and hands and brushed his teeth, he stood in his dressing-room with a glass of gin, regarding an open drawer of laundered shirts.

He selected one that was silk and cotton combined and shook it open. Though he could see himself in the full-length mirror, he barely noticed. The pleasures involved in putting on the shirt were almost entirely tactile. The skinlike feel of the material swept him all the way back to his youth and the gift of a dozen shirts that his father had brought from England to celebrate young Kurtz's entry into manhood.

Handstitched, French-cuffed and long-tailed, each of the birthday shirts had been wrapped in tissue paper and packed with a pair of collars in its own magenta box and each of them had *Rupert Kurtz* discreetly printed on a label sewn to the inside seam on the right-hand side. Studs and cuff-links had been a part of his father's gift—the first that Kurtz had owned: silver studs and bloodstone links, each stone set in an oval silver frame. Kurtz had green eyes. The bloodstones had been his mother's suggestion. Though his father had concurred with the choice, he had thought them ostentatious. *Perhaps,* he had said as an aside, *you can manage to lose them...*

Kurtz did up the buttons slowly—taking his time and savouring little mouthfuls of gin as he made his way from top to bottom.

One always loses one's first pair of cuff-links, his father had said, *around the time one loses one's virginity. At least it was so when I lost mine.* Kurtz had been sitting—his father standing—in a club on York Street.

Kurtz gave a toast to the ghost of his father—tall and straight and grey as himself in the mirror.

The loss of one's virginity, back then—his father had continued—*was considered a formal affair, worthy of formal attire—though a business suit would do. Whether you lost it with a girl of short acquaintance in a foreign city or a prostitute in a local brothel, you owed the occasion some respect. You never, of course, considered losing your virginity with someone known to either your parents or your friends.*

Kurtz selected a sombre tie and knotted it. Green with a maroon stripe. He had managed not to lose that first pair of cuff-links and he wore them now. When he had lost his virginity, that was all he had lost. In London, Ontario.

Dressed, he wandered through the bedroom, idly looking for his missing envelope—gone now how long? He had only just discovered its absence today.

He turned on the lights that displayed his ivory collection set out on shelves against one wall, glassed in from top to bottom—the display case sitting on a black marble ledge, waist high. Beneath the ledge, locked in behind latticed doors, he kept his other collections—the ones not shown to visitors, but only on occasion to intimates: the photographs in wooden boxes; the toy lead army; the Chinese shoes. The ivory collection had some renown. New York and Paris curators had come to view it. It had been appraised by experts from the great museums. It was priceless, even in spite of having been given a price. The age of some of the pieces precluded the possibility of replacement. Most of them were African—a few were from Dieppe—and more from Southeast Asia and Japan.

The envelope was nowhere to be seen—and not in any of the drawers he opened. It was not—why would it be?—in the conservatory overlooking the city and not in either the dining-room or kitchen.

How could one have lost it? Where could it possibly be?

He glanced at his watch.

It was getting on for seven-thirty. He would look for the envelope again tomorrow. It must be in the office. Maybe in the car. Somewhere. Nothing disappears. Completely. *Does it?*

He turned out the lights displaying the ivory. He left a few lamps burning for his return. He put on his outer garments, finished his gin, took up his umbrella and left. In spite of wind and weather, he would attend the opening of Slade's exhibit at the Fabiana Gallery. More than the paintings drew him there. It was her. It was Fabiana—and the thought of standing beside her—close enough to smell her skin.

A few minutes later—the journey being so short—Kurtz started up the steps of the Fabiana Gallery on Cooper Street.

Someone else was coming up behind him and they seemed to want to pass. A man and a woman. The woman spoke.

"Is that you, Rupert?" she asked. Kurtz turned.

Olivia Price stood before him, smiling. Griffin Price was standing just beyond her—sleek and balding—with one tanned glove against the door.

"Olivia," Kurtz said stiffly. "Griff." They shook hands.

Griffin acted as porter while his wife and Kurtz went through.

"You a fan of this Slade fella, Rupert?" he said. "I wouldn't have thought he was your cup of tea."

Kurtz said: "I'm always interested. A person has to keep track of the trends, you know." He did not say Slade had once been his patient. "How have you been, Griff? You went off to Poland, or somewhere."

"Prague," said Griffin. "To the glassworks, and so forth."

"Oh, yes," said Kurtz, "the glassworks and so forth. Did you pick them up?"

"Did, indeed," said Griffin, giving up his alpaca overcoat to a man in a white jacket. He brushed his hand through imaginary hair and straightened his tie. "I'm thinking of having them duplicate some of our Eskimo stuff—you know, birds and things—seals and things—polar bears in glass. That sort of thing. Sell them in hotel shops and airports. People like to take a little something back from here that doesn't have *Toronto* or *Canada* written all over it. Something discreet and classy. Glass is classy. And if it says *MADE IN PRAGUE* on the tag, so much the better." He took a martini from a passing tray—removed the olive on its stick and laid it back where the glass had been before the tray moved on. "We have to get the souvenir market back from the Taiwanese and the Koreans. Put it in the hands of Eastern Europeans. They're counting on us, now, to do something for them—take out the Asians and put them back at tinware and bisque. One thing they never got a handle on, Rupert: that little touch of taste that gives an object class. Paste and lacquer—that's what they're good at. Agreed?"

Kurtz gave a non-committal nod and wondered if the speech was over. Griffin Price was drinking his martini. He seemed to be noshing on the glass—holding it firmly to his lips and leaving it there. His teeth were like tiny pearls—each one perfect and all of them the same size. His pale blue eyes were shaded by dark, luxuriant lashes—the kind you see on expensive dolls, Kurtz thought. He remembered Griff as a boy—ten years Kurtz's junior. His hair had been fine and fair and the contrast with dark brows and lashes had been remarkable. He had seemed, then, somewhat lost—a boy who needed protection and reassurance. Part of this, doubtless, had to do with the events that had traumatized him.

Griffin's father—whose name was Alex—had been what used to be called a roué. He had made a point of always having European mistresses—dark-haired women who looked as if they ought to be in films, but never were. Griffin's wife, Olivia, bore some resemblance to these women—tall, slender, patrician—with the classic beauty shared by all three Wylie sisters. Alex Price would have eaten her alive, but had died before he got to see her. He was killed playing polo at Palm Beach—his wife and children looking on—his current mistress off in the clubhouse. Everyone remembered that day—the pony falling—Alex Price going down with it and the pony rolling over on him, crushing his ribs and puncturing his heart. Ventura Price and two of her three sons barely went into mourning. Martyrs and millionaires in a single stroke. But Griffin, who was the youngest, had worshipped his father and long after Alex's death, the boy remained bewildered and bereft. The mistress went back to Spain and was never heard of again this side of the water. Not an untypical story, Kurtz thought, as he surveyed the antechamber where they stood with their drinks before going in to the paintings. Nearly everyone in this room, he mused, has violence somewhere in the family background—the violence always on an operatic scale—Verdi, not Puccini. Never Wagner. Tasteful—but fullblown; a generation of weddings sung by tenors and sopranos—with all the dark basses and contraltos waiting in the wings....*La forza del destino...*

Here, Kurtz thought—as he watched Fabiana's guests over the rim of his glass, are the children of all those violent marriages—thirty and forty years old, the progeny of a dozen dead millionaires and two, maybe three dozen Palm Beach widows. The rest, in Fabiana's antechamber, were either self-made and home-grown or had *come by jet*, as the saying goes—Brits and Yanks and Krauts and South Americans—Argentinians, Brazilians—exiles from Chile.

Kurtz took a small round of toast with a mushroom on it and popped it into his mouth. He swallowed it whole. He wondered where Fabiana might be. And Julian Slade.

Slade had once been his client at the Parkin Institute. This had been three years before, when the artist had first showed signs of schizophrenia. Kurtz had treated him then and had been intrigued by Slade's unique reaction to what was happening to him. There had not been any fear in the man, but only gratitude. *I look forward,* he had said, *to my life as a madman. When does it begin?*

Kurtz had smiled at this impatience. But with Slade, it was hard to tell if he was joking or being serious. His expression rarely changed and his voice, which could modulate in volume, never modulated in tone. His paintings had then been white on white—with holes torn through the canvas. Eyes that were blinded and mouths that were screaming. Slade's favoured word back then had been *shreds*. Kurtz had been dazzled, but kept his enthusiasm to himself. As for Slade, he fell in love with Kurtz—aesthetically—and became, in this way, his disciple.

Having mounted an exhibition of his torn and punctured paintings at the Pollard Gallery, Slade had wanted to dedicate them all to Kurtz—*the man who released my demons*. But Kurtz had forbidden it. The paintings were too alarming. And, while he was impressed, a part of Kurtz had been shaken by what he saw.

The Pollard Gallery had been divided down the centre with an avenue of potted lime trees. The canvases showed a variety of tortured figures—all of them wearing white—and each with its share of punctured features and torn parts. Running beneath the paintings was an aluminum eavestrough—one trough on either side of the room, each of them feeding into a wide aluminum pan at the far end. By some ingenious means a bright red liquid ran from the painted figures into these troughs. They "bled." Above the collecting pan was Slade's intended *pièce de résistance*—a portrait of the artist with *my shredder in my hand*. The shredder was a flaying knife.

The effect had been electrifying—just what Slade had intended: *like walking in on forensic surgery*, he told Kurtz. The exhibit—and the Pollard Gallery—had been closed the next day by the police. Someone of influence had complained and Pollard was charged with *showing indignities to the human body*. Ultimately, the gallery owner had his day in court and was cleared. Julian Slade left the country and did what he had always wanted to do. He went to Spain and studied the works of Goya, and he went there a good deal wealthier than he had been before the *Shreds* exhibit. By the end of the third day following that event, every single one of the canvases had been sold.

Neither Pollard—whom Kurtz could now see standing on the far side of Fabiana's antechamber—nor Slade—who had still not put in an appearance—had divulged the name or the names of the buyers. The buyers, in their turn, were silent—though Kurtz, in time, was made aware of what had become of the paintings. They hung on the walls of his clients.

Griffin Price could seem so beguiling, Kurtz thought as he watched him remove another olive from another martini. With his cornflower eyes and his pearly teeth and his pensive smile, he was like the beautiful child he had been that day he had watched his father being lifted from the polo field. But the man that heartbroken child had become had a heartless streak that verged on the sadistic. He fancied himself as something of a social critic and his pronouncements were larded with implications of cruelty—all of them delivered in an even, almost casual tone. "I think that Julian Slade is the Mengele of art," he said, dipping his finger into his martini and sucking on it. "It intrigues me just to imagine what he will imagine next to improve the human race."

Kurtz blinked.

Griffin regarded the olive on its stick and set it carefully back on the waiting tray—waving the waiter away and dipping his finger back like a diver into his glass. "Wouldn't you agree, Rupert?" Griffin was smiling. "The human race needs another Mengele to bring it up to date."

Kurtz thought: *if I look at him now, I won't know what to say.* Luckily, Griffin went on with his speech while Kurtz pretended to search for a handkerchief. Around them, the hum of other conversations broke from time to time to let the music through from the room where the paintings were still in hiding beyond the doors.

"In Prague," Griffin said, "I had a vision when I was standing in the glassworks." He was on his third martini, now, and very slightly drunk. This gave his voice a kind of purring edge—the voice of someone dreaming, hypnotized and not quite present. "There were all these men with mechanical buffers polishing, polishing bits of crystal. Turning them, turning them, making them perfect. And I thought: *if only we could do that to ourselves; shape ourselves that way.* And my vision was..."

Griffin looked through his martini glass at Kurtz and said: "my vision was that we are ready for another version of the human race. The final honing." He drank the martini and looked at Kurtz straight—still with the smile. "Isn't that sort of what our pal Julian meant when he tore things to shreds? All those paintings of people flayed—torn away from who they were..."

"I guess so," said Kurtz, who didn't want to commit himself to what Griffin was saying. "Maybe."

Griffin looked around for somewhere to put his glass. "There's another side to this, you know," he said.

"Oh?" Kurtz had spotted a woman on the far side of the antechamber near the front door. She must have just arrived.

"Yes," said Griffin. "And this is where you come in—the king of psychiatry. I mean—if there are new forms of human beings, then it follows there must be new forms of madness... Yes?"

Griffin let the proposition hang between them. He could see that Kurtz was distracted.

"What are you looking at?" he asked.

"Nothing," said Kurtz. "Just an acquaintance—who happens to be your sister-in-law."

"Pray God not sister Amy," said Griffin.

"No," said Kurtz. "The other one."

Peggy Webster, who was chic and unadorned, stood off to one side, alone. She was the eldest of the famous Wylie sisters and, in Kurtz's youth, had been a prize. She was austere without being aloof—reserved, but not unforthcoming. She was known for her devotion to the past and could tell you anything you wanted to know about the city and its people—the sources of its wealth and the sources of its staid traditions. Most of the great families—great, so-called—had adhered to social patterns that had been established in the early eighteen hundreds. Admittance to this core group was rarely granted—and only if the credentials presented were impeccable. Like most pioneer colonial societies, the rules of conduct were limiting and uncreative. *More British than the British* had been the motto then, which Griffin Price translated as *More Torontonian than Torontonians*. This was the pool of genes from which the Wylies had emerged. The Websters—one of whom Peggy had married—were another story altogether.

Besides the old Toronto society, there was the new. This, Griffin would tell you, is common to every culture—but the difference between one *new* society and another lies in the uniqueness of the given *old* society. It is the old society that is being aped—and what is being aped depends on where the old society got its values. In Toronto, Griffin said, they were got from snobs. So *snobbery* was aped—and, while snobbery itself is bad enough, the aping of it is vacuous. Money turned the key, as always—and what this produced, according to Griffin Price, was *a social class of rogues and brutes dressed up in pinstripe suits and screwing everything in sight. Metaphorically speaking, of course...* Needless to say, in Griffin's opinion, the Webster clan had been spawned by rogues and brutes.

When Peggy Wylie said yes to Ben Webster, he had once said to Kurtz, *the whole of Rosedale fainted dead away*. And Kurtz had thought: *metaphorically speaking, of course.*

It was the marriage of its decade—the one that saw the first of the great Wylie houses pass into other hands. It did not, of course, pass into other hands so long as Peggy was in residence—but its fate was sealed. And the fate of its neighbours. The tide was only turned when the pinstriped brutes discovered life on the heights uptown and the delights of Russell Hill Road. In the meantime, real-estate barons and media stars were *playing house along the Bridle Path and other horsey lanes* (also Griffin's description) in a semi-rural district called, of all things, Bayview—where there were neither bays nor views of bays—nor views of anything but other houses. This, according to Griffin, was what Peggy Wylie had feared the most—the invasion of the tasteless hordes whose money would put the old world to shame because it was passed about in living-rooms.

There she stood. "Waiting," Griffin said, "as always, for the world to turn without her."

Her husband, Benedict, shouldered his way through the crowd by the bar and returned with two glasses of wine. If Griffin Price could be said to dislike Ben Webster, Kurtz could be said to hate him. He hated him for reasons of which even Webster himself was unaware—reasons that had their seat in school, where Ben had been a king and Kurtz had been a joyless subject. Ben had been blessed with physical beauty and grace. He had all the sports in his limbs and his feet from the day he was born—and none of the classic numbness in the skull that so often, in boys, goes hand in hand with physicality. Ben had his personal fortune started before his graduation from St Andrew's College. He got it from establishing a taxi service, using his father's cars and his brother, John, as a driver. They ferried fellow Andreans to football games and dances. This way, he ended high school with several thousand dollars in the bank.

What Ben Webster needed next was a way in through the door to his dreams—and that was Margaret Wylie, known as Peggy. He wooed her shamelessly. She was given heirloom pearls and rings which had been his mother's—the last of his own great possessions. Peggy was also brought to heel by Ben's awareness of her fear of him. He frightened her to death. His physical presence—his energy—his eyes—all these were terrifying to her. He was—and he remained—electrifying. And there they stood—together, side by side a perfect melding of upward mobility and class, victor and victim, man and woman.

Now, Griffin Price was talking to a couple unknown to Kurtz. Kurtz began to wander around the room. He wondered where Fabiana was. It was not her habit to have her guests stand around drinking so long before an opening. Normally, Fabiana was prompt and a good stage-manager—an excellent host. But this night there were complications. Slade had not yet put in his appearance, and Fabiana would not declare the exhibition open until he was standing beside her. Kurtz also wondered if she was nervous of the paintings awaiting them beyond the closed doors in the next room. She was admiring of Slade—but guarded about the reaction his work was bound to receive. He had never failed to challenge his audience. Witness what had happened to Pollard and his gallery. And there was always an overpowering sense of menace staring down from a Slade canvas. Perhaps Fabiana was even grateful he was late. Reinforced by a few extra drinks—on this occasion only—her clientele might withstand the shock of what would shortly confront it.

Suddenly, a flurry of excitement out in the hallways caused the patrons to turn in that direction, standing on tiptoe trying to see whoever had arrived.

Slade at last?

No. It was John Dai Bowen and the Berrys. Hardly a letdown.

Everywhere the Berrys went in public, John Dai Bowen—with his camera—was certain to be there. For all her great beauty, Emma Berry could not abide her picture being taken. She was known to the press as *The Elusive One* and *The Ghost Queen*. But the epithet by which she was known at large was *The Surgeon's Wife*. Maynard Berry himself was not without talent when it came to elusiveness. He was afraid for his hands—and never greeted anyone with a handshake. If making a public appearance, the hands were always safely tucked into his jacket pockets—a public stance for which he was almost as famous as his wife, who used the most extraordinary means and ruses to protect her features from the camera's eye.

Emma Berry was small—a tiny, perfect figure of exquisite proportions. The word *petite*, however, did not apply to her. She was not a china doll. She was not a delicate flower. She had a dazzling, energetic presence and was quite incapable of an ugly gesture. Her skin, it seemed, had a genius for radiance. John Dai Bowen knew this too well and had tried every trick in the book to make a record of her beauty for posterity. So far, he had failed.

This night, in fact, John Dai was a member of the Berry party. His little round body was the perfect complement to Maynard's fox and Emma's swan. He was their cat—overfed, overgroomed, overpetted. He adored the attention of his own fame—and he adored even more the reflected glory of the company he kept. The well-known sibilance of his whispered asides was catlike, too—the chatter of a hunting cat about to pounce.

Emma was veiled. This was her disguise for the present affair. As if she could hide behind an openwork veil—but it offered enough of a screen to thwart John Dai's camera—and that was what mattered. Like Fabiana, Emma generally favoured black—but on this occasion she wore a gown that was midnight blue. It was drawn in tight at the waist and its skirts just revealed her perfect knees. There was a jacket, worn open over the bodice—and the veil was held in place with a small blue rose made of silk. A second of these roses, with its petals spread, was tucked into her cleavage. Maynard held her by the elbow as they made their way into the antechamber where Kurtz stood watching.

John Dai hovered. Perhaps when Emma sipped her wine, the veil would be raised. But no such luck. She declined all refreshments. John Dai wandered off to see who else was present.

Maynard nodded at Kurtz—but did not speak. Emma looked away—but not out of malice. She was hoping that Fabiana might be nearby, since they were friends. Kurtz, as they passed, could smell Emma's perfume. *Calèche.* It drifted in the air, holding her in place even as she moved on. Precisely at eight-thirty, the music stopped and Fabiana Holbach, wearing a black wool sheath with a short-sleeved gold brocade jacket, led her distinguished guests into the gallery. Her publicist, Lillianne Tanaka, had arranged that a small number of eminent collectors had been invited, whose tasteful sensibilities would be traumatized by Slade's paintings. *If we can send a minimum of five people out of here mortified by what they've seen, within two hours there won't be an unsold canvas hanging on these walls.*

Fabiana had inwardly winced at this. She certainly wanted the collection to be sold—but she hoped the moving force behind the sales would be genuine admiration—not mere notoriety.

Now, with drinks in hand and high on expectation, seventy-five hand-picked patrons stepped through the opened doorway in their silver shoes and patent leather pumps and stood, all at once, immobilized at the centre of a large white room. "I always forget how huge it is," Olivia Price said to Kurtz. "I wonder what they used it for in its brothel days."

Kurtz did not reply. He stood with Olivia and the others, herded and silent, all of them pressed together at the centre of the room like people finding shelter on an island in a storm. They stood this way for almost a minute, gazing from side to side to see which path the storm might be going to take. The lighting all around them was dim and only the glowing shapes of the paintings could be seen—gigantic in size and seemingly waiting to burst into flames.

Lillianne Tanaka, wearing scarlet and brushing her long black hair away from her face, stepped up onto a rostrum that sat dead centre in the room. "Welcome to the Fabiana Gallery," she said. "We are pleased that you have come in spite of the rain." Her voice was broken—filtered through two packs of cigarettes a day—and her hands, that kept brushing her hair aside, were shaking with excitement. After the weeks of calm and calculated preparation for this moment, Lillianne had finally succumbed to nervous tension. "Please," she said, "give welcome to Fabiana Holbach..."

Everyone applauded. Lillianne's tension had taken hold of the whole room and as Fabiana made her way through the guests, she, too, could be seen to be nervous. Her hands could not manage to lift her skirts as she climbed up onto the rostrum. Her pupils were enlarged and her smile was fixed.

John Dai Bowen was having a wonderful time. The group of young women whom he called *The Charity Bimbos* was out in force. Over-dressed and overzealous, they made what John Dai had dubbed as *The Bimbo Wars* to see who could throw the most outrageous parties in behalf of this week's psychotics—this month's disease—this year's Third World disaster. John Dai adored the crass and the vulgar almost as rashly as he worshipped class and beauty.

Fabiana managed to smile at the over-enthusiastic applause. "Before I present Mister Slade," she said—and cleared her throat. "Before I present Mister Slade, I want to say how pleased I am—and proud—that so many of you have come to do honour to this brilliant artist..."

"Where is he?" someone shouted.

Laughter.

"Patience," said Fabiana, with another smile. "He is here." She paused, and looked around. "When the Pollard Gallery was closed and Tommy Pollard retired, I had the good fortune to inherit Julian Slade, along with two or three others of Tommy's incomparable stable. Thank you, Tommy...." She waved. "All of us miss you in the art world, but we are always more than happy to have you in our company."

There was a smattering of applause and Tommy Pollard blew a kiss to Fabiana.

"Now," Fabiana said, "comes the moment. Ladies and gentlemen—my friends—please welcome—Julian Slade!"

Fabiana began the applause which spread out over the room and the antechamber beyond in waves. She reached out her hand. The Red Sea of patrons parted. Julian Slade came through—and the guests closed in behind him, still applauding.

Kurtz immediately saw that Slade was ill. His body, always thin, was now emaciated. Sturnusemia? AIDS? It was impossible to tell without a closer view, but clearly—all too clearly—Julian Slade was dying.

His face, which had once been remarkably beautiful, was haggard now, and bearded. He wore dark glasses—a further sign of illness, of intolerance to light. His clothing had been chosen to offset the shock of his condition—a brightly coloured harlequin jacket made of suede and velvet, patched together in shades of blue and grey and burgundy. The trousers were made of burgundy leather and the shoes were bright yellow espadrilles. When he stood on the rostrum beside Fabiana, he made a full turn so that everyone could see him. But he was silent.

Fabiana said: "Mister Slade is a master of trickery. His trick tonight is silence. He refuses to speak to us. He will make no statement—he will answer no question. I have here his written communication..." She unfolded a piece of paper and looked at Slade. "You're sure about the silence?" she said.

Slade nodded vigorously and drew a smile on his face with his finger.

"All right," said Fabiana. And then she read from the paper. *"You will see here...savage acts which have been done too long in darkness. It is my belief they should be done in the light. And to that end—these paintings."*

Fabiana did not appear to have been prepared for these words. She turned the paper over, but there was nothing more. She gave Slade a nervous look. She folded the paper and kept it tight in the palm of her hand.

"Ladies and gentlemen," she said, "I take pride in this moment, and in this company, to introduce you all to the latest collection of paintings by Julian Slade!" With this, she waved her hand at the doorway and someone, taking the cue, brought up the lights so the paintings could be seen. Everyone turned full circle. There was a collective intake of breath.

Fabiana said: "Julian Slade has called these paintings *The Collection of the Golden Chambers.* They are the largest canvases he has ever produced. Two of them are sixteen feet in length and ten feet high—one of them larger still. Because of their size, there is only room for twelve to be hung. When told of this limitation, Julian said: *"If there is only room for twelve, then only twelve shall exist."* She looked at the silent harlequin beside her. Then she said: "we know that Mister Slade wants the paintings to speak for themselves. And they do—as you shall see. I invite you now to peruse them at your leisure—and I thank you, once again, for coming here this evening to celebrate the talent of this young and brilliant artist."

Before he was engulfed by the mass of patrons who still had not looked at the paintings, Slade made a curious gesture which was barely seen by anyone but the man for whom it was intended. He turned in Kurtz's direction and raised his arm as if to say *Ave Caesar.* He made Kurtz a bow—and was gone.

While this was happening, Fabiana also disappeared into the crowd.

Kurtz turned to the nearest wall of paintings. They were lit with a bank of lights that were more theatrical than was usual. Looking around, Kurtz could see that the gallery and all the people in it were touched with a golden hue that was oddly sensual—and it was not until he'd drawn a bead on the canvas closest to him that he realized it was covered with gold leaf.

This was not true of every painting in the room. Some had less than others—but all had passages of gold somewhere on their surface. They were, as Fabiana had promised, gigantic in size, and the theme of *Golden Chambers* was borne out in every one of them, though Kurtz thought *Golden Dungeons* might have been a more appropriate title. Regarding them, he was swept with alternate spasms of heat and cold—as if a fever was coming on.

Each individual canvas was perfectly self-contained and needed no reference to the surrounding canvases to make its point. The collective effect, however, was electrifying.

They hurt, Kurtz thought, *my eyes....* For a moment, he had to squint to see them.

Also, they were overwhelmingly sexual.

Kurtz stepped forward alone, passing from each to the next like a man performing a slow march.

Every golden chamber had a name: *The Golden Chamber of the Missing Children, The Golden Chamber of the Hunt, The Golden Chamber of the River Gods*, etc. Crowds of bodies, most of them nude, were spilled before him as he walked—and there was not a single female figure among them. Slade was a master draughtsman, and his evocation of this multitude of naked men and boys was painfully erotic. The exuberance of the figures lured the viewer in through the eye, but once the eye was caught, they burrowed on to the groin.

Kurtz considered himself to be as textbook straight—in the sexual sense—as a male can be. He was therefore shocked to discover that his penis stirred as he gazed at these men exposed in the golden light. He was also forced to acknowledge he was being aroused by the scenes of torture and degradation. In his mind, a kind of buzzing began to sound and the channels behind his eyes began to swell with pressure.

What Kurtz saw, as he passed along the unfolding canvases, was a panoply of naked men in thrall of other naked men, males in thrall of being male, boys and youths in thrall of masculine strength—and strength itself in thrall of force. Kurtz had never seen figures—even in life—so naked as these. Every hair and every nuance of veined muscle, every toe and finger, every penis and nipple, every folded, curving buttock was exposed as if prepared for manipulation or consumption. And yet, there were no erections—no overt invitations to engage in sex—no depictions of the act itself. But, equally, each and every figure was rampant with sexual menace and power—even those who were displayed as victims. It was unnerving—but Kurtz could not look away. Neither could he close his eyes. And when he made the turn and faced the wall that had been behind him, he was stopped in his tracks.

The painting hanging there was *The Golden Chamber of the White Dogs*—a triptych, and the largest work in the whole exhibit. Nothing that Kurtz had so far seen—in spite of its power—had prepared him for this. By the time he had viewed each panel of the triptych from left to right, he was in full erection—aching with shame and confusion. No man alive had ever produced this effect on Kurtz, and he was mortified.

His face must have shown some inkling of his groin's condition—a flush of sudden colour in his cheeks, perhaps, notorious for their whiteness. Or the dry, hot parting of his lips—the need for air—the abrupt intake of a breath that got no further than his throat before it choked him. He drew out his handkerchief and snapped it open like a fan and coughed into its folds.

"Sort of gets to you, doesn't it," said an unfamiliar voice—male and hoarse and impertinent. Kurtz took a step away to one side before he looked at the fellow—a small, neat man with a flattened nose and sleek red hair.

"Have we met?" said Kurtz—and put away his handkerchief. He was hoping to throw the man off his scent.

"Don't think we have," said the redhead. "But I know who you are. You're Doctor Kurtz. My name's Shapiro."

"How do you do?" said Kurtz, with excessive formality—withdrawing his hand from where it had deposited the handkerchief. But Shapiro did not reciprocate—both his hands remained plunged to the depths of his trouser pockets.

"That one over there—" Shapiro jerked his chin at *The Golden Chamber of the Missing Children*, "gave me a hard on. But this one here—" he rocked back onto his heels and eyed *The Golden Chamber of the White Dogs*, "it makes me want to come. I mean—I'm already wet in my underwear." He looked up at Kurtz—sweating and smiling—very slightly drunk—thinking he was just being friendly. Even in spite of his own now waning condition, Kurtz was disgusted. He wondered how on earth such a creature had been allowed through the doors, treating the paintings as if they were an exhibit of blatant pornography.

But then Shapiro said something that caught Kurtz by surprise. "It's a sad, bad day," he said, "when a man can't accept his own desires—even with them staring him straight in the face. But I'll bet you every man in this room is looking into these paintings and saying, *no—it's not me in there. It's someone else.*" Kurtz noticed, all at once, there were tears in Shapiro's eyes. Not welling over—but filling the cups of his lids—and forcing him to bite his lip to keep them in their place.

Kurtz looked back at the painting before him. It was, of course, the product of madness. He knew that. A perfect rendering of the schizophrenic nightmare that passed for Slade's reality. He turned and glanced sideways in order to verify the content of the other paintings already seen. Yes—absolutely—these were the chambers of Slade's existence— the caves through which he clambered, passing on his way to the ground of the common world—or the little bit of the common world he could share, in his schizoid condition, with other human beings.

"I'll leave you now," Shapiro said. "I need a breath of air."

This time, he did put out his hand and Kurtz took it—noting its sweat—into his own. "Goodbye," he said. "Mister..."

"Shapiro." The man gave a small, quick smile. "I trust we'll meet again, Doctor Kurtz," he said. "But not, I hope, in your office." This had been meant as a joke, but neither man laughed. Shapiro made his way to the door and Kurtz turned back to the painting.

The Golden Chamber of the White Dogs was eighteen feet long and painted on three separate canvases. The centre panel was ten by eight and the others four by eight. It could be displayed, as now, flat from end to end, or it could be shown as triptychs are shown in churches, with the shorter panels open at an angle. The figures in the painting were gathered in a darkened blood-red chamber, the chamber itself contained and limited beneath a gilded arch that spread from end to end of the picture.

In the centre panel, three men sat at a low, white table. One of these men had his back to the viewer—and his was the only figure fully seen. The others were partially obscured by the table itself and by three standing figures—one of whom had both arms raised with what appeared to be a severed leg—not human—in his hands. The focus of attention was a shallow metal basin into which all six men were gazing. It could not be said they were staring—only gazing, and the feeling this gave was one of casual horror. Lying in the basin was what appeared to be a monkey's head, partially wrapped in a blood-stained cloth. A large white dog stood in the foreground—bull-like and shark-eyed—its muzzle reddened, presumably with blood.

In the left-hand panel, a bleeding male torso was suspended from somewhere out of sight beyond the golden arch. Two white dogs, more like pigs than bulls, and hairless as the others, were lying on a ledge that was strewn with golden straw. Below them on the floor, another white dog was nervously pushing its snout towards a human hand that was reaching from the darkness at the painting's edge.

In the right-side panel, two more white dogs were seated with their backs to the viewer, yearning upwards in the direction of a metal table on which a young man was stretched in agony. His back was arched and one knee was raised and both his arms were held out to prevent whatever was going to happen to him next. His head, with its eyes filled with terror, was thrown back over the table's edge towards the two watching dogs. Beyond the table, two men stood in conference—one bending forward to support the raised left leg of the supine figure. At the extreme edge of this panel, the buttocks and one leg could be seen of a departing figure—someone either fleeing from the scene or going away to do the bidding of the others.

The whole of the chamber was bathed in red and gold light—fading into a tunnel of smoke and shadows, some of which spilled out almost into the foreground. Later, Kurtz would discover that tar was the medium used to create this darkness. And at the far end of the chamber, visible to some degree in each of the panels, the walls were topped by wooden stakes—each one bearing a white-faced, grimacing human head—severed and bleeding.

Kurtz was mesmerized. Somehow, the painting soothed him. It verified his fears. But it also informed him that fear was wonderful. It told him there was nothing in the whole wide world of madness that was not the property of sanity as well. The figures told him that—with their golden skin and their tangible flesh. Their inflammatory nakedness was an open invitation to join in what could only be seen as the beauty of madness—and the gift of power that madness bestows.

Dear God, Kurtz thought, as he forced himself to turn away. He felt ill with excitement.

He must find Fabiana—or that other woman, Lillianne. It was imperative that someone be found in this room who would buy *The Golden Chamber of the White Dogs* and make a donation of it to The Parkin Institute of Psychiatric Research...

Someone surely could be found who would be honoured to make a gift of wonder to the mad.

Some time before the evening was over, John Dai Bowen achieved a notable success. Good as his word that afternoon to Kurtz in his office, Maynard Berry took his wife's arm and walked her once around the paintings, ending as Kurtz had done at *The Golden Chamber of the White Dogs*.

"Look," he said to Emma, "do you see the heads?"

Emma looked away. "Horror doesn't interest me," she said.

"It should," said Maynard. "It is, after all, how I make my living."

Emma was silent for a moment before she said: "yes." She glanced then, sideways, at each of the panels. The dogs, but nothing else she saw, had more than once invaded her dreams. Prowlers—sniffing at her heels. She turned away.

"Can we leave?" she said.

"Indeed we can," said Maynard.

They stepped away and collected their coats from the attendant in the antechamber. Emma declined to put hers on, but wore it around her shoulders—dark, rich furs which made a perfect frame for her pale, bright face beneath its veil.

Maynard drew her towards the door. They waved good-night to Fabiana and the attendant let them through. A white Mercedes limousine awaited them at the curb.

Emma paused on the top step. She unclipped the blue rose and drew off the veil.

"That's better," she said—and took a deep breath. To her left, the park beyond the palings was lit with lamps and the shiny skins of rain-wet trees. The rain itself had ceased and the night air held the slightest portent of green. Maynard went down the steps before her. Emma reached out for the rail—and almost fell.

A flash-bulb went off in her face. *Damn you, John Dai Bowen. Damn you!*

She fled—and the limousine with her.

5

Once inside, Lilah dried off the hood of the baby buggy with a towel. She was cold—and eager for her tea. In the kitchen, she found that an envelope had been pushed beneath the door between the houses and, intrigued, she sat down to read the message.

Dear Miss Kemp, she read. *We have something important to tell you and would be delighted if you could join us for tea upon your return. Most sincerely, Honey and Rob't Holland.*

At last. Lilah was being invited beyond the door.

Having put on her cotton dress and a clean pair of shoes, she decided it was best, even when calling on people with whom you shared a roof, to observe the formalities and take your purse. Kissing Peter Rabbit's shoes, she popped them in amongst the combs and Kleenex and snapped the bag shut. She then unbolted her side of the door and knocked.

Almost at once the bolt was drawn in number 38 and the door was pulled open.

"There you are, then, dear Miss Kemp!" said Honey Holland—who towered above Lilah, smiling down at her from a flat, blue-eyed face. "Do please—please come this way."

Lilah was led through a small, cold kitchen that looked to be little used, and on into a hallway.

"Isn't this weather perfectly dreadful?" said Honey Holland. It was a question that required no answer.

They came to a living-room where a fire had been laid in the grate but remained unlit. Lilah began to wish she had worn a sweater. Like the kitchen, the living-room was cold and sterile—though every opportunity for warmth and charm had been offered by the architect. Its ten-foot ceilings and deep-set windows were Victorian gems. The Hollands, for whatever reason, had made nothing of these features. Their colour scheme was bland and their furniture looked barely used, as if to say the room did not appeal to them.

A man even taller than Professor Holland came sloping into the room from somewhere off to the left and extended an enormous hand in Lilah's direction.

"Dear one," said Honey Holland, "this is our neighbour, Miss Kemp... Miss Kemp—my husband, Robert."

"We've met," said Robert Holland. "Putting out the garbage."

"Yes," said Lilah. She looked around for tea things. There were none. Nor had a tea-tray been evident back in the kitchen.

"Would you care for a glass of sherry, Miss Kemp?" said Robert.

"I would, indeed."

"Do sit down," said Honey—making an all-inclusive gesture that took in the floor and the window bays and the fireplace. Lilah sat on a dark blue sofa whose springs were in bad repair.

Robert returned with a tray of bottles and glasses and once the sherry had been poured and handed about, Lilah said: "what is it you want to tell me?"

Robert went and stood by the fireplace—stretching one arm along the mantelpiece. This appeared to be a pose he was fond of. He coughed in order to draw attention to himself—and gave Lilah one more smile. *Big, aren't I*, he seemed to be saying. *Large fellow, well-dressed. Impressive...*

Honey sat on a chair directly in line with the window and said: "we have news, Miss Kemp—and I'm not sure how you'll take it."

"News?" said Lilah. "What sort of news?"

"We are *leaving!*" said Honey explosively. "There. I don't know why— I've been dreading telling you. We aren't to be neighbours any longer."

"I see," said Lilah.

Honey's face clouded. "Oh—but we were so concerned," she said. "I mean, we've shared these premises such a long time. We didn't want to upset you."

"That's all right," said Lilah. "I'll be fine." In fact, she would be more than fine. The Hollands had taken no interest in her whatsoever, the whole time they had been in residence. "Where are you going?" she asked.

"Australia," said Honey.

Lilah said nothing.

Robert gave a cough. "Excuse me," he said. Perhaps he had thought that Lilah would be more impressed.

"I have been offered tenure in Adelaide," said Honey.

"I see."

"And Robert has found a publisher there."

"Well, then—I suppose you ought to be congratulated," said Lilah.

"Thank you." This was said in tandem.

Lilah finished her sherry and stood up. "Perhaps I should go now," she said. "I have a great deal to do."

"Of course."

"Bye-bye," said Robert Holland—still on display by the fireplace.

"Yes," said Lilah. "Goodbye."

She began walking back towards the kitchen. The house had people in it besides the Hollands, she now discovered. There was someone right up there at the top of the stairs... One of *them*. The dead.

"We will be leaving soon," said Honey. "It all came about so suddenly. You will be disturbed, I'm afraid, by the movers banging things about in a week or so..."

Lilah had almost achieved the door to number 38-A—which still stood open.

"Can you tell me," she said, turning back, "if the house is to have an occupant after you leave?"

"Oh, yes. How careless of me. Oh, yes indeed. There will be another professor very shortly after we've gone."

"I see."

"He's a single man, so I understand. Divorced. Has a dog, but I trust that won't bother you. I gather he's been teaching—this chap—at Harvard—but I can't remember what."

"What...?"

"What he's been teaching. Anyway—he's coming back here. He used to live in Toronto. Was born here, I think. Such a nice man. Everyone says so."

"Do you know his name?"

"Name?"

"Yes."

"Robert!"

"Yes, my dear?" Robert said from the living-room.

"Can you remember the name of the man who's going to be living here after we've left?"

"Marlow," Robert shouted.

"Marlow," Honey repeated—turning back to Lilah. "Professor Marlow. And, yes, I've just remembered—he's a psychiatrist."

Lilah heard none of this.

She had fallen to the floor—and it took some time to revive her.

THREE

*Beware of all enterprises that
require new clothes.*

Henry David Thoreau
Walden

1

Kurtz often ate alone at a restaurant called Arlequino's. Its cuisine was an interesting meld of Northern Italian and Southern French— Mediterranean, but inland oriented. Not a great deal of seafood was offered on the menu—pasta was prominent but not dominant—veal and chicken were plentiful and everything was cooked with herbs and served on plates that had been swabbed with olive oil. Meals could be made from soups and three-green salads, supplemented by a large selection of breads that were baked in-house. Baguettes and crusty, fat Italian loaves could be carried home—as well as pastries, cheeses and ten kinds of olives. Arlequino's was Kurtz's restaurant of choice for all occasions—solo dining, business luncheons and midnight suppers provided equal pleasures in its quiet elegance.

Three days after the opening of the Slade exhibit, Kurtz took his midday meal at his usual table, unaccompanied and without accoutrement. No briefcase, no *Financial Post,* no telephone. Kurtz, on rare occasions, would accept a call while dining—if the denouement of some emergency was pending or if Kilbride, his secretary, had been told to forward a call from overseas. Otherwise, he looked on the telephone as a necessary evil that should be kept in its place—the office and the home. Cellular devices were anathema and Kurtz regarded their increasing appearance in public venues as a sign of the grossest insensitivity. If a client who was his guest at luncheon arrived with such a contraption, he would be told to leave it with the *maître d'.*

This day, Kurtz ordered a warm breast-of-chicken salad and the remains of a bottle of Montrachet he had begun the day before. Sitting, before the meal arrived, over a glass of Saint-Raphael, Kurtz lighted a cigarette and looked about him. The restaurant was long and narrow, with a single row of tables on each side to accommodate the diners. One wall, darkly mirrored, had a banquette that ran its full length. The other wall—Kurtz's wall—had no banquette and no mirror. The tables were all of uniform size and covered with white linen cloths. The lighting throughout cast a burnished rose aura and the mirrors, though smoked, provided a startling clarity—a source of light, rather than its reflectors.

Kurtz, all at once—and quite off-guard—was caught by the image in the mirror of Fabiana Holbach. She was seated to his right, four tables off, with her back to the wall. Opposite, but sufficiently to one side not to obscure his view of Fabiana, was a female companion. Kurtz took a slow scan of the faces in profile beside him and verified that Fabiana's luncheon-mate was Tina Perry.

Tina Perry was small and tough and spent her life pursuing golf and tennis balls. She was wearing white, which showed off her tan—and her hair, dyed honey-blonde, was cut with stylish eccentricity extremely short. Rumour had it that Tina Perry was a lesbian, though the rumours had never been substantiated. She had no female companion and, in fact, no companion in her life at all. She was long divorced from a man called Gordon Perry, who happened to be a client, on and off again, of Kurtz. There was a great deal of money shared between Gordon and Tina Perry—some if it hers and some of it his and all of it, combined, the source of much bitterness and wrangling. When Tina left Gordon, she had only barely escaped with her fortune intact. Gordon Perry's lawyers had been a good deal more effective in court than Tina's had been and most of what had been mutually held had remained in Gordon's hands.

Kurtz regarded Fabiana now in the mirror. She gave no indication of any awareness of his presence in the restaurant, while he found it difficult to look away from her. Kurtz had once loved Fabiana to the point almost of desperation. And then she had married Jimmy Holbach.

It had long been assumed by everyone who knew him that Jimmy Holbach would not return from the Amazon region. He had gone there four years before to investigate mining prospects and had disappeared, presumably into another life. He had been the kind of man for whom civilization was a prison. It kept him from his roots, which were grounded somewhere in barbarism. Constraint was death. For Holbach, the only response to being alive that made sense lay in bearing arms against everything else that lived.

He had waged a war against Kurtz for possession of Fabiana and precisely five years after he had won that war, he had no further interest in her. The same, by then, was true of Kurtz. He stepped away into a life without women—almost the life of a misogynist. As for Fabiana herself—she was lost between her fear of Holbach and her disappointment that Kurtz had not been more ruthless in his bid for her. It was her contention that Kurtz had let Holbach win—and she had been wary of him ever since.

Sitting there, Kurtz was overwhelmed with regret. He had not expected this. Fabiana had been gone from his life, in the passionate sense, for quite a long time—and all that had remained of her was her sexual presence in his imagination. But he had, till now, excised those parts of his interest in her that might have been called *loving* or *spiritual, intellectual* or *admiring*. She had been a lost cause—done with and finished. Kurtz had been reconciled—though it took a good while—to defeat.

Now—there she was.

Kurtz finally turned his attention back to his plate. It hurt, now, to see her. He wished she had stayed out of sight where she belonged. Her forays into view were increasing. *Out of sight—out of mind.* That had been better all these years, when he had successfully blotted her from memory. Now, she was there again—flesh and blood and all too visible.

Sitting there over his salad and his Montrachet, Kurtz was reminded of why one eats and drinks: to be filled—to be sustained. To live. The same was true of that part of him that had been emptied when Fabiana married Jimmy Holbach. It had been starved. Kurtz himself had refused to feed it. Now, it was forcing itself on his attention. *Fabiana.*

How does one catch her? he wondered. *How did one catch her before?*

She had wanted him, once. She had needed him in order to survive.

That was the ticket. *Need.*

Kurtz could not, of course, declare his need for her. That would be demeaning. But some way—surely—could be found to lead her back into his sphere of influence where soon enough and certainly Fabiana would rediscover her need for him.

Need. Feed.

An interesting rhyme.

In an interesting locale.

With an interesting view.

Kurtz drank wine and was content. He would watch her openly and let her find her own way back into his presence. He was, after all, a curator of remedies for need.

2

Every Friday Oona Kilbride took lunch with her friend, Bella Orenstein, at Motley's Bar and Grill on Spadina Avenue. She had been doing this now for three years and, to tell the truth, she would give it up in a flash if Bella were not so devoted to the place. The food, being Motley's least important consideration, was not terrific and the atmosphere had overtones of a double life. Oona suspected that, by night, Motley's Bar and Grill served a different clientele than the one it served by day. Remnants of this other patronage lurked in the washrooms and spilled across the floors in the form of stains that were reminiscent of stains she had seen in horror films and bad dreams. But Oona set these complaints aside for Bella's sake.

As Oona functioned in the world of Rupert Kurtz, so Bella functioned in the world of Austin Purvis. Both had been at the Parkin Institute for years—each as a secretary—each in a classic mould. Each was devoted, for entirely different reasons, to the man whose status defined her own. All ambition for feminist equality had been cast aside. Neither woman thought of herself as a minion—but that men with secretaries preferred those secretaries to be female was an accepted fact of their lives. *Sic transit Gloria Steinem.*

Oona Kilbride was tall and tailored. She had locked herself inside this ideal the moment she realized, aged fifteen, that she was never going to fill out through the chest and never, as a consequence, achieve an appreciative boyfriend. Her mother had not been helpful in this— giving Oona counsel that included everything from deprivation therapy to breast enlargement exercises. Her final offer was a gift of implants which Oona declined. This way, Oona gave up men before she had even experienced a boy—and her disdain for all things sexual was born.

It was not, however, disdain of the dismissive kind. It was disdain in the sense of forswearing. She would attempt no affairs—she would not even have male friends. She would leave men where they were, in a world of their own making. She would develop skills which men eschewed—but without which a man is unable to function in a man's world. This left her two choices—wife or secretary. (The whores she acknowledged, but she had no desire to join them.)

Wifery was dismissed. There was nothing in her make-up, Oona decided, to provide a basis for motherhood. She had an intense dislike of children—especially female children—which she had fostered even as a child. Other little girls had bored her to death with their dolly problems and their wet pants and their ridiculous aspirations to be space-women and nurse-people. Oona forswore their company more vehemently than she did the company of boys.

This left *secretary*—and Oona had applied herself to this estate as she might if she had decided to be a neurosurgeon or a prima donna.

Thus, she had come to Kurtz as the most highly recommended secretary in the entire medical profession. Bar none.

It is not required of secretaries that they like the person for whom they work. It is best if that person can be admired—but friendship is not required. Kurtz, it was clear, could never gain Oona's affection. Nor could he gain her respect. He was too ambitious—too aloof for either of these. But she did admire him. She saw what others saw—his creative research programmes, his ability to charm the birds out of the trees (an unfortunate phrase in the age of sturnusemia) and his talent for leadership. Under his direction, the Parkin Institute had been manoeuvred into the first rank of psychiatric research—and Kurtz had also garnered as its staff the finest psychiatrists that money could buy.

So it was that Oona had become a legendary appendage—Kurtz's right arm—his memory bank—his way-maker—his guardian-at-the-gate. She became not *Oona*, but *Kilbride*. Clearly, Kurtz could barely function without her. Kilbride knew this. But he did not. It was news that awaited Kurtz down the road.

Fridays, Motley's Bar and Grill was crowded with an amalgam of university students, Parkin staff and people from the garment industry who came uptown at week's end to indulge in food that was not Asian. Farther south, Spadina Avenue was awash with dim sum. At Motley's there was no such thing as cuisine. There was only food.

Bella Orenstein had been a regular customer for so long she had been accorded what Frank, the waiter, called a *table for life*. Bella ate her lunch at Motley's every workday. Oona did not know how she stood it. The noise could be deafening—a combination of recorded music and student ebullience. *Students always shout their conversations,* Oona noted. A simple exchange of sports enthusiasm could sound like the climax of group sex. It always made Oona vaguely uncomfortable.

"Tell me what your week has been like," she said to Bella while they waited for their martinis to arrive. Bella always ordered doubles—two or three of them, depending on her state of mind. Oona never had more than one: *a single—as befits me.* Bella had not even smiled at this. She seemed excessively distracted, even for her.

"What on earth is the matter?" Oona asked.

Bella, who was older and less at ease in life than Oona, lighted up the first of several pre-lunch cigarettes and looked around in the hopes that drinks would arrive before she would have to speak.

"I wish Frank would come," she said.

"You're avoiding my question," said Oona.

"No, I'm not. I just don't know what to think about it, that's all."

"Think about what?"

"Doctor Purvis has lost another patient. The third this month."

"Suicide?" said Oona. These things happened.

"No, no," said Bella. "No, no. His people don't kill themselves. At least—they haven't for a long while. No—it's losing them in the other sense. They just don't turn up and then he discovers they've gone on to someone else."

Oona blushed. She knew where some of these patients were going, and it embarrassed her. They were coming to Doctor Kurtz—but Oona had assumed that Bella must know this. Feigning innocence, she offered a loss of her own.

"Doctor Kurtz has mislaid an important document," she said, "and is blaming me for its disappearance. At least, Doctor Purvis doesn't blame *you* for the loss of his patients, I assume."

Bella looked down at her hands. "No," she said. Then she said: "you shouldn't let him blame you, Oona. It isn't proper. You're a professional."

Oona had, in fact, more than slightly exaggerated in saying that Kurtz had blamed her for the loss of his envelope. The fact was, he had done no more than ask her if she had seen it. But she wanted Bella to feel that the trauma of loss was common to them both. Bella lived on the melodramatic edge of life, where every gesture had an extended meaning and where every event was accompanied by music—violins, pianos, drums. This, at any rate, was Oona's sense of her friend's perceptions and, therefore, of why the loss of a patient from her doctor's roster could seem like an earth-shattering calamity.

"Doctor Kurtz says that whatever is in this envelope he's lost," Oona said, "is the most important document of his career. I don't know what I'm going to do to help him, since I never saw the thing to begin with."

Frank arrived and set down their martinis.

"You want another one, Bella?" he asked.

"She hasn't even had this one," said Oona.

"Bella?"

"Yes, thank you, Frank. I will have another."

Frank departed.

Bella, who always wore a hat, put her hand on the back of her head to hold the hat in place, and drank over half the martini in a single gulp.

Then she said: "three patients in one month, Oona. It has to mean something."

"I'm sure it does," said Oona, sipping with practised nonchalance. "But what?"

"Well—it doesn't mean that Doctor Purvis is slipping, I can tell you that much."

"You don't need to be so defensive."

"I'm sorry. Forgive me. It's just so...troubling. You see, I think Doctor Purvis is losing his patients because of something...I don't know. I think that something may be going on at the Parkin that we don't know about, Oona. A research programme—something. Perhaps a programme into which these people are being fed."

Bella gave Oona a long, intense look.

"Will you promise me something?" she said.

"Anything," said Oona.

"Will you promise to tell me if there's something going on that I don't know about, that you think I should know about. For Doctor Purvis's sake?"

"What makes you think I'd know anything you wouldn't know?"

Bella sat back. "You work for Doctor Kurtz, Oona. That's why."

"Well..." Oona could think of no defence.

"Staff is supposed to be kept informed," said Bella. "Especially senior staff, like Doctor Purvis."

"All right," said Oona. "I promise."

Bella looked away—and then back. Then she leaned forward—reaching for and preparing to light another cigarette.

"It's Doctor Kurtz who gets the missing patients, isn't it?"

"Yes." There.

"Thank you. I mean—I knew it, but I wanted you to say it."

"I simply assumed..." said Oona, and shrugged.

"Don't assume anything," said Bella. And then she said, in her most dramatic fashion: "the times are out of joint, Oona. The times are out of joint."

"Yes. Well," said Oona. "Who have you lost this time?"

"Most recently a man called Warren Ellis."

"Ah, yes. He started with Doctor Kurtz last week."

"I think you should know that Warren Ellis may be in trouble," said Bella.

"He wouldn't be a patient if he wasn't."

"No, no," said Bella. "I don't mean trouble—I mean *trouble*."

Oona said nothing.

"What are you going to have for lunch?" Bella finally asked. "The dreadful shrimp or the dreadful scallops?"

That was better. Bella was smiling. By the time she had started her third martini, Warren Ellis and his troubles would have ceased to be the subject of her conversation. Though not of her concerns. Bella Orenstein, unlike Oona Kilbride, was more than her doctor's secretary. She was secretly in love with him, and she carried his burdens everywhere she went.

3

Warren Ellis first wore women's clothes when he was five years old. Caught in his mother's closet one afternoon while she entertained her lover, Tony Bloor, Warren believed he could escape their notice by pretending to be someone else. Emerging from his hiding place, he wore a large black hat with a veil. Also, the long-sleeved jacket of a silver evening gown which covered him to the knees. Warren's mother and Tony Bloor were naked on the bed, engaged in a rocking motion which reminded Warren of his father rowing a boat.

"Is that you, Warren?" his mother asked, looking out from beneath Tony Bloor.

Warren had his answer ready.

"No," he said. And left the room.

At boarding school, Warren was cast as Katherina in *The Taming of the Shrew*. This was to constitute the second time he dressed in women's attire. Warren was twelve years old by now and a veritable "beauty," with all his mother's classic features and his father's poise and gravity. He was a sensation. Several parents complained that "a girl from Branksome Hall" had been brought in to play the role. And the boy who played Petruchio was beside himself with desire. He became so disturbed by Warren's charms that he failed an English exam.

Another boy who began to view Warren Ellis differently around this time was a prefect with the unlikely name of Shirley Ashcroft. Whatever had persuaded his parents to call him Shirley was not in the public domain. Rumour had it that Ashcroft senior had been threatened by the loss of an inheritance if he did not name his son for some obscure ancestor buried in history. It hardly mattered. The boy, once christened, was brutalized by his name and became an instant brawler the moment he was thrown into the company of other boys. His rage at being Shirley drove him to excel at all things male and menacing and, as will happen in boarding schools, these qualities elevated him to what amounted to kingship. As king, he was entitled to take whatever he wanted, whether it was food on the table, a bed by the window or the person of Warren Ellis.

There was another element at play in Shirley's designs on Warren. The boy's father, Hedley Ashcroft, was a senior partner in the Beaumorris Corporation—the source of Warren's wealth. Shirley had caught the innuendo at home that a schism was developing between his father and Warren's family over control of Beaumorris, and he thought it might be rewarding if he could help to widen it. His loyalties were not unlike a patriot's—*my father, right or wrong.*

Primarily, however, Shirley Ashcroft was looking, in his own words, for *someone to bonk.* But a boy's idea of bonking and the thing itself are two different stories. Especially at boarding school, where bonking would be best described as rape. When Warren Ellis hoisted his bathrobe— shouted *no!*—and started running down the dormitory hall away from Ashcroft that night, the king had deployed a few of his pack in neighbouring rooms. Warren was finally tackled and returned to his cubicle. A dozen of Shirley's acolytes gathered to watch. Having jammed Warren's scrotum and penis down between his legs so he looked more or less like the girl he played in skirts on stage, Ashcroft had his boyish way with him—covering him with sperm and shame.

For the briefest moment that night in the dark, Warren Ellis saw his mother as a sympathetic figure. *Getting bonked,* he decided, *is the inevitable result of saying no.* It would be some time before he got the language right to express this thought, but the thought itself would return to haunt him in ways he could not begin to imagine at the age of twelve.

Warren's mother, Freda Manley, never gave up her own name. Eddie Ellis, Warren's father, was not the first of her husbands, nor her last. He was, however, Freda's most ardent and devoted lover—and the father of her only child. That Freda Manley, in her race to the top, had paused long enough to produce a son had left those who knew her stunned with amazement. Their amazement, however, turned to dust when it became quite clear that having Warren was merely her way of securing her place in line for the Ellis millions. The word *voracious* had been used to describe her appetite for men of wealth. But her sister-in-law was a more discerning witness. *The feastings of Medea,* Ethel Beeman said, *paled in comparison.*

Ethel, born an Ellis, was Eddie's beloved elder sister. One day her husband, John Clare Beeman, was eaten by a shark while swimming off Palm Beach, Florida. Ethel—something of a mystic—took this to be a sign it was time for her to withdraw from the world of feeding monsters. She sold her house on Ocean Boulevard and took up winter gardening in her Rosedale greenhouse. Her residence on Cluny Drive became increasingly a haven for Warren, as his parents' marriage was torn apart.

Freda had gone through several lovers since Tony Bloor had rocked with her all those years ago. Most of them were passing fancies—amusements—and lasted no longer than a month or two. Some, however, were serious contenders for Freda's next marriage vows—providing, as they did, access to power she found irresistible. One of these was Gordon Perry, who stood in the living-room one day and said to Warren: *I'm thinking of marrying your mother. What do you have to say to that?* Warren, who instinctively feared Gordon Perry the way he might have feared a crocodile, said to him: *if you come near my mother again, my father will kill you.*

Gordon Perry, for whatever reason, departed. It could not be said that it was because of Warren's threat. Gordon Perry knew Eddie Ellis too well to believe that he would do another person harm. No. It was for some other reason which neither Warren nor Freda could fathom. He was troubled by his health, he said. He took a holiday—a long one—and came back to the Beaumorris offices looking fit and tanned—and tense.

Gordon Perry, around this time, began to see a psychiatrist. The one he chose was Rupert Kurtz. He told no one why he needed help. And the battle for Beaumorris supremacy went on.

Here is what happened. No sooner had Gordon Perry vacated Freda Manley's bed than Hedley Ashcroft took up residence there. This meant, in Warren's previous image of it, that one after the other, Freda had *gone rowing* with three Beaumorris partners. Since she and Ethel Beeman were the other two partners, there was no one left to go rowing with. Warren, by then, had endured his encounter with Shirley Ashcroft and now he recognized what it was his mother was doing. She was bonking her way to the top—and somewhere before she got there, she was going to find Warren standing in her path—and she would bonk him, too, if he did not watch out. This was the first indication he had that bonking was not what it seemed to be. The word *no* took on new meaning.

<u>4</u>

By the time Freda Manley made her move on Hedley Ashcroft, Eddie Ellis was living exclusively in hotels. His encounters with his son were conducted in lobbies and dining-rooms on formal occasions—or on the run, when Warren was being driven to and from his school on the city's outskirts.

Towards the end of the year Warren turned fifteen, he had a phone call from somewhere in Mexico. His father's voice was oddly jolly when he said he had *come down here to lie in the sun and reconstruct my life.* When he returned, he promised, he would *come back home a brand new man.* This, it turned out, was all too true. In his absence, Eddie had discovered the ethereal qualities of drink. The world, so unbearably empty of hope, could be made to disappear in the mists of tequila and gin. There were fewer meetings now in hotel lobbies or dining-rooms. Instead, they sat on the sides of beds high up above the city, eating room-service clubhouse sandwiches and drinking, in Warren's case, forbidden wine. After his father died, it came to be that Warren's favourite food was what you got from room service. The smell of it and the taste of it were inextricably layered into the texture of his father's presence.

Eddie had always been a gentle man with a passion for love without violence. If his wife could not respond to this love without a breaking down of doors, then Eddie was prepared to let her go her way without a sound. Nothing could induce him to make a spectacle of his love.

When the divorce was final and Eddie had given up everything—including his dignity—a meeting of the Beaumorris Board was called to discuss the redisbursement of voting stock.

Warren had been delegated by Aunt Ethel to see that his father attended the meeting in a sober state. As many will know who have to deal with the crafty side of alcoholics, there is nothing short of death that will keep them from their drink. Eddie had perfected his strategies over time. Tequila, vodka and gin, kept in plastic bags, had been sewn into the linings of the curtains in his suite at the Four Seasons Hotel. Bottle-pockets had been created on the undersides of chairs. If he was eating with Warren in the coffee shop, he would have himself paged—slip to the bar where double margaritas would be waiting by pre-arrange-ment—and return to Warren claiming the phone call had been cause for celebration. Drinks would be ordered. The world would spin. Warren, now seventeen, caved in for love and let his father go. What else could a person do for a man so riddled with pain?

And so it was that Warren failed that day to bring his father in a sober state to the boardroom high in the Baycorp Building. What he brought instead was a man who thought he was Fred Astaire. As the meeting came to order, Eddie rose from his chair and made a charming speech in which, like Lear, he divested himself of his kingdom. The difference was that he made the speech while performing a tap dance up on the surface of the table. Kicking ashtrays and water glasses aside, he gave a fair imitation not so much of dancing as of what it felt like to be a dancer.

In one dazzling moment at the end of this performance, he leapt nimble-footed to a window-sill and from there delivered his peroration. Warren was thinking what tiny feet his father had—and what beautiful shoes he wore. Ethel was praying for a shark to rise and carry her away into oblivion. Freda sat frozen—apprehensive at last—between her would-be lover, Gordon Perry—and the man she was soon to marry, Hedley Ashcroft. If Eddie was so inclined, he could cut her off from her voting stock in this moment.

Eddie finally said it had been his extraordinary privilege to have endured their treasons. The burden of their wounds, he said, had been his joy. He had but one sorrow, he said—that Warren, his son, had been left to carry him alone. *Forgive me,* he said, holding Warren with his eyes. *I love you—and that is all the excuse I have.*

Then he said: *it is such a lovely day, I think I'll just step out for a breath of air.* And he opened the window and began his fall.

Warren, never afterwards knowing how, had reached him in time to grasp his hand. He stared down into his father's face and saw him smile. And then as Eddie had intended, he slipped away and was gone. Only Ethel came to the window. She was the one who brought Warren back from the edge of it and said to him: *we get to keep him, now—just you and me.*

Two weeks later, Freda Manley married Hedley Ashcroft.

5

Time passed. Warren survived. He received—among other more personal artifacts—precisely half of his father's voting stock. Eddie, ever forgiving, had left the other half to Freda.

Warren's residence until he came of age was in his father's house with his mother and her new husband. It was a living hell. Once nineteen, however, and graduated, he went to live with Aunt Ethel Beeman and took up wearing pale grey suits, cut to reveal the splendours of his small, taut body. His face took on the appearance of an inquisitive angel. His watchful eyes were betrayed by the set of his mouth. *I will not speak,* it said, *till spoken to.*

Warren did not strike out entirely on his own till he was engaged to be married, at which time he had the first of his revenges on his mother.

Claiming his father's furniture, he moved it into a house of his own on Crescent Road. This left Freda Manley in the somewhat alarming position of having to give up her bed.

For six years, Warren sat in his corporate office, vigilant to the point of rigidity. His door was always open. Survival at Beaumorris depended on knowing who was passing through the corridors. All movement ceased on the day in spring when Hedley Ashcroft, aging, at last fell ill.

A phone call came from Hedley's secretary, Arlene Phillips.

"I think this will be of interest to you, Warren," she said with a negligent tone that did not imply the world was about to end. "Mister Ashcroft has now been transferred to intensive care."

"When?"

"Half an hour ago," said Arlene Phillips. "I've only just been told."

Warren's heart began to race. His mouth went dry and he tried not to cough.

"Does my mother know about this?" he asked.

"No," said Arlene. "She is still at Palm Beach. You're the only person I've told and the only person I intend to tell. Of course, the others will find out soon enough. I saw Mister Perry in the hall about an hour ago. He was on his way to one of his sessions with Doctor Kurtz. He gave no indication he was aware of Mister Ashcroft's condition."

"What do you think I should do?" said Warren.

"Meet me in the boardroom," said Arlene Phillips. "Right away."

The Baycorp Building was forty storeys tall. The top five floors had been leased to the Beaumorris Corporation. The boardroom was on the thirty-sixth floor.

Arlene Phillips was standing there by the long sleek table with its quorum of yellow chairs. She was a good deal taller than Warren—six feet to his five-eight—and she had never, for anyone, made the concession of wearing low heels. She was towering there in the muted light—an imposing red-haired figure in shades of green and grey that were so discreet it could not be told where one left off and the other began.

In her hand, she held a single piece of paper. She would not sit down and she spoke to Warren as if she were an intelligence officer sending a minion out on a mission.

"I've brought you this," she said. "Study it and put it in your pocket. You already know the details—but you tend to get flustered where figures are concerned." She showed the paper to him—8 1/2 x 11—a standard piece of office letterhead.

"I've made a little diagram here," she said, and ran her finger along some lines she had drawn in red and green between the names and figures listed there, showing the dispensation of voting stock. "The red line is the configuration of holdings that must be avoided if you expect to survive...."

"Survive?"

"Survive. Don't make faces, Warren. And don't go pale. It's just a word."

"I see."

"The green line is the one you want. Simple. Follow that and..."

"I'll come to the Emerald City?" said Warren—but his voice was dead when he said it.

Arlene Phillips smiled.

"Good for you," she said.

She crossed the room towards the door that led to Hedley Ashcroft's office—and her own. "I'll be in here waiting for calls," she said. "There's no word yet. He's still hanging on..." She stopped herself in mid-sentence.

This was the very room where Warren's father had gone to his death because he had failed to "hang on" to Warren's hand.

"I'm sorry," said Arlene. "I seem to have a knack today for saying the wrong thing."

Warren shrugged.

"Thank you," he said, "for the diagram."

Arlene waved a deprecating hand.

"Don't leave it lying about," she said. Then she smiled. "Once you've memorized it—eat it."

"Ush!" said Warren.

"Speaking of lunch," said Arlene, "I think it would be an excellent idea if one day—*very* soon—you took Mister Perry to lunch at Vermeer's."

"What?"

Warren sat down as if he had been pushed.

Arlene spoke from the open doorway.

"I know you have problems with Mister Perry, Warren. But if you want to survive..."

Warren covered his ears.

"...an alliance must be struck," Arlene finished.

Warren nodded and lowered his head.

The door closed.

The first thing Warren saw when he raised his eyes was the window from which his father had fallen.

All the windows—six of them—were reflected in the table top—with its almost black mahogany veneer—polished every morning by four Oriental men in green coats. When Hong Kong money and Japanese money had started to flood the boardrooms of Bay Street, Hedley Ashcroft had fired all the Portuguese women previously hired to clean the offices and had made a point of hiring Vietnamese and Chinese men exclusively. No Japanese were available as cleaners and Hedley had confronted one of the Chinese gentlemen—he always called them "Chinese gentlemen"—and offered him a bonus of twenty dollars a day if he would tell everyone, in Hedley's own words, that he was "a Jap." The man had refused and been given his walking papers.

Seated at the table, Warren laid out the diagram Arlene had given him with its red and green lines. The red-line version showed how Freda Manley could maintain control of Beaumorris after Hedley's death—and the green-line version favoured Warren Ellis.

The Beaumorris charter included a proviso which stated that, if anyone should manage to acquire control of fifty-one percent of the voting stock, that person could force the remaining partners to sell their holdings to him—or to her. As things stood now, there were two possible scenarios—and the linchpin in each was Gordon Perry. In the red-line version, Freda won the day. She would inevitably fall heir to Hedley's stock, and although it would not, by itself, give her fifty-one percent, it would make her holding large enough to cement her alliance with Gordon Perry. Together, they would take over. In the green-line version, Warren could triumph—but only if he and Aunt Ethel managed by some miracle to bring Gordon Perry into their camp. But how might that be done, since Warren had spent the last ten years driving Gordon Perry from the door?

Warren shoved the page away and looked at it with disgust. The window from which his father had fallen cast its reflection as if to catch him in its frame.

He was just another of Freda's men—doomed, as his father and Hedley Ashcroft had been, to perish in her shadow. She would eat them all—like Uncle John Clare Beeman's shark—and spit out their bones.

Oh, God, Warren thought, *I am living in a world of monsters.*

Standing up and pushing aside the tall-backed chair, he folded Arlene's piece of paper and put it in his inner breast pocket. At the door, he looked back one last time at the silent, haunted room where both his father and his stepfather had made their wars and lost and won. Both had sat in that chair up there at the table's head and both had striven for mastery in the bed of Freda Manley. Both had lost. Now, there was Gordon Perry.

Bedrooms and boardrooms, Warren thought as he turned away and closed the door—*they have a lot in common. Someone is always getting bonked.*

6

On the day Hedley Ashcroft was moved into intensive care, Kurtz was confronted by an agitated Gordon Perry. The Beaumorris Corporation was in a state of crisis—and while everyone was trying to put a good face on it, a sense of panic was pervasive. Gordon Perry arrived in Kurtz's office in obvious distress, claiming that he would soon be called upon to save Beaumorris single-handed. Also claiming that, because of personal problems for which he was already undergoing treatment, he was not at all sure he was going to "make it." *Making it,* in Perry's terms, meant surviving the consequences of Freda Manley's fast approaching widowhood. Would he, or would he not, take Ashcroft's place in Freda's bed?

Kurtz maintained a calm demeanour and, having gone through a series of questions and answers concerning Gordon Perry's obsessive concerns, he prescribed an especially high dosage of diazepam and sent his patient home to *face the future without anxiety.*

When Perry departed, Kurtz himself took a single Valium. Ten milligrams.

Kurtz, like any deft administrator, possessed the skills of a cardsharp. The hand was quicker than the eye, especially when shuffling the personalities in his grasp, and dealing them onto the table in new arrangements. His expression never betrayed his intentions. It gave no hint of what was hidden behind his eyes—to say nothing of what was hidden up his sleeve.

As a practitioner of psychiatric therapy, he was influential—and not only in his own profession. Kurtz had clients who ranged from psychotic killers to cross-dressers and anorexics. His Rolodex read like a *Who's Who* of prominent citizens, including an ex-minister of finance, a network news anchorwoman and the president of one of the country's largest banks. It was doubtful the worlds of commerce and communication could function without him.

Kurtz never thought of his supplicants as patients in the classic sense. They were not "diseased." They came to him to bargain for their freedom. The majority of them—including Gordon Perry—were the prisoners of fear, in thrall of penchants, desires and obsessions that threatened to destroy them; certainly, that threatened to destroy their peace of mind, their ability to function.

When Gordon Perry had gone his way that afternoon, Kurtz sat for half an hour and pondered his clients' problems: the impending death of Hedley Ashcroft—the voracious appetites of Freda Manley—Gordon Perry's vulnerability—the crisis within the Beaumorris Corporation. Kurtz, months earlier, had foreseen the possibilities of such a crisis as he monitored the Beaumorris situation. He always took a keen interest in clients whose corporate funding policies might prove helpful to the Parkin. It was because of that interest that he had recently taken the decision that caused Bella Orenstein so much distress. He had placed Freda Manley's son, Warren Ellis, on his own case list.

When Warren Ellis had first sought psychiatric help, he had come to Austin Purvis. Kurtz regarded Purvis as one of the best practitioners in the building. Warren Ellis had seen himself, in some ways, as a murderer. This was after his father's hand had slipped from his own, and Eddie Ellis had fallen to his death. For months, the offending hand had been useless to Warren—paralyzed even in the simplest of gestures. It would not hold knives or spoons or forks—it would not turn pages—it would not pick up a pen.

Austin Purvis had got Warren out of this predicament by convincing him his fingers, one by one, were innocent. Warren must stop judging them. He must give them back their freedom. And this, for a time, worked.

Now, however, on hearing of Hedley Ashcroft's condition, Warren suffered a relapse. In the past, he would simply have put through a call to Purvis and made the appropriate appointment. In the present scheme of things, Warren had no experience of how Doctor Kurtz might deal with him, given his state of panic. To date, their relations had been cool and cordial. But he need not have worried.

Kurtz nodded sympathetically as he read Kilbride's transcript of Warren's call. First Gordon Perry—and now the Ellis boy...with incapacitated fingers. An intolerable situation. For Warren—or for Kurtz, whose own fingers insinuated themselves into the stuff of every life they touched. Setting the telephone message aside on his desk, he thought further about the whole Beaumorris crisis. As he pondered, his interest in Warren Ellis increased. It became acute.

7

Lilah was returning from Wong's Groceteria when she next saw Kurtz in the flesh. This happened on Avenue Road, the site of both Wong's and of Kurtz's residence, The Citadel. It was snowing, but gently. Large, wet flakes as big as quarters floated down from unseen clouds.

Kurtz, walking beneath an umbrella, came towards Lilah at such a slow pace he seemed to be lost in meditation. Meditation or medication. He had the look of someone steeped in Ativan—a drug that, for Lilah, caused a kind of sleepwalking reverie. She doubted that Kurtz would see her. His eyes were lowered.

Lilah pulled the baby carriage into the nearest doorway—(Ardaths, the Beauty People)—and watched him pass.

Marlow will get you, she thought. *He'll be here any day now—and then you'd better watch out, Mister Kurtz.*

Lilah closed her eyes. *If you try to shout, he'll smash your head. He will throttle you for good...*

That was what it said on page 94 of *Heart of Darkness.* Lilah had memorized it.

Kurtz stepped in towards Wong's and lowered his umbrella. Lilah was astounded. She thought of Kurtz as being so utterly a creature of fiction—a paper man without human needs—that it was a shock to see him enter a grocery store. He was going to buy food, as she just had.

Of course he wants food! He wouldn't be well written if he didn't!
Still...

She wondered what he might purchase.

What do such men eat?

Delectables or simple food? Lilah could not remember. No one ate much in *Heart of Darkness.* Their hunger there was of a different kind—and could not be satisfied with what one bought in grocery stores.

She left the shelter of Ardaths' doorway and continued down the street towards Lapin Lanes.

Once home, Lilah set her provisions out on the kitchen table where she could see them. She was going to bake barmbrack in memory of Ireland. If money could not be found to return her there—then the smell and taste of its food might do it.

Nutmeg, flour and butter. Yeast, of course, and sugar. Eggs, salt and currants. Candied peel. Sultanas. Milk, and a baking pan.

Dublin rose up before her. And all its magic names. Donnybrook. Dollymount. Drumcondra. *From Drumleck Point to Dalkey, I have leaned against the sky—with Dublin Bay behind me, and Dublin in my eye...*

That had been Nicholas Fagan's song. His favourite. They had gone, then, together through all its streets—drinking ale in its pubs and wine in its hotel bars. Fagan and his pub crawls—the greatest privilege she had ever had. He would take his favoured students with him—sometimes a dozen of them, sometimes only one—and he would give them the story of all the men and women, children, dogs and cats who had ever stepped from books in the English language. And he would sing. He would get them all to sing. *With Dublin Bay behind me, and Dublin in my eye!*

One night, a woman whose name, even now, Lilah knew by heart had said to Fagan: *sing us your favourite!* Her name was Moira.

Fagan told her *Dublin in My Eye* and they all stood round and sang it—Moira with them, a scarf tied round her hair—a glass of Jameson's in her hand. And then she had said: *now sing us your favourite favourite!*

And so it went, that happy night, from Fagan's favourite-favourite to his favourite-favourite-favourite and so on, on and on. And on.

All that singing. And the woman called Moira. And Fagan—roaring out all the names of all the men and women, all the dogs and all the cats and all the children who came forth from books.

A book is a way of singing, Fagan had said to her. *A way of singing our way out of darkness. The darkness that is night—and the darkness that is ignorance—and the darkness that is...*

What?

Lilah could not remember.

One more kind of darkness.

Which one was it?

Books are a way of singing.

Lilah, with dusty hands, hurried into the bedroom and brought *Heart of Darkness* back to the light and sat with it at the table.

Fagan had told her something. Said something. Written something. And Lilah had pasted it into this book—because it had to do with books and what books were—much more than songs—songs, yes, but more. Where was it?

She pushed aside bowls and pans and bags and bottles and floured the pages with her fingers...

There.

These characters drawn on the page by the makers of literature, Lilah read, *are distillations of our thwarted selves. We are their echoes and their shadows. They move us through our muddied lives at a clarified pace.*

What we cannot describe, they articulate. What we cannot imagine, they reveal. What we cannot endure, they survive.

Lilah could hear Fagan speaking even as she read:

If I were to propose a text for the twentieth century, it would be Joseph Conrad's Heart of Darkness. *As subtext, I would nominate Mary Shelley's* Frankenstein. *Nothing better illustrates than these two books the consequence of human ambition. On reading them again, I fell away from my complacent view that nothing could be done to stop us, and took up my current view that the human race has found its destiny in self-destruction.*

Fagan had written this more than thirty years ago as part of an essay. Lilah had asked him to sign her copy of it. Now, it was there in her kitchen. If only she could bring him forth as she had brought forth Kurtz.

Suddenly, she remembered the third and final darkness. Fear.

8

Three days later, Warren had lunch at Vermeer's—not with Gordon Perry, as he had been urged, but with Ethel Beeman and his fiancée, Leslie Drew. He had been, already, once to see Doctor Kurtz and had a second appointment that afternoon. For now, the recalcitrant hand was more or less behaving itself. It had returned, as from leave, to active service.

A word about Vermeer's. As a restaurant, it was *non pareil*. Not a day went by without at least one visiting celebrity being found at its tables and the élite of every world—from politics to business to the arts—ate there as a matter of course.

The layout was circular, presented on two levels. As a consequence, everyone sat in plain view of everyone else. There were no cozy tables tucked out of sight—no booths or private rooms. You went to Vermeer's to be seen and if you did not wish to be seen, you ate elsewhere.

When Warren walked in out of the rain that Monday afternoon to join Ethel Beeman and Leslie Drew, the first person he saw was his mother.

Freda was seated at the centre table in the cockpit. She was more alive than Warren had seen her in years. Her Palm Beach tan was a rich shade of bronze. Her teeth, which one could count from across the room, were blinding white. A person could not begin to tell she was about to be a widow for the second time in her life. Her voice rang out. Her perfume dominated the air. And there beside her was Gordon Perry—sitting in all her lights. The shape of his face was deceiving. His brutal eyes were made to seem benign by the roundness of his features. His hands, Warren noted, were empty—as always. Gordon Perry needed no props to emphasize his presence.

Every eye in the room was on Freda Manley. In spite of the season, she was, as usual, wearing her sable coat, and had cast it off in such a way that its skirts made a pool of fur behind and to the sides of her chair. She ate with gusto and panache—cracking molluscs and biting through their flesh as if they were her enemies. Her hands, all through the meal, made waving motions over the table as various dishes were delivered to be refused or accepted. When she wanted more wine she thrust out her glass at the *maître d'* with a jangle of silver bracelets that could be heard twenty feet away. Her eyes rarely left her food until she was finished feeding.

The poor waiters—three of them—tried to avoid walking on her coat every time they approached her, and as a consequence, the food they proffered on spoons and in ladles sometimes landed on the tablecloth. Finally, exasperated, Freda—pointing down at her coat—was heard to say to one of the waiters: "walk on it! Walk on it! What do you think it's for!"

Warren cringed, felt his fiancée's eyes turn towards him—and took advantage of the menu.

"It's appalling to see her sitting there with all that food, while her husband lies dying," said Ethel Beeman. "It confirms my opinion of her entirely. She lives for death."

Warren said: "I wonder what she'll do when she hears he's actually died."

"She'll order champagne," said Ethel—"and Gordon will drink it out of her shoe."

Leslie Drew laughed. At once, however, she recovered herself and raised her napkin. "Excuse me," she said. She was a pale girl—with straight blonde hair and brown, frightened eyes. She wore dark colours, navy blue mostly, and charcoal grey, and she always wore flat-heeled shoes. Warren had come upon her in an elevator at the Parkin Institute. He thought she was a patient, but in fact she was a student. She wanted, she had told him, to work with autistic children. In Ethel's opinion, she was one. *Trying to get an expression to cross her face was like asking the Venus de Milo to pass you a sandwich.* Nonetheless, Warren loved her—and she was not, like most of her class-contemporaries, a fatuous fashion plate. She was merely dull.

Warren was watching his mother manhandle a piece of lobster when he saw Arlene Phillips enter the restaurant behind her. *Oh, dear,* he thought, *this is it.*

Arlene would not remove her coat. She carried an umbrella beneath her arm—clamping it there as if it were a swagger stick. She wore, as always, green. Her red hair was hidden beneath a stylish black fedora and her eyes could not be seen. She spoke to the *maître d'* and accepted his directions. The subject of her search was Freda's table. *Where else,* Warren thought, *would she go with such exhilarating news?* He pulled at Ethel Beeman's sleeve and said: "it's happened. He's dead."

Ethel closed her eyes and murmured a tiny prayer for Hedley Ashcroft. Even enemies deserved respect in death. She did not, however, think: *God bless him.* She merely thought: *he's gone. So be it. Amen.* When she opened her eyes and looked into the cockpit, Freda had received the news. Gordon Perry had risen when Arlene approached. Now he sat down. He reached out for Freda's hand in sympathy, but she refused him. Gordon sat back. Freda sat forward. She placed a piece of lobster in her mouth.

Warren watched. His mother chewed as always, mouth open, teeth flashing, eyes half-closed—her fingers gleaming with rings and melted butter. He saw Gordon Perry blanch every time Freda picked up the crackers and pressed them against another bit of shell. He thought of her, in bed with Gordon—and, indeed, in bed with Hedley and with his long-dead father—crackers in hand and teeth in place—and always with her piece of paper with the dotted line for signing at the ready.

Ethel said to Leslie: "I hope you are paying attention, my dear. It would be wise to take note of how the news of your firstborn will be received. One more corpse to feed on."

Freda was dabbing at her lips with her napkin. She accepted an envelope in her other hand from Arlene and threw it down on the table. Arlene stepped back and Warren could see that she was offering condolences to Gordon Perry. Doubtless because he would be the next of Freda's victims. Then Arlene looked up, saw Warren watching and nodded. She took leave of Freda and Gordon and began to make her way onto the upper level. Freda did not even say goodbye. Instead, she summoned a waiter and ordered champagne.

When Arlene reached their table, Warren stood up and invited her to join them. She declined.

"Mister Ashcroft is dead," she said, "as you will have guessed. He did not regain consciousness. However, I was with him two days ago in company that included his lawyers. I have brought you this, as instructed." She handed Warren an envelope. "It contains the same news I have just delivered to your mother—though I see..." she looked down at Freda "...she has still not bothered to read it. What it does, Warren, is give you one last chance. I hope you take it. And I wish you

well." With that—and a nod in Ethel's direction and in Leslie's—
Arlene Phillips walked away and was gone. She had left the restaurant
before Freda Manley gave a cry that could be heard at every table.

"What on earth...?" said Ethel.

Warren had just finished reading the message Arlene had left behind.
It informed him that Hedley Ashcroft had split his voting stock—leaving slightly more than half of it to Warren—*in memory*, so it said, *of my
predecessor.* It would considerably strengthen Warren's position. The
residue had been left to Freda, but it was not enough to give her automatic control of the Beaumorris Corporation.

"She has just read this," said Warren—handing the piece of paper
to Ethel.

Below them, Freda threw down her napkin and stood up. Gordon
Perry had turned pale. He was wondering, perhaps, if control of Beaumorris was worth being caged with the woman let loose before him.
Freda pushed over her chair. Silence fell over Vermeer's. Only the
kitchens, steaming and hissing beyond their doors, could be heard.

Pushing waiters from her path, Freda crossed the floor and stood
directly below her son's table. The deadly piece of paper had been mangled in her hand. She raised it at Warren.

"Nothing you do can save you now," she said. "No matter what you
have up your sleeve—I still have Gordon Perry!" Then she threw back
her head and laughed and said while she pointed at poor Leslie Drew:
"and all you have is that pathetic bitch!"

9

Two hours later, Warren sat in Doctor Kurtz's office—folding, unfolding
and folding his right hand—relaxing it and making it into a fist again.
He had told the psychiatrist what his mother had said.

Kurtz was sympathetic. He also urged Warren to be conciliatory with
Gordon Perry.

"I've tried," said Warren.

"Then try again," said Kurtz.

Anything, to prevent the disaster of an alliance with Freda Manley. If
the Beaumorris Corporation went to her, its philanthropic focus would
be altered to favour schools of economics. The Parkin Institute would
be the loser—and so would Kurtz. Not that he could say so. Not that he
had any right to interfere in his clients' lives beyond these walls. But...

He stood up.

"Would you excuse me, Warren?" he said. "I have a matter that requires my immediate attention." Kurtz went over the carpet towards the door. "Make yourself at home," he said. "I won't be any longer than fifteen minutes."

He then came back to his desk and fumbled amongst some files that were sitting there. "Oh, yes..." he said, "I shall need these..." and, leaving the top of his desk in disarray, he made his exit. The door went *click* and Warren subsided.

The view from the windows was dull and non-informing. All it showed was a sky full of doomed birds. Warren had no interest. He stood and walked once around the room—squeezing his nervous hand into a ball and releasing it, as before. Returning to his place, he glanced at the mess of files and papers on Kurtz's desk. His own file...the file of a man called X...the file of a woman whose name was indecipherable...and the file of Gordon Perry.

Gordon Perry's file.

The file of Gordon Perry.

Warren coughed.

His hand relaxed.

He reached.

He read.

Client's desire is to dress athletic youths in women's clothing and...

Warren closed his eyes. He turned pages.

You have no idea, Client says, *how overpowering the image is of a boy in a Balenciaga. Mini-skirted, tight-waisted with spaghetti straps. And the boy with shoulders out to here...*

Warren thought he was going to faint.

He verified the name of the file.

Gordon Perry. No mistaking it.

He turned more pages.

Client spoke of his friend, E.E... of their profitable partnership and of how he, Client, had soured that partnership by bedding E.E.'s wife...

My father, Warren thought. And my mother. Gordon Perry sits here and discusses my father and my mother...

Client was deterred from pursuit of E.E.'s wife by E.E.'s son, who said...

Now Warren repeated it aloud—precisely as transcribed in Kurtz's file: *if you come near my mother again, my father will kill you.*

There.

He was magnificent, said Client—Warren read. *Sixteen years old and shoulders out to here...*

Warren sat down.

"Oh, God," he said to the room at large. "It's me."

On the page, Kurtz had written: *now that Client has fallen in love with the son, he has made it a family affair.* There was an exclamation point—and then Kurtz had written: *of course, I did not say so.*

Warren looked back at the sky beyond the window. But the voice he heard in his mind was not his own. It was that of Arlene Phillips. And she was saying: *it gives you one last chance. I hope you take it and I wish you well.*

10

So it was that on the day of Hedley Ashcroft's funeral, Warren Ellis arrived alone at the doors of Timothy Eaton Memorial Church on St Clair Avenue. He moved down the aisle looking neither left nor right. He could see his mother seated far away at the front, facing Hedley's unopened casket with its mound of white chrysanthemums. Ethel Beeman was seated there, too. And the hated Shirley Ashcroft. And Shirley Ashcroft's hated wife. And Arlene Phillips. And Gordon Perry. They were all strung out along the pew as though they were contaminated—no one sitting close beside another. All in black—and Freda still and ever with her black sables.

Leslie Drew was not in evidence. She had escaped, as Warren had intended.

Kurtz was standing near the back. His eye, till now, had been on Gordon Perry and Freda Manley. *How aptly named she is*, he was thinking. Then he saw Warren moving down the aisle and smiled.

Done, he thought. *And well done.*

Warren came at last to his destination.

He sat down firmly. He took Gordon's arm.

Freda turned and stared.

There was a woman sitting there. Young, by the look of it. She wore a trimly tailored black linen coat and a small black hat with a veil. Beneath the coat, a black silk dress. Balenciaga. She wore real pearls and carried a black alligator bag. Long kid gloves reached up beneath the sleeves of her coat. *Who the hell was this?*

Earth with its dark and dreadful ills / Recedes and fades away, the choir sang.

Freda felt distinctly ill at ease. She fussed with her furs and fidgeted with her handkerchief. The hymn was coming to an end. The words *O grave, where is thy victory? O death, where is thy sting?* flew up to heaven.

Gordon Perry sang a long *amen*—and slid in closer to the figure at his side.

All at once, Freda turned. Her mouth fell open. The profile beside her had come at last into focus. It produced a low and masculine cough.

Freda leaned away and stared in horror. "Is that you, Warren?" she said.

Warren knew it was best to have his answer ready.

"Yes," he said.

And he gave his mother a dazzling smile.

FOUR

*Club: An assembly of good fellows
meeting under certain conditions.*

Samuel Johnson
Dictionary

1

In recent times, it seemed to be increasingly inevitable that, just as April began, the season took a step backwards into winter. What had been promised was withdrawn—the bare skies clouded and the gentle rain, which at first had seemed so warm, became a storm of ice pellets. As expectations climbed, the snows descended. There had already been a week of this when, all at once, the trend reversed itself yet again and the temperature rose by ten degrees. The first wary starlings began to collect in the trees and the air was filled with the first breath of green. Mornings and evenings were misted. Twilight was extended half an hour. It was a time, for some, of exploration.

A man named Robert Ireland walked through the first of these evenings with his hands in his pockets and his mind on his destination. He wore the traditional trench coat and scarf—the scarf folded neatly showing a brown-and-yellow tartan at his throat. Though an ill-paid academic, Robert was also a man of private means and need not ever have walked. But he liked to walk and often he went out for hours on end and moved through the streets of Rosedale while the sun went down. Dusk was his milieu—dusk, and the hours that followed it. As the sun descended, Robert Ireland set his shoes to the sidewalk and left the safety of his car.

He would choose a street and park his Jaguar there, watching the people come and go. He had no interest in what they did—he wanted only to see who they were and where they were going. If they carried shopping bags or walked with dogs or moved in pairs or singly through the streets—these things did not matter. Ways of walking mattered. Slovenliness was not to be tolerated. Straight backs and energy—these were of interest. Eyes that were watchful—these were of interest. Boys with baseball caps and catcher's mitts—these were of interest. Especially those who could throw the ball in the air and catch it while walking—those who could roll the ball down their arms and flip it into the mitt—those who could do all this while riding a bike or standing on a skateboard—these were of interest. Those who in spring and summer wore rugby shorts and, in the wintertime, trousers cut to the shape of their buttocks—these were of special interest. These were his targets.

He would watch them pass and witness where they went. Which roads they crossed—which gates they chose—or, lacking gates, which drives and walkways they chose—which lawns they crossed—which doors they entered. Houses with visible numbers were of particular interest. Such addresses could be researched. Names could be assigned.

Each street and all streets. He had parked on them all and cruised them all. As the sun went down, he would open the door and step out into the air, his shoes impeccable—his gait serene. He seemed so benign—his expression revealing nothing. Only his hands told a story, shoved as they always were in his pockets. Shoved and gloved. Robert always wore gloves. Trim, tan, soft leather gloves—the kind with which you can pick up a dime. And the scarf—in any season—was always the same: two shades of yellow, brown and black.

On this particular evening—in the dusk, it so happened, that preceded Marlow's arrival in Toronto—Robert Ireland moved through the mist as one who could find his way through any state of darkness. He was adroit at this. His feet never strayed towards the gutters, nor onto the lawns of strangers. They found the pavement and avoided its pitfalls. They were never soiled, these feet—these shoes. In no way, ever.

There was a park in this vicinity. In the park there was a baseball diamond. In the wintertime, there was an outdoor hockey rink where, once or twice a week in the evening, music was played—recordings and tapes that were broadcast over public speakers. Men and women, boys and girls would skate to this music. Also on Sunday afternoons in what was known as *the family hour*. Other times, hockey games were played—pick-up games like the games of ball in the summer and of rugby in the fall. Anyone could play in these games—a father on occasion, or a wistful aging athlete of the kind who haunt such playing fields beyond their time. Mostly, however, these were boy games—adolescent games—the games of puberty.

Now it was early spring—and cool—and boys in the park would be clothed in windbreakers, jeans and baseball caps. Also in Converse and Nike hightops—the shoes of heroes—not like the shoes of Robert Ireland. Robert had no heroes. Only reverence for the young.

As he moved through the mist this evening to the park, Robert made a catalogue of his assets. Internal resources—external possessions. His display of these assets was spare to the point of being no display at all, which is to say that none of the truths about Robert Ireland were evident in anything he showed. Not his wealth—not his predilections—none of his academic brilliance—none of his emotions. Nothing. The lectures in eighteenth-century history which he gave at University College were invariably—word for word—the lectures he had given there for eleven years. He never looked up from his text. He opened his binder—stood at the lectern—read—and departed. He did this twice a week.

He lived behind a high stone wall in a large stone house whose rooms were hunter green and shades of burgundy. The paintings he displayed were hung between shelves of antique books and English silver. The appointments—he called them appointments—were tasteful, carefully assembled pieces, exclusively Georgian, every chair and every table brought from England. He owned nothing French. He hated France and detested all things French, including the language, though no explanation of this was ever offered. He drove a Jaguar XJ6. Its colour could not be named. Grey came closest to describing it—the hue, perhaps, of a shadow.

On the day of his walk through the dark, Robert was forty-two years old. Forty-two—curly-headed—slimly made and attired entirely in variations of tan and russet. Entirely, that is, except for his yellow tartan scarf. Even his underwear was khaki, though faded due to overwashing. His skin was a natural shade of bronze—a sign of his Celtic genes. His eyes were brown. Robert had never been married—he had no siblings and was orphaned. A man somewhat older lived in a cluster of tiny rooms at the top of the stone house and descended every morning but Thursdays to make Robert's breakfast, tend the garden and keep things in order. This was Rudyard, who went through his life with no last name.

Before he reached the park, it was necessary for Robert to cross a three-way intersection. He paused on the lip of the curb and savoured the wild, wet smell that rose from the nearby ravines. It reminded him of the grassy smells that had permeated his childhood adventures there, when he had seemed to be alive. He was nothing now but a spirit—though life or something like it burned in his groin from time to time. Such times as these, when poised beside the crossing, he knew precisely where he was going and what the consequence of his going would be.

The updraught carried him over to the other side—bearing him along with the swirling mist. The street lamps had now come on and their aureoles led Robert forward. The mist itself was lit from within with the last of daylight and he could see his hands, when he removed them from his pockets, with their leather skins and red-stitched outlines. His steps quickened.

At the gates to the park, he paused again. He listened for birds—but none was heard. Perhaps the D-Squads had already been, though it should have been too early in the season for that. There was certainly a chemical odour hanging in the air. So far, so good. He would not call out. The announcement of his arrival must be visual only. I am here, his shape would say, as he went beyond the gates and made his way along the gravel path to his quarry.

This was to be a boy called Arnie tonight, who rode home every afternoon from school on the Glen Road bus, descending at Binscarth Road and walking, most often alone, from Binscarth to Edgar Avenue to Clairmont Road, where he turned—it seemed reluctantly—towards a tall, grey stucco house with three green roofs and an empty driveway. Number 82. There was never anyone home to greet him, and Arnie, very often, would let himself in and come back out with his baseball cap reversed and sit on the steps of the porch with two cans of Pepsi and a sandwich.

Arnie had said that this time he would bring a friend.

Robert went deeper into the park towards the clubhouse there—a small wooden building with toilets and a large communal room where people could exchange their boots for skates and vice versa. A wide, deep porch gave shelter from the weather—and a vending machine that never worked was supposed to deliver candy bars and gum.

Two boys were sitting on the railing, waiting. Arnie was one of them and a boy with a grin was the other. Arnie said: "this is Steven. Don't call him Steve—he hates it." Steven went on grinning. He did not stand up. Perhaps he was under the impression Arnie had been kidding him about the details of their rendezvous in the park. Perhaps he did not quite believe he was about to enter the world Arnie had described. Perhaps, on the other hand, he knew that Arnie had told the truth—and he recognized the jeopardy he was in and was merely nervous. He had been chewing gum behind his grin and now, with Robert standing there, he gave up chewing. His mouth stood open—the gum caught up behind his teeth. His eyes froze.

"I want to see the money, now," he said, surprised that his voice did not break.

Robert got out his wallet and removed four hundred-dollar bills. "Two for you—two for Arnie," he said.

"Cool," said Arnie. "Let's go."

Steven got down from the railing and pulled his leather windbreaker tighter in around his neck. On his back, there was a single word: WOLVES. On his sleeve, there were several emblems—each denoting a separate sport. Capping the top of the left-hand sleeve there was a yellow *C*—which stood, Robert knew, for *Captain*. Arnie had brought him a prize. He would pay him something extra.

2

There was a house on Scollard Street that was divided into a workplace and a residence. The residence was upstairs. Downstairs, there was a shop at the front and a studio at the rear. In the window of the shop, a series of pictures was on display which offered blow-ups of the city's most famous faces: Fabiana Holbach—Barbara Davey—Helena Schleeman. Plain gold letters spelled out: *JOHN DAI BOWEN—PHO-TOGRAPHIC PORTRAITURE.*

Robert led the way. He had left the Jaguar on Hazelton and they had walked from there. Now, he went up the steps to the side of the house and rang the bell. Arnie and Steven stood behind him—gazing back across the road through the mist. There were no people there and no parked cars. Snow that had not yet melted lay in the gutters. Arnie seemed unconcerned, but Steven—given that he was new to all this—was dubious about the empty street.

"Shouldn't there be someone there?"

"There's lots of people in the houses."

Steven lifted the gum from his mouth and threw it out towards the sidewalk.

A buzzer went and a voice said: "yes?" It was a man's voice.

Robert said: "I'm here."

The voice said: "come up."

The door made a clicking sound.

Robert went through and the two boys followed.

They stood in a mirrored hallway—with a stairway directly in front of them.

The mirrors were clouded with a copper underlay and the light they reflected gave the immediate effect of being displaced in time. Steven removed his baseball cap, not knowing why—something a grandparent might have told him was proper in another age. Arnie, who had stood before in this hallway, began to undo his jacket—a heavy wool version, with fewer badges, of the one Steven wore. Robert stood at the bottom of the staircase and said to them: "after you."

Arnie went first, then Steven. Robert heard them whisper something sibilant—possibly rude—but could not decipher what it was. No matter.

Rejoinders were not his forte. Saying nothing, he merely watched them rise. He did this standing perfectly still.

Following after, he reached the top as John Dai Bowen stepped forward through an open door. There was a landing, not very large, with a Persian carpet on the floor and elaborate glass and silver sconces hung on the walls between other mirrors of the kind below. John Dai was something over thirty-five, but looked to be nearer twenty-five. He was small and brilliant and fey. Tiny would be the word—tiny in the way that adults who are perfectly proportioned appear to have the bodies of children. John Dai's hands were so small and delicate they were more like paper butterflies than hands—and he used them extensively, endlessly brushing back his pale fine hair from his pale round face. He wore a tailored waistcoat over a striped blue shirt—the stripes being almost black against a shade of blue more often found in coloured photographs than life. In every way conceivable, John Dai Bowen was the physical opposite of Robert Ireland. He was a man in flight, who rarely landed.

On the other hand, his manner could be confidential—almost conspiratorial, as though a secret was always about to be revealed. He delighted in making everyone feel that no one else existed for him but the person being confronted. He would draw each one aside and turn his head in such a way as to exclude a whole world of onlookers and lower his voice and say such things as: *what do you think of this weather?* Or: *do you need to use the bathroom?*

Others—watching—would be convinced the world was being reshaped. Now, he bent forward in Steven's direction, put his hand on Steven's arm and whispered: "the living-room is right through there." He nodded towards the open door.

Steven went through and Arnie followed. John Dai hung back—but only long enough to look at Robert and roll his eyes at heaven. Robert, of course, made no response. Flamboyance, like almost everything else, was beneath him.

In the living-room, known in John Dai's circle as the *salon,* there were three Victorian sofas and several small Victorian chairs. All were covered in shades of yellow—some with velvet, others with silk. A large collection of antique photographs was displayed in silver frames on the tops of various tables, large and small. The paintings on the walls were mostly early Canadian portraits in the style that was current in the 1840s and '50s. Children stood in clusters beside their parents, with centre-parted hair and tiny shoes. None of the artists had mastered the foot, and few had mastered the hand. The faces all looked outward, black-eyed every one of them—cracked with age. Dogs barely larger than rats were tethered to children's wrists by means of coloured ribbons and all the little boys had caps that were either worn or carried. Some of the little girls held unidentifiable bunches of flowers. The parents, for whatever reason, had all been painted in funeral clothes—perhaps because they were the best thing owned—and the children all looked doomed. There was not a single smile in the whole display, though whether this was because of the age they lived in or the artist's failure to master teeth was not self-evident. One thing was clear; it was an age of apprehension.

A fire was burning in a small Victorian grate and a tray with cigarette papers and a bowl of Colombian marijuana had been set conspicuously in front of it. Off to one side, there was a second tray with an array of bottles and glasses. On a third tray, four loaded cameras sat amidst clusters of candies wrapped in coloured papers. Banks of lights—already in place—were permanently fixed in tracks that webbed the ceiling.

"The bedroom is that way," said John Dai. "You will find two robes on the back of the door. When you return, you need not remove them until we have enjoyed some chat and a little dope."

Arnie led Steven away.

Robert said: "are the others here?"

John Dai nodded. "In the dining-room," he said.

Robert removed his trench coat and scarf and hung them in the hall. He did not, however, remove his gloves.

Both men sat down. Robert looked at his watch. John Dai smoothed the tops of his thighs. Both men fell silent. When the fire popped, John Dai rose and placed another piece of cedar in the grate. Outside, the mist proliferated—thickened with smoke, its colour altered. What had been grey was yellow. It came to the window panes and streaked the glass as rain would have done. "God is crying," John Dai said in his little-boy voice. "That's what my mother always said…"

"Did she?" said Robert. And looked the other way.

3

The Club of Men met once a week.

There were rules:

No physical contact with the models.

Models are not required to give information regarding their private lives.

Masks will be worn by the membership to protect identity.

Members are forbidden to speak one another's names.

All requests for poses will be given, unsigned, in writing.

One print of each pose shall be provided free of charge to each member. Further prints for a fee.

Two elected members will be responsible for procuring models. All models shall be amateurs. Professional agencies will be shunned because they keep records. Gratuities to models must be paid in cash.

The membership of the Club of Men shall not exceed one dozen.

Arnie and Steven were persuaded, finally, to remove their robes at a quarter past seven. Each had been encouraged to anaesthetize his inhibitions with marijuana. Drink was never offered to male models because of its debilitating qualities. For half an hour, the two boys presented themselves—untouched—to the assembled membership, seven of whom had arrived for the evening's entertainment.

Arnie was already known to some of these men and his presence was often requested. As with many lonely boys, there was a streak of sadism in Arnie and this could be encouraged to a degree that provided interesting poses. Those who favoured Arnie also favoured the notion that a boy could force them to perform those acts they were otherwise ashamed to consider. *Oh, no! Don't ask me to do that! I've never done that before!* There was something in Arnie's smile and the way he thrust himself at the camera that was thrilling and dangerous. He had a way of staring down the lens that could produce erections for the most impotent viewer. The power of his sensuality lay in his violent availability. There was nothing, it seemed, that Arnie in a photograph could not persuade a person to do for him.

Steven, being a virgin to this situation, was at a loss to know how to show himself. He had never been desired before, except in his own imagination, where all the world desired him as its lover. But not as its beloved.

Men were not objects of desire in Steven's world. It would be unmanly to think so. The size and potency of his penis could be envied—but not desired. So it was that his initial display of nakedness was much the same as it would have been in any school locker-room. Because of his youth, Steven's maleness, in this present company, was gauche and therefore charming. Reason had already told him what was wanted of him—but nothing had informed him that in providing what was wanted, he was giving up his freedom. To be chosen was to lose his right to choose. In his dreams, he was a rapist—but in these strangers' dreams, he would be raped.

All at once, a hurt expression bruised his face. He gained an unusual beauty. For all one could tell, Steven had never been naked before this moment. Embarrassed by its flaccidity, his penis began to rise. His hands—for the first time ever—went down to cover it.

Most of the men who inspected Arnie and Steven were masked. Only Robert and John Dai Bowen were barefaced. Neither Arnie nor Steven spoke. Because of the marijuana they had smoked, their perceptions were delayed. This prevented the need for speech.

At eight o'clock, the picture-taking began. A large silver bowl had been placed beside the tray of cameras and candies, into which each man had dropped a folded piece of paper. The paper was blue—one sheet per member.

Drinks were refreshed and, with glasses in hand, the membership stood back at this moment in order to create a suitable arena in the centre of the room.

"Gentlemen—are you ready?" said John Dai Bowen—stepping towards the bowl.

There were murmurs of assent. One or two cigarettes were lighted. Each man stood by himself as if entirely alone. There would be no contact now until the photo session was concluded. It would take just over an hour and a half.

John Dai selected the first sheet of paper and opened it to read. His lips moved over the words—but silently. Once considered, the instruction provided its own inspiration. A master both of lighting and of lenses, John Dai moved with surprising speed, once he had determined what was wanted. His wrists gained instant control of themselves and his hands flew over the panel of dimmers, pushing light into unlit corners and removing it from others. He conjured music that emerged from unseen speakers—barely audible but universal. He selected cameras—each one fitted uniquely with a different lens—each one preloaded—power-driven for rapid shooting.

His first instructions were for Arnie, into whose ear he laid the bones of a story. "You are alone," he said—and he turned the boy away from his audience. "It is Sunday night," he said, "there is no one in the house but you..." By the time he raised the camera, Arnie was lying back in one of the yellow Victorian chairs with one hand rising towards his nipples and the other descending through his pubic hair towards his penis. *One-two-three-four-five* frames were shot this way until the boy had aroused himself. John Dai stepped forward and drew a tube of cream from his pocket. "Your hand is dry," he said aloud—as if there were no one there but Arnie and the camera. "Use this," he said, and laid the tube on Arnie's thigh. *Six-seven-eight-nine-ten-eleven...*

Arnie was instructed to rise from the chair and to seek a partner. "There can only be one..." said John Dai, "...because he has never done this before..."

Arnie moved now, fully erect, across the open space before the fireplace and turned in Steven's direction.

"Tell him you want to show him something," said John Dai, hurrying to crouch in front of the fire.

"Hey! I wanna show you something." The look was coming, now, into Arnie's eyes. He was going to make something happen tonight that had never happened before.

"Tell him you need his assistance," John Dai prompted.

Arnie's hand was on his erection. He offered it to the camera's lens. "I need your 'sistance," he said—but it was not the dope that slurred his speech. It was expectation.

Along the walls, the men in masks stood silent as the paintings at their backs. The black-eyed children and their sombre parents could not look away.

Arnie's hands made motions.

"Lie on the sofa, Arnie." This was a whisper.

Arnie lay on the sofa nearest the fire. His skin was gleaming with lubricant and sweat.

"Steven," said John Dai.

Steven stepped forward. Drugged. Debauchable.

Twelve-thirteen-fourteen-fifteen... All the way to twenty-five.

"Stop," said John Dai. "Not too far. You have to make it last."

"Stop," said Arnie. "You got to make it last."

John Dai laughed. "No," he said. "*You* have to make it last."

Arnie lay back and placed one hand behind his head. Steven sat up—but Arnie did not see him. Arnie was looking at the fire.

"Your turn now, Steve," said John Dai—rising to select another folded sheet of paper.

"Don't call him Steve," said Arnie. "He doesn't like it."

"I beg your pardon," said John Dai. "*Steven.*" He was smiling.

Someone laughed.

John Dai unfolded the blue instructions. Once he had finished reading them, he said: "my goodness!"

He selected another camera. Two.

Moving in where only Steven could hear him, he said: "I want you to lie on this table..."

Steven lay back against his elbows.

John Dai handed him a condom. "See what you can do with this," he said.

So it went.

In the time remaining, more blue sheets were unfolded and two hundred frames of film were exposed. Less and less was said. More and more was done. The sound of it was entirely the sound of wheezing cameras and of liquid hands.

When it was entirely over and the boys had gone to the bedroom to dress, the Chairman of the Club—a man called Peter Horvath—raised a final glass and made the announcement with which their meetings came to an end every other week. "Gentlemen," he said, "next time, the wonderful mystery of girls."

"Hear! Hear!" said the others—as if they were a parliament—and dispersed into the night.

Robert Ireland returned to the park with Arnie and Steven. The mist, by then, was almost a fog. Neither boy spoke.

Robert said: "I'll be in touch," and went back out through the gate to his car. Not once, until that moment, had he removed his gloves.

4

A certified cheque had arrived by courier from the Beaumorris Corporation and was signed by Gordon Perry. Made out to The Parkin Institute of Psychiatric Research, it was a donation of half a million dollars earmarked for research. A note, which Kurtz had slipped into his pocket, simply said: *Thank you. Gordon P.*

Kurtz—in his office—had smiled when he saw this. His *arrangement* had played through smoothly to the end—and here was the pay-off in his hand.

What a delightful image it made in memory—the image of Warren Ellis in his impeccable ensemble—*with shoulders out to here*—walking up the aisle of Timothy Eaton Memorial Church to meet his destiny. It might have been a wedding, instead of a funeral. Even Kurtz, who had not the slightest interest in such things, was approving and admiring of the Balenciaga's effect on young Warren's figure. Well—that was only as it should be. Kurtz, after all, had an obligation to fulfil Gordon Perry's dream as precisely as possible, if he wanted the Beaumorris Corporation to go on funding the Parkin.

My, my, my. It had been quite a ride, bringing those two men together.

Kurtz laid the cheque on top of his desk and gave it a little pat. *Half a million dollars. Half a million dollars...*

Half a million dollars for research.

Kurtz considered the various projects being pursued at the Parkin. His own pet programme concerned what he called *The White Mind Theory*, which was currently being carried out by Doctor Sommerville. Originating with Kurtz, *White Mind* was a form of therapy involving sleep induced by sound-infusions of white noise. Years before, white noise had been introduced as a pain suppressor in dental operations, where its use had been a qualified success. Kurtz had seized upon it as an anaesthetic device and had been making some progress with it when he was appointed Director and Psychiatrist-in-Chief of the Parkin. It had then been necessary, because of his added work load, to turn the project over to Doctor Sommerville, who was young and energetic and an enthusiastic supporter of the programme. Ian Sommerville was equally a supporter of Kurtz's theories in general—and had been a protégé while still a student. Half a million dollars would go a long way in his behalf.

There were only eight patients undergoing treatment at the moment. Six of them were manic-depressive; one had been traumatized when forced to witness a killing. The eighth was a man known to Kurtz as *The Paranoid Civil Servant,* a patient so severely troubled that Kurtz had moved him now three times into different therapeutic courses, all of which had failed to eradicate his psychosis. Each of the eight subjects rested in a separate unit, each unit soundproofed and lit with amber light. White noise was all they heard—and, as they slept, each was fed intravenously and each was bagged for waste elimination. Each was temperature-controlled and monitored by a separate attendant. The use of amber light and personal attendants had originated in Kurtz's observations of midwinter beehives—*those somnolent pleasure-domes where the lullaby never ends...*

Theories had abounded over time on the uses of sleep as a curative for mental disorders. Few had been successful, though a man called Cameron had come very close to success in a programme conducted at Montreal's Allan Memorial Institute. Cameron's experiments had included what he called *psychic driving*—a method involving tape-recorded messages introduced subliminally during sleep. But the use of white noise was unique to Kurtz and Sommerville, and Sommerville's pursuit of it was currently *the great white hope of sleep therapy*—a phrase that gave Kurtz pleasure.

He sat back, lighting one of his Sobranie cigarettes. The smell of them irritated Oona Kilbride and whenever Kurtz vacated his office, she rushed in and turned on the air conditioning at *high* and left it on until his return.

There was also the work with drug therapy being pursued by Doctor Shelley—a programme Kurtz was extremely keen on. Shelley was also his protégée, a woman of intense dedication and enormous talent, whose vision of re-created lives was almost literary in its imaginative applications of science. While chemotherapy lay at the heart of Shelley's thrust, she was also conducting concurrent experiments in the field of thought transference, which she preferred to call *motivational impulse cross-communication.* Here, she was regarded as a revolutionary, having introduced non-scientific theory into the bloodstream of science itself.

There were other experimental programmes in place at the Parkin— but Kurtz was most profoundly interested in those being conducted by Sommerville and Shelley. And most especially by Shelley. Sommerville was good, but Shelley was braver—more daring.

Half a million dollars...

A quarter of a million each?

Kurtz closed his eyes.

There was something else.

There was *The Golden Chamber of the White Dogs.*

Not worth—and certainly not calling for—the outlay of half a million dollars. But a sizable portion thereof might be spent on it. Seventy-five or a hundred thousand—which would include, of course, Fabiana Holbach's commission.

A gift of wonder to the mad.

The thought of Slade's canvas slid to Kurtz's groin—just as the painting itself had done so mysteriously when first confronted. Naked power was a property of males—and Kurtz was now discovering, with less chagrin than at first, that he was elevated by its image.

"I *will* have it," he said out loud.

The sound of his voice brought him forward in his chair.

Did I speak?

Yes.

Kurtz pressed the button that would summon Kilbride. When she entered, she noted the lit Sobranie but said nothing.

"Get Shelley up here," said Kurtz. "And Sommerville. Tell them I have good news."

"Right away." Turning to go.

"And would you get Fabiana Holbach on the telephone as soon as possible."

"Yes, Doctor." Walking to the door.

"Kilbride?"

"Yes?"

"Are you an art lover?"

Oona did not know what to say. Doctor Kurtz's questions were so often loaded, a person must be guarded with her answers. "I dare say our definitions of art might differ," she said. "But judging art by my own standards—yes. I am, largely, its lover."

"The Parkin is going to have a masterpiece in residence, Kilbride. I want you to be the first to know."

"Thank you, Doctor."

Oona knew very well that she had been *the first to know* about a dozen things in the last year. But she knew she was not the recipient of Kurtz's bulletins because of his admiration of her. She received them simply because she was there more often than anyone else when Doctor Kurtz boiled over with enthusiasm. That he reached the boiling point at all was a rarity. That he reached it in another person's presence was practically unheard of. Now, she said: "which masterpiece is that, Doctor Kurtz?"

"You remember Julian Slade, the artist?"

"Yes, indeed."

"His masterpiece."

"I see."

"It will hang in the foyer. It will be the very first thing that people see when they enter the Parkin Institute. It will lift them off the floor and drop them in our hand."

"Yes, Doctor." *Lift them off the floor? Drop them in our hand?*

"That will be all, Kilbride."

"Thank you." Go.

Kurtz had decided that Julian Slade could be credited with having conducted research on a scale with Sommerville and Shelley. He had decided to split the Beaumorris money accordingly. He had decided that Slade had explored mental illness as avidly from the inside and with the same scientific skill as Sommerville and Shelley had explored it from the outside. He had decided that *The Golden Chamber of the White Dogs* transcended art to become a scientific statement. *For a desperate disease—a desperate cure.* Montaigne had written that—and Kurtz had read it while still an intern. He took out his fountain pen and wrote it down on a piece of stationery. He would quote it at the unveiling. He would see that it was included in the info-kit. He would make it his motto.

When Shelley and Sommerville had come and gone, Kurtz allowed himself only a brief moment of unbridled contentment. He knew too well that nothing can be taken for granted. Even a signature on a dotted line can be nullified by the letters *NSF*. Not that the Beaumorris cheque would bounce—but others had, from other sources—bounced or been withdrawn or failed to materialize. The thing was—not ever to relax. Not ever to rest on your laurels. Not ever to forget the dictum: *the harder I work, the luckier I get.*

Yes.

Beaumorris funding was a *fait accompli* and, therefore, he must put it out of his mind and move on to the next.

The next what?

Kurtz had been going to say *score.*

Well. No. *Objective.*

That was more acceptable. *Scoring* sounded like something done on the street by sweaty men with rolled-up sleeves and trousers made of some inappropriate material. Over-anxious, pushy men, whose meetings were always held in second-class hotels—men who smelled of beer and hamburgers. That was *scoring.*

To gain one's objective, on the other hand, one sat in high-flown offices and did one's deals in boardrooms or the back seats of limousines—even, if the players were of a certain station, in the salons and parlours of private homes...

Salons and parlours, Rupert?

Well. You know what I mean.

Kurtz sat forward.

Onward.

He had asked Kilbride to provide him with a few significant files—and they were now sitting on a tray by his left elbow. These were in aid of his next objective—what he called the *Appleby Project.*

This was entirely a financial consideration. Appleby was the latest of an unbroken line of Canadian press barons who were precisely that—*Lords.* Beaverbrook—Thomson—(Black, still in waiting, untitled)—and Appleby; all had begun their careers in Canada and all of their triumphs had culminated in Fleet Street. Appleby's lordly name was Parkdale. His title was barely ten years old—but his money could not be counted.

Kurtz was proceeding on the assumption that his Lordship might be interested in establishing an *Appleby Wing* at the Parkin. Could a man ask more?

Kurtz knew the answer to this, of course, was *yes*. Still, it was his duty—and his job—to set the wheels in motion that might capture

Appleby's attention. This was where the files at his elbow entered the picture. One of them contained the psychiatric exploration—by Kurtz, himself—of Richard Appleby, the only son of Lord Appleby of Parkdale. A mother-lode of useful information.

Kurtz drew the file from its place and opened it. He pressed the appropriate button and said: "I don't wish to be disturbed, Kilbride—not for the next hour."

"Yes, Doctor Kurtz."

Kurtz released the button—and began to read.

Richard Appleby's problem—as he put it to Kurtz—was *terminal impotence.* It had begun when he was seventeen and he was now approaching thirty. In all that time, he had not been involved with a single woman, though several had caught his attention and one of these had been Amy Wylie. Richard was a fiction writer of sorts, though none of his books—there were three of them—had sold beyond two thousand copies. It was not so much that the books were bad—they were simply too esoteric to win the attentions of a reading public devoted to fictions in which the heroine was beaten, raped and left for dead—and to paperback biographies of drugged celebrities. In recent times, Richard had been in the process of courting a new idea for a novel that, so far, had eluded him. He described this affliction as being not unlike his other: *both pen and penis fail me.*

Kurtz had not been the least bit concerned about Richard Appleby's impotence. Nor, for that matter, had he cared if the young man produced a dozen masterpieces or never wrote another word. What Kurtz had wanted from him was access to his father's fortune. More importantly, he had wanted access to the progenitor, himself—*both of fortune and of boy.*

As always, when Kurtz discovered that Austin Purvis had another rich or influential client, he conducted the usual raiding party. *Best for all concerned if I take over here...*

And, as always, Kurtz had asked Richard to provide him with an essay concerning his reasons for seeking psychiatric help in the first place. Such writings could turn up what Kurtz called *trigger-words and phrases*—images, names and places that otherwise lay buried out of sight in the patient's mind. This way, Kurtz also garnered useful information that was, in fact, none of his business as a psychiatrist. Such things as income data, the contents of wills and the details of marriage settlements. He knew a great deal more than he should about the dispensation of monies and possessions within families and corporations—details that otherwise belonged behind locks in a lawyer's office.

Regarding his father, this is what Richard Appleby had written:

My father prefers to be called Lord Appleby of Parkdale. It is not a title I will inherit. I am glad. Seventy-eight years ago, my father was born on Rebecca Street in that part of Toronto from which he derives his title. The story of his rise from abject poverty to the British peerage is too well known for me to tell it here. It has, in any case, been told with greater skill than I could muster, in Anthony Blore's *Anatomy of Power*. I would not, however, imagine I could tell the story of my father's life in the first place. I am a novelist and all I know of him is lies. I trust the implications of this are clear. For me, the reading of novels has been my only access to certain truths—and I stand in awe of the truth-bending done in books such as *Anatomy of Power*, regardless of their entertaining style.

My father is not a suitable subject for fiction. He belongs in a film—best played, perhaps, by Sidney Greenstreet. As sinister as that. As large. But not with Greenstreet's sense of style. My father has no sense of style. He wears what his tailor tells him to wear. He is not even capable of choosing a suitable tie. His face and his voice and the smell of his clothes I can tell you. But not the man who hides behind these things. That man has never revealed himself to me and I have only his name and his wayward presence in my life to tell me I am his. My sister, Rose, and I have been granted permission to occupy those spaces in his résumé left open for *Offspring* and *Issue* and *Children*. We have played no other role. In childhood, we were simply *there*—at the back of his mind—and he drew us into focus only long enough to choose our schools and pay our bills...

Beyond the windows, the April clouds were darkening. Rain had not been predicted—but there it was. At any moment, it would begin to fall. Kurtz turned on his lamp—and continued to read.

It was not for nothing that my father chose Parkdale as the title by which he would enter the House of Lords. He came from generations of English labourers—miners and factory workers—whose suffering began in the dark satanic mills of Northern England and ended in the dark satanic mills of Southern Ontario. Driven—more by despair than hope—to emigrate in 1895, my father's forebears landed in the underground forges of Massey-Harris on King Street West in Toronto. The box-house squalor into which my father was consequently born not only shamed him, it enraged him. He never forgave his parents for having forced him to inhabit this hell through what he called their *inability to improvise. They had no dreams,* he said. It never occurred to them, he claimed, to resist the powers that kept them in their place. *The first thing my mother taught me,* he said, *was how to tug my forelock. So I cut it off.*

In this way, he was wonderful—zealous and energetic in his refusal to stand in place. He would have made an effective communist revolutionary, but he chose the other side. Parkdale, the place, would be made to pay for the humiliation he had suffered in its streets. He would do this not by exposing its inhuman living conditions, but by closing its gates and locking the people in. The message was clear; by its failure to resist, the working class of Parkdale had condemned itself to eternal obedience. Its motto, he believed, should be *submit or perish.* His way of saying this was curious. On the masthead of the *London Daily Globe,* the flagship of his empire, he placed the following declaration: *THE PEOPLE HAVE THE RIGHT TO BE THE PEOPLE.*

Privately, of course, he added: *piss on them all.*

That my father should believe such things was the mark—so he told me—of the self-made man. Not for him, *submit or perish.* Never. He fought his way out—and those who didn't fight did not get out because *they lacked the boots and the brains—the balls and the brass—to throw off their chains—and get off their ass!* I often heard him chanting this little verse, singing it, almost—shoving the words through barely parted lips as he thrust out his chin in order to shave his neck. *You sit there and listen,* he would say to me, when I was six or seven—and I was made to sit on the toilet in his presence while he shaved and bathed and dressed himself. It was the only time I saw him, day to day, and the only time he wanted me to see him. He wanted to teach me how to be a man before I was eight years old, he said. *After eight, too late!* His bulk in a bathrobe was terrifying. He once exposed himself to me—held up his privates in his hand and said: *these rule the world—don't you forget it.*

You can guess the rest. It is too trite to tell. If my father's life cannot be told in a novel or a biography, but only in a film, my life cannot be told in any medium. I am someone of whom it is always being said: *who is that man in the corner?* The man in the corner has nothing worthy of exposure. He does not want to rule the world.

The source of Richard's impotence had declared itself. Mason Appleby was just another Caesar. The problem was, his career—to date—had not made clear which one.

The time was coming when Kurtz and his Lordship would meet. The Appleby Lecture was to be given this year, at the University of Toronto, by an Irishman—Nicholas Fagan. Appleby always turned up for these events, which served as an annual homecoming—allowing him to touch base, see his children and deal with what remained of his Canadian interests.

His Lordship was aging. Kurtz could not delay their meeting. It would have to be arranged during this year's lecture season.

How, Kurtz wondered, *does one capture such a man?*

Certainly not by flattery. Nor by suggesting bequests in the name of science. There must be some other way. A parallel in aims.

That's good, Kurtz thought. *A parallel in aims.*

Submit—or perish.

Kurtz sat back, relaxed.

Outside, in the world, it began to rain.

5

Marlow took possession of 38 Lowther during a week of burgeoning puddles. The moving vans had *MAYFLOWER* written on their sides, which seemed entirely appropriate for a man returning from Massachusetts. Marlow directed the whole operation wearing a Burberry and carrying a rolled-up umbrella. He was brisk and confident with the movers—but also sympathetic. The stairs were narrow and steep—with a landing part way up where a sharp turn had to be made—and in spite of the fact that some plaster was cracked in the process, Marlow never raised his voice or complained.

Lilah watched much of this through the half-opened door between the kitchens—or from a place on the sidewalk opposite the house, where she stood beneath her umbrella. She heard the rest through the walls.

Marlow. Marlow. Charlie Marlow, she kept repeating. *Charlie Marlow. Charlie Marlow. Please.*

Kurtz.

How would she broach the subject? When?

She must tell him, of course. She must put it to him straight: *you are to go to The Parkin Institute of Psychiatric Research and bring Kurtz back down the river...*

No. She could not say that. It was impossible. To begin with, there wasn't any river. There was just the symbolic river, running through the city streets—but how could she possibly expect a stranger to understand that? All because his name was Marlow—Charlie Marlow—and because there was this other man named Kurtz.

I let Kurtz out of Heart of Darkness, *Doctor Marlow,* she could say. *Right here—from page ninety-two.* And she could show him. She could even take him to the Metro Library. That he might understand. *This is where it happened,* she would tell him. *Here. Right here...beneath these cotton fibre trees...*

No.

How could he possibly believe her? He would tell her she was crazy and she would have to say to him: *Yes, I am.* Her D-card would give her away: *Lilah Mary Kemp—Schizophrenic—takes Modecate and Infratil. Outpatient, Queen Street Mental Health Centre.*

She sat on her bed and listened as Marlow bade his movers goodbye. He had bought them a case of beer and they had been drinking it for the last half-hour. There must have been an army of them. It sounded like a regimental mess hall through the walls. They laughed. They cheered. They shouted. They sang.

A dog howled—but not with pain. He was obviously singing, too—joining in—being one with the others. An all-male chorus.

Lilah had forgotten there would be a dog. Not that she minded. Dogs had always been kind to her. It was rabbits they chased. And birds and squirrels. But not Lilah Kemp. This dog's name was Grendel. That was interesting. Who, then—and where—was Beowulf?

At last, the movers left and the *Mayflower* sailed off down the street. The front door shut—and, after it, the door of the vestibule.

Lilah heard Marlow moving through the house—approaching. She was determined that he should make the first move. This was proper. This was right. He would have to come to her. He would have to declare himself. *I am Charlie Marlow.* She would not have to tell him who he was.

She heard him rap at the kitchen door. She heard him push it wide. She heard the dog, Grendel, clicking across her linoleum.

"Miss Kemp?"

It was him.

She got down off her bed and moved without a tremor through the short, dark hall towards the summer kitchen, which was hers, with its view through the door of the smaller kitchen beyond.

"How do you do," she said—when she was finally in his presence.

"I am well," said the man, whose height was not a great deal taller than her own.

Say your name.

"My name is Charles Marlow," he said. He was smiling. "I've just returned from Harvard University, where I've been working these last five years. You, of course, are Lilah Kemp. It's a pleasure to meet you."

"Thank you," said Lilah. "I can say the same."

There was a short, somewhat awkward pause, in which Lilah forgot to invite Marlow to be seated. He said: "this is Grendel, my dog. I'm sure you two will get along. He's not the least bit aggressive, now that he's old."

Lilah reached down and gave the dog her hand—which he sniffed, while he wagged his tail. *Grendel.*

"Look here," said Marlow. "Why don't you come through now and have a drink with me. I'm rather partial to the cocktail hour—and I would enjoy your company."

Lilah said: "yes. I would like that." And then she said: "you go on back and I'll join you directly."

Marlow nodded and retired to the other side of the door. Grendel went with him.

Lilah hurried off to her bedroom and picked up a spare copy of *Heart of Darkness*—not her own, with its Fagan pastings. *I'll just sort of take it through and leave it somewhere where he can't avoid it,* she was thinking. *I'll just sort of let him see it—but not a word. I won't even mention it. I'll just...*

She left it on Marlow's kitchen table and went on through to the living-room.

"I've lit the fire," said Marlow. "Someone very kindly left one laid for me. Was that you, Miss Kemp?"

"Oh, no," said Lilah. "that would have been the others. The Hollands, who were here before you."

"Well, that was kind of them."

"No it wasn't," said Lilah. "They put it there for show—like everything else about them."

Marlow listened to this and laughed. "You certainly are forthright," he said.

"I have to be," said Lilah. "My life depends on it."

Marlow nodded. His smile began to fade. An interesting woman—though clearly, there was something odd about her.

"I'll take sherry," said Lilah.

"Good for you," said Marlow. "Sweet or dry?"

"Dry," said Lilah. "Sweet is for sick people."

"Yes, of course," said Marlow. "I'll be right back."

He walked out around her and went to the kitchen.

He was gone some time.

Lilah prayed.

Grendel snoozed by the fire.

When he returned, Marlow carried some bottles and glasses on a tray. Lilah's sherry was already poured and he handed it to her.

"The conspiracy continues," he said.

"Oh? What conspiracy is that?"

"Someone left me this on the kitchen table," he said—and drew Lilah's book from his pocket. "*Heart of Darkness*," he said. "Ever since I knew I was coming back to Toronto, everywhere I go, there it is. Friends have given it to me—people have joked about it. *Oh how funny!* they say to me. *Who would have believed it?* Stuff like that..."

"Who would have believed what?" Lilah asked. The sherry was superior. Marlow was drinking something golden called Ricard. It smelled like licorice.

"Well," he said. "As you know, my name is Marlow... And I've come back home to Toronto to work at The Parkin Institute of Psychiatric Research..."

Lilah nodded. She held her breath. *Say nothing.*

"And—it's just sort of crazy—the kind of coincidence that happens once in a lifetime, but—the Psychiatrist-in-Chief at the Parkin Institute is a man called..."

"Kurtz."

Marlow laughed. "That's right," he said. "It's crazy! *Heart of Darkness—Kurtz* and *Marlow*—and now, Doctor Kurtz and me, Charlie Marlow—at the Parkin Institute. Who ever would have believed it was possible?"

Lilah said: "I would."

She did not, however, tell him why. That would have to come later, when she knew more about this man who stood before her. As *Marlow*, he was something of a disappointment. He wasn't bearded. He didn't

128

have a seaman's walk. His eyes were not squinty. In fact, he was not right at all. She had expected someone who looked like Joseph Conrad—and what she got was someone who looked like a soldier in civilian clothes—taking the weekend off—parading around in a wool checked suit with a dog at his heels.

On the other hand, *Marlows* were not a dime a dozen. She would have to accept what she got.

6

Charlie Marlow was not yet fifty, though his eyes were ageless—old one minute, young the next. Hooded and widely spread in an oval face, they gave the impression cats' eyes give—of watching something in the middle distance that cannot be seen by others. His skin was yellow, like cream on its way to becoming butter, and his hair was iron-grey and stood up short and straight from his head. He never wore a hat, his father having told him years before that wearing hats would make him go bald.

Marlow had no women in his life at the moment. His mother was dead—he had been an only child—and his wife had died while they were both still young—in their early thirties—and Marlow could barely recall her. Her name had been Charlotte—which had caused a lot of friendly jokes and confusion. *The Charlies are coming for dinner,* people used to say. It all seemed such a long while ago, in another world entirely. Time and distance had cut him off from remembrance of it. So many years had intervened and his time at Harvard had taken up five of them. He was a dog man, now—with Grendel as companion. Grendel and memories—not of Charlotte. Charlotte was best forgotten. She had caused him so much pain.

They had been a popular couple, uniquely gifted, attractive in their mismatched way. Marlow wasn't all that big—five-feet-seven—a lightweight in pounds. Charlotte had been a giant, which is why she had died. Her heart gave out. It stopped in the middle of a sentence while she was giving a lecture on molecular biology. Marlow had not been there. Two months after her death, he discovered she had been having an affair with one of her students—a girl called Allison Mowbray. Allison had been the one who'd phoned the afternoon of Charlotte's death. She had whispered hoarsely to him down the line: *Professor Marlow's dead, Marlow—why not you?* Marlow had not understood. He had thought it was a student prankster, seeking some kind of revenge for having been failed in an exam.

Charlotte faded from his memory over time as he came to realize the wife he had known was someone Charlotte had invented for his consumption. It couldn't matter less, in retrospect, that she had been a lesbian. It mattered only that she had failed to tell him she was going to leave him; not by dying, but by going to live with Allison Mowbray. Here, all unwitting, Allison had again been his informant. Her letters to Charlotte turned up in Charlotte's chiffonier and, in the very first of them he scanned, he saw himself described as *that hateful little yellow man.* The words being quoted were Charlotte's. She had written, apparently, to Allison saying: *when I finally leave that hateful little yellow man, I will bring all my love to you and we will live on that forever...* When Allison had written out these words in her letter to Charlotte, she had added: *most people don't understand how wonderful it is to hate.*

Yes, they do, Marlow thought at first. And then: *not* wonderful, *Allison, no. But liberating.*

Harvard had saved him with its old-style academies and old-world havens. Cambridge, Massachusetts was a special blessing. Marlow had always been a sucker for a garden laid out beyond a picket fence. Old houses charmed him. He basked in the presence of history. This was why he was particularly happy to be situated now on Lowther Avenue.

The houses on Lowther, though old enough, were a hundred years younger than Cambridge houses. The gardens were not as spacious. William James had not walked over to Harvard Yard, nor had T.S. Eliot gone to eat at the Athens Olympia past the houses here. Nor had Gertrude Stein walked here—nor Thornton Wilder. But others had. The continuity, till now, had been maintained—of place, of loyalties, of kind.

He had always loved Toronto; not the whole of it—but parts. He loved the St George Campus and was glad to be back on its greens again, beneath its gothic horrors. *The buildings are so damned ugly,* he said, *you miss them for the charm of their deformation.* This was not true of the newer buildings: the Library and the Parkin Institute. These were monstrosities of another kind altogether—flat-slabbed paste-ups of glass and concrete that had passed for *architecture* in the deadly years when the whole world sucked its thumb, eyes closed in self-satisfaction.

Still, there were pleasures here to which he looked forward with great excitement. Old friends, once fellow students, with whom he could work again—patients, whose progress he could monitor, eager to know how each had fared. Colleagues not of his discipline whose work he admired and whose books he had read—scientists, law professors, professors of English.

"What do you do, Miss Kemp?" he asked.

"I'm a retired librarian," she told him.

"Surely you're too young to be retired."

Don't butter me up, she wanted to say. But instead, she said: "I'm older than I look."

She was an odd little thing, Marlow thought, with her wide-set eyes, her powdered face and her madcap hair. And the weight of all those unsaid words held back behind her lips. He knew there was something pent-up in there, but was not yet aware of the schizophrenic cause of it. Strange, though, the way she had pounced on Kurtz's name—and his own—with such intensity. It was only a bookish connection, after all— no different than a Romeo bumping into a Juliet on the dance floor—or an Emily living next to a George.

On the other hand...

Marlow used literature as psychotherapy. He believed in its healing powers—not because of its sentiments, but because of its complexities. No human life need ever be as knotted as Anna Karenina's life had been—since the living had the benefit, as she had not, of her own example. Many a suicide had been thwarted because of Anna's death. The trouble was, with books, that no one read any more. That way, trains still claimed many victims.

Marlow had previously lectured in psychiatry at the University of Toronto, just as he had done at Harvard—but his practice had been at the Queen Street Mental Health Centre. Now, it was to be at The Parkin Institute of Psychiatric Research. This, for Marlow, was greatly exciting. It was known to be the ultimate accolade if one was chosen to practise at the Parkin.

"Would you care for another glass of sherry, Miss Kemp?"

"I shouldn't," she said. "But I will."

It was such a pleasure—such a relief—just to be standing in his company at last, she could not give it up.

"Would you care for some barmbrack?" she asked. "I made it only yesterday."

"I would be delighted," said Marlow. "I haven't had barmbrack in years."

"I'll go and cut it, then," said Lilah. "And I'll bring it back buttered on a plate."

They made their way to their respective kitchens and, as Marlow was taking an extra nip of Ricard, he heard his neighbour singing beyond the open door. It was a song he had never heard—but he would ask to hear it again. It was enchanting.

From Drumleck Point to Dalkey,
I have leaned against the sky—

With Dublin Bay behind me,
And Dublin in my eye.

7

Were it not for her love of her boss, Austin Purvis, which had fixed her in place for over twenty years, Bella Orenstein would never have come to work at the dreaded Parkin Institute, where everyone was mad and, sometimes, one person killed another and other times, the bodies of suicides crouched in the cabinets of darkened washrooms, waiting for Bella Orenstein to turn on the lights. Often, returning from her lunch hour—spent in the tropical haven of Motley's Bar and Grill on Spadina Avenue—Bella would pause, while she drew to the end of a final cigarette, and gaze with wonder at the grey, dead walls before her. Above the doors, a wide brass plate proclaimed *The Parkin Institute of Psychiatric Research*, but the building itself was incoherent. It seemed, in its design, as disconnected as the sorry minds it harboured.

The Parkin—intended as a centre for creative psychiatry—had been housed, as if through spite, in a concrete fortress of remarkable ugliness. It was twenty-four storeys high, though all you saw from the street was evidence of twenty. The other floors were underground and were called *Subsidiaries One to Four*, as if the words *basement* and *cellar* had been excised from the language. Bella thought of these places as *Dungeons One to Four*, and dreaded going down there. Upstairs, all the windows—hermetically sealed—had one-way clouded glass, which made them look, to Bella, like the eyes of a blinded idol. Inside, it was all red marble and burnished brass and the interior had about it an air of pervasive secrecy, since not a single door stood open along its corridors. Because of the marble floors, people in leather heels could be heard approaching for what seemed like hours. But they would pass without identity and might as well be walking on sand.

"I hate it here," Bella said one day to Oona Kilbride. "I wish I had the nerve not to come back...." And perhaps some day, her lunch hour having slipped away, she would not return, but go on sitting at her table in Motley's Bar and Grill, sipping her vodka martini—double—while the music played and the students danced. If only Doctor Purvis would imbibe from time to time. If only she could persuade him to come down—*come down from the dreaded tower...*

But, no. He would not come down. It was his life, up there on the eighteenth floor, tree tops below him: *safe, safer, safest;* the dedicated purveyor of sanity, locked in his place, with his back to the street and his face to the setting sun. *My favourite hour of all,* he had said to her once, *is twilight, Mrs Orenstein.* How often she had left him gazing from his windows at just that time of day. Nothing of the city to mar the prospect before him—only the reassurance of the St George campus spread beneath him, with its ring of pseudo-Gothic façades, each one fronting the wisdom of the ages: *the great, good houses of learning,* he would say. *The great, good house of books; the great, good house of history; the great good house of law,* et cetera. Set pieces, all. He came from that tradition. Not that traditions bound him. But popular venal innovations in psychiatry held no interest for him.

Post-modern theories about the insane appalled him. *We are not here to drag them willy-nilly back into our world!* he had yelled one day at Doctor Shelley, who was overly fond of somnificating her patients. *We are here to drag our perceptions forward into theirs!* Doctor Shelley, furious because he had yelled at her in front of her students, had flung her clipboard in his face and broken his nose. *You self-ish tyrant!* she had screamed at him. *Why would you deny the insane the comforts of civilization?*

Bleeding profusely, Doctor Purvis had refused all aid and, turning at the elevator doors, had shouted back at Doctor Shelley: *you won't be satisfied till every last one of them is sitting, sedated, in his allotted place at McDonald's!*

It was like a vaudeville act. Thank heavens, Bella Orenstein recalled with a smile, the elevator doors had folded Doctor Purvis out of sight at just that moment, leaving Doctor Shelley alone with her students, her pills and her bloodied clipboard.

Today, there was a Scotch mist—and the birds had begun or were about to return to the city, which meant that spraying would soon commence in earnest. Sometimes, if birds escaped from a spray-site, they ended up dying or dead in the gutters. It was *too depressing for words,* Bella thought, *and the saddest thing in all the world. Aside from Doctor Purvis...*

Did she call him Austin? Not to his face. *I would never do that.* But in her mind he was Austin more often than not—and sometimes, *Austin, dear.* Nowadays, however, he was increasingly thought of as *desperate Austin* or spoken of aloud as *poor Doctor Purvis.* Something dreadful was happening to him and Bella could not figure out what it was.

He was constantly agitated—much too often seen to be perspiring, and his speech had become a weapon—sharp words, tersely spoken. Even to Bella—whom he called *Orenstein* with an exclamation point when he summoned her into his office.

On these occasions, his anger always had to do with missing patients. *One more gone!* he would shout at her. *I won't have any patients left, if I lose any more!*

For the briefest moment, on hearing this cry of anguish, Bella wondered how Doctor Purvis could possibly be under the impression he had not already lost his patience. Her mind was falling into a mode that was more and more raddled—a mode in which words became jumbled and took on all the wrong meanings. To calm herself, she drank even more—though never so much that she became incoherent. At its worst, the extra drink might lead to a spelling mistake or an added trip to the washroom.

As more and more patients vanished into the venue of the Psychiatrist-in-Chief on the twentieth floor, Austin Purvis became more and more accusatory. Bella—already paranoid—settled into a state almost of shock. What had gone wrong that so many were leaving? The thought that Doctor Purvis might be guilty of some misdemeanour crossed her mind. The words *improper conduct* entered the scene. Female patients had been known to exit the Purvis sanctum with tears in their eyes. Bella could not deny it. She had offered them Kleenex and a chair. None of them mentioned anything about inappropriate behaviour. None of them charged Doctor Purvis. But still...a woman in tears—a trembling woman—a woman who requested assistance in finding the washroom...

No. It could not be so. Men, also, had been shifting away from Doctor Purvis to Kurtz: Warren Ellis, Allan Morowitz, David Purchase and... Why could she never remember his name—the one who always looked as if he had just escaped from custody—frantic and breathless? The one whose sessions with Doctor Purvis Bella so often had to interrupt, fearing that violence was being done. Well—whoever he was, he had gone on to Doctor Kurtz just as the others had done—without explanation and without apology.

And now, there was to be this other person sharing the Purvis suite. Doctor Marlow. Bella had been instructed, quite arbitrarily, to share her services—to *do* for Doctor Marlow as she *did* for Doctor Purvis. *Do. Did. Done.* They never ask. They just throw down the workload of a giant and walk away as if they'd paid you a compliment.

Well. It would not be easy. What with Doctor Purvis in such a state and the birds returning and the plague increasing. Everything happens at once. And then it rains.

Marlow was delighted. He would be sharing the services of a secretary with his old friend, Austin Purvis, a colleague with whom he not only had taken classes in Montreal and Toronto, but with whom he also had done a year of special studies at Bristol, in England. Austin Purvis was, in fact, two years older than Marlow—the disparity being accounted for by the fact that Austin had thought he was going to be a neurosurgeon. He had not come over to psychiatry till Marlow was a first-year student. They had been, at that time, inseparable. But, later, Austin had not approved of Charlotte—having sensed, before Marlow, the hidden enmity in her. Austin—not unlike Lilah Kemp—had a troglodyte's ability to penetrate the darkness of other people's caves. Instinct informed him—though he would deny that.

The woman Marlow met in the antechamber separating his own and Austin's offices was hardly credible as a secretary for one psychiatrist, let alone for two. Her name was Bella Orenstein and a quaver in her voice made Marlow wonder if she had just finished weeping or was about to begin. He could not fail to note that although it was some time after ten o'clock in the morning, she had not yet removed her hat. It was a bowl-shaped straw affair with a ribbon round its middle—the bowl turned down so its rim made a shadow in which Bella's eyes could not be seen. Marlow, in time, would discover his initial reading of this woman was as wrong as it could be. She would prove to be a lesson in misguided first impressions. For the time being, however, Mrs Orenstein remained an extraordinary choice for the work she must accomplish.

Marlow could see quite clearly that Austin Purvis had aged dispro-portionately, having leapt ten years ahead of his contemporaries—excessively balding, excessively haggard, excessively tense, excessively tired. There was a certain distraction about him that had not been evident before—and Marlow wondered if Austin had suffered some debilitating disease from which he had not yet recovered.

Their greeting, on the other hand, was cordial and filled with genuine affection. Austin was clearly relieved (that was the word for it) that Marlow had returned. The feeling Marlow got was that Austin had news to impart—or a story to tell that could barely contain itself—though neither news nor story was immediately forthcoming. His distraction was of a kind that Marlow had seen too often over his years of practice. It was the distraction of a man on the verge of breakdown—the distraction of a man who would deny he was distracted the moment he was challenged. *Me? Me? There's nothing wrong. I'm just...*

Distracted.

On the morning Marlow first appeared on the eighteenth floor, an episode occurred that gave him pause, though nothing could be done about it because it happened beyond the closed door of Austin's office.

Marlow was standing beside Bella Orenstein's desk, exchanging pleasantries, when all at once he heard the voice of a woman rising steadily beyond the door.

"Austin, I beg of you," the woman said, "come and look at them! Talk to them!"

Marlow noted that Bella's hands clenched—but she said nothing.

"I'm asking for your help," the voice went on. "It is your duty as a doctor to assist me."

Austin's voice could be heard, but his words were indecipherable.

"Austin, please," the woman said.

Marlow looked at Bella to see if she was prepared to explain—but she did not.

Austin said: "no—not yet..." the first clear indication that he was angry with this woman who, so clearly, was at odds with him.

"Why?" the woman said.

"BECAUSE I AM UNABLE!" Austin shouted.

There was a pause.

The door opened.

Marlow stepped back to clear the passage to the outer doorway.

The woman who came forth was obviously in distress, though equally capable of control. While her hands shook, her voice did not. The door did not slam—she pulled it closed behind her with an efficient *click*—nothing more.

"Good-morning," she said to Marlow.

Marlow nodded. The woman was beautiful, but should not have been. Her mouth was set in such a way that her jawline was pulled to one side. Her face was long and narrow and there were circles beneath her eyes. Yet the impression of beauty was very strong. The openness of her expression, perhaps. The sense of wholeness in the way she presented herself. She stepped towards Bella's desk.

"I'm sorry, Mrs Orenstein. I'm sure you must wonder what on earth that was all about." The woman smiled—but it was a tight smile—a nervous reaction, automatic. "Tell Austin I apologize. Tell him... Tell him I won't continue to press the matter. He'll understand." She turned to Marlow. "I hope I haven't delayed your appointment with Doctor Purvis," she said. And she made her way to the farther door.

"I'm not a patient," said Marlow. "It's quite all right."

"Thank you," said the woman. "Goodbye."

And she left.

Marlow caught the faintest whiff of her scent—but could not identify it. Hair—and skin—and silk, perhaps. Not perfume.

Bella was watching him.

She smiled.

"That was Doctor Farjeon," she said. "Forgive me. I should have introduced you."

"Not at all," said Marlow. "She works here?"

"No. Well—yes. And no."

Marlow laughed. "Which is it?"

Bella said: "Doctor Farjeon is on the staff here, but for the last—I don't know exactly how long—but for several months now, she has been assigned to the Queen Street Mental Health Centre. She works with children."

"I see," said Marlow. "But I must say, that's odd. There *are* no children at Queen Street. It's not in the hospital's mandate."

"I realize that, Doctor Marlow. But Doctor Farjeon has received—so I believe—some sort of special dispensation. She has a group of children there under unique circumstances but that's all I can tell you."

"Thank you."

Marlow considered for a moment, hovering in the doorway of his own office. Then he said: "Mrs Orenstein—I know this may be privileged information, but... Is Doctor Farjeon a patient?"

"Of Doctor Purvis?"

"Yes."

"No, Doctor Marlow. She's not. That would be improper."

"Of course. I just wondered."

"Is there anything I can do for you, Doctor Marlow?"

Marlow said: "my books and papers will be arriving in an hour or so, Mrs Orenstein. I'll just go in and wait for them."

"Yes, Doctor."

Marlow walked through into his office.

It was larger than he'd expected. There was a lot of shelf space. The desk was more or less standard—a large teakwood table, with a minimum of drawers. The chairs were relatively elegant leather affairs. There was nothing on the floor—he would have to provide his own rugs or carpeting. The windows looked out to the east—whereas Austin's looked out to the north and the campus. Marlow's view was somewhat discouraging. It showed a length of College Street and a range of deadly architecture—most of it stopping short of the Parkin building's height.

"Well," he said to the room. "Here I am."

He set his briefcase on the desk-top and took out a prized possession—always the first thing displayed wherever he worked.

It was an axiom set behind glass, with a dull metal frame. For the moment, since it could not be hung for lack of a picture hook, he set it up on a shelf behind his desk.

"There," he said. "present and accounted for."

The axiom, taken from G.K. Chesterton, ran as follows:

> *The madman is not the man*
> *who has lost his reason. The*
> *madman is the man who has lost*
> *everything except his reason.*

This was where Marlow began the treatment of every patient.

The speaker on his telephone made a clicking noise. Mrs Orenstein said: "excuse me..."

"Yes."

"Doctor Kurtz would like to see you, Doctor Marlow."

"Is he here?"

"No, he would like you to go to his office."

"And where is that?"

"On the twentieth floor, Doctor Marlow."

"Thank you."

The speaker clicked off.

Marlow thought: *that's interesting. Mrs Orenstein said* Kurtz *and* Marlow *in the same sentence and didn't even pause...* Then he thought: *well, it takes all kinds...*

$$8$$

Kurtz himself said nothing regarding their names. He had seemed, when they had first encountered one another in Boston, not to have noticed. But he could not have been unaware of the coincidence.

Although they each had worked at Queen Street, it had been at different times. Marlow had heard Kurtz speak at conferences, but they had not met until a few months ago, at the interview in Boston that led to Marlow's appointment. Kurtz had taken him, after the interview, to the Ritz for lunch and Marlow had thought at the time it was an odd thing to do— given the fact that other candidates were on the list that day, and they were not taken to lunch. He certainly knew of Kurtz's reputation, and clearly, the opposite must be equally true, or this new position would not have been won. Not that the Psychiatrist-in-Chief makes all such decisions alone—but he must approve them, and can veto them.

That morning, up on the twentieth floor of the Parkin, they were cordial in their greetings—shaking hands across the desk. Kurtz rose—but that was the only conciliatory gesture he made. Marlow had already noted that Kurtz had summoned him into his presence, rather than coming down to greet him. A strange man. Aloof. But courteous.

"I thought I might show you around, if you have the time."

That was better.

"It will take a while," Kurtz continued—still seated—still not having offered Marlow a chair, "for you to get to know your colleagues—but that is as it should be. Too many introductions can swamp the memory, don't you find...? Besides which, you're bound to know a good many people here already."

Marlow said: "yes." He was waiting for some statement of welcome, which had not yet been forthcoming. It amused him. He wanted to like this man, but already had begun to think of Kurtz as being unnecessarily cool.

Kurtz said: "you will become acquainted with the range of our researches here at the monthly meetings. There will be one on Tuesday. Each of our research programmes receives an update on these occasions—and those of you who serve here as practitioners..."

Serve?

"...are given an opportunity to ask questions. And to answer them."

"Answer?"

"Yes. We take a great interest, here at the Parkin, in one another's work—in one another's patients—in one another's methods." Kurtz then made an expansive gesture and gave a rare smile. *"No input—no output.* Yes?"

Marlow thought: *oh, dear. Am I to live by catch phrases here?* Then he said: "of course."

Kurtz stood up.

"I'll take you around, then," he said. He looked at his watch. "I don't have much time for this—but one or two vital locations should suffice, to give you an impression."

"Thank you," said Marlow.

Although he did not yet know it, the die had been cast between them and the game was begun. His impression of Kurtz, *in situ,* was of someone who played with heavily loaded dice—but he did not know why that need be, since Kurtz already had the winnings in his hand. Could there be more to win than what he had?

Within weeks, Marlow would know how naïve that question was—and he would laugh at his own innocence. But that was not now. That was later.

When the grand tour was over, Marlow returned to his office to see if his things had arrived. They had not. But Bella Orenstein had laid out some papers on his desk and, having noted that he smoked, had also provided him with an ashtray. She had still not removed her hat—and he began to realize that, perhaps, she never would. An image arose of Bella Orenstein lying hatted in her bed—presumably with Mister Orenstein lying at her side—and he wondered if he, too, was hatted. A bowler, perhaps. Or a hunting cap that glowed in the dark... He did not yet know that Mister Orenstein had long been dead.

Mrs Orenstein explained that the papers on his desk would give him some indication—though it was incomplete—of his case load. The first of his patients would turn up tomorrow. The files provided were those of the first week's appointments. Mrs Orenstein also explained that attached to each file was an explanation of why each patient had been allotted to him. Some had been dissatisfied with their present psychiatrists—others had lost their psychiatrists to *attrition.* She did not explain her use of this word. *Was it retirement?* Marlow wondered. *Death? Had they been fired?* He decided it was best not to ask.

When Bella Orenstein had gone and he was alone, he pushed the papers around and glanced at the files. These latter were not set out in alphabetical order, but in order of arrival, beginning at ten o'clock the next morning. *Findley—Baldwin—Berry—Wylie—Wertz...*

On seeing the name *Berry*, Marlow closed his eyes and invoked his gods. *Would it be her?*

He reached for the file. Yes. *Emma Berry. The Surgeon's Wife* was coming back to him. Coming back to Charlie Marlow, where she had begun her quest for survival six long years before.

The note—in Bella Orenstein's hand—that was attached to the file was brief. *Mrs Berry,* it read, *especially requested to resume her treatment with you. She had been, until six months ago, with Doctor Heather McNaughton, of whom she expressed some frustration. B.O.*

Marlow set the file aside. He would take it home and read it that night. Emma Berry's appointment with him would not take place until three o'clock the following afternoon.

Emma Roper. Emma Berry. Emma Beautiful. Emma Damaged. Emma Desperate... She was all of these—and he dreaded the thought of what might now have become of her. The door had been open, when

Marlow left, for her escape. Something had closed it in his absence. He would search for that information in her file. For now, it was enough to anticipate her presence in his life again. She had moved him in the past—to such an extent that Marlow had been in the gravest danger of falling in love with her. Which, of course, was forbidden. But Harvard had intervened and saved him—though he realized now it had not saved her. He hoped—and yes, he prayed—that she was not beyond the point of no return. *A person can go so far so quickly, if help is not at hand.*

He would see.

Emma Berry had been the mother of a six-year-old child the last time he had seen her. A girl whose name he could not remember. That, too, would be in the file. Emma had wanted the child, but the child—it seemed—did not want her. The schism between them had begun, in Emma's words, *when they cut the cord.*

Marlow could see Emma now, in his mind, her beauty marred by tears, her hair falling forward as she leaned towards her hands. She wept as women had been taught to weep in another time and place—silently, covertly raising her fingers to brush away the tears. The sort of weeping women did in Victorian novels—the weeping of the brave—the weeping of the stalwart. There was always something vaguely theatrical in everything that Emma did. Not that her feelings were unreal—but her performance of them had a calculated edge to it. And why not? She had been an actress, once.

She had seemed like a novice when it came to her own life. She behaved as if every natural feeling she had must be a mistake and needed explaining. Justifying. Someone to tell her how to live. *I'm afraid,* she would say. And then look up and ask him *why?* And then, *I'm sorry.*

She was filled with hate—and despised herself for it. She hated her parents—she hated her husband—she hated his family—she hated her beauty—she hated her fame. She was always in hiding—in behind the perfect image Maynard Berry had made of her with his knives and scalpels and layerings of skin. She hated her life.

But she did not hate her child.

Her child hated her.

What does that mean? she would say to Marlow.

She sees you, Emma, as you are. And she knows you hate yourself, he had said.

Because she was inside me, she knows me from inside out. Is that what you mean?

Perhaps.

He would not have said it that way. But certainly, the child being carried could not have resisted the tensions surrounding its hiding place. The thought, at least, was interesting—if unscientific.

Emma.

Yes. He had loved her.

No other patients had moved him as she had. She was more than merely vulnerable—she was raw. And she had lost all track of how to treat her wounds.

Marlow had always been afraid for her. She was one of those people who step out blindly in front of cars. Who fall down lighted stairwells. Who drown in empty pools. And now, she was coming back into the care of someone who would have to resist her, even as she approached.

Marlow set her file aside and turned to the rest.

The first of his patients was this fellow Findley.

Marlow lighted a cigarette and opened the dossier.

Bella's note simply said: *has threatened to sue Parkin Institute if forced to remain with Doctor Rain. B.O.* No explanation was offered of why Doctor Rain was unacceptable. Or, indeed, if Doctor Rain was male or female, brilliant or stupid, present or absent. Perhaps Doctor Rain, if he invited suits, had become a victim of Bella's *attrition.*

Marlow opened the file.

Ah, yes. *A ranter.*

And a *writer. Novels. Stories. Plays...*

Patient Findley's first name was *Timothy.*

Marlow had never heard of him. He perused a few pages. Something caught his eye that he liked. A transcript. Findley was saying: *you know, Rain, we do the same thing, you and I. We're both trying to figure out what makes the human race tick. And the way we do that—both of us— is by climbing down inside other people's lives to see if they're telling the truth or not. Most of us are lying, Rain. That's what I've discovered...*

Marlow smiled.

...lying and afraid we'll be found out. So afraid, in fact, that most of our days are taken up compounding the lies we told the day before...

Marlow flipped the page.

...don't you think so, Rain?

Rain had not agreed. *No...* he said.

Bella's voice cut in through Rain's response: "your things are here, Doctor Marlow."

The known was knocking at the door and Marlow's world was once again made up of equal parts of what he knew and what he did not know. He had been wary, up until today, of going back into practice after being so long in the lecture hall. But for him, the lecture hall had become a sterile place—so long as he was the speaker there. He was back out, now, in the fertile world—where theory could not protect him from the chaos of other people's lives—and the mayhem of reality.

At the end of Kurtz's tour, they had stood together in the lobby where *The Golden Chamber of the White Dogs* had been newly installed. Kurtz made a deceptively nonchalant gesture. "A recent bequest," he said.

Marlow stared up at the triptych, which he had earlier missed, having parked in the campus lot and entered through the rear door.

The painting looked back at him without a sound. Footsteps echoed through the hallway beyond it, but the golden chamber itself, that should have been filled with noise, was mute.

Marlow stood in its presence, mesmerized. The thing was a hymn to violence. Its rightness—given its location and however vile its message—was what alarmed him most. It could not be refuted—it could not be refused.

Kurtz said: "it tells us who we are, Marlow. Each and every one of us. That is the wonder of it."

Yes. And the horror.

Marlow looked over and saw that Kurtz had closed his eyes.

9

The next day, Robert Ireland had his monthly session with Rupert Kurtz.

Kurtz sat back and watched his client settle into the chair beyond the desk. Kurtz was curious.

"Why are you wearing dark glasses, Robert?"

"I want to," said Robert.

"I see. So—you've gone into hiding again. Is that it?"

"Yes."

"What have you done this time?"

Robert eased his buttocks from side to side and stared at his hands.

"Gloves again, I see," said Kurtz.

"Yes."

"Well..." Kurtz attempted joviality, "...one can't be too careful, can one—what with AIDS and sturnusemia..."

Robert said: "I don't have AIDS or sturnusemia."

"You know I didn't mean that, Robert. Don't be childish. Why are you wearing gloves?"

Robert did not answer.

"Robert..."

Kurtz had lowered his voice into its gentle, parental register.

"What?"

His client was sullen.

"You know we have an agreement."

"Yes." Looking away.

"Well...? What was it, this time?"

"I did it again."

"I see."

"In front of other people."

"Yes. Well. Who? The usual?"

"Yes. But..."

"*Yes—but?*"

Robert was silent. He stared at his knees.

"*Yes—but*, Robert?" Kurtz said.

"I wanted..."

"Yes?"

Kurtz waited. But he knew he must not wait long. The impetus to tell had been set in place and he must get his client to go the distance until the whole of what he had to say had been said.

"Robert?"

"Yes."

"Don't stop. Tell me. Are you saying the whole thing happened again?"

Robert nodded. Speechless.

"You had another vision."

"Yes."

"The same way—during orgasm?"

"Yes."

Robert, now, was clearly frightened. His voice had tightened.

"And in the vision?"

Nothing.

"Robert—*in the vision.*" Now the time had come to force it. "*In the vision*, Robert. *In the vision*, what? Did you do it?"

"YES!"

Robert stood up, having shouted.

"Yes," he whispered.

Kurtz watched and waited. He knew what to do. He knew what not to do. What to say. What not to say.

Robert sat back down, with his hands gloved and fisted—pressing hard against his groin.

"How?" said Kurtz. Gentle.

"With a razor."

"Yours with a razor? Or someone else's?"

"Mine."

"I see."

There was silence then and Kurtz sat patiently awaiting the next step. He knew what it would be—but he could not request it. This had to happen of Robert's free will.

Then it did—just as Kurtz had anticipated.

Robert reached inside his trouser pocket and drew out a slim, black leather sheath.

"I'm sorry," he said—as he always said in this moment. "I won't buy another."

And he handed the slim, black leather sheath to Kurtz.

It contained a straight razor—silver, folded, etched and lethal. Which Kurtz deposited in his desk. As he always did. Until the next time.

Coiled in his chair, Robert Ireland subsided.

"Good," said Kurtz, "you have done very well."

When Robert had departed, Kurtz looked down at the drawer which contained the razors. *Robert himself should be drawered,* Kurtz thought. *And the key turned. And pocketed.*

He stood up. Some birds, too—pigeons—were rising beyond the windows. Perhaps the D-Squads were in the street. Perhaps a spraying was taking place. Kurtz did not go to see. The sprayings always made him uneasy. They were too reminiscent of spraying in another time and place—his dreams, where fire was sprayed on the bed where he slept.

He walked to the farthest end of the room and looked down over the campus. There was Robert Ireland—walking. Even toy-size, Robert was identifiable. The gait—the pocketed hands—the way the head was held. What was he doing there now, passing up and crossing the grass in front of Convocation Hall? Mingling with the students—none of whom he greeted—none of whom greeted him. Off to give a lecture, perhaps: *Burke's Reflections on the Revolution in France* or *Frederick the Great and the Hanoverian Alliance.* Kurtz could not avoid the image of Robert Ireland standing at the lectern, arguing against the French Revolution with a razor in his pocket.

Kurtz had other clients who, like Robert, should be prevented and pulled in from their perverse activities. Brought, so to speak, to psychic heel. But he was waging the war of necessities—and in order to survive, he needed those activities to continue. It was part of his scheme—his plan. He wanted to see what could be accomplished by giving what he called *permissions. Let a psychosis have its way with a client*—and see what the client would do in return for permissions having been given...

As with Gordon Perry. As with Robert Ireland and the Club of Men. There had been no returns, as yet, from the Club of Men—but they would come in time. Kurtz was acting there as his own monitor—a voyeur watching other voyeurs—a voyeur of voyeurism—not a voyeur of masturbating boys and girls. It was the membership itself that Kurtz observed. There would be no dividend from some of them. But—others... He counted them over in his mind—and their monies—and their inclinations, both as watchers and as philanthropists. More than one of them had reason to be grateful to the Parkin Institute.

And then, there was the question of the children themselves—all of whom had malleable parents, credulous parents, persuadable parents. People did not want to know so many things—and what a person refused to know could surely be as useful as what a person did want to know. In terms of raising money.

That boy who had recognized him—the one who had tried to emasculate himself at Queen Street—he had still not spoken to Doctor Shelley about that boy. Perhaps he should have consulted her before his own little field test of her results. But her results had looked so promising. And the drug combination so simple. But something had gone wrong that need not have gone wrong. Kurtz could not blame Shelley. She was not aware of her own involvement—she had merely provided a convenient means of coercion.

Then there was Doctor Farjeon. It was clear she was going to be a problem. Till now, he had avoided her as stringently as she avoided him. He might have to begin some enquiries. It depended on what she knew.

Shelley, on the other hand, was a natural ally—and he needed her. More than that, he wanted her allegiance. She was a brilliant technician in the field of biochemical psychiatry. She was also a splendid manipulator. She had the requisite spirit for the programme Kurtz had in mind—but he was not entirely satisfied she had the will for it. *One must want so carefully,* he thought. *One must want so precisely what one wants to achieve. Have. Advocate.*

Kurtz looked out at the slated roofs below him. *Academe.* The whole world of knowledge, down there struggling for articulation. Struggling to clarify what is and give it all a name. Naming. Defining. Quantifying. Quantumizing. Everyone preparing for the past to repeat itself—as if the past was a continuum and that now did not exist. He thought of all the pens and pencils poised above the pages spread across the desks and tables down below him. *Academe,* with its inky fingers and its chalky hands—hovering over the pages—waiting to be the first to bring a sentence to its close—*I will put a period here... No—here... No—here...*

And when the past has been defined, Kurtz was thinking, *not one of them will have the courage to say:* it is over.

He turned back into the room.

Where was his envelope, with all his fine thoughts in order? And all his findings enumerated.

He went to the door and opened it.

"Kilbride," he said, "you remember my saying I had lost an envelope..."

"Yes, Doctor Kurtz. But that was some time ago."

"Do look for it again. I very badly want it."

"Yes, Doctor."

"It was my father's stationery—a legal-sized envelope with the single name *Kurtz* on the flap. In black."

Kilbride had been typing, but she rose at once and went to the filing cabinet. She had already done this before in the initial search for the missing envelope. But, if Doctor Kurtz wanted her to go through it all again... then go through it all again she must.

She began with the letter A. It would take her two hours—till lunchtime—to search every file and fail, yet again, to yield an answer.

The thing is gone, she said to herself. *Why can't he let it go?*

10

There had been no two o'clock patient. Marlow was grateful. He was so nervous about Emma Berry's arrival he would not have done justice to another patient's problems. His nervousness was not entirely apprehensive. Part of it had to do with the anticipation of seeing a woman of whom he had such fond memories. He had puttered about rearranging books and hanging his diplomas—which was required—and trying to decide where Emma should sit. Which light would be most flattering—most comforting to her? How should he greet her? *Hallo, Emma!* Or, *how do you do, Mrs Berry?* Pocketed hands or open arms?

One thing was certain. The room needed something living in it besides himself—a vase of flowers—a potted plant. He opened his door in order to consult Bella Orenstein, but she was not at her desk.

Marlow had just turned away when Bella stepped out of Austin's office.

"Oh, Mrs Orenstein," said Marlow. "I was wondering…"

"Coffee?"

"No, no. I… this is embarrassing—but I'll be frank. My next appointment is with someone I rather look forward to seeing…"

"Mrs Berry. Yes. She was eager to see you, too." Bella went to her desk and deposited some files.

"I noticed yesterday, through the open door, that Austin has one or two African violets…"

"Yes. They're mine, Doctor Marlow. I grow them on his window-sill."

"Do you think I might borrow a couple. Just for this afternoon."

"Of course you may. Which colour would you like?"

"Purple. The dark ones."

"Yes. I thought so."

Bella went over to Austin's door and knocked.

No sooner had she gone inside than Marlow heard the sound of approaching steps in the corridor.

Emma.

He fled to his office and closed the door.

A bare two minutes later, Bella Orenstein was standing there, holding the door open to let Emma Berry through. Then she said: "oh, Doctor Marlow. The florist has delivered these…" and, walking through, she placed two pots of African violets on the edge of his desk.

"Thank you, Mrs Orenstein."

"Not at all," said Bella—and took her leave.

Emma had not moved an inch. She was standing as if waiting to be given permission to enter farther into the room. She was still alarmingly beautiful—though somewhat wild-eyed, which made Marlow wonder for the briefest moment if she had been drinking or was drugged. The *wildness* was a lack of focus—a seeming inability to bring her gaze to rest on him.

"Hello, Charlie," she said.

"Emma." He nodded. He felt as if he must cross the room and escort her to her chair. He did not, however, move. Instead, she took a step towards him and stopped.

"It seems like yesterday," she said. "Same man—same woman. Different room."

"Yes."

"It's good to see you, Charlie."

"Thank you. And the same…" He waved his hand to one side.

Emma turned away. Then back again—as if she had not decided whether she would stay.

Watching her, Marlow had the immediate impression of someone trying to break free from some impediment. Her black sable coat was flung open wide as if it gave her claustrophobia. She moved—just as he remembered—at a dancer's pace, with her toes pointing out and the shape of her legs revealed by clinging layers of white silk. Her stockings were white. Her shoes were white. She wore white gloves. She came, at last, towards him. "I have just been to church," she said, as she put out her hand. "Forgive me if I'm late."

"No problem." Marlow smiled. The claim that she had come from church was so patently a lie, he did not even bother to comment.

Except for the outfit, she looked very much like the photograph Marlow had seen in *Toronto Life*, where Emma had been displayed—full page—in black and white above a caption that read *The Elusive Surgeon's Wife*. Maynard himself had written to the magazine demanding an apology because the caption had made it seem that he was the elusive one. He did not deny his wife was seldom seen in public—but he wanted it known that he was not in retirement. He got his apology, but the photograph had done its work. Emma had been seen. The woman it revealed, with her wide-set eyes, had a hurt expression, as if the flash of John Dai Bowen's camera had slapped her across the mouth.

Marlow offered her a chair and set the African violets where she would see them when she looked at him.

She said she was coming back to him because she still could not sleep. Six years ago, the cause of her insomnia had been her fear of sudden death.

Is this because of your accident? Marlow had asked. *A kind of nightmare?*

No, she had said. *It is more like suffocating. Being suffocated.*

How?

By someone in the dark.

Someone you know? Or a stranger.

Strangers. Not one—but many.

Marlow had known that before her marriage Emma had been an actress, and before that, a prairie girl—from a town somewhere in Saskatchewan. She had told him about the town and about its churches. Or what she called its churches—its library and its movie theatre. She lived through books and films and television. She lived entirely through other people's lives.

Between my bouts with Madame Bovary and movie stars, I had no life at all, she had told him. So I began to make it up. From the very first moment I was conscious, I wanted to be anyone but who I was. I called myself Emma. Not my real name... I started wearing lipstick when I was ten. By the time I was twelve, I was already hiding my suitcase, packed, beneath my bed.

So you went away and became an actress?

Yes. An actress. And a good one. She had smiled, then—and added: *the trouble with being an actress is that you only get to borrow those lives. I want a life I can keep. But not my own. I hate my own.*

The room, then, had filled up with silence.

Now, Marlow looked at her closely, and saw the tension in her face. He said: "you said you had just come from church, Mrs Berry. Was that the library—or a Cineplex?" He was smiling now, hoping to divert her from the evident depression she was in.

"No," she said. "I mean I have really come from church."

"I see." He knew she was lying—but could not guess why.

She looked away. Her hair fell forward and then she pulled it back away from her forehead. "I go there from time to time to seek forgiveness," she said.

Marlow said nothing. *Perhaps she goes there in her mind*, he was thinking. He waited.

"I also go there to pray," she said. "For survival." This seemed to cause her some embarrassment—the saying of it. She still did not look at him. "Not that I deserve it, Charlie."

Marlow watched her—noting various details which he would later put on paper.

"What makes you think you don't deserve to survive?"

"What I've done. What I'm doing. There's hardly anything left alive in me, Charlie." She looked out the window. Marlow's view of her was framed by Bella's violets. "Every moral authority in the world will tell you it isn't right to kill yourself. But it's what I'm doing."

"You look alive to me," said Marlow.

"Yes. I'm sure I do. I look alive to me, too. But..." She shrugged and crossed her legs—the same as ever—the slim calves rising to elegant knees. Suddenly, she smiled at him. "And you're alive."

"Yes."

"That's another reason I want to come back to you. You're like a blood transfusion. I'm not afraid, in here with you. Am I a vampire, Charlie? Is that what it means?"

Emma looked away again. She sobered. Marlow watched her and did not speak.

"Life sucks," she said. "I always used to think that had a sexual connotation. Now, I don't think so. I think it means exactly what it says. Life is a vampire. Yes?"

"I wouldn't have said so," said Marlow. "But it makes an interesting picture."

There was a pause. Marlow realized she was trying to formulate whatever she would say next. It was not, apparently, easy.

Then she said: "I don't want to die, Charlie. Don't let me die."

"I'll do my damnedest," he said.

The light was altering beyond the windows. Nothing could be heard from the street. The room itself appeared to be holding its breath.

Finally, Marlow said: "tell me about your husband. And your daughter."

They talked then, for half an hour, about generalities—the fact that Maynard had been raised to the pantheon of North American plastic surgeons. The fact that Barbara, now twelve, was still not reconciled to Emma. The fact that Emma was still not reconciled to her husband's family—or the memory of her own.

Finally, Emma rose and began to draw on her gloves. Marlow had forgotten how small she was until he stood beside her again and realized he was looking down at her.

All at once, her purse fell to the floor. Marlow retrieved it for her.

She thanked him and put out her hand.

Marlow turned away, hoping she had not seen his expression. Looking at her skirts in the moment he had reached for the fallen purse, he had noticed for the first time the small bright flecks of red that might have been design, but which he now recognized as blood.

"Are you on your way home?" he asked.

"Perhaps," she replied. "I don't know."

"I suggest you consider it," he said. And she was gone.

Marlow closed his eyes, fighting off the impulse to follow her—to re-enter her life, altogether. Her fear of sudden death, that had once seemed so uncalled for, now seemed logical and necessary. Real.

11

The whole of Marlow's house had once been other than it was—a Victorian family house where children had cavorted on the staircase, spawned by a doctor with three successive wives, all of whom had died the deaths of heroines lifted from melodrama—tragic deaths at unseemly ages, caught in the throes of happiness, torn one by one from their mutual husband's arms by appendicitis, plague and childbirth. Someone's sighs could still be heard as Lilah bent her tracks from room to room.

I hear you, she would mutter as she caught these phantom sounds that rode on the draughts from open doors. *Good-morning,* she would say. *Good-evening* and *Good-night.*

Lilah, at first, had thought she was in the presence of all three wives—but it soon became clear that only one of them remained. The other two, for whatever reason, had abandoned the house—as the husband had done. *A spirit only remains to solve its problems,* Lilah knew. To solve its problems—or to come when bidden by the living. Of all the husband's children—more than a dozen—only one small boy remained with his mother. This boy had died on the kitchen table—killed by a surgeon who had tried and failed to cut away a tumour from his brain.

Lilah gleaned this story as she moved through Marlow's house in her effort to sort out the chaos of his belongings. Marlow had invited her to help him unpack the cases of books and the cartons filled with paintings and photographs and prints. He had thought this would be a good way to get to know her—and to let her discover a little more about him. Lilah had been more than willing—though she could not say why, in his presence. This, after all, was Charlie Marlow who had come to save them all from Kurtz—and she had to guard against revealing her ambitions for him too soon in case she bungled the telling of it and irritated him.

Besides the dog, Grendel, there was now a cat. Lilah, however, saw more of the cat than Marlow did—and was fearful he might have it banished. She set up a box for it in her own bathroom and encouraged it to spend as much time as possible in her part of the house by putting down endless bowls of milk on her kitchen floor. Marlow was not helpful in this exercise. He tended to leave the door open between the two kitchens—and it stood that way increasingly, night and day.

The cat took more advantage of this than Lilah did and was soon free-ranging in every part of the house. When Lilah apologized, Marlow claimed he hardly ever saw the creature and said it must be invisible. This way, it was settled that the cat was there to stay.

Marlow got to see the feline intruder on an average of once every two or three days, when a tail or a pair of ears that were unmistakably those of a cat were glimpsed for an instant over the edge of the stairs or poised in the depths of a chair as Marlow passed along the hallways to and fro. Food was put down and vanished in the night while Grendel slept at the foot of Marlow's bed. The box of litter in Lilah's bathroom was certainly used.

Lilah's name for the cat was Fam—for *familiar,* as in witchcraft. Fam was grey. She would come and sit on Lilah's window as the sun went down and she would stare past the flowers in their pots and seem entirely content to be there half an hour, no more. The view and the evening, for whatever reason, were meaningful ingredients of her past—some other house and time, perhaps, when she had been content. When the sun was gone below the rooftops, Fam hopped down and returned to her invisible mode.

One day, while Lilah was hanging pictures beside the staircase—in places prescribed by Marlow and marked with pencilled *X*'s—Marlow returned to the house in the early afternoon.

"Are you all right?" Lilah asked.

"Yes," he told her—but it was clearly a lie—an excuse not to talk about whatever it was that was troubling him.

In Lilah's mind, there could only be one problem confronting Marlow. This seeming depression in which he had returned must have to do with Kurtz. She decided it was time to make her first move.

While Marlow cooked and served himself some scrambled eggs and toast—which he took with a bottle of wine—Lilah brought her handbag and sat across from him at his kitchen table.

"What do you think these are?" she said—and handed over a small neat package of folded tissue paper.

Marlow opened the package—looked at the contents and said: "they're slippers." And then: "sort of old-fashioned, too."

"Indeed."

Marlow examined them. "They're awfully small," he said. "Any child wearing these would be barely old enough to walk."

"Who says it was a child?"

"Well, it had to be, didn't it," said Marlow.

"Not necessarily."

"A doll, then."

"Not a doll," said Lilah. "No."

Marlow looked at her. She was gleam-eyed—a sign of something pending.

"Are you on medication?" he asked.

Lilah did not answer. Instead, she said: "animals wear shoes, too. Sometimes."

"I beg your pardon?"

"Animals wear shoes, too," said Lilah. "Some animals. Some times."

Marlow was careful to remain perfectly serious. "Which animals?" he said.

"Rabbits," said Lilah.

"Snowshoe rabbits?"

"Plain rabbits. Cottontails."

"I see."

"You don't believe this, do you."

"Well—I wouldn't mind a little evidence," said Marlow. He had decided to ride it out—and see what happened.

"Give me just two shakes," said Lilah, and went off into her own part of the house.

Marlow could hear her throwing things around in her room. *This should be interesting,* he thought.

After a moment, Lilah returned, triumphant.

She handed a small, square book to Marlow. The light in her eyes was wonderful to behold. She was a child again—and it was Christmas. Marlow wondered what on earth was happening.

"Open to page 25," she said.

The book was *The Tale of Peter Rabbit* by Beatrix Potter. Marlow sighed and did as he was told.

"So?" she said. "What does it say there?"

Marlow read: *"Peter was most dreadfully frightened..."* Like me, he thought.

"No, no. Bottom of the page. Read that."

Marlow read: *"he lost one of his shoes..."* and stopped.

"Go on."

"...among the cabbages..."

"And the other?"

"...and the other amongst the potatoes," he finished.

"See?" said Lilah. "He lost them on page 25—and there they are, right here." She held up the shoes.

What gave Marlow pause at that moment was not the little book in his hand or the impossible presence in this woman's life of a literary character. It was his own inner voice saying: *yes—they do look like rabbit shoes...*

"Where did you get these?" he asked—still holding up the mask of innocence.

"I've had them since I was five years old," said Lilah.

Someone must have given them to her. A toy.

"They're my talisman," she said.

"I see."

Marlow handed them back to her and watched her as she folded them lovingly into the tissue paper. It was only then he noticed that she was trying not to weep.

"You don't believe me, do you," she said—not looking at him.

"Yes," he said. "I do. They're Peter Rabbit's shoes."

Lilah saw through his patronizing tone in an instant.

"You're making a terrible mistake," she said. "I'm trying to tell you something—but you're just as blind as all the rest."

"In what way, blind?" Marlow maintained an even tone.

"We are all in terrible danger," said Lilah. "But no one cares."

"I care. Explain it."

She looked at him.

"No," she said. "You're not ready, yet."

Then she stood up.

"I hope you enjoyed your little laugh," she said—rather grandly.

Oh, dear, Marlow thought. *Hurt pride.* "I wasn't laughing," he said.

All of a sudden, Lilah yelled at him with terrible vehemence. "Some-times people tell the truth!" she shouted. "Sometimes, people aren't lying!"

Then she turned and left the room.

Marlow sat there, sorry and exhausted.

Emma Berry had come back into his life. And Kurtz was his master. Now this. Peter Rabbit's shoes.

The truth.

12

Paula Phalen had been silent now for six weeks. Her shaved head, like the heads of her companions, was not the result of fashion or of fever. It was the result of her own repeated habit of tearing out her hair. When other methods failed to prevent this, Eleanor Farjeon had decreed that Paula's head must be shaved like the others. That made eight.

The eight were now ten. Two more had turned up in the last month. Eleanor Farjeon could see, of course, they were a group—but because of their silence, she could not tell why. Clearly, there were flickers of recognition. When Paula had arrived, for instance, two of the other girls in the ward and one of the boys went over to her at once and traced the features of her face with their fingers. This was their greeting. Nothing was said.

The hair-pulling had started immediately. It had seemed, almost, to be an act of jubilation—as though perhaps Paula was signalling her joy at being with people she knew. The baldness of the other children could not have been the only spark of recognition—but it was the only thing besides their silence that all of them shared. Some were more violent than others. One, before arrival at the ward, had run through a glass door—evidently not by mistake but as a gesture of defiance. Another had tried to kill an attendant with a chair—and nearly succeeded. One boy had tried to pull his penis from his body. That was Daniel. The boy who had run through glass was Todd. Sandra had wielded the chair. The rest were docile. Or so it seemed. It was best, however, not to turn your back. The violence sometimes came from stations of absolute tranquillity.

Eleanor watched through the window, knowing she could not be seen. She was standing in the antechamber of the observation room in the special ward that had been set aside for her brood at Queen Street. This was a Friday. Tomorrow, she would rest. She had never been so tired in the whole of her life. Mostly, the tiredness reflected frustration and the depths of despair she had reached when unable to convince the others that her theory about these children was valid. Kurtz had forbidden her to speak of it. He had called her an undisciplined practitioner of personal theories and had urged her to take a sabbatical. Austin Purvis had turned away from her just as she had begun to think he was her ally. Losing him meant the loss of her only real hope of getting others to pay attention.

Now, there they were. Her charges, sitting in the sunlight, unaware that she was there. She smiled. *My brood.* Some of her colleagues had thought this *offensive terminology. Condescending. Possessive. Trivializing.*

Fuck them.

Eleanor could see her reflection in the glass. She had a mess of dark hair that made a perfect frame for her thin, plain face. She had what one man claimed—a long time ago—were the saddest eyes in the world. And her mouth was crooked. She was enviably underweight—so her women friends said—but she thought of herself as bony and flat-chested. She often folded her arms in self-defence—her shoulders rounding forward and her head tilted sideways. She wore clothes as if born to be a couturier's mannequin. She was never less than elegant, but had no notion of this. It was simply the way she was. Now, however, she was dead inside her clothes. A corpse. Her arms were numb and her neck was sore. She massaged the back of it.

In the observation room, Paula was sitting on the floor on one hip. She was wearing a cotton dress—excessively plain. This was true of all the clothing worn by Eleanor's brood. They could not have belts or bows or ties of any kind. They all wore slippers or went barefooted. The boys wore jump suits with zippered fronts.

Paula was making designs on the floor with her finger. Road-making. Map-making. Over against one wall, on an exercise mat, a boy whose name was Adam was masturbating with another boy whose name was Aaron.

The two A's. Masturbation happened. No one paid attention. If Paula had looked up, the effect would have been the same if she had seen them scratching their armpits or playing with their toes. It had no sexual content. It was just another male activity performed as bleakly as all the rest.

Isabel wore gloves. She chewed her fingers. She would fold her hand and put the whole thing into her mouth, lock it in place with her teeth and suck and chew on it for hours. The gloves were meant to prevent her from pulling off her nails.

Eleanor laid one finger against her lips. It smelled of ink. Her pen leaked. Eleanor's *nicotine stains* were blue. She shifted from one hip to the other.

These children were not really children except in the eyes of the law. The youngest of them was fifteen and the oldest, nineteen. They were all a hundred. She had received the first of them not quite a year before. Then, of course, she had no context into which to fit them. That had not emerged until later—probably with the arrival of a boy called William who seemed to be known to the others in ways that provoked more reaction among them than any previously shown. William's entrance had almost caused speech—and Eleanor's heart had leapt in expectation. Sounds had been made—strangled attempts at words— and crying had been a part of it. Weeping. William was greatly loved.

He was a sweet-faced boy of seventeen. One of those kids whose fate can be read at a glance. A car would kill him—or a gun would go off. He would die of AIDS or of sturnusemia. Someone would steal all his money. His parents would abandon him. All of this was there in his eyes. William would open all the doors in the world with a smile—and some-one would slam them all in his face. Someone—but not everyone. That was the difference. William was like a magnet. Horror would find him in a multitude—William and only William. He had been born for this.

Of course, it was nonsense to think so. Irrational. Crazy. But the facts bore it out. He was disaster prone. Yet his entrance had been a cause for celebration—and relief. The others had behaved as if William had just walked out of a grave. He would sit in the middle of the room, in the first days, and the others would come and pet him like a dog. His smile had broken Eleanor's heart from the moment she saw him. He became the centrepiece of her crusade. Something devastating and shared had been done to these children. Something had touched them all and crippled them. Their vocal cords, like the vocal cords of trouble-some dogs, might well have been cut. Their tongues torn out. They were bereft of language—except of the language of pain and rage. First one and then the other.

They ate with sullen manners—all of them intensely well-behaved. This came, in Eleanor's view, from their lives before this life in which they shared. They stood well; they moved well. They could make a graceful gesture. They could walk as if they knew where they were going. Then—all at once—it would stop: the walking—the gesture—the gracefulness. Like an ill-driven motorcar, the movement would lurch into the wrong gear and they would stumble and fall or knock something over or begin to cough.

They were all alike. They looked alike. In fact, they looked so much alike, there were moments of androgyny when you could not tell which sex was which. More than likely, the shaved heads gave that impression. Bald, they were all one being. Amoebic.

They would gather in a circle and stare at the same place in space. They would sit holding hands. They would stroke one another. They would lie in one another's arms. They were refugees from nightmares. They would sit, sometimes, for forty-eight hours or more without closing their eyes.

Yes. But, whose nightmare was it?

Whose?

Which bastard had done this to them?

Eleanor thought she knew.

And she had tried to tell—and been silenced.

Now, she watched her brood with desperate exhaustion. Friday. Thank you. One more dead week. Tomorrow it would be Saturday. And she would sleep.

Eleanor turned away. She could watch no more.

There comes a moment when even the dark will not hide what is there. She had reached that moment—and could not walk through. She wanted—more than anything—light.

FIVE

...his dream must have seemed so close that he could hardly fail to grasp it. He did not know that it was already behind him—somewhere back in that vast obscurity beyond the city...

F. Scott Fitzgerald
The Great Gatsby

1

There is a large brick house at the end of Beaumont Road, the street in Rosedale where Lilah Kemp had been a child. This house was currently owned by a man who, at first, did not take up residence but lived in a hotel downtown. His name was Gatz, but that was just about all that was known of him. When the vans at last rolled up and left his furniture on the lawn about a year ago, he still remained a mystery. All that was known was the price Gatz had paid for the house and the fact that his first name was James.

All the women living on the street immediately fell in love with him. His fine brown hair, his blue-grey eyes and his rangy frame turned all their heads, and the invitations for drinks and dinner went out before the vans had departed. No wife was visible, though rumour had it a woman had left him recently. A child was mentioned, but never named.

There were servants who—as always—were the source of much incorrect information. They sat on summer chairs in the yard between his house and the house next door. They did this while smoking cigarettes and drinking tea. There was a maid, a cook and a butler. Gardeners came by once a week in a small green Japanese truck and cut the grass and did miraculous things in the flower beds.

The maid was the worst of them for talk. She might have been a novelist. She spoke with such conviction and her flourishes were so ornate that every sentence was believed—and every detail memorized. Gatz was *a South American drug lord—a Kennedy relative—a dealer in arms—a man with show-biz connections*. The woman who had left him was *a movie star*. The child had been *fathered by Michael Jackson— Elvis Presley—Madonna*. If the maid had said that Gatz kept a kangaroo, it would have been believed. She lasted in his service three weeks only, replaced by a girl from Argentina who spoke no English.

Gatz himself was rarely seen. He did not respond to the invitations for drinks and dinner. Hopes were dashed and hearts were broken. The word went round that he was in mourning—*trying to forget a very sad thing that had happened to him long ago.* When asked what this might have been, the informers shrugged and said, *he killed a man once* and then added, *by mistake.*

Around the time James Gatz moved into his house on Beaumont Road, a large white limousine began to appear in the city's streets with a kind of regularity that soon began to draw amused attention. *There it goes again,* people would say, as they watched it passing down Yonge Street at three o'clock in the morning or at four o'clock in the afternoon. When it parked, it seemed to have found a basking site, as a creature of the sea would do, and in time it took on a name of its own, since no one could identify the occupant. It was known as *The Great White Whale—* which people said with a smile—and one day its basking site would lie at Gatz's door. It was inevitable.

Gatz was a figure of such great mystery that his name had taken on a kind of legendary status. Few could tell you what he did—but everyone could tell you who he was. Nobody got it right—but that is how it always is where riddles are concerned. Gatz was no different in this respect from the occupant of the Great White Whale.

Marlow's first encounter with the white Mercedes came late in its career. He was one of those who knew its occupant, even though he had never ridden there. He knew her at first for the simplest of reasons— because she was his patient. But over time, as her visits to him increased, the simplicity of their relationship evaporated. As her symptoms multiplied, Marlow the psychiatrist became, yet again, the victim of the one condition and circumstance forbidden to his profession. In the latter pages of her file, he had written and underscored the words: *against my will, I am still in love with The Surgeon's Wife.*

Those who knew Emma socially knew her as the wife of Maynard Berry. In Marlow's earlier time as her psychiatrist—before the Harvard years—he had gained a vivid picture of the Berry marriage. Maynard had chosen Emma for her restored and augmented beauty; she had chosen him for his money. Their marriage was a paragon of expedience. Its face was pulled as taut and expressionless as the faces of the surgeon's patients.

2

After Marlow had gone down to Harvard, he had lost all track of Emma until his return. Her life had been entirely closed to him. Now, as they spoke during her visits to the Parkin, and from what he heard from others, he was able to piece together a picture of her current life.

Of an evening, over time, Emma sat at her dining-room table alone with her child. The child's name was Barbara. This, as a name, had not been Emma's choice, but Maynard's. Everyone in his family had names like that: Barbara, Carson, Ezra, Annette, Estelle. Perhaps they were named that way because their lives in every other way were devoid of panache. All the women wore their hair pulled back and done in knots that were clipped and pinned and tied with silver ornaments and velvet bows. They dressed from Chanel exclusively. They rarely, if ever, smiled. It seemed—perhaps from some experience in the womb—they believed that smiling was a form of social suicide. Their eyes were uniformly black and they all wore the same magenta shade of lipstick. The men wore navy blue suits and were never seen without them. They lived in rooms apart from their wives and Emma could not imagine how they had got their children. By appointment, perhaps, during visiting hours.

The Berry family specialized in expressionless condemnation. Not a muscle had moved in Estelle Berry's face when she first regarded Emma as a future daughter-in-law. This was after Emma's accident, and after Maynard had performed his surgical miracle on her face. *Short,* Estelle had said to the room at large, and then, to Emma: *and tell me— who are your people?*

Emma had never answered that question, which had not endeared her. Estelle spent the rest of her life turned away.

Emma had endured all this in order only to secure her place in the world to which she aspired—the world where fabulous people flowed from one encounter to the next in sable coats and velvet shoes. That no such world existed did not occur to her. She had got it out of biographies and cut it out of magazines where the lives of actresses and presidents' wives were written about and photographed in living colour. Estelle herself had been one of these: *the Chairman's wife.* Now, of an evening, Emma sat at her dining-room table alone with her daughter.

As they ate, the Surgeon operated. Clocks were always ticking through these hours—clocks and watches—the clicking of knives and forks and spoons—the endless dripping of saline solutions—the cutting of veal or chicken or beef—the layering of grafted skin. Emma too often imagined this juxtaposition—the table where Maynard operated and the table where she ate, afloat side by side in the same pool of light. While his hands were powdered, she dusted salt across her plate.

"Will you go out again tonight?" Barbara asked.

"I don't know," said Emma.

"Will Daddy be home before I sleep?"

"I don't know, sugar."

"He's never home. Not ever," said Barbara. She was dividing her vegetables into camps: the carrots vs. the peas.

"Eat your peas. Stop playing games."

"It's not a game," said Barbara. "It's a war."

The telephone rang.

Emma set down her fork and dried her lips with her napkin. She drank some wine and waited.

The maid, whose name was Orley Hawkins, brought the telephone into the dining-room and set it down beside Emma. "For you, Mrs Berry."

"Thank you," said Emma. "Don't take Barbara's plate until she's finished her vegetables." And then: "hello."

Barbara watched—bent above her carrots—looking sideways along the table.

Her mother's expression altered only slightly. A smile began—but faded. All she ever said on the telephone was *yes* and *no* and *hello* and *goodbye*. She always seemed to know who was calling—and, after every call, she would send the telephone away with Orley and start to fold her napkin. It was always the same. The napkin would be folded up in squares and then unfolded again with the same precision. It would then be set aside and wine would be poured. Emma never failed in this moment to light a cigarette. Clearly, judging from her expression, she was already partway out the door to wherever it was she was going. Barbara could feel herself fading from her mother's gaze—feel herself disappearing, sometimes slowly, other times like a light going out. She would sit there in darkness, waiting for Emma to bring her back into being.

Emma said *yes* and *yes* and *no* and *yes* again before she said *goodbye*. Orley retreated with the telephone. Barbara heard her in the hallway, dialling and telling the driver, Billy Lydon, to bring the limousine.

"So, are you going?" said Barbara.

"Yes," said Emma. The cigarettes were then produced.

Barbara said: "if I promise not to tell Daddy, will you tell me who it is?"

Emma flicked her lighter open, producing a small blue flame. Then she stood up. "Finish your war," she said.

"I'm not hungry."

"Tough. No armistice, no dessert." Emma went along and leaned down to kiss the top of her daughter's head. Barbara leaned forward, out of reach. Emma gave the kiss with the palm of her hand instead.

"Don't pat me," Barbara said. "I'm not a dog."

Emma was already leaving the room.

"Good-night, sugar," she said. Thank God her back was to the child—otherwise Barbara would have seen the look of panic in her eyes. She wanted desperately to run, but she forced herself to walk to the staircase. The knot inside grew tighter. Hotter. The man she was going to meet made terrifying demands on her imagination, and these were the cause of both fear and exhilaration. It was not always so. There were clients whose needs were so dull they could be met with the flick of a wrist and the application of a Kleenex tissue. There were also clients who required certain cruelties she had problems feigning—wanting more often to laugh than to sneer. But the man with whom she was now about to launch the long night's ride was one whose requests had never failed to fill her with provocative anticipation. To begin with, he always required her to dress in white.

Looking back from three steps up, Emma saw beyond the darkness of the hallway the child alone at her table in its pool of light. The clocks were ticking—all of them in unison. The Great White Whale would soon be parked in the driveway, waiting—while further north, where the city began to end, Maynard bent above his patient and said: *this isn't going to hurt.* The usual lie. Told in the usual tone. *I am God,* the voice said—always coming from above—*and I can destroy you, if you don't lie still—without a word—and let me do this to you.*

On the fourth step, Emma turned away and hurried on. It was eight o'clock. By nine, it would have begun. By twelve, it would be over.

3

Barbara Berry thought of herself as an orphan. The only person who ever entirely acknowledged her existence was Orley Hawkins and Barbara had a strong suspicion this acknowledgement was somehow linked to money.

"They pay you to pay attention," she said to Orley one day in the kitchen.

"You think so, do you?"

"Yes."

Barbara was defiant—but already she did not believe it. The moment she had said it, she knew it was not the truth. Orley could not love anyone she had been paid to love. It wasn't in her. Mostly because she had no interest in spreading herself around where there could be no return. She had done that—and it hurt.

"I'll tell you what," said Orley. "You give me one good reason why your mom and dad should pay out good money to have me come in here and pay attention to a stranger."

"I'm not a stranger," said Barbara.

"Who says I'm talking about you?" said Orley. "I'm talking about that other kid who was in here a moment ago making dumb accusations."

Barbara blinked.

"You do remember her, don't you?"

"I guess," said Barbara. And then she said: "I'm sorry, Orley."

"That's okay."

Orley was drinking beer from a can while she broke up beans into a bowl. Barbara tasted the beer and hated it. "Ugh!" she said. "How can you?"

"It's grown-up stuff. Not like that wine you drink."

"What wine?"

"God, girl! You must think I'm blind."

Barbara sank a bit lower in her chair. Orley eyed her from beyond the bowl of beans. "You'll give yourself curvature of the spine," she said. "Sit up."

Barbara straightened.

Orley said: "you can grow up and be a drunkard, if you want to. It's none of my business. I just wish you wouldn't spill wine all over your dresses—'cause it won't come out in the wash."

"Orley?"

"Yes—what?"

"Do you like being black?"

"What the hell kind of question is that? Boy! Something sure got into you today. Miss Impertinence." Orley drank beer and broke beans. "Do you like being white?" she said.

"I don't know. I never thought about it."

"Well—there you are, then."

Barbara went to the fridge and got out a can of Pepsi.

Orley said: "black people think about being black all the time. Not that a person wants to. But a person has to. Otherwise, you die—like Bobby."

Barbara wished she hadn't brought it up. She hated the story of Bobby Hawkins. It made her feel as if she had done something wrong.

"Do I like being black?" Orley said. "The answer is *yes*. Most emphatically. What I don't like is white." She smiled at Barbara. "Sometimes..."

"Bobby's been dead now a long time," said Barbara.

"That's right."

"How long?"

"Almost twelve years."

"Almost me," said Barbara. "As long ago as me."

"You got it."

"Is it true you owned a store and everything?"

"Unh-hunh. We had what you call a franchise. Mac's Milk."

"Was it fun?"

"No. It was hard work. Never much rest. Just the two of us to do it—me and Bobby—and we had a girl come in through the summer. Summer was always busier—kids wanting pop and stuff."

"Did you make a lot of money?"

"Some. It was getting better. But a franchise is no prize."

"That rhymes."

"Unh-hunh. I'm a poet."

Barbara knew that Orley was going to tell about Bobby—and part of her wanted to hear it—and part of her did not. It was the worst of all the stories she had ever heard. Even worse than her father's stories about the accidents people had with fire.

Orley said: "that was the awfulest thing, I guess. The timing. Aside from the event itself—them killing Bobby. We had just begun to turn the corner. We had just begun to make it, you see. Money in the bank—stuff like that."

"Yes."

Orley and Bobby Hawkins had come to Canada long before Barbara was born. They had come up from Washington, D.C. because of the war in Vietnam. Bobby did not believe in that war—and neither did Orley. Bobby said more black Americans were killed in Vietnam than any other kind. He said he would go to Canada alone if Orley did not want to go. They were not even married then. That happened here.

Orley said: "you know what happened was three teenage boys come into the store one night real late..."

"Yes."

"...and they stuck us up and killed that poor girl. Rose Teller."

"Yes."

"And we telephoned the police. It was real, real late. Mac's Milk stores stay open all night."

"I know."

"Summer and it was hot. And there we were with a dead girl. So..."

Orley set her beer can aside and threw the last of the beans in the bowl.

Barbara waited.

Orley never cried when she told about Bobby. Other times, she cried. But never recounting Bobby's death.

"When the police came, I was inside the store and Bobby went out to meet them..." She waited for a moment and folded her hands. "He went out with his arms wide open and Rose Teller's blood on his shirt. He was walking right up to them and he was saying: *so glad you come...* And they shot him."

Bang.

"Because he was black—and he was there."

Barbara did not speak. She could hear the seltzer sizzling in her Pepsi.

Orley took a final swallow of her beer. "Every time I see them spraying to kill all those starlings, I wonder when they'll start in spraying to get rid of us—just because we're black." She put the beer can down. "Sometimes," she said, "I would like to take a gun and go back down there. I would like to stand right there where he was—and shoot somebody myself. Because they're white. I might just do that, some day."

Barbara sat frozen.

Orley had never said that last thing before. It had not been a part of the story. Out loud.

Then Orley said: "I could use another beer, if you felt like walking to the fridge."

Barbara brought the beer and said: "do you really mean you'd kill someone?"

"Sure. Why not?"

"Because they're white?"

"Give me a better reason."

Barbara thought about it. "It isn't right to kill people, Orley. Not for any reason."

"Are you telling me this? Are you telling me? You certainly got a lot of nerve, today. Don't you tell me what to do and what to think."

"You tell me what to do. And what to think."

"Because I'm older. I'm older than you. And I'm in charge here."

"You're not my mother."

"No. But I'm the next best thing—you better believe it."

"At least my mother's a mother."

"What the hell does that mean?"

"You never had children. You don't know anything about it."

Orley looked out the window and tried not to speak.

Then she said: "isn't it time you went and did that homework you brought back from school?"

Barbara stood up and went to the door.

"Don't forget your Pepsi," said Orley.

Barbara came back to the table, picked up her drink and left the room. After she had gone, Orley said *damn* out loud. But the thing in her mind remained unsaid—the story of how she had aborted Bobby's child after Bobby died. The story of how, in her rage, she had decided there would be a different kind of killing than the kind that Bobby Hawkins had suffered. The kind that would deny the world another victim. Now, twelve years after, Orley regretted that decision. She missed the unborn child that, at least, would have been her own. What she did not regret was the rage. The rage was still a source of satisfaction. She had vowed that she would foster it until the day she died—and up until now—including now—she had succeeded.

4
—

Now it was May and the fine spring rains had begun to bring the world alive again. Gatz went out and stood in his garden beneath an umbrella.

It was a Sunday and far away beyond the ravine that broached his garden he could hear some church bells ringing. He wore a pale blue shirt and a cardigan of navy blue wool. His trousers were white and his shoes were white and he looked as if he should have been standing on the deck of a yacht and not beside a swimming pool in a Rosedale garden.

He was lonely. It was awful. Nothing filled up the spaces left by his absent child and her mother. Gatz had tried everything. He had even moved strangers into his house. These were not, in the strictest sense, employees—but on the other hand, they accepted his hospitality as payment for their presence. A few of them shared his bed—the last of these being a girl called Susan Clare. Prior to her there were two other girls and a boy. Gatz felt no affection for them. All he wanted was their touch and the weight of someone else by his side. The boy had rather a pretty face and long, red hands. He played the piano, but could not play anything Gatz enjoyed. It was the same in bed. The boy apparently expected to be courted. He lay back waiting for Gatz to make the first move. Gatz did nothing the boy expected of him. It was a disaster. And after he had moved out, Gatz heard he had fallen ill with sturnusemia and died.

The time with Susan Clare had been no better. She read a lot of books and gave a fair impression of maturity. She was studying Eastern religions and did elaborate exercises lying on her back beneath a sunlamp in the Florida room. In the long run, however, Gatz despaired of her. He had no talent for patience and she kept insisting that he wear a condom. When he refused, she sat on the bed cross-legged and began to lecture him. He hit her, then, and she had to be sent in a taxi to the

Wellesley Hospital, where she told the doctor who stitched her lip that, in the dark, she had fallen downstairs. No one who knew him ever told the truth about James Gatz.

Now, in his Toronto garden, he experienced a vivid memory of his Texas childhood. His Pa had beaten him—almost killing him—when Gatz was nine. The usual combination of alcohol and fury had brought it on—his father driving him backwards through the rusty screen door because Gatz had failed to complete some chore or other. His Pa had needed very little excuse to launch into one of his rages. Ever since Gatz's mother had left them, the boy had been beaten with words and with fists once a week or more. She had gone down the road with her suitcase and Gatz, in his mind, could still see her standing beside the highway as the dust blew up around her and took her away. She had ridden off on a Greyhound to Houston—and always ever after Gatz had thought of that bus as the whirlwind he had been told about from the pulpit.

He was then the only target, besides the horses, of his Pa's violence. In time, the man had crawled beneath the sheet with his boy and had wept and wept and wept, while the calloused palm of his hand had ridden flat up and down the boy's dry torso until the boy had realized too late that his Pa meant to take him the way he had seen his mother taken. And so it was that Gatz, aged ten, went down the road with his own valise to follow his mother into the whirlwind, but he never found her.

What he found instead was the hidden commerce in his own situation. A ten-year-old boy with sundried hair and eyes the colour of grey-blue flowers can make a fortune from his story—so long as the story has all the right ingredients. Gatz then discovered the value of public relations, by which in time he would come to his fortune. It is not what you are that matters, but what you appear to be. The word *face* entered his vocabulary.

Choosing the doorsteps of various agencies—avoiding the police and opting for churches and charities—he claimed that his parents had abandoned him. He trusted his father would not dare follow him yet and he guessed that his mother's disappearance was permanent. Where, after all, could the whirlwind take her but into some bleak motel with strangers, once it arrived in Houston. That was the end of her. Gatz had never seen his mother again. As for his father—some chance encounter might still produce him. A man who beats you from his door can always beat his way to yours.

This was the only time young Jimmy Gatz gave up the integrity of his person for advancement. The boy who had fended off his father now turned willingly to others. He used the physical glamour of his youth to catch the attentions of the rich who patronized the hotels and clubs where he worked as bellhop, parking valet and barman. He even had cards that read: *J. Gatz—Available*—a message so demanding of inquiry that it rarely failed to produce results. He already knew the word *available* is the most provocative word in the language.

The card was handed out sparingly. Gatz was not about to squander himself. He wanted a great deal more than money—he wanted advancement. He gave the card to both men and women. Whatever was required of him, he performed with ingenuity, tact and efficiency. But he used every opportunity to project a sense of vulnerability. This, for the most part, brought him into the company of clients who were susceptible to charm. It also protected him from violence and opened those doors that lie beyond sexual gratification, where mentors introduce their protégés to education and business opportunities. By the time Gatz was twenty-one, he had a bursary that took him east to Maryland—and by the time he was twenty-eight, he had married Marianne Prager of Baltimore and had come so far from his ride in the whirlwind that if his Ma had seen him, she would not have known who he was.

The city beyond the ravines made Sunday noises while the grass turned green beneath the rain in Gatz's garden. A robin came and ran quick-footed through a bed of bulbs that had begun to sprout. It stopped then in the way that robins do—head cocked and beady eye searching for movement. Gatz, beneath his umbrella, watched. Since the D-Squads had begun spraying, robins weren't so numerous. The fingers of his free hand folded compulsively in against his palm. He wanted someone else's hand to hold. *Marianne—Anne Marie.* His hand was now a fist. *Come home...*

It rained some more. The bells stopped ringing. Gatz turned around and—lowering his umbrella—went back inside his empty house. The robin stabbed the earth with its beak and ate. Gatz, for his part, had made a decision. He would give a party—and the whole world would come.

5

Emma had been intrigued with the house on Beaumont Road ever since she had first encountered it on one of her early runs to collect its neighbour, a man called Royhden.

"Who is it lives in there?" Emma said, as he climbed in beside her one night.

"Gatz," Royhden told her—and he shut the door with a bang. "You don't want to know him."

Eric Royhden, like others, often used the excuse that he was *going for a very long walk* when he left his front door to meet her. Comfortably incognito in the back of the Great White Whale, Emma did not worry about discovery; it was the problem only of her clients. She was often amused by their tactics. One man always came to her in running shorts. Another always brought his dog. Royhden, being unmarried, only had his servants' sensibilities to contend with. Still, he was nervous of their opinion and never went for his *walks* until he knew they were far away at the back of the house, watching one of the television sets he had provided for their entertainment.

"Why don't I want to know Gatz?" Emma asked.

"Because," said Royhden, "he is notorious."

"Notorious for what?"

"He's a raving alcoholic, to begin with."

Emma laughed. "Nonsense!" she said. "Men are always saying that about their rivals." Then she added: "someone said the very same thing about you the other day."

Royhden was not amused.

Later, after Emma had seen Gatz standing on his lawn, she had pressed for more information. Royhden had nothing further to say—but when Emma brought the subject up with her husband, Maynard said: "I've been told he's in what is known as damage control."

"You mean he's a surgeon, like you?"

Maynard laughed. "Hardly," he said. "It's damage control of another kind entirely. People hire him to protect them from the press."

"I don't understand."

"Business people—law firms—developers. They don't want people prying."

"Have you met him?"

"No."

"You're lying."

"I never lie to you, Emma. You lie to me—remember?"

She stared at Maynard—knowing she could not defend herself. His smile, on the other hand, had something of forgiveness in it.

Still, she could not forget Gatz. He hung around in the back of her mind and once in a while, she conjured him deliberately. A man with sad eyes who stood on his lawn in the twilight must be, somehow, her twin. This way, Gatz took up residence in Emma's dreams, and his figure, larger than life, became the measure against which other men had to match their importance. Like all the men in women's dreams, Gatz held out a helpless hand and gave the appearance of having landed on the earth only in order to find her. Emma knew, of course, there was no such man alive—nor ever had been. She knew very well—too well—that every man is a trickster, hiding either impotence behind a blue-veined hand or dominance behind a little boy's smile. Still, there was something in Gatz's stance as he stood on his lawn that was truly forlorn. The angle of his shoulders had the ring of truth to it—sloping forward, hunched against the onslaught of some loneliness that seemed so absolute that he was like a man made ill by it. If that was the case, it was an illness Emma understood, having suffered from it so long herself. The illness of absence—not the absence of the world at large, but the absence of some specific other—the other half of self—the missing half of who you are.

So it was that Emma had Gatz close at hand in her mind for some time before she first encountered him in the flesh.

As happened at all the houses of Toronto society's upper echelon, an invitation arrived one day which called for the Berrys' attendance at Gatz's splendid residence on the evening of May 14th. *Wine and dancing and a midnight collation* were announced.

Orley said: "sounds like the Old South to me," when she heard about the midnight collation. "Not my style," she told Barbara.

"I wish I could go. It sounds so romantic," said Barbara.

"Romantic is as romantic does," said Orley. "If I was you, I'd stop reading all them Victorian novels and get real."

On the night of the event, Barbara watched from the dining-room table as her parents came down the stairs to depart. It was rare enough to see them together under any circumstance—but to see them dressed together, each of them so beautiful, both of them so perfectly matched, was an even greater rarity.

Emma wore red and a white silk rose. Maynard was in evening dress—black tie and patent leather shoes. Emma had forgone her usual defence against the onslaught of eyes that could be expected on such occasions. She went unveiled and her evening bag was far too small to hide behind if photographers were to be present.

"Looks like there's someone she wants to take notice," said Orley.

When they were gone, Barbara said: "there's a girl at school who swears Mister Gatz seduced her older sister."

"Take note of the fact," said Orley, "that somehow there is never a girl at school who swears she has been seduced herself by the likes of Mister Gatz. Thank God I was never anyone's older sister. Fastest route in creation to being called a tramp."

Though she failed to say so, Barbara suspected that Orley could be right. She could think of at least two other girls at school who claimed their older sisters had been seduced by famous men. One by a rock star. And the other by a baseball hero. Then there was the Holtz girl—Isabel. Isabel had been absent from school since just after the new year. Rumour had it she was in the insane asylum on Queen Street. Her sister Ruth would not talk about it much, but she did say Isabel had been seeing an older man and had tried to *run away from home to go and live with him!* Or something. This seemed extremely romantic, somehow— *to be locked up in the loony bin because you had gone mad for love.*

Barbara herself could have told a tale or two. Not about her older sister, since she had none. But about her mother. Tales that happened to be true. Which is why Barbara never told them. It occurred to her that others might have untold tales of escapades that were true. People rarely talk about what really happens to their sisters—mothers—fathers. And they never talk about what really happens to themselves. By some unnamed agreement—to which Barbara herself adhered—it wasn't done.

A marquee had been raised in the back yard and a dance floor had been laid above the pool. In the Florida room, there was a real palm tree and the staircase had been decorated with garlands of bougainvillaea and hibiscus. Emma expected that the next thing she might see would be a flight of cockatoos landing on the chandeliers—or flamingos standing in the hall. Maynard, however, was not impressed. He said that people who had honest money did not have palm trees in their Florida rooms. Emma asked: *what do they have?* Maynard said: *the Atlantic Ocean.*

Waiters wearing pale green jackets and bearing silver trays of champagne, white wine and rosé made their way through the horde of guests. Red wine was offered on brass trays carried by others who were dressed in shades of plum and burgundy. The band played out on the terrace— beyond the pool—with the music dominated by a saxophone.

Everyone seemed to know everyone else—though this was not entirely true. Very few, except those who had employed him, knew Gatz himself and there were also many who only knew one another by reputation or *by defamation*, as someone said. There were divisions in this society which everyone recognized but which no one admitted to—divisions that had to do with where one lived and how one had got one's money. This was the same as any other society, but here it was marked by the vehemence with which one refused to mingle. A curt *hello*—the touching of fingers only, never a handshake. Gatz's invitation had consequently been declined by certain important figures—not because of Gatz, but because of his guest list. Fabiana Holbach, for instance, did not attend. Nor Kurtz. Nor Benedict and Peggy Webster. Nor Benedict's brother, John. Nor Gordon Perry. Nor Warren Ellis. Others, too, had sent their regrets. Eric Royhden, his neighbour, would not be caught dead in Gatz's house. It stood to reason—Gatz having done some damage to a Royhden business partner.

Freda Manley, on the other hand, had been delighted to accept. Gatz had been her champion in preventing the publication of a book about the Beaumorris Corporation that would have done some harm had it been published. Freda was already moving on to a new conquest—a young man from Uruguay, who was her escort that night.

Olivia and Griffin Price were there. And John Dai Bowen. And all the charity bimbos John Dai despised and all the glamour queens he worshipped—plus the O'Flahertys, who were richer in real estate than anyone could tell. Rumours of bankruptcy plagued the O'Flahertys—or had, until Gatz stepped in with rumours of a libel suit in the O'Flahertys' behalf.

Patti O'Flaherty, whom John Dai had photographed on more than one occasion at her husband's request, was perhaps the most flamboyant guest at the party. She had a way of bursting into every scene as if it had been created in her behalf. It would be fair to assume that Patti had once appeared on the stage—since every word she uttered and every gesture she made was larger than life and twice as loud. This night—she went out on the dance floor above the pool and insisted on dancing the Charleston all by herself. She was not an insignificant figure. Patti was tall and rather thin and given to wearing lacquered wigs of blue-black hair. The Charleston had been chosen as her vehicle presumably because she had worn a dress of beads and fringes—a dress that shimmered as she danced and showed off the slimness of her hips and the bounce in her bodice. When her performance ended, many applauded—and many more, including Emma and Maynard Berry, retreated into the house, determined not to see the second act.

It was at once a party like any other, and a unique celebration—unique because nobody really knew why they were there—except to discover why others were there. Some had felt it would be dangerous not to attend. Who could know what might take place? Who could really tell what sort of power Gatz wielded and to what extent he wielded it? And over whom—unless one was there to assess the guest list.

Gatz himself was the least apparent presence of the occasion. He was glimpsed, but never cornered. No one would come away from the evening claiming to have had a conversation with him. Pleasantries had been exchanged. Some doors had been closed, which made it seem that Gatz might be cloistered with a preferred guest—but when the doors were opened, it was never Gatz who appeared, but others in combinations that were common knowledge.

No one danced with him. He chose no partner. Many guests departed as they had arrived—never having once encountered their host.

Emma searched for him everywhere, but saw him only once at a great distance. This had been as she stood on the staircase looking down into the grand hall crowded with people passing to and fro between the reception rooms, the Florida room and the terrace. Gatz had been standing for the briefest moment over against the door that led to the library—and he took up a glass from a passing tray and turned with it to toast some woman whom Emma had never seen before.

It so happened that Olivia Price came down the stairs at that moment and Emma touched her on the arm.

"Do you know who that is with Mister Gatz?" she asked.

Olivia said she hadn't the foggiest notion. After which, she turned to Emma and said: "does he interest you?"

"Yes," said Emma. "He does."

Olivia smiled and fingered the pearls at her neck. "Be careful of him, Em," she said. "Rumour has it he killed a man once."

Emma was smiling, too.

"I know," she said. "Do you believe it?"

"I'm not sure," Olivia replied. "He certainly is mysterious. I saw him on television once. It was around the time he prevented that book about the Beaumorris Corporation from being published. You know, the one about Freda Manley."

"Yes."

"Well—it was never explained how Gatz had pulled that off. As a lawyer, he seems almost to have a closed operation. No one knows anything about it. Or about him. And he keeps it that way. On this television item—I guess it was on the news one night—there was an extensive interview with the book's would-be publisher—and with the book's author— but when it came to Gatz, he refused to be interviewed. I mean," said Olivia, "it seems sort of crazy, doesn't it, since he won the case. Anyway, after Gatz walked away from the reporter who was doing the item, the reporter said: *this man has managed to bring all inquiry into the affairs of the Beaumorris Corporation to a halt. He refuses comment. Standard practice for James Gatz.* And that was it. I mean—he didn't say a word. Amazing, isn't it. And he gets away with it all the time, apparently."

Olivia then went on to ask about Maynard and Barbara and how they were. But Emma was not listening. She was looking for Gatz—and Gatz was gone.

In her dream of him that night, he was dancing with someone beneath a marquee on Emma's lawn. The saxophone continued to play as if it had played her all the way home and into her sleep. No one else moved through this dream but Gatz and the unknown dancer. Emma herself was a mere observer. There was, however, one other figure whose presence, Emma would think on waking, must have been prompted by Olivia's remarks on the stairs. A dead man lay on the grass. In the dream, Emma thought she knew him. Awake, she did not.

<u>6</u>

It so happened that Emma Berry was among Marlow's patients the following day and halfway through their session, she said to him: "you ever hear tell of a man called Gatz?"

"The troubleshooter? Yes," he said.

Emma said: "I'm in love with him."

"That's odd," said Marlow—attempting as always, diffidence. "You've never mentioned him before."

"We've never met," said Emma.

"I see. So you love him from afar."

"I guess you could say that. But it doesn't feel that way. I was in his house just last night."

Emma told about the party and Marlow said he had understood that Gatz was reclusive and was never seen at other people's parties. What might have brought on this sudden outburst of sociability?

"I think he was hoping to meet someone. My impression is that he's unbearably unhappy. Lonely."

"*It's lonely at the top*," said Marlow.

"It's lonely at the bottom," said Emma.

Marlow swivelled in his chair. "What makes you think you're in love with him?"

Emma said: "I like lonely people. I have an affinity for them."

"Am I supposed to accept that as an answer?"

"Don't back me into a corner, Charlie," Emma said. "Don't push."

"I'm here to push," said Marlow. "That's my job."

Emma was still. Even her hands did not move.

Marlow said: "you want to take him riding in the back of your limousine?"

Emma looked away.

They had discussed the Great White Whale and, to some degree, what happened there, but Emma had not kept track sufficiently of what she had said to Marlow—nor was she aware of the nature, yet, of the danger she was in from the progress of her condition. Marlow was all too aware of this—of how badly she needed help. She was a woman walking in her sleep, telling her story without the protection of consciousness. There were moments when he was tempted to force her to take some cure—a rest home—a clinic. But she eluded him by insisting that *any moment I will stop and lie down*—that exhaustion would claim her and bring it all to an end.

Once, she had asked him point-blank if he thought she was a nymphomaniac. His answer had been *no. In fact,* he had said, *you are anything but.*

What am I, then?

Manic-depressive. Marlow had not said so. She was riding through a version of it—a psychic storm that could not quite be defined. In many ways, she was a set of variations—in the musical sense—on the theme of panic. Technically, yes—manic-depressive. But he was not prepared to give her condition a name. The depressive side of her rode too often in tandem with the manic side, in a kind of joyless exaltation—a jig being danced in a flood of tears. She was a catalogue of contradictions.

One thing, however, was clear. In Lilah's terms, Marlow might have described Emma as an incomplete conjuring—as if, in being summoned, only half of her had come forth. In his own terms, he had been prompted to think of her as one of a set of multiple personalities—stranded out in the open, abandoned by her corporeal host—an incomplete identity with nowhere to hide, no body into which to retreat. It could be said that, if such a phenomenon existed, Emma Berry was a perfect example of an ethereal being. And yet...

And yet...

She sat there before him—living and real. He could smell her hair. He could hear her breathing. Was she any different, when he came right down to it, than any other woman of substance whose mystery could not be pinned?

Yes. She was.

Physically, she was Maynard Berry's re-creation. But she had not yet found a surgeon who could re-create her spirit. Someone else had to prove she was alive. She could not provide the proof of it herself. *To live and breathe is nothing,* she had told Marlow, once. *To want to live and breathe is everything.*

This could be why she courted danger, Marlow surmised. Why, when there was blood on her skirts or stockings, she was flushed and feverish. Why, when she said *Gatz,* she raised her fingers to her lips, as if to verify the shape of his name.

Marlow tried smiling. "Are you asking me to arrange a meeting with Gatz?"

"Perhaps you could leave me on his doorstep in a basket," said Emma. "Isn't that how it works in novels?"

"Not in good novels, no," said Marlow. "Perhaps in Victorian penny-dreadfuls."

"Written by women who all have three names," said Emma. Then she fell silent—utterly.

Marlow said: "you seem to have given up all your efforts to save your own marriage. I have to tell you that, in my professional opinion, you are in danger of throwing it away—and your daughter—for no better reason than your refusal to come to terms with your recklessness. I cannot help you if you will not help yourself."

"Maybe I don't want help."

Marlow was silent.

"I have rights," said Emma. "To my dreams. I have rights. I have the right to fulfil them."

"Yes." He was tired.

"Then give me permission."

"I can't do that. I'm not your priest—I'm just your doctor."

"Doctors are supposed to help."

"Not by handing their patients a box of matches."

"You forget," she said, "I have already, once, been burned."

Emma stood up. Pulling on her coat, she crossed the floor and looked from the window. "There's a fog coming down," she said. Her voice was hoarse. She turned. "Forgive me," she said. And departed.

Marlow heard the door click shut—and then the silence of her absence. She had left, in the chair, a small white handkerchief. He picked it up and held it to his nose—and put it in his pocket. The handkerchief had not been perfumed. All he could smell was white.

7

Robert Ireland had been aware for some time that Julian Slade had once been Kurtz's patient. He knew it from Slade himself, whom he had first encountered on one of his evening walks. Slade had been cruising in Cluny Park and he and Robert had their eye on the same young man.

This had been before Slade had been stricken with AIDS. He had not yet mounted the exhibit known as *Shreds,* though some of its paintings had already been completed. Slade had been diagnosed as schizophrenic and had refused medication—*in behalf of my demons,* as he said. He was still a young man with a breathtaking figure and the face of a mischievous saint. He carried knives and scissors in his pockets and, when he took his pick-ups home, the first thing he did was cut their clothing from their bodies, which produced the most excruciating tension. He never, however, cut flesh or drew blood. He played at terror all the way through to the end of orgasm—a game which, if obediently played by the boy on his bed, could produce a reward of pristine clothing in which the boy would depart. The cut-up shirts and jeans and underwear went into a box in Slade's studio.

In Cluny Park, Robert had known who Slade was—but Slade had not known him. Their conversation in the evening light had been about danger and Slade had soon recognized in Robert a kindred spirit. *You carry anything?* Slade had asked, with something of a smile. Robert had said yes and produced—very slowly, as if exposing himself to Slade— the silver razor of the moment in its leather sheath.

Slade had been impressed. He had showed Robert two pairs of scissors and a hunting knife. The two men had sat, then, side by side on a dark green picnic table, with their feet on the seat and their fingers touching. But nothing had come of it. They were on the same side of the sexual quotient and each of them needed a pliant other to complete the circle. The boy with the apprehensive smile and the pale hair falling into his eyes—the same young man they had each been pursuing—was the one they each required. In the end, it was Robert who retreated from the chase. He had preferred the fantasy version of what would take place between Slade and the boy to the reality of what might have happened if he had taken the boy, himself.

This way, Slade and Robert met—acknowledged one another—and parted. But when the *Shreds* exhibit opened to a storm of protest and the Pollard Gallery had been closed because of it, Robert Ireland had been the first to approach Tommy Pollard and make a purchase. He displayed it between the shelves of books and English silver along with the rest of his modest collection. Modest in numbers only. Among the paintings hung on Robert's walls there was a Thomas Eakins, an Alex Colville and a Francis Bacon. There was a Cocteau drawing of French sailors, a Bakst design for a Nijinksy costume and a Tchelitchew self-portrait done in ink and coffee grounds. This was the extent of it, barring one or two drawings which he exchanged for others when he tired of them.

Robert was not greatly social—but on occasion, he would invite a few acquaintances to dine with him—never more than three or four at a time. Neither he nor Rudyard—his man, as Robert called him—was proficient enough in the kitchen to provide a suitable meal for guests and, consequently, all such affairs were catered. Robert knew of three or four private catering services whose dinners were exquisite and whose people were discreet. He never catered from restaurants or other well-known professional services, fearing that his habits and his proclivities—to say nothing of his precious possessions—would become known in too wide a circle and thus become the subjects of gossip and speculation. Robert lived behind a high stone wall in a thickly stoned house for a reason. He wanted no one in his life who had not been invited into it. He wanted no strangers but the strangers who peopled his sex life, which he lived, for the most part, incognito—in the privacy of hotel rooms and the Club of Men.

On the first night of the mid-May fog, Robert gave a dinner party for Kurtz to which he invited Fabiana Holbach and John Dai Bowen. It had crossed his mind to invite another female guest, but the only woman of interest to him—Emma Berry—was unavailable. Kurtz arrived first and was early. Robert, not being ready to come down, had instructed Rudyard to show Kurtz into the library and to provide whatever drink was required.

Kurtz went in and stood before the paintings with a Scotch in his hand. The room was not overly large, but it reflected Robert's tastes in every way. Clearly, it begged the question of appropriate dress. A man must wear a tie in such a room. His shoes must gleam. A jacket must be worn. In the fireplace, a large piece of cannel coal was being consumed by blue flames. Beyond the leaded windows, the fog took on an English hue. Kurtz smiled. Robert had a way with atmosphere—right down to the weather.

Kurtz turned to the Slade canvas.

Unlike the *Golden Chambers* series, in which Slade had given a title to each painting, the series called *Shreds* had been numbered. One through thirteen. *Number Thirteen* had been the self-portrait. Robert Ireland had bought *Number Eight*.

Kurtz stood back and looked at it sceptically. If Robert had wanted it, what did that say about the painting? That it was nothing less than sadistic erotica? Surely, Robert had understood he was buying more than that. And had wanted more than that. The painting was wonderfully accomplished. As always, with Slade, the draughtsmanship and the sense of texture were masterful. As always, the surface was brilliant. And—as always—the subject matter was terror.

Elements of Francis Bacon, whose work was hung on the opposite wall, were in evidence here. The melting eyes—the open mouth neither screaming nor laughing, but a human bellows for the last breath. The bleeding, helpless arms, hanging down as if death had already occurred, and the thrusting neck of the victim—pushing the head with such force that it gave the appearance of springing forward from the canvas. And—just beneath the frame—the blood-pan, resting on an eighteenth-century gaming table.

Kurtz stepped forward to examine the pan and found it was only half-full of something red that looked suspiciously like wine. The blood-lines were stained with it where they poked through the canvas—and the tracings of past bleedings had the same wine patina. He wondered how to set the thing in motion—but could find no evident device with which to do this.

He moved away again and drank from his glass. The single piece of ice that floated in the Scotch made a bell-like noise against the crystal. Kurtz savoured the flavour and swallowed. He folded his arms and tilted his head to one side.

Number Eight.

This particular figure—unlike the others in the series—was depicted as being clothed in shreds. Like a Goya torture victim. In the other paintings, some of the figures had been nude, while others were clothed in sumptuous gowns and robes. This man here was a beggar, perhaps—or a slave. His skin had an olive complexion. His shirt and trousers were white—and had the look of peasantry about them—the trousers belted with rope, the shirt full-bodied and lacking buttons. The painted aspect of this attire showed it to be already ragged and torn. The shredded aspect—done, as Kurtz recalled, with what Slade called his *flaying knife*—cut through the canvas in parallel downward strokes. All cuts were vertical. None had been violent strokes—nothing was slashed—as was true of the other paintings. The shredding had been accomplished in much the same manner as Robert must have shaved away the pubic hair from a boy he had talked about once—with lingering, sensuous strokes—each stroke a considered work of art. Whatever rage was evident in Slade's other shreddings had been tempered here with a disciplined hand. Kurtz, in his mind, could hear the slow, hoarse voice of the knife as it broke through the canvas skin—not unlike the voice of Robert's silver razor...

"Hello, Rupert."

Kurtz did not turn. His hand closed more tightly around the glass.

"You like that painting, don't you."

It was Fabiana.

She had entered the room so quietly, he had been completely unaware of her.

"Yes," he said. "I do. I like all of Slade's work. Hello, Fabiana." Now, he turned.

Fabiana was wearing black, as always—with a red silk belt at her waist. "The fog out there is terrible," she said. "Which is why I'm late."

Kurtz went on watching the painting. He did not want to look too openly at Fabiana.

"How do you turn it on?" he asked, nodding at the blood pan.

"Over here by the door," said Fabiana. "I know, because I helped Robert install it. He likes to make people think it's magic. So we put the switch back here, where he could activate it without going near the paint-ing." She demonstrated. The device was silent. The wine-blood began to flow. "Frankly," she said, "I believe such paintings belong in galleries." She turned it off. "A work of art is not a toy. It's the one aspect of the *Shreds* paintings I don't like. Brilliant—but they rely on a gimmick. Not good."

Kurtz did not agree, but said nothing.

"I love this room," said Fabiana, turning away from the painting. "I mean, I love the rest of it. The furniture is gorgeous, isn't it. And I like the other paintings. I advised him to buy the Bacon. That was a real coup." She paused. "The Cocteau is so saucy," she laughed. "And the Colville so severe. Do you know, sometimes his work actually frightens me more than Slade's? It's true. Something dreadful is always about to happen, but you rarely know what it is. Or was. Sometimes the dreadful thing has just occurred..."

Fabiana looked at the Colville and Kurtz said of it: "it's nothing but the surface of the sea. Dead calm."

"Yes," said Fabiana. "but someone has either just drowned out there—or will, as soon as you turn away. I find it eerie and forlorn. That's the other thing about a lot of Colville's paintings—they're unnaturally quiet. The word *menace* seems appropriate."

"You don't like him."

"I didn't say that. I do like him, as a matter of fact. His paintings. It's the tension I like. There is absolutely no way you can watch them without a knot beginning to form in your stomach."

"Watch them?"

"Sorry? What?"

"*Watch* them. You said *watch*."

"Did I? I wasn't aware of it. I guess that's right though, isn't it. At least it is for me. I think that paintings should be watched—not just *looked at*. Not just *seen*. That's what the tension's about—the watching—the waiting—the silence." Fabiana was drinking gin and now she had some from her glass. Two gold bracelets on her arm fell back against each other and made a clicking noise.

Kurtz was watching her avidly. He knew her well enough to know that, in this moment, she would not look back at him. She was deeply preoccupied.

Finally, he said: "the last time I saw you, you were having lunch at Arlequino's."

"Oh?"

"Yes."

"When was that? I have lunch there a lot. Who was I with?"

"Tina Perry."

"Oh, yes. Tina Perry. Money, money, money." Fabiana smiled. "She's one of my backers."

"I wish she wasn't."

"Good heavens, why?"

Kurtz said: "she's crude. Brassy. Tough as nails."

Fabiana said: "she's a hell of a business woman, Rupert. So am I."

They fell back to silence for a moment. Each of them drank. Then Fabiana said: "the one thing I don't really like about coming to Robert's house is—he won't let you smoke."

More silence.

And then Fabiana said: "Rupert..."

"Yes."

"I need help."

"Help?" His heart began to race. She was turning in his direction—coming back to him. She needed him...

She walked away from him.

"I'm lost again, Rupert," she said. "The way I was before." She sat down in a straight-backed chair. A Quaker chair, with a rush seat. All her glamour fell away. She was just a woman dressed in black with her face turned down towards her lap where her hands with their burden of drink were folded. "Maybe it's just the aftermath of mounting a show like Slade's. I don't know. Everything in you is geared to the rush of getting it hung and opened—and sold. Then suddenly, *bang*—there's nothing and all you have left is your own life. And I..." She sighed. "I don't have a life. Not beyond my work. All at once, it seems to be four o'clock in the morning, every waking hour of the day."

The coal in the grate began to fall apart with a series of slides. Lanslides. Mountains falling. Yellow flames joined the blue.

"Jimmy's back," she said next.

Kurtz took a deep breath.

"Back?" he said.

"Yes." Fabiana pointed at her head. "Up here. And I can't get rid of him. I can't escape him. I'm a hostage, Rupert. Literally. He's holding me against my will."

Kurtz waited. Fabiana's description of Holbach was apt. He was a terrorist, in his way—a hostage-taker. *Use—and dispose. Kill, if you must.* Men did that to women. Some men to some women. It was a fact. And when they left—if they left—they left their victims in captivity. Sometimes for life. Holbach had been gone now for some years, but he evidently still held the keys to Fabiana's cell.

"If you're in trouble," Kurtz said—knowing better than to approach her physically, standing back near the Colville sea—"then I'm here to help you."

"Yes," said Fabiana. "I know."

Then she looked at him, set her drink aside and drew a handkerchief from her evening bag. Kurtz could not help but think of the words *worn down*. She wiped her eyes and blew her nose and sat for a moment, with the handkerchief displayed like a flag of surrender. "It's always the same," she said. "The minute he gets back in, he destroys me all over again."

"I can set up a session for you whenever you like."

"Thank you. Yes. I would like that."

Kurtz turned away to the fire. In his mind there was something like a shout of triumph, but nothing of that was in his voice. "You can start the way I ask all my...people to do..." He might never say *patient*, but he could not bring himself to say *client* to Fabiana. "You can write a précis. Try to put your problem on paper. Why you want help—why you need it. Who you think you are—how you see yourself. Putting it on the page, you have a chance to articulate it without interruption. I always find this works, as a way to begin."

"You're sly, Rupert," she said. But she was smiling when she said it.

Kurtz went so far as to give her a short bow. "It's my genius," he said. And he, too, smiled.

Fabiana looked up at Slade's painting. "He's dying, you know."

"AIDS?"

"Well," said Fabiana. "Everything. AIDS. Life. Schizophrenia. Not a great combination."

"It produced great art."

Fabiana looked at Kurtz and sat up straighter in her chair. She gazed at Slade's painting. "He was your patient, wasn't he?"

"Yes."

"What did you make of him?"

"The usual. Troubled. Defiant. Bedevilled."

Fabiana smiled. "Bedevilled, you say. That's interesting, Rupert." She drank. The painting remained her focus. "He thought you were a god."

"Did he." Kurtz was noncommittal. Slade, it was true, had been something of a disciple as well as a patient. He believed—naïvely—in what Kurtz was doing at the Parkin. Naïvely only in the sense of Slade's having no scientific insight into madness—only the insight of one who was mad. Still, it had been exhilarating for Kurtz to have a believer at his feet. *When does my life as a madman begin?*

Fabiana said: "he saluted you at the gallery. Did you see that?"

Kurtz had seen it—but said: "no."

"Yes," said Fabiana. "He thinks the world of you." She looked at him. "I'm not so sure I'll feel safe in your hands," she said with amusement. "As a patient, I mean."

Kurtz now wanted to change the subject. She was getting too close, too soon.

"Next week," he said, "we will have a man of real stature in our midst."

"Oh, yes? And who might that be?"

"Nicholas Fagan is coming to the university to give the Appleby Lecture."

"I must go to that."

"Well—that's why I brought it up, actually. You see—I won't be here when he arrives. Fagan, I mean. And there's a dinner party being given—and I've been put in charge of seeing that Professor Fagan has a companion..."

"So?"

"I think it should be you."

"Me? Oh, Rupert, *please!* I can't possibly."

"Why not?"

"He's a god, Rupert."

Kurtz gave one of his rare smiles. "Well, you've been sitting here with me this last while—and I'm a god. Or so you say. According to Slade."

Fabiana subsided. She did want to meet the man. Fagan had exerted some influence on her reading life.

186

"What do I have to do?" she asked.

"Pick him up at his hotel. Get him to Marlow's house for drinks—and get him to the dinner party."

"Charlie Marlow who was married to Charlotte O'Neill?"

"That's right. He works at the Parkin, now."

"And the party—where's that?"

"The O'Flahertys'."

Fabiana laughed. "Oh!" she said. *"Them."*

"Yes. *Them* because they're Irish, like Fagan—and because they offered."

"All right. I'll do it. And thank you for the opportunity, Rupert. Otherwise, Professor Fagan might have slipped through town without my knowing." Then she said: "why can't you be there?"

"I'll be there for the dinner party—and there for the lecture. But I'll be on a plane from Chicago earlier, so I can't be there for the Marlow affair."

Fabiana stood up. She finished her drink—and gazed around the room, with its books and paintings and English silver. "Poor Robert," she said. "Lives all alone and has no one to share this with."

"Oh, I don't know," said Kurtz. "We're all alone. And Robert at least has Rudyard. For myself—I don't feel sorry for Robert. This is his sanctuary. And that's what he needs."

He did not explain.

Fabiana took his arm. John Dai Bowen had arrived and could be heard in the front hall. Fabiana began to lead Kurtz from the room. "And your sanctuary, Rupert?" she said. "Is there one?"

Kurtz said: "no. I have no need." And they walked away from the books and the Georgian chairs and the English silver and the burning coal. Away from the tensions of Alex Colville's sea and Julian Slade's white shreds.

Out in the hallway, greeting them, John Dai Bowen said: "do I have news for you!"

Good, Kurtz thought. The rest of the evening would be spent in vacuous gossip—none of it of any consequence, all of it ribald and bitchy and true.

8

The fog had not crept in on little cat feet. It had not descended like a curtain. What it did was capture the city and hold its people prisoner for three days.

It was a thick, pervasive fog—tumbling and yellow. Amber. It was diseased. It exuded poisonous odours and fetid, unidentifiable smells of the kind that came from the earth, as if it had been digging there in cemeteries and thick lagoons of human waste. This fog also carried the residue of deadly chemicals being sprayed by the D-Squads. Because of this, there was a roaring trade in surgical masks for those who could make their way to stores and hospitals. But, in time, the supplies ran out and the people reverted to the old-west style—a city of frontier bandits done up in red and blue bandanas.

Public transport ceased to run on the surface. Only the subways continued to function. Above ground, the streets and avenues filled up with abandoned private vehicles until, at last, the Works Department sent out trucks to pull them aside. People got lost, as they do in blizzards, a few paces from their own front doors. So many calls went out for assistance, that the telephone service broke down twice from overstimulation.

Bandits of the dictionary's kind turned up and did a lot of damage. Stores and houses were robbed as a matter of course. A woman was stripped and raped in the middle of Yonge Street where it intersected with Carlton/College. No one responded to her calls, thinking she was merely lost. She walked in naked to a bank, where the guards arrested her for indecent exposure. The rapists were never found. There were other crimes and indiscretions. The ravines filled up with Leatherhead beatings. The parks filled up with Moonman orgies. It was a startling, crazy time—a sinister *mardi gras* in which the city itself was masked.

Unfortunately, before the fog descended, the D-Squads had been out in several locations, mostly in public parks where starlings were now collecting in earnest. Huge congregations of birds, including other species—blackbirds, cowbirds, grackles—filled the trees with clamouring chatter and, were it not for their imminent demise, the whole event was otherwise a raucous, joyous celebration of life. But the D-Squads quickly found them and went about their work with stringent efficiency—every gesture having been orchestrated during their winter exercises. The setting up of barriers, the placing of the hoses, the trotting figures in yellow moving with military precision were all reminiscent of riot control. Then the commencement of spraying, the falling-rising-falling swirls of dying, panic-stricken birds and, finally, the funeral mounds of raked-up feathered corpses, and the dreaded smell of flesh and chemicals on fire—and the yellow flags unfurled and hung from the trees, as if the trees had been guilty of a crime by spreading their branches too invitingly for the avian invaders.

As always, when the process had been completed, the tanker trucks and the yellow Land Rovers rolled away down the streets to the sound of loudspeaker voices announcing whatever quarantines had resulted from the operations: *ALLAN GARDENS OFF LIMITS TILL SEVENTEEN HOURS! SIBELIUS PARK OFF LIMITS TILL ZERO SIX HOURS!* Et cetera. Some—mostly senior citizens with extended memories—said prayers. Others—mostly children—applauded. It depended on what one knew about the past—and the young, for some time, had been sheltered from all history containing episodes of chemical warfare—the dawning of the atomic age—the news of holocausts of any kind involving the gassing of victims—the First World War—Vietnam and Desert Storm. Auschwitz. The yellow flags were raised in behalf of human survival and none may disparage them. By law.

Lilah, it so happened, had gone with the baby carriage that day to the University Bookstore on College Street. This was a large, grey building with slim, high windows and—in part—glass panels in its roof. Once, it had served as the home of the Toronto Reference Library—but when that library was carted off and expanded to become the Metropolitan Toronto Reference Library on Yonge Street north of Bloor—the old grey building had become a bookstore—and one of the best in the city. Lilah had gone there many times to browse—simply to be with books— just to stare at the rows and rows of pristine copies of *Madame Bovary* and *The Brothers Karamazov, Death in Venice, The Sound and the Fury* and *The Pillow Book of Sei Shonagon*.

Round and round the islands of shelves, Lilah would walk with a measured pace, reciting the titles under her breath, as one might utter prayers in a cloister. *War and Peace, The Trial, David Copperfield... Pride and Prejudice, Gulliver's Travels, The Turn of the Screw... Ulysses, The Last of Cheri, The Good Soldier...*

All the words are prayers—this was Fagan—*and all the men and women merely pray-ers...*

The siren went.

A voice on the public speakers said that *everyone must stay indoors until the tankers have departed.* Lilah did not mind. It would give her time to visit more islands.

All at once, there was a great commotion beyond the glass skylights and the shapes and cries of hundreds of birds—more than likely pigeons—could be seen and heard, echoes and shadows only—nothing of substance. There was a roaring, racing, rushing flurry of wings and of feathers—voices—doves never shouting, only fleeing—sparrows muted and smothered as children might have been trampled in a human stampede—grackles squawking—blue jays calling...

And then—a sudden, total silence.

Lilah had been staring up, watching, with one hand raised to her lips and the other caught at the back of her head, its fingers splayed to support her tam-o'-shanter. There was a thump—as if a stone had fallen against the glass. But it was not a stone. It was an escaping bird, throwing itself against the skylight in its terror—falling dead and retracting into an oval ball, as it might have done if a human hand had held it.

And there, where it had died against the glass, the perfect shape of its final moment was spread across the pane, with every feather etched, wings wide, tail splayed, head turned in silhouette, beak standing open to exhale the final breath—a dove of grey dust against a yellow light.

Lilah stared. And withdrew both hands to her sides.

A signature. An autograph. A signing of the self...

Fagan again. He seemed to be in her mind at every turning.

When had that been—a *signature—an autograph?*

A window-pane.

In Dublin.

Yes. There in the alcove—Fagan explaining.

There were four of them—five—it made no difference. In Lilah's memory, they might have been alone, the two of them. But she knew there had been others. *Fagan's favourites* on one of his pub crawls. And this was an alcove—a cornered place with a window to one side. And Fagan writing with his finger in the steamy perspiration on the glass. *N.F., L.K.* and the initials of whoever else was present—and the steam on the window running—*there, you see?* Fagan had said. *Like Keats, our names are writ in water.* And the names—the initials—had run away down the panes, dissolving in the instant they were made.

This is the world without books, Fagan said. *Do you see it there, forgotten where it was. Gone already and not one minute old. But now,* he said, *look here...*

He had reached then, farther out to another pane in the window, swiping it clean with his red-dotted handkerchief. And, as if by magic then, there had suddenly been words.

Not words a person could read in the second they were revealed, but words, it was certain, in the English language.

> *You taught how I might youth prolong*
> *By knowing what is right and wrong,*

How from my heart to bring supplies
Of lustre to my fading eyes.

Cut with a diamond into the glass.

"Who put it there?" Lilah had asked.

"A woman known as *Stella*," said Fagan, "whose real name was Esther Johnson. All her life, ever since being a child, she had loved and revered her mentor, Jonathan Swift. He, too, had loved her. They never married—but that," Fagan told them, "is another story. I wanted you to see these words—look upon them and touch them with your fingers. Life and love," he said, "are twin ephemera—but words can tell of them forever."

Swift and Stella. Never forgotten. Remembered entirely through words.

Lilah stood less rigid now and gazed at the imprint of the bird above her—the imprint of all birds now imperilled. But something had been said of them there on the glass, and would remain. *Once we were*, it said. *And now we are.*

She looked away then with a rush of Stella's lustre in her eyes and, because of this, she almost failed to see the sign that was hanging there by her shoulder. She did, however, see it when she had put away her handkerchief and was preparing to move to the next archipelago of books.

THE APPLEBY LECTURE
will be delivered
by
NICHOLAS FAGAN
Professor Emeritus
Trinity College
Dublin
May 27th
7:00 P.M.
Convocation Hall

Even as the siren went to free her from the bookstore, Lilah was still immobilized—with her finger on Fagan's name.

9

As the fog was rolling in, Gatz grew restless. What he did for his living was rarely a source of distress to him. So many people in his past had treated him exclusively as a source of gratification that it gave him pleasure, now, to watch the current victims of his expertise stumble and fall in his path. But it left him appallingly alone.

In the evening, he went down on foot to the corner of Bloor and Sherbourne streets, where he purchased a book of photographs and a package of candymints in the local drugstore. The photographs, by a man called Willard, were exclusively of Texas and the cover showed the very heart of the world from which Gatz had fled. The desolation of the WesTex dry flats stretched in all directions. A road cut through it that led to the living—so you were told if you grew up there. The photograph caught him because of its sepia-coloured earth and the dying green of things that tried to survive. It also caught him with its depiction of dust—the grey sand mist that filled the air. This was the very stuff and texture of his childhood and, all at once, as he saw it there on display, he had a longing for it he could taste.

When he and Marianne Prager were married in Baltimore, Marianne had said: *I will never let you take me there, to Texas. It has the look of a place that kills.*

It was true. It did. Although it also had its own perverse beauty and a population—Gatz did not think of them as perverse—who not only survived WesTex but also thrived in it. Gatz had never known how—or why they bothered. For him, it had been a killer because of his father. The landscape merely augmented what had already been a life-and-death situation.

Marianne Prager had a way of killing love that in men would have been called abusive, but in women, was called revenge. In women it was justified, because men were demons bent on destroying women. In men it was justified because women were unfaithful sluts and ambitious whores. Gatz had bought none of this until Marianne began to tear him down in the eyes of his child and, finally, took his child away from him entirely. Clearly, she had never intended to stay with him. Clearly she, too—as his father had done—had thought of Gatz as a workhorse, a stud and a source of extra security. When she left him, most of his money went with her—even though she had money and real estate of her own.

Above all else, she had deprived him of his child, Anne Marie. Anne Marie, as she left him, had called back over her shoulder: *I love you—* but caught in Marianne's grip, she could not resist the force that impelled her forward into the waiting limousine.

The love Gatz had for Anne Marie was fed by his desperate need to excise the memory of his father's abuses. He had wanted never to be away from her, but always to be in her company. Marianne had said it was a sick relationship and encouraged her mother to intervene. Laura Meade Prager had done just that—with a battery of lawyers. The fact was, Marianne was jealous—jealous, in part, of Anne Marie, who had caught the attentions of Gatz so entirely—but mostly jealous of Gatz, who provided the improbable and unacceptable news that all fathers were not monsters. She, too, had suffered as Gatz had suffered—though, in her case, the abuses had carried the patrician stamp of bribes in the form of sorrel hunters and water spaniels. Also the great hotels of London and Paris where she lost her virginity first to her father's fingers and then to the whole of his immaculate person. He had died before Anne Marie was born—a cause, for Marianne, of celebration.

How had he won her, Gatz wondered. And how had they stayed so long together? Eight years. Nine, if he counted the dreadful remembrance of that final year which ended with Anne Marie's departure.

He could not deny that, in the beginning, his desire for Marianne had been a facet of his ambition. She came of a "great" family—a coalition of bankers: the Pragers and the Meades. Their bloodlines went all the way back, in American banking, to prerevolutionary times.

The words *American banking* and *prerevolutionary*, taken both singly and together, were enough to catch an ambitious young man's attention. But when they were combined with the image of Marianne Prager, *recently returned from her studies in Paris*, they were irresistible. As for Gatz, he was then newly launched upon a phenomenal career as a lawyer with the Baltimore firm of Daniel Cody. Cody had put him through law school—*Harvard, with strings*—and had been the last of the mentors to whom Gatz made himself available.

Cody himself had been ambitious for the marriage—and, being a close friend of Laura Meade Prager, was instrumental in bringing Gatz and Marianne together. Childless, Cody had nothing to lose and everything to gain by the alliance. Laura Meade Prager had similar thoughts. Young James Gatz had everything a mother could want for her daughter—the truth of his background being entirely unknown and what was known being so entirely brilliant: his extraordinary talents, his physical graces, his connection to Cody and Cody's own impeccable reputation and considerable fortune.

It took a year—and they were married. Gatz made it all the way through to Anne Marie's fifth birthday without a single indiscretion. That was when he took her to see where he was born—and told her the story of his life. Granted, it had been the story of his life as vetted for a five-year-old. But the truth of his roots was revealed—and the look of them and the air in which they had thrived. Gatz had felt it was only proper that his child should be able to verify her bloodlines—to understand the dust that was in them and the burning sun that warmed her veins.

When Gatz had returned from that journey, the first of Marianne's accusations had been levelled—and from that moment onward she had been his persecutor and his cancer, maligning him at every turn. This way, he had turned from all other women with the same frozen regard he held for Marianne—lost to every tenderness, bewildered by every desire. Raising his glass, as Emma had seen him do, to the woman by his side—whoever the woman might chance to be—Gatz had all the requisite charm of a ladykiller. His problem was that, buried in his heart, that description carried another meaning altogether, literal and lethal—and the cause of all his pain. There was, it seemed, no one in all the world to whom he could find his way—who, loving him, would not betray his trust and invoke his fury.

Standing now on the corner, waiting for the lights to change, Gatz had a vision of his father walking in the dust. It was engendered by a sense of unease that his father's batterings had become his own.

The familiar figure in Gatz's mind was moving towards the corral where the horses were kicking up a storm, as they did on any summer day when they moved in numbers. His father's hands, which had always been red and raw, were hanging at his sides, unmoving. He walked, Gatz's father, the way that shot men walk in the movies—stiffly falling towards their destination, their feet never leaving the ground. Gatz couldn't think why he saw him so vividly that way. More often than not, he had seen his father bearing down on him with one or both hands raised.

The lights changed. Gatz could only tell this was so because the traffic had altered its direction. He placed a peppermint in his mouth and raised his handkerchief to cover his nostrils. This, too, brought him back to where he had been before the whirlwind had carried him off—stumbling through dust storms between the rattling barns and the flapping screen doors of the house. The weight of the book in its carrier bag at his side was comforting. It reminded him that even in this northern city, the weight of his past was with him—and that was a good thing—never to forget what had driven you to where you were.

Crossing over the Sherbourne Street Bridge, he saw the great white shape of a limousine roll by his shoulder. It slipped through the fog without a sound—but its passing weight disturbed the air and the fog appeared to be making way for it, slewing out to either side and frothing upward before it closed again and the car was gone. It left a trail of exhaust in its wake which Gatz could smell, in spite of the handkerchief held to his face.

He wondered if it had been the same white limousine that parked from time to time in the street near the house of his neighbour, Eric Royhden. If it was, then it must be the Great White Whale of which he had heard so much erotic speculation. *There's a whore in the back of that car who can blow a man to heaven.*

Gatz and Royhden were never civil to one another. Royhden, if he could get his way, would have Gatz removed from the street. Beaumont Road was not a fit setting for one who made his living protecting crooks, especially when the crooks had done in your own best friends and business partners.

Gatz started over the Glen Road Bridge. The cold air rose from the ravine below. It made a vain attempt to lift the fog—but the fog had too much weight to it. Beyond the bridge he would come to Beaumont Road—the turning which would take him home.

Parked not more than a dozen feet from the corner was the phantom limousine that earlier had passed him on the other bridge. It was so completely hidden in the fog that he almost walked right into it.

He cursed, but barely aloud.

He stepped out farther into the road. He was secure, now, in the absolutes of the geography. His house would be at the end of this street, perched—as the whole street was—above the pitches of that dark ravine. The great white car was parked beside the low stone retaining wall on the south side—the off side, where the houses were below the roadline, lost among the trees—now doubly lost in the sea of fog.

Gatz heard a woman's laughter.

He paused. The car was on his right. Its rear door opened—and the glow of its dim interior smudged the dark with ruby-coloured light. A form very briefly eclipsed this view as someone—surely Royhden—got out and stood, unaware of Gatz, about ten feet away. Inside, against the black leather seats, Gatz could see the elegant juxtaposition of a woman's legs as they were crossed one over the other.

There she was—precisely as rumour had painted her. A woman in a dark dress, seated in an amber-ruby glow—with elegant legs and a fluttering hand.

The door closed—and she was gone.

The great car moved on into the fog—making, as it must, for Gatz's end of the street, where it would turn, perhaps in his own driveway, in order to achieve the homeward part of its journey. Gatz turned to his neighbour and within three minutes had the identity of the woman in the limousine. Emma Berry. He realized her name had been on the guest list of his party, and he wondered how it could be that he had failed to see her there. Perhaps she had not, after all, attended.

What he did know was that, when he saw Emma bending forward in the amber light — a trigger had been squeezed. A gun had fired. Someone had shot him — that was the effect of it.

10

Emma had seen him there in the fog. The sight of him caused a stutter in her breathing. Hope so seldom paid off, it had startled her to find him standing outside her mind since he had barely left it for the past week. *What are you doing out there?* she wanted to say.

She supposed these were the signs of obsession—and in some ways, they made her feel foolish—like a star fan who has lost control of reality. But that was the least of it. Overall, she felt charged with a kind of energy that Marlow would have recognized at once as manic, but which Emma herself took as being a gift of stamina in a failing moment.

In the mirror as she passed, she saw the bright-eyed woman she had been warned of, but she refused to take that woman's medication. Instead, she took up a bottle of vodka and carried it to her bedroom. The first thing she did behind the closed door was go into her bathroom and clean her teeth.

After that, she turned on the shower and sat in a blue wicker chair and listened to the water streaming down beyond the glass doors. She poured more and drank more vodka. She stood up and lighted a cigarette and wiped the make-up from her face and listened to the water streaming and washed her hands and dabbed her cleavage and the undersides of her breasts with *Calèche* and placed a drop of it on her tongue and wiped the steam from the mirrors and saw what she had not known—that she was talking—or was it singing?—and she leaned on the palms of her hands, the cigarette smoke curling up from between her fingers—and stared at the woman before her and the room in the mist around that woman and she listened to the water streaming and for half an hour she stood there, hung there that way, caught in the frozen animation of her desire for Gatz and for Gatz's hands that would come and lead her away. *Truly,* she was thinking, *for the first time ever, there will be more of me alive than there has ever been before.*

And yet—they had still not met.

Finally, bathed and robed, she returned to her bedroom.

She opened her closets and gazed at what was there.

What, she wondered, *does a person wear for such an encounter?*

As Marlow would have predicted, she opted for white.

The telephone had still not rung the next night as Emma sat with her mid-course cigarette. Barbara, who was wearing the uniform of her school, was sitting as usual in semi-darkness, halfway along the table. Her plate was empty. She was drinking, as she was allowed to do on rare occasions, a glass of sparkling wine. A rosé. Emma, as always, was drinking red.

The clock seemed almost as agitated tonight as Emma was. Barbara, on the other hand, was serenely calm. She barely moved. The long strands of her white-blonde hair had been braided into plaits, each with a green bow to match her uniform.

"Will you be going out tonight?"

"I don't know yet."

"Then why are you dressed like that?"

"Because it makes me feel better."

"Aren't you well?"

The telephone did not ring.

At ten o'clock on the third night of the fog—Emma sat on Barbara's bed. The phone call she had waited for still had not come. Nonetheless, she had put on the white dress, as before, and the white silk stockings and shoes.

Barbara was reading.

"What's the book?"

"Wuthering Heights."

"I see." Emma smiled. "Where are you in the story?"

Barbara said that Catherine had just married Edgar.

"Oh, yes. That bit."

They sat.

Emma said: "do you like her?"

"Catherine Earnshaw?"

"Yes."

"Of course not. She's stupid," said Barbara.

"I see. Stupid."

"Don't you think so?"

"No. I never felt that way about her at all."

"Well, I do. She loves Heathcliff—but she marries Edgar. I think what will happen is that Heathcliff will kill her in a fit of rage—and it will serve her right."

Emma laughed. "You want too much!" she said. "That's not how it ends at all."

"It isn't?"

"No. Of course not. You don't kill people you love."

"Sometimes you do."

"Oh? Who, for instance?"

"Othello kills Desdemona. George kills Lenny."

"Who's George? Who's Lenny?"

"*Of Mice and Men,* by John Steinbeck."

"And they love each other?"

"Yes. Lenny's simple-minded. He kills a woman, not meaning to. So George has to shoot him to protect him from himself." Barbara sat forward and hugged her knees. "Othello kills Desdemona in a fit of rage—so why not Heathcliff and Catherine?"

The telephone rang.

Emma stood up. She was not even aware of crossing the room. Before she knew it, she was at the door.

"Mother?"

The telephone rang again. Surely Orley would answer it.

"Mother?"

"What?" This was a whisper.

"If I was Heathcliff, I would kill her. Wouldn't you?"

Orley was calling from below. "For you, Mrs Berry."

Emma turned back towards Barbara. "No," she said. "And you aren't Heathcliff—you're Barbara!" She was smiling. "Good-night," she said. And she blew a kiss. Gone.

The sound of her descending steps was the sound of someone running towards an open door. The word *escape* came into Barbara's mind. But later, when the draught of Emma's departure blew through the house, the word in Barbara's mind was *rage*.

11

Emma's driver was a man called Billy Lydon. He was small and dark with hard black marbles for eyes, set in the face of a cherub.

Long before Emma appeared, Billy had brought the white Mercedes into the spill of light that fell from the *porte-cochère* in front of the Surgeon's house on Highland Avenue. He was nervous of the fog, having already driven through it yesterday afternoon. His greatest fear was of banging into the rear of another vehicle. This would cause embarrassment, not for his mistress but for her guest. Anything requiring an exchange of information with another driver or an encounter with the police was to be avoided at all costs. The Surgeon's Wife unconditionally guaranteed the safety and privacy of her clients. To date, there had not been a single indiscretion and Billy wanted to keep it that way.

When Emma came down the steps, Billy got out to let her into the back seat. Orley, when she had called down to tell him he would be driving that night, had said this was to be a champagne excursion. This meant the provision of chicken sandwiches, green pears and a Boursault cheese besides the wine—and a mix of white and yellow roses. Billy had scurried to put all this in place, thinking they must be going to meet someone of extraordinary importance. Champagne excursions were normally reserved for cabinet ministers and visiting celebrities who had been given Emma's name as far away as L.A. and New York. So when Emma said to him *Beaumont Road*, he was astounded.

"We been to Beaumont yesterday," he said. What he really wanted to say was: *you ain't goin' to blow champagne on that prick Royhden, are you?* Emma put him straight with a laugh, because she knew what he must be thinking. "Not Mister Royhden," she said—and reached out to pat his cheek. "We are going to his neighbour, Mister Gatz." And she gave him the number of the house. Billy had rarely seen her so happy.

From Highland Avenue to Beaumont Road is a very short distance. They broach the same ravine. Even through the fog, the journey was over in less than five minutes. Billy descended and went up the steps and rang the bell of Gatz's house. For a moment there was no answer. He rang again.

Emma had rolled the window down and sat bolt upright, staring out so she would see him the instant he appeared. She wanted to shout at Billy, *stand aside!* But she remained mute, her hands turning white with tension in her lap.

All at once, he was there. His hair was full of light. Behind him, she could see the massive distance of the hallway leading to the staircase curving off to the left—the staircase from which she had watched him toast the anonymous woman. Gatz seemed immensely tall, standing up as he was on the steps and looming over Billy who was backing down into the driveway.

The door closed and darkness fell. She heard Gatz coming to the car and she sat back all the way on the farther side. When Billy let him into the light beside her, his head was bent forward and she could not see his face. She could already smell his hair and his skin as Billy shut the door and went around to the driver's side and slid in behind the wheel.

Gatz was leaning back into his corner, adjusting his frame to the shape of the seat. His legs, in pale flannel, were drawn up slightly at the knee and his shoulders were twisted, cantilevered to the rest of him. Neither of them spoke. They did, however, look at each other. They should have smiled. They should have laughed. But there was not a sound.

The great white car rolled down the street towards the turning that would lead it deepest into the ravine. As it began its descent, Emma said: "don't speak..." Leaning forward into the aura of Gatz's body, she began very slowly to undress him.

They did not come back until dawn.

Gatz said: "please, I want you to come with me into my house."

Emma said: "I don't go into customers' houses." Then she added: "but I've already been in yours."

"I knew you were there before. At least, I supposed you were..."

"Yes."

"Now, I need you to be there—with me."

Gatz was adamant. He wanted to bring her all the way into his life. He forgot that in order to do so, he would have to lure her all the way out of her own.

"You're bleeding," she said. "I'm sorry."

Gatz had not been aware of it. He smiled at her. "So are you," he said.

Emma looked away. She would have let him kill her. There had been moments when she knew he almost had. His fingers had torn her, and his mouth, having tasted every part of her, had closed so firmly over her breasts that even as she urged him on, she caught the image of flesh being eaten and had tried to drive him off, pretending it was any other kind of frenzy but fear.

She could not imagine where the cruelty in him was centred. She did not, therefore, know how to answer it. He called her everything but *Emma*—all the names of all his enemies and the name of his wife—but not his daughter's name. He called her by his father's name. Never her own. She accepted that. This was Gatz as he was, and she had learned, over time, that her job in the Great White Whale was to bring her lovers back full circle to themselves. All the way out into danger and all the way home, like a lunatic passing through the phases of the moon, to safety.

But for herself, beyond the limousine, she would not even have her protective cover as *The Surgeon's Wife*. That, too, would be over. In Gatz's house, Emma would be herself alone. She dreaded this.

"Please," said Gatz.

"I'm cold," said Emma.

"Not in there, you won't be."

Emma took a deep breath and let it all the way out.

"All right," she said. "I will go."

It was just like making an entrance in a play, she decided. *You can't turn back for safety in the wings.*

In the hallway, Emma stood and stared at the great, high dome above her. Blue glass shone with artificial light—as if the moon were out there beyond it.

"Shall we go up?" said Gatz.

"Up?" said Emma. "I—could we sit for a few moments?"

She turned towards the tall, polished doors that stood open at the end of the hall.

"The Florida room is just what I need, right now," she said, and took three steps towards it.

"No," said Gatz. "Please, come up with me now to the part of the house you've never seen..."

Suddenly, Emma said: "there's someone there. Who is it?"

"What?" said Gatz.

"There's a man. In the Florida room."

"Just the butler. Come on..."

"No. Not the butler." Emma stepped forward again. The man was wearing a raggedy coat—old and torn and dirty. His hands were in his pockets. He was staring at her hard.

"You had best," he said, "stand out of my way."

Emma saw him move forward. She turned to Gatz for the answer.

Then the old man stood in the hallway and said to Gatz: "Jimmy? It's me." Later, there was gunfire—and after that, oblivion.

<u>12</u>

The phone call came at seven o'clock on a Tuesday morning. The city was still held captive by the fog. A policeman whose name was either Harley or Varley rang through to Marlow at his house on Lowther Avenue and told him he was to come at once to a house on Beaumont Road. Marlow's first thought was *Gatz*. Gatz was that street's most notorious resident.

Of course, he was right. It was all beginning to fall into place with dreadful—and dreaded—precision even as Harley/Varley talked. The police. Yes. A death. Yes. Murder. Possibly. Emma.

There. It was done. The ending Marlow had feared.

Yes. He would come at once.

No. He would not tell anyone where he was going.

Harley/Varley offered to send a car for him. *The fog, you know. It's treacherous.* Marlow accepted—*as long,* he said, *as it doesn't arrive with its siren blaring.* He needed no more sirens now than the ones already singing in his head.

When Marlow arrived, there were two police cars and an ambulance in the driveway besides the Great White Whale. The police cars' windows were open, their radios bleating with sheeplike voices. Slow spinning shafts of red light split the fog through which Marlow walked until he came to the steps. To his right, he could see the fallen figure of a man in a dark blue uniform. This was Billy Lydon—though Marlow was not aware of his name. He lay on his face with both arms flung out before him, his fists full of gravel. One foot was twisted back towards the bottom step just inches from where Marlow stood.

The policeman whose name was Harley or Varley greeted him in the hall.

Just as Gatz had brought Emma, Harley/Varley now brought Marlow over towards the curving staircase. Like Emma, Marlow turned back. Where Emma had seen the raggedy man in the shadows, Gatz now lay in the light. Harley/Varley said: "that's him," the way people say *there's the floor* or *that's the ceiling.*

Marlow had never laid eyes on Gatz, who had played such a negative role in the lives of so many people. He was stunned by the gentle, boy-like features of this man he had heard was so harsh and dislikeable.

"You know him?" said Harley/Varley.

"No," said Marlow.

Gatz had been shot in the chest. He lay on the green marble floor in a mass of his own blood. A palm tree leaned above him and a pool of clear water was at his back. Somewhere, a fountain played—but it could not be seen amongst the giant ferns and the bougainvillaea vines.

Harley/Varley said: "your patient is up here, Doctor."

"Thank you," said Marlow, and he turned and followed the man along the curving flight of the stairs.

Passing through another hallway, they came to another, shorter staircase—this one uncurving—with a door that was shut at the top. Here was that part of the house that Gatz never opened to other eyes. Emma was in there somewhere, refusing to speak to anyone but Marlow. It was she who insisted he come—so he went up these last steps alone.

There was a den with empty shelves and an empty desk—books piled up by the hundreds on the floor. Paintings that had not been hung sat facing inward like children playing hide and seek along the hallway leading to Gatz's bedroom. And in the bedroom itself, the scent of Emma's perfume—cigarettes and *Calèche*. Marlow could not yet see her—but what he saw instead left him speechless.

A vast, barren floor without rugs or carpets—a bed so large that it almost took up one whole wall—and a single shelf of photographs—every one of them framed in silver—and a series of floating bureaus and cabinets, each of them on casters, each one pulled or pushed at will so its door or drawers could be reached and opened wherever Gatz might be in the room.

The photographs were all of one woman and one child. Marianne and Anne Marie. There were twenty of them. Twenty or more. No less. The woman never smiled. The child must have lived for laughter. The difference between them was alarming. Marlow guessed who they were. Gatz would frame his saints in silver. The rest of the world was framed in wood and turned towards the wall.

In the centre of the floor, a pair of black slippers had been shed, as if Gatz had been in flight when he removed them.

But it was the bed that stopped Marlow cold. It was a wide, vast field of smooth green sheets. Smooth, that is, except high up near the wall on the left-hand side—the side that was nearest the shelf of photographs. There, a sort of nest had been made. No other word would describe it, since it was shaped as a bird would have shaped it to the contours of its own body. Here, the contours had been those of Gatz. Curled. Tight. Pulled in around itself—the embryo shape of a child afloat in amniotic fluid. It was the saddest thing Marlow had ever seen.

Emma said: "hello, Charlie." She was behind him.

She must have come, Marlow guessed, from Gatz's bathroom—off beyond the floating cabinets.

He turned to her and she gave her smile. She was not quite there—and he feared for her, but all he said was: "hello, Emma."

She was carrying her shoes in one hand. With the other, she idly—or with seeming idleness, like a casual visitor—opened the doors of the cabinets as she passed them, one by one.

"Gatz's clothes," she said.

Suits. Jackets. Sweaters. Shirts.

Marlow barely looked. He was staring at her white dress, the front of which was covered with blood. It occurred to him for the first time that she might have killed Gatz—that hiding inside her all along had been the need to dispense with someone. Anyone—it wouldn't matter who it was by the time she got to him. He would just be the last of her lovers, whoever that happened to be. So many men had used her—and she had been used so willingly, thinking that was how she would survive. But a part of her knew, while she had been with each of them, that what they wanted of her made them hateful. There was always the aura of laughter about her attitude to them while, at the same time, she waited for one of them to love her not as The Surgeon's Wife but as Emma. That had never happened, apparently, till Gatz. Even then, he might have turned out to be like all the rest. What if he had wanted her to be the woman in the photographs? Perhaps she had killed him for that.

"Can I have a cigarette, Charlie? I've completely run out."

Marlow crossed the room and stood with her while she took a cigarette and accepted the light he offered. Then she passed him—heading towards the bed.

Watching her standing at its foot, with her shoes in one hand and the other hand with the cigarette straying up to push back her hair, he thought: *she might as well be standing over his grave.* The wide, green expanse of it, with its cornered nest, was like that—a place to mourn.

Emma sat down on the floor and leaned her arm against the sheets. She looked at the photographs.

"The last thing he saw every night," she said. "The first thing he saw every morning."

"Yes." Marlow laid an ashtray on the bed near her elbow and stepped away again.

"This is his blood," she said, looking down at her dress.

"Yes," said Marlow. "I supposed it was."

"Do you think I killed him, Charlie?" It was almost as if she didn't know the answer herself.

"I don't know," said Marlow. "You'll have to tell me." He was thinking about the injection he would have to give her sooner or later to bring her back. Sleep first—then reality. But not yet.

"His father did it," she said.

"I see." Marlow was still not certain. "Tell me what happened."

"His father did it."

"Yes. You said so."

Emma laid the end of her cigarette in the ashtray and turned it like a key. "He was waiting when we got here," she said. "And he said, *I want my boy back.* And I didn't know what he meant because I didn't know who he was. Then Gatz said, *I thought you must be dead, Pa, it's been so long.* And the man said, *it doesn't matter how long it's been. You owe me. I'm entitled...*"

Emma thought about it. Then she said: "Gatz went down to him. In the Florida room. I could hear them yelling at one another. I went into the dining-room and sat at the table and waited. Ten minutes. Maybe fifteen. It was only just beginning to be light outside. I know that. I saw it from the window, the sun coming up through the fog. Then the gun went off and I went running. I don't remember the rest. That's all I remember. Running—and the sound of water. And I think there was another shot. Outside."

The chauffeur, Marlow thought. Yes.

"Then I was up here and that's all I can say about it. Except that my dress is covered with blood."

She must have held him, but the image of it was blocked.

Emma looked over at the photographs.

"That woman's name is Marianne," she said. "And the other is his daughter, Anne Marie."

"Yes."

"What are you doing, Charlie?"

"I'm giving you a shot. It will help you sleep by the time I get you home."

"You mean I don't have to stay here?"

"No. You don't have to stay."

"I never go into houses, Charlie. It's dangerous."

In the bathroom, Marlow had found some rubbing alcohol. He rolled up her sleeve and swabbed her arm and gave her the injection. "Now," he said, "we can leave."

He helped her up and led her across the floor towards the door. She looked back from there, but she did not speak. They went away, leaving her silence in Gatz's room.

On the bed, the ashes from her cigarette were blown from their container and scattered across the sheet when Marlow closed the door.

On the stairs, Emma said: "is he there?"

Marlow said: "no. They have taken him away."

A girl and a woman—the maid and the cook—were sitting on chairs in their night attire. The cook was weeping and the maid was trying to comfort her.

Emma stopped in front of them and said: "I'm sorry."

They did not even know who she was. But the maid, who was quick and astute and who had been many times in Gatz's room, took one look at Emma and decided: *it is her.*

She thought it was Marianne. *So typical,* she also thought, *that a woman who has caused such pain should not return until it was too late.*

This was not unlike the thought that would be uppermost in Emma's mind for the rest of her life. The words *too late* would never let her be.

Beyond the door, as Marlow led her through, the fog made one last effort to hold the city. Later that morning, it rose like a beast and was gone. And Gatz went with it.

SIX

*We shall live! The music is so
gay, so joyful, and it seems as
though a little more and we shall
know what we are living for, why
we are suffering... If we only
knew—if we only knew!*

Anton Chekhov
Three Sisters

<u>1</u>

All afternoon, while he lay on the bed, Benedict Webster could hear the children playing down by the water's edge. And while he sweated in and out of dreams, he made and remade the image of the lake, correcting it as he remembered more, adding fish and rocks and depth and above it all the sky with its fires and the pale blue wash of its blinding light.

Moira—wearing red—is twelve, he was thinking. *Twelve and blooming—becoming dangerous. Carol is only ten and I have no interest in ten.*

But Allison...

Allison is fourteen, now. Fourteen, with budding breasts like magnets and when she sits in that careless, childlike way with her legs splayed open and last year's bathing suit pulling up tight against her thighs, I can see the escaping pubic hairs like shade against the pale blue cloth and I want....

To lick them.

In Ben's dreams that hot afternoon, his sweat became the lake in which his brother's daughters swam and his own pale hair became the flowing weeds entangled with their legs. Lying on the bottom of the bay, looking upwards, he was only vaguely aware of the light beyond them—more aware of how slowly and seductively they swam. His arms kept rising to embrace them.

Moira dove beneath the surface and brushed his hair aside and looked right into his face and smiled. *I know about you*, she said. As she rose away from him he tried to run her ankles through his hands and he could hear her saying to her sisters: *Uncle Ben is down there drowning.* Carol said: *let him. I don't care.* But Allison turned above him in the water and sank until she was beside him. She seemed so tenderly concerned. She kissed his forehead and lifted up his arms and placed his palms like open mouths against her breasts.

Hold on, she said. *I won't let you die.* And she began to struggle upwards, taking him with her.

Ben could feel her nipples pushing at him and growing hard. Her bathing suit in the dream was made of tissue paper, and it now began to dissolve. Ben's head was pressed between her thighs and she held him there with the motion of her swimming, pulling his face up tighter so that his lips were forced against her as if she wanted him to enter her with his tongue.

The light around him began to flicker.

Maybe he was going to drown.

Breaking the surface of the water also broke the surface of the dream. Someone had shouted. Had he done it, or Allison? Ben was alone on the bed like a body lying on a raft. Allison—out beyond the window, down by the water—laughed at something Carol had said and Moira said: *beat you to the rocks!* and Ben could hear them leaping into the bay and swimming towards the point.

He swung his legs out over the edge of the bed. His underwear clung to his erection, wet and cold as if he really had emerged from the lake. He walked across to the window and pulled aside the translucent curtains hanging there utterly still in the breathless air and he looked out over the terraced lawns of dying grass towards the bay where the girls were swimming.

All he could see was their gleaming arms and bobbing heads. Allison was winning.

There was a boy there, standing on the dock with a towel around his waist, and Ben supposed this must be one of the Shapiro boys—whatever their names might be—he could never remember.

Their father must have brought them while Ben was dreaming. The Shapiros were friends of Ben's brother, John. They often came up for the Victoria Day weekend. This year, however, Shirley Shapiro was going to be absent—which disappointed Peggy Webster. Ben was all too aware that his wife detested Shapiro, and could tolerate him only because of Shirley, who was a childhood friend of all three Wylie girls. But Shirley had begged off coming to the lake, so Shapiro had brought his sons instead—the ones who were always getting into trouble. Ben was nervous of them. They seemed entirely devoid of personality, sullen and largely silent. Their only asset was the way they moved. They moved like animals, without a sound. They never smiled. About a year ago, they had started breaking into their neighbours' houses. Not to steal, but just for the hell of it—leaving notes in people's beds and cupboards saying: *Boo-Boo Was Here.* Or: *Shit-face Was Here*—and sometimes: *Fuck Off, Charlie!* or: *Scream! You Asshole!* Charming.

The Shapiros were in the process of splitting up. Shirley was having an affair. Everyone but her husband had known what Shirley's decision would be, long before she finally made it. When it happened, Shapiro settled into a permanent despair. In order to placate his sons, whom he could not control, he enlisted them in his rebellion against what their mother was doing.

Long a casual weekend toker, Shapiro began to encourage his sons to share his dope in Shirley's presence—and by the time she finally left them, the boys were smoking pot every day.

Shapiro bought his marijuana from a man on Regent Street, whose clientele included John Dai Bowen. It was John Dai, in fact, who had introduced Shapiro to the dealer, a Chinese man who also ran cocaine and whose name was Jason Lee. As always, John Dai had an ulterior motive.

Aside from being the city's leading "society" photographer—he was also famous in a smaller circle as the owner of a large collection of erotic photographs. Ben Webster was not a part of this circle—but he had heard the rumours of it for a long time. Once, about three years ago, he had been shown some prints of four or five of those photographs and had—then—been mildly amused. His amusement had to do with the fact that he knew one of the subjects—a well-known TV sportscaster. It would not be strictly accurate to say these photographs were obscene. Most of them were aesthetically tasteful. What made them interesting was the fact that all the photographs were of naked men, some of whom—like Ben's friend—were well-known public figures. A few of them even sported erections (*sported* was John Dai's word for it) while lying on one of John Dai's famous Victorian sofas.

Lately—so Ben was told—those who had seen the newest additions to this collection had begun to mention how young a few of the recent subjects were. Sixteen- and fifteen-year-old boys were not uncommon, whereas in the past, the subjects had all been in their twenties or thirties. There were also, so Ben was told, some photographs of girls. Not women. Girls.

Sipping from his glass of wine, John Dai would watch the viewers' faces carefully. He never offered to tell the ages of his models. He waited for the connoisseurs to bring the subject up. They never did. He found this curious—provocative and exciting. He came to realize that in their silence was acquiescence, and he began to wonder how far he could go before someone would object. This was why he had introduced Shapiro to the Chinese man on Regent Street.

Shapiro's boys were just fourteen and twelve—and John Dai sensed that, given their basically defiant attitude, they would be more than happy to pose for him without their father's consent. But John Dai didn't want to take that route. He wanted Shapiro to tell him: *yes, it's okay with me....* Something about a parent's permission appealed to John Dai. It aroused him. In fact, as he lay in bed one recent night, his masturbation fantasy had been entirely based on asking Shapiro if he would allow his two young teenage sons to be photographed in the nude.

And did Shapiro want to watch?

John Dai's orgasm coincided with the voicing of that question. The answer would have to wait for tomorrow's fantasy. Ben's informant had told him all this with evident relish.

How come you know so much about Bowen's orgasms? Ben had asked.

That's the part Bowen enjoys the most, when he tells you.

Oh.

Now, Ben stood by the window watching the Shapiro boy in the towel. It was the older boy, he assumed, whichever that was. He was certainly the biggest. Five-feet-eight or nine. His hair was cut short—a sort of mousy, nondescript colour—and he had big ears. Ben smiled at this. He had big ears himself and they had been the bane of his adolescence. Big ears, big hands, big feet—he'd felt like an ape, awkward and clumsy until his full growth had filled out the rest of him.

The girls, having reached the rocks beyond the point, had clambered up and were sitting there now in the sun. The Shapiro boy waved. They did not wave back. Typical. Either they were too stuck-up to acknowledge him or else it was a teenage ploy: *pretend we don't see him. Make him wave again.*

Girls. It was ever thus.

Ben wondered what would happen if he himself waved. Would the girls wave back? Allison might—with that strange, almost disturbing innocence of hers—but Moira would not. Nor Carol. Carol would just ignore him—but Moira might even give him the finger. Moira might not understand precisely what was in Ben's mind—but she knew it was a form of hunger and it made her angry. His gaze was like an invader, always catching her off guard.

Now, as Ben was watching, almost idly—even dreamily—he saw the Shapiro boy drop his towel.

Jesus Christ! The kid was naked.

Jesus Christ! He's masturbating. Right there on the grey dead grass above the dock. And all three girls were watching.

Ben was riveted. *Quit that!* he wanted to shout—but he didn't.

Quit that. Stop that. What are you doing...?

But he knew what the boy was doing. It was what he had been doing himself—taking each of the girls in his mind, one by one.

Ben's hand, already flat against his belly, slid down inside his shorts.

His focus remained on Allison, as if the dream were being extended where he stood beside the window—but his gaze, unavoidably, was on

the boy, whose flashing hand was quickening its pace as his naked buttocks began to convulse.

Way off over the water, Allison had risen and was climbing down into
the lake. Carol, moving as if perhaps she had been told to hurry, followed her meekly without looking back. Only Moira remained on the
rock—and she was standing facing the boy and shouting at him.

Ben could only vaguely hear the words. *Asshole. Asshole. You asshole!* Then she stopped abruptly, climbed down into the water and followed her sisters, already making for the farthest visible shore.

The Shapiro boy turned around when he saw they were gone. He
hung the towel across his shoulders and made his way up the terraced lawns towards the house. Ben, for the first time, noticed he
was wearing running shoes. Otherwise, utterly naked—just the shining emblem of his youth and generation, a pair of pristine Converse
hightops—blue with a silver stripe and yellow laces. He bounced as
he walked, from heel to toe, and Ben could see that he was
whistling—hissing between his teeth, his lips slightly parted. Eyes as
dead as glass.

You wondrous bastard, Ben was thinking. *Here I am behind this curtain—hiding in my underwear—and you stood up in front of everyone
and took them one by one.*

Jesus—the nerve—and the wonder of it.

Ben went back and sat on the bed. He dried his fingers on a piece of
Kleenex and threw his shorts across the room into a corner. He thought
of Allison—blue and white in her melting bathing suit—and he wondered what she was thinking. Far out beyond the point, she was leading
her sisters towards the farthest shore—while down below them all the
lake filled up with men and boys who yearned to reach up through the
light to hold the flashing limbs in place. Did Allison know the lake was
full of men and boys? And if she did, did she rage against that fact as
Moira had or was she—maybe—smiling?

Why not come smiling, he pleaded with her, *all the way to the
inevitable? Look,* he said to her—even moving his lips to say it—*that
boy is just a boy—and I'm a man and I have rights...*

He shivered.

Rights, he thought.

He hadn't known he was going to say that.

Rights.

I have rights.

Reaching for a cigarette, he waited fully thirty or forty seconds
before he lighted it—holding the lighter in his drooping hand and the

cigarette dangling from his lips. Then he flicked the wheel and sprung the flame and took one deep and long inhalation.

Lying back and setting the golden lighter aside, he lay on the bed and thought again about his brother's children. Allison. Moira. Carol.

And his rights.

2

There were three Webster cottages—one for each of the Webster children. They were clustered on a promontory of wooded land on Lake Joseph, in the Muskoka area north of Toronto—cottage country. The Websters had owned the promontory since the 1890s.

The tradition of summer cottages had been a part of Canadian culture since late in the nineteenth century—and while the tradition was basically middle class, the upper-middle class to which the Websters belonged tended to populate areas, such as Muskoka, where their wealth protected them from encroachment. It was true that few sites existed which did not look out one way or the other at someone else's cottage—but none of the cottages was crowded by the walls of another. Stands of trees and tall-grass meadows were spread between them and, in the Websters' case, large outcroppings of rock formed barriers that guaranteed them a maximum of privacy. Muskoka is situated at the southern rim of the great Canadian Shield—and the rock in question was rust in colour and covered with green and red lichen. Its smooth, large shapes gave rise to such landmark names as *Elephant's Back* and *Giant's Shoulder.*

It had long been the custom in this society to open cottages—and have the first swim—on Victoria Day—which always falls on a long weekend towards the end of May. Families gathered and made the trek by car—an event that gave rise to Friday-night and Monday-afternoon traffic jams that had also become a tradition. On arrival, dogs and children spilled out over the landscape, while exhausted parents unpacked the cars and started the evening meal.

Through the winter, the Websters—like many others—hired local residents to act as caretakers. Consequently, every spring, beds would be made up, furniture stripped of its dust covers, deck-chairs set out and all the houses aired with pine-scented breezes. Most of the local cottages, having been constructed at the turn of the century, were made of wood—most often cedar. Wide plank porches fronted these houses under roofs and each had a screened-in section where meals were eaten and rainy afternoons were given over to board games and quizzes.

Hammocks sprouted between the trees—canoes and rowboats were pulled from their winter trestles—and motorboats and outboards made the first waves of the season.

This year, the weather had been exquisite. A week-long, out-of-season heat wave had made the swimming a joy and lying in the sun—in spite of the UV factor—an obligation. A person could not return from the cottage without the year's first layer of tan. It was *de rigueur*.

The senior Websters' lives had been prime examples of the whims of fortune. Each had been born with money—each had been profligate. Too much was spent on trappings—too much invested in foolish speculation. Their children were sent to private schools—John and Ben to St Andrew's College and Ruth to Bishop Strachan. In London, the whole Webster clan would stop at Claridges—in Paris at the George V—in New York at the Plaza. Even when totally broke, they lived this way. By the time the children were ready to take their place in the world, there was nothing left. The great house was sold, the great cars dispersed and the paintings auctioned. Mary Webster was persuaded to give up her heirloom jewellery in order that Ben could impress Peggy Wylie. Every last precious thing was sacrificed—from Persian rugs to Meissen china—in order to provide the children with one more token of wealth and station—a pair of shoes—a pinstripe suit—a hair-do from Leonardo's. The one thing never released from their grip was the trio of Muskoka cottages. They were sacrosanct.

Slowly, the children's marriages fell into place, and with them, the trappings of new wealth—*nibblings*, as Mary Webster had called them. Ben married Peggy Wylie. John married Susan Bongard. Ruth married Howard Marks.

When he died, Oliver Webster had been in financial disgrace and limbo. But when his will was read, it was discovered that a fortune had been salted away and set aside in Switzerland, which only his death could protect from creditors. Two million dollars. *For those of you who will wonder why we suffered the absence of this money while I lived,* Oliver had written to his heirs, *I have only this to say: better late than never, better now than then.*

Two years after probate, the will offered up its cash. One year after that, Mary Webster died. More dividends.

A silence fell.

And then, the disasters began again.

Ben and Peggy Webster were childless and, by all appearances, they meant to stay that way. Given Peggy's reserve, it was not a subject she was willing to discuss. She had married into a family of unlikely wealth and sinister power (sinister was Olivia's word for it) and, in spite of her devotion to tradition, she had not fulfilled the traditional demand of such a marriage—the farrowing of offspring. There should be *at least two*—and more would be welcome. Children were marriage-fodder—a means to more power. Ben Webster's brother, John, and their sister, Ruth, had parlayed their genes into seven progeny—three girls to John and four boys to Ruth.

Ruth had married a man whose suicide had rocked the Webster family. Howard Marks had leapt from the Glen Road Bridge with a rope around his neck. He hung there under the bridge for a week before his body was discovered. A newspaper then revealed that Howard Marks had been leading a double life and was suffering, at the time of his death, from AIDS. Ruth did not remarry and never returned to society. She lived in seclusion in Nassau. The Marks boys were sent to schools in Switzerland in order to escape the scandal of their father's demise. The name of Howard Marks was never mentioned again in Webster circles. His double life became a double death.

The Marks children still returned each summer to their mother's cottage, where they took up residence with their father's sister, Hilda. Hilda Marks had never married, but was devoted to the children. This inheritance from her brother was a dream come true.

Still, it had always seemed to Olivia that her sister Peggy mourned the lack of children—and she suspected the fault lay in Ben. Ben Webster had been a great womanizer before his marriage—great to the extent that Peggy had feared she would be the victim of much infidelity. No other woman had appeared on the horizon, however, and Peggy had stopped talking about Ben's philandering as soon as they were married. Her reticence where private matters were concerned became almost legendary. It was not that she was cold—it was just that she seemed to have no temperature at all. Someone had said of her: *Peggy died at birth.* However unkind this comment had been, Olivia could not deny its authority. The speaker had been Eloise Wylie, their mother.

Death at birth was a common Wylie experience—or so it seemed to Olivia Price. Jar babies. Peggy. And the child Olivia carried herself—soon to be, she was now quite certain, a victim of abortion. She no longer cared that the child—or *Voice*, as she called it—was past the age when aborting it would be considered safe or proper. Four months plus. Too late. But never too late from Olivia's point of view. If only she could pass the child to Peggy. *A high-thrown ball to a wide receiver. End run. Touchdown!*

Peggy had once loved Ben. In a guarded way—carefully. The boy-man image had been appealing in its fashion. He had been generous to her—kind and thoughtful—considerate. It seemed, for a while, that he had really wanted her to be happy. He gave her leeway with the house—providing the money for its restoration and furnishings without a word of complaint—without a single question. He was proud of what she accomplished—praised her for it—showed the house off: *look what Peggy's done!* He also gave her credit for his own reformation.

She had been patient with him. She had forgiven his indiscretions, no matter what they were—losses of money—his loyalty to men who were obviously crooks—his vanity—his violence—his childlike flamboyance. His connivance with his brother, John, to damage the careers of one or two businessmen downtown who once had slighted him; men who had disparaged Ben because he had wanted what they had wanted and they had got it and he had not. Ben had a schoolboy's sense of vengeance, which Peggy had curbed by reminding him that vengeance was a waste of time, when you wreak it on men who would soon enough wreck themselves, if you left them to it. She taught him the value of the redistribution of energies—drawing him away from the uglier aspects of his behaviour and urging him to concentrate on behaviour that would bring him respect and admiration: his sense of generosity—his delight in her own happiness. *Spread it around to others,* she told him—smiling when she said it. Confidence was all he lacked, she had decided. Ben's was a classic case of bravura masking insecurity. The boy who had used his father's motorcars to taxi his schoolmates for a fee had been—in fact—a boy who was ashamed of his father's failures and terrified by the prospect of poverty and loss of face.

This way, Peggy came also to understand Ben's relationships with women. Basically he was emotionally immature—nothing more and nothing less. Adults do not make demands of others—they make demands of themselves.

For a while, Ben and Peggy had succeeded in living this way almost in harmony. As Ben *grew up,* Peggy *loosened up.* (That was Olivia's version.) They could be seen at public functions actually laughing together—arms linked—outgoing—trusted—trusting—a couple with whom you wanted to be friends.

Then it ended. Ben wanted more. Peggy wanted less. One advanced—the other retreated. The Ben who had been subverted returned for an encore. In business, he became, yet again, the bully in the schoolyard—the king come back from exile, rallying his supporters, thumbing his nose at his enemies—taunting them, taking up arms against them—reclaiming his territory. In his private life, he returned to the sports field—took up, exclusively, the company of men—began to trim and flex his muscles—to look at himself excessively in the mirror. Only Peggy knew the cause of all this—and she never spoke of it to anyone. Certainly not to Olivia, the favoured sister who once had received all her secrets.

The cause had been Ben's commencement of an affair with a woman ten years his junior. But the *commencement* of this affair was as far as Ben had got. The woman had turned him down at the bedroom door. She had laughed at him, apparently, and in effect had said to him: *you must be joking!* Ben had returned from this shock to his pride in a state of rage that had been the most frightening spectacle of loss of control that Peggy had ever witnessed. It was then that, running from his presence, she had fallen on the ice and suffered the broken leg that everyone was told had been the result of a *skiing accident.*

As sisters, the Wylie girls had been—and were—as different one from the other as sisters could be. Each had chosen a totally different route through life—as travellers might who came to a crossroads where three directions are offered. Each of the three ways was taken—and the sisters turned back from time to time only to wave to one another—or to call out one another's names. Amy, who was youngest, had gone the furthest distance—Olivia, the second furthest. But Peggy had barely gone any distance at all. There she was—just around the corner from where she had begun—a Wylie daughter—a Webster wife.

Peggy usually enjoyed her times at the cottage, but this year regretted Shirley Shapiro's absence. She had never been fond, on the other hand, of Shirley's husband. *He's disturbed,* she told Ben. *There's something funny about his ideas. He's too acquiescent—too accommodating. If selling his mother was a condition for promotion, he'd sell her. He's also secretive—furtive—wanting something he never describes...*

Ben thought differently. Not that he had any great liking for Shapiro. But, in his opinion, Shirley was a slut...

Peggy said: "you weren't a slut, of course, when you brought down every woman in your path."

"Men aren't sluts," said Ben. "They can't be—unless they're homos."

"Oh?" said Peggy. "That's interesting."

They were seated on the screened-in porch. It was the evening of the swimming incident—of the Shapiro boy's display, which Ben had not mentioned to Peggy. They were drinking vodka martinis, to which Ben was partial. Peggy could not care less what she drank, as long as it wasn't overly bitter.

"I'm fascinated about your claim that men can't be sluts," she said.

"Except homos," Ben chuckled.

"Explain."

"A slut spreads her legs, Peg. Simple as that."

"Thank you," said Peggy. "Charming."

"And the wider she spreads 'em, the more of a slut she is."

Peggy looked away.

"*Wide, wet and weady!*" said Ben—in a sibilant, supposedly girlish voice.

"For heaven's sake, Ben. Clean up your act. I didn't ask for this kind of conversation."

"Sorry. Forgot. You're a lady."

"I'm not sure you ever knew it."

They fell silent. The old war started so easily.

Peggy said: "why is Shirley Shapiro a slut? Given what you've just said."

"Ran off with a kid half her age—that's why. Spread her legs for the youth of the world, that's why. Took one look at him and wet her pants. That's why."

He was angry. That was standard where sex was concerned.

Peggy said: "he's not half her age. He's over thirty. And he's decent. Not what you're describing at all."

"Have it your way."

"Thank you," said Peggy. "I will. I prefer the truth."

Ben stood up. "Want any more?"

"If you mean another martini—yes. If you mean any more of this conversation—no."

Ben did not reply. He took her glass and went back into the cottage.

Peggy looked down at the dock and out towards the point. It had been so lovely here, once. Now, the view itself remained and would survive. But her view of it would not. Its placidity was being destroyed by her own agitation.

How did I get here? she thought. *How did I get to this moment?*

3

Ever since her contretemps with Marlow concerning Peter Rabbit's shoes, Lilah had gone into a private mode. This was dangerous, as Marlow knew—now that he realized just what her condition was. It could drive her back to her demons—back to her visions. She was spending more and more time in her own quarters. Sometimes, returning from the Parkin, he would find the door between their kitchens closed—and once, he found it locked.

He wondered what she was doing in there and he would try to entice her out—but she would not come. Fam came and went by another route—out through Marlow's window, in through Lilah's door. Grendel, who had come to expect Lilah's hand to greet him, lay more and more asleep in a kind of mourning.

May was now in its final week. Lilah's sullen version of spring cleaning was to dust and realign her books on their shelves—and to air the blankets from the baby buggy. These, she spread on her window-sill. In the yard, a few scrawny flowers had begun to make their appearance— hyacinths, scilla, primroses—all in a state of shock from the chemicals descending over the city—and from the lack, this past week, of rain.

The high board fence between the yard and the lane yielded a view of prowling cats and occasional dashing squirrels. Beyond it, Mrs Akhami could be seen day and night in her kitchen—*when was she ever out of it?*—cutting, slicing, stirring, sifting.

Lilah had now been twice to Mavis Delaney for Modecate in the past five weeks. She was due to go again—but the thought of the journey depressed her. She wanted to avoid the streets, where everything she loved was threatened by D-Squad activities. The guttered corpses of birds were everywhere. Moonmen were also everywhere—and Leatherheads. Best to stay put. If she felt an episode approaching, she could always take a vitamin pill—an Infratil—a Cogentin—a dream pill...

Most of Lilah's books were paperbacks—not just because they were cheaper, but because they were handier—more practical. And she liked the covers: Penguins, mostly, with their haunting, period images— Marlow's river steamer—Heathcliff's moors; and the New Canadian Library with its reproductions of paintings—also Canadian. Susanna Moodie's pioneer roads, the pioneer clearing of trees. *Oh, world without books—what would you be?* Lilah did not dare to think. Her world would have no population at all, if someone had not put it there with pens.

When Lilah had last gone down for her shot, Susanna Moodie had failed to materialize at the Queen Street Mental Health Centre. But Lilah had seen the groundhog with her young, up from her burrow and browsing on the grass. Two young. Only two, from a beast whose litters in ordinary times would have numbered four or five.

Roughing It in the Bush. Life in the Clearings. Wild Animals I Have Known, War and Peace, Madame Bovary... These were all of a similar height. Lilah fingered them into place, having kissed each one.

Moby Dick. Don Quixote. Pride and Prejudice. Death in Venice... She never put them in order. There would never be order on her shelves again, since the Rosedale Public Library had burned to the ground. Her inner eye could no longer seek for titles that way. Somehow, *order* had put them in jeopardy. It had been the cause of her own disarray. The obsessive precision that set authors out in alphabetical order had sent Lila racing up and down the aisles that fiery night in futile pursuit of her favourite titles—all of them in flames, impossible to save. Now, she made saveable sets of miscellaneous titles—grabbable, throwable, heavable, tossable sets that defied the alphabet—but preserved the language.

Lilah paused.

Beowulf.

Grendel.

The book fell open on the floor—as Lilah would say—entirely of its own accord. *I had nothing to do with this.*

On the open page she read:

In the black night, then, came gliding the walker in darkness...from the moor, then, under the mist hills, Grendel came walking, wearing God's anger...

Lilah could hear him, snuffling at the kitchen door.

Come bring me through.

Lilah went down the hall, unlocked and pushed the door wide.

Grendel was there, head down, tail beating low against the furniture, his backbone undulating, his opaque, sea otter's eyes glancing up at Lilah for approval. He was in the prime of life but had been to the wars on more than one occasion. His ears had been torn and his muzzle had been slashed and his haunches bore the evidence of two Alsatians having caught him in their jaws on Hawthorne Street in Cambridge, Massachusetts. Grendel was a pale, honey-coloured Labrador and he slept each night on a small settee at the foot of Marlow's bed. He wore a leather collar. Red.

In his mouth he held a soup bone brought for him from the butcher's by Marlow, who bought the bones by the bag and kept them in the freezer.

Lilah looked at the dog for evidence of God's anger. There was none—*unless the bone itself...*

"Come through," she said.

He did—and this was the first of the placable gestures made from either side of the divided house. Lilah, returning to her books, felt less oppressed. An open door, after all, lets in the air.

Grendel followed her, lay on the floor and dropped his bone on the open copy of *Beowulf.*

"That's right," said Lilah. "The cave you shared with your mother was full of bones."

Grendel wagged his tail, took the bone between his jaws and began to gnaw on it with the side of his head turned down to the floor for support.

Lilah picked up the book and gave it a swipe with her sleeve. She noted the residue of spittle Grendel had left on the page.

Marlow had told the story of Grendel's mother and her savage brood and her savage death. She had lived in the home of a well-known lawyer named McCarthy, and McCarthy had trained her to become a guard dog. Thinking to have an endless supply of beasts with frenzied stamina and killer jaws, he had refused to have her spayed. Thus, for a while, McCarthy had Grendel's mother and four of her offspring guarding his house and offices. That time ended after the dogs had attacked a woman and mangled a child. Then, it was decreed that they all be destroyed. This, in due time, was done—but not before Grendel was born and left without a parent. Marlow found him, six months old, in a death-row cage at the Toronto Humane Society, doomed by his mother's history. Marlow, however, had sympathy for monsters. The mad were deemed *monsters*—maligned and harried. He decided he would set things right, and took the dog home. Seeing in the gentle eyes and soft honey colour a nature that was anything but monstrous—and in honour of all who are wrongly judged—Marlow named him Grendel.

Lilah approved of this story, finding in Marlow's new ending a signal that to be deemed unacceptable is not to be doomed.

4

Marlow was making grilled cheese sandwiches—a favourite. The secret—aside from the Forfar Extra Old Cheddar—was in using olive oil, which gave a warm Mediterranean innuendo to the flavour of the toast. He had also prepared a salad of Boston lettuce and tomato slices with a classic dressing—vinaigrette augmented with a single teaspoon of lemon juice. Charlie liked the balance of tartness to lay against the cheese on his palate. And with all of this—a bottle of Merlot. And before it—a clouded glass of Ricard—and precisely three cigarettes. Matinée Extra Mild Slims. Since returning from Harvard, he could not imagine how he had smoked American cigarettes for five years— and lived.

Routine—discipline—patterns would save him. *Say it again, Charlie,* he would say to himself. *Routine, discipline—patterns.* Coming home to Toronto had been more traumatic than he had imagined it would be. The tensions at the Parkin were completely unexpected. And, of course, the disaster of Gatz and Emma.

As for his old friend, Austin Purvis—what on earth was happening there? The anguish in the man was palpable. Distracted—driven—sometimes even speechless, as if he had no words to explain what the problem was. And melancholy as if he had discovered life was ending, or...

Marlow lighted the second of his cigarettes. Then he got up and turned on the gas. The smell of the cheese was tantalizing and pleasing. It soothed him, as he stood there, pressing a plate on the sandwiches so they would brown more evenly.

This was the joy of weekends. You got to have your own way with time. You made your own rules—and broke them. Or someone else—intruding—broke them for you.

All at once, there was a voice in the yard behind the house—and Grendel was barking.

"Hello! Hello! Hello in there! Hello!"

It was a woman's voice—not panic-stricken, merely persistent.

Marlow went to the door and opened it. Beyond the screen, the evening was blooming just as if it had grown in one of his flower beds.

"Hello? Is someone there?" the voice asked.

"Yes. But where are you?"

"I'm at your gate—on the far side, in the lane."

It was Lilah who insisted the gate be kept locked. *Heathcliff might return.* The first thing she always did in the morning was unlock her back door and check the garden gate—procedures that were reversed at nightfall.

Now, Marlow pushed out through the screen door and let it slam behind him. This set off another round of barking from Grendel, who was in the yard. *How had he got in the yard?* When Marlow reached the gate and had turned the lock and withdrawn the bolt, he said: "you should know I'm still in my robe and slippers. It's Sunday. I apologize."

Grendel came over and stood beside him, damp and smelling of freshly dug earth—holding something cold and fetid in his mouth. Marlow could feel the dog's tail slapping against his calves.

He pulled the gate open and stood to one side.

"Thank you," said a shape that looked for all the world like a fugitive from *The Playboy of the Western World*—a shawl drawn over its head and held in place at the neck by one fisted hand. He could not quite see the woman's face. "I'm looking for my cat," she said.

"Do please come in," said Marlow—who had become a beacon for mosquitos. "Don't mind the dog. He's harmless—except to other dogs."

He led the way towards the kitchen door—noting that Lilah had peeked out and then withdrawn from her own kitchen window.

Grendel followed with a large, decaying glove—a glove so large it must have been a giant's. Once inside, Marlow turned to look at his visitor.

A woman with luminous eyes—the largest Marlow had ever seen—revealed herself by drawing her woollen shawl aside. A mass of entangled red hair surrounded a round and almost mischievous face—almost so because of the way it presented itself to the light. There was something impertinent and challenging in the way this was done—the whole head tilted, the face itself a moonful of possibilities.

He recognized her instantly.

"My name is Amy Wylie," she said.

"I know," said Marlow—and smiled.

"You do?" she said, stepping back—adjusting the tilt of her face—looking at him, now, directly.

"Yes," said Marlow. "I've read your work. I give it to my patients."

"We've never met," she said. "I live up there through the lanes a block or two—on Boswell." She made a vague gesture, indicating the world beyond the door.

Amy Wylie was a poet—and a good one; sometimes extraordinary. She was in her thirties now, but Marlow had first encountered her when she was in her early twenties and still a student. She had staged, in those days, a hunger strike for endangered species—setting up a tent in the wolf compound of the Metro Zoo, where fellow students kept her alive with orange juice and tea during a three-week siege. In the end, she was arrested and was forcibly hospitalized. Marlow had been called in then, to make an assessment of her mental state. He had also encountered her eight years later when she had been a patient in the Queen Street Mental Health Centre. He did not, however, like to say he remembered her there. Amy Wylie obviously did not remember meeting him in either circumstance.

"Would you like a cup of tea?" he asked. She looked as if she had been starving herself again.

"I'd like a drink," she said. She had cast the shawl aside and he saw that she wore a torn woollen cardigan over a pale cotton dress, the collar of which sat up, though askew. He wondered why—in this heat wave—she wore a sweater. The shawl she explained with the single word *mosquitos*, as she threw it down.

"Of course," said Marlow—and he walked to the counter. "I was having a glass of red, myself. Would that do?"

"Yes," she said. "Nicely."

She was also wearing tall grey work socks and running shoes. The work socks were the kind that kept you warm in winter but always made you itch. They also had red tops. Marlow had worn their counterparts years before in the days of his youth when he'd marched up over the mountains and through the wilderness of the Yukon.

"Do I smell cheese?" Amy asked.

"You do. And if you'd care to join me—there are two toasted sandwiches there—just made."

"Thank you," she said, and drew a hand-rolled cigarette from a flat tin box that squealed as she opened it. "The lid sticks," she said.

Marlow made room for her at the table—brushing some magazines aside and setting out another plate and another paper napkin. "Sit," he said—and gave her the glass of wine.

She drank the wine almost straight down—and, seeing this, Marlow set the bottle on the table. She lighted her cigarette with a shaking hand—and poured a second glass. This time, she drank it more slowly.

"So—you've lost your cat," Marlow said, sitting down across from her—pushing the ashtray in her direction.

"Yes," she said. She was looking around the room, candidly snooping for helpful information—something belonging to a wife—something belonging to the children he must have—a man his age, in a house this large.

"The cat's name is Wormwood," she told him. "Perhaps you've heard me calling him..."

Marlow shook his head.

"Are you warm enough?" he asked, referring to the mysterious sweater.

"I'm never warm enough," she said.

"I see," said Marlow.

"It is always freezing where I live. I don't have any heat, you see—and the house keeps chilled till July. It's because I'm afraid of fire. I'm also poor—though I choose to be."

Her candour was not the least bit dramatized. When she said *I'm also poor,* she might as well have been telling him her weight or height or the colour of her hair. It was just another statistic.

Marlow stood up and got the cheese sandwiches—sorry he would now have only one for himself—and laid them out on the plates. "Would you like a pickle with that?" he asked.

"I would, yes," she said.

Marlow got the pickles—Polish dills—out of the refrigerator and opened them and put them on the table with a fork beside them. Amy was watching him—smoking her cigarette and holding it as Europeans do between her thumb and index finger—pinching it in the process, making it bulge at one end, flatten at the other.

"Has Wormwood been missing for long?" Marlow asked, sitting down.

"Weeks," she said. "He's probably dead—but I can't bear to admit that, so I go out looking for him—calling. Red," she added. "He's a red-head, like me."

"Had he been with you long?"

"Three years. Four. Yes."

"There is a cat who turned up here. But she isn't red. She's grey."

"That would be Gigi," Amy told him.

"Yours?"

"No. An alley cat. I used to feed her when I was still feeding cats. Grey all over—somewhat aloof?"

"A trifle more than somewhat," Marlow laughed.

"You give them a home?"

"Who?"

"Cats. Wild ones. Alley cats."

"No. Just the one."

"Take more than one," said Amy. "Take all you can. Get them off my back." She reached for her sandwich. "Fill up the house with cats. It will help save the birds."

Marlow gave a tentative smile. "You don't like cats?" he said.

"I didn't say that. Wormwood has been my friend for a very long time. I love him. But the alley cats are killing birds because no one will feed them. I mean that no one will feed the cats. Or the birds. It's against the law."

"Yes," said Marlow. "I know."

"Someone has to save them," said Amy.

"Who? The cats?"

"Of course, the cats. They're in danger. So are the birds."

Her eyes flashed over her last bit of sandwich.

"I don't quite know what you mean by *save the cats*," said Marlow. "Save them from what?"

"Extinction."

"Oh." He was dubious. "I see."

"Somebody's trying to kill all the animals," said Amy. "Birds. Dogs. Cats. All of them."

Marlow did not respond. He knew as well as anyone did about the spraying of the birds. But *dogs, cats, all the animals?* Amy Wylie's vehemence was startling and he recognized it at once. It was the vehemence of someone out of touch with reason—the vehemence of someone obsessed.

"I've found two dogs, three cats—a squirrel and a rabbit out there," she said. "In the laneways—dead. Some of them shot—some of them strangled. Thrown down. No one believes me, but it's true. Seven animals. Dead. And I found them all in the last week."

"But who do you think would do such a thing?"

"Someone. Anyone. D-Squads. Everyone," she said. Her voice had flattened. "No one wants animals any more. They kill them all the time. The way they kill the birds. They want the world entirely for human beings. It's quite deliberate."

"I see."

"Do you think you could open another bottle of wine?"

"I'd be delighted," said Marlow, and did so.

Amy fell silent. Her tin box of cigarettes made a squeal again, but that was the only sound aside from Marlow's struggle with the cork. He was playing, to some degree, for time. And the return of memory. What had it been, he wanted to recall, that had caused Amy Wylie to be kept in the wards of the Queen Street Mental Health Centre? Another hunger strike? He could see her now quite clearly in his mind, tied into a restraining device—looking up at him blank-eyed and yelling. But the yelling in his memory was inarticulate. Nothing could be conjured of any cause.

The cork popped.

"There," he said—and put the bottle on the table.

"You've seen all the dead birds, I suppose," said Amy.

"Yes," said Charlie. "Those I've seen."

"Dead birds. Dead animals," she said, as Marlow filled her glass. "And you think," she said, as she raised it to her lips, "there isn't a reason?"

"Of course there's a reason, so far as the birds are concerned. Sturnusemia," said Marlow. "But..."

"Don't say *but*," said Amy. "I know very well who you are, Doctor Marlow—you're a psychiatrist, and you have no right to step aside and say *but*. *But* is for idiots and infidels."

Marlow looked down at his hands. He could not endure her gaze. It was entirely unnerving. He poured himself a glass of wine. *All along, she's known who I am and didn't say so.* "How did you know," he asked, "who I am—and what I do?"

"I know the name of every person who lives along this laneway. All the laneways. I can name you every one—except their wives and husbands. Are you married, Doctor Marlow?"

Marlow shook his head.

Amy said: "I solicit for aid. Not for me, of course. I need nothing. But the animals—the birds need us all. And the cats."

"How many cats do you have?" he asked. "Besides Wormwood."

"None. It's the birds I have. Hundreds. That's why I'm asking you to take on the cats. And someone else the dogs. And someone else the squirrels—someone else the rabbits. Someone else..."

Marlow waited.

Amy had faltered—could find no words. Her lips moved, but there was no sound.

Then: "I feed them every day," she said.

"You do."

"Yes. The birds. At least, I try to. Some days..." She drifted off again, away from him.

"Yes?"

"Some days..."

Marlow watched. A cigarette was burning between her fingers. She seemed not even to know it was there.

"Some days, I can't get out," she said. "The door gets jammed."

"The door gets jammed," Marlow repeated. He was trying to keep her going until she had reached some part of her story he would recognize—a landmark or a name that would mark her condition.

"There's someone, you see, who's trying to stop me."

"Oh."

"Don't say *oh* like that. It sounds as if you don't believe me." She pushed away the plate beside her elbow and poured herself another glass of wine. "I can't understand—I never have been able to understand—why other people don't understand. If your door is jammed and you haven't jammed it yourself, then someone else must have done it. Wouldn't you say so? What else could it be, besides another person. The wind couldn't do it."

"No."

"A dog couldn't do it."

"No."

"A cat couldn't do it. A dog and a cat want in, not to be locked out."

"True."

"Only a person could do it."

"Yes."

"Who?"

"I don't know."

"Do you have a real cigarette?" she asked. "I would like a real cigarette."

"Yes. Here..."

Marlow pushed his packet across the table. Amy fished for one, but she seemed, for a moment, incapacitated. Her fingers couldn't manage the packaging—the pushing up and the taking of an individual cigarette. Marlow did it for her and she bent in carefully over his proffered lighter and pulled her hair to one side, avoiding the flame. Fear of fire. A sign. And not the only one. The rest of her gestures were truncated jabs— unfinished reachings. The glass could be got to her lips—but that was all; the glass and the cigarette and the bending forward and the leaning back. *Clearly,* Marlow thought, as he watched her, *these are paranoid-schizo signs—the jerkiness—the brevity of focus—the stilted speech... Lilah, but in worse shape.* He wondered when Amy had last seen a doctor.

"Did I bring a bag?" she said.

Marlow said: "no."

"I always have a bag," she said.

"A purse, you mean?"

"A bag. With food."

"You might have left it by the gate."

"No. I wouldn't do that."

"Perhaps you forgot to bring it. You were looking for Wormwood, after all."

"I think I should go." She stood up.

Even though he wanted his privacy, the suddenness of her decision to leave surprised him. He had thought she would stay with him longer. She was nervous now—agitated. A certain look had come into her eyes.

"Is there something I can do for you?" he asked.

"No," she said. "No. Just... No."

She was looking around the kitchen, as if she expected Wormwood to be sitting there—or an object, perhaps imagined to have been mis- placed. The phantom bag? Marlow would have recognized the signs if he had known more about her immediate history. Later, he would realize that, when she had risen distracted from her chair, it was the first in a sequence of serial gestures which now began to unfold with increasing precision.

Amy crossed to the cupboards that ranged beneath the sink and its counters. She dropped to her knees and opened them one by one. "No—" she said—"no—" she said. "No," as each one failed to reveal whatever it was she was looking for.

Then she stood up.

Marlow stepped back and watched.

Amy went around behind the gas stove, which sat more or less in the middle of the room, and began to open and close the cupboards that were clustered there.

"No—" she said—"no—" she said—"no...."

Marlow closed his eyes and prayed. *Don't let this spread to the rest of the house,* he was thinking. *Don't let her get to the cupboards in the dining-room...all that glassware.*

Then she was coming around the stove towards him.

"I want a bag," she said.

Bag.

Marlow handed her a plastic shopping bag. *Wong's!* it shouted—red on white. Amy went around again behind the stove and he could hear her rummaging and pushing things about. This, too, was Lilah-like—looking for *The Tale of Peter Rabbit.*

He followed without haste to see what she was doing. He wanted to speak her name—but he knew he mustn't. Whatever this was, it was not an event that would brook interruption.

Amy was throwing cans of Campbell's tomato soup into the bag—like painted hand grenades. *Bam! Bam! Bam!* Her hair had fallen completely over her face—and her kneeling figure resembled that of a person pulling frantically at something stuck in the ground.

"Bag," she said yet again—and her hand went out towards him.

Marlow handed her a second shopping bag. *Wong's.* Amy took it and began to fill it with corn flakes boxes and Harvest Crunch boxes and bags of granola.

At last, she stood up, completely out of breath. She pushed her hair from her face and ran the back of her wrist across her mouth. She looked from side to side and failed to see him, so it seemed.

"I came with something," she said. She spoke with perfect clarity—but not to Marlow.

He crossed the room to the chair onto which she had thrown her shawl and he picked it up and held it out in her direction.

Grendel—ignoring the giant's glove—had watched Amy's rummaging from a sitting position. It seemed that people dug for their bones in the strangest places.

Amy now had nothing left to say. She made a move for the door and Marlow opened it. As she lifted up the shawl to place it over her head, the bag of soup cans thumped against the wall and chipped the plaster.

Never mind, he thought, *it's done.*

Amy was moving with an almost hypnotic sense of direction—pulled magnetically out towards the gate. The light from the door broke through the dusk to let her pass. Marlow watched her fumbling with the latch and went down the walk to help her—but before he got there, she had managed to solve the puzzle and was gone.

"Miss Wylie?" he whispered. He didn't want to call. It seemed, some-how, unseemly.

He spoke her name once more, out loud—*Amy Wylie*—but there was no reply. Listening, he could hear the sound of her footsteps as she moved away to the west, where the laneway met with others northward bound—the ones that would take her home to Boswell Avenue. The yards and gardens along her route seemed to be lapping at the high board fence that ran from end to end of this rutted thoroughfare for garbage trucks and cats and crazy poets. Marlow turned around and closed his gate and started back towards the house. Lilah, again, was watching from her window, but this time she did not retreat.

Then it was that Marlow heard the first of the sounds that stopped him dead in his tracks. It was not, he thought, a human sound—though he knew it was a voice. Something was being strangled.

He turned towards the gate. The wailing voice rose up against what-ever it was that wanted it to stop. A pang of incomprehensible horror caught at Marlow's bowels. He had never heard a thing being killed before with such exquisite clarity. The sound of it came in spirals up whatever throat was there—and fought against the silence being demanded of it.

I have to move. I must, Marlow thought.

At last, he did.

By the gate, he was caught by the final cry. Not a scream—for a scream goes on forever, once begun. This was a high-pitched shriek—and then it stopped.

He moved through increasing darkness towards the silence.

It did not take long before he fell. It was inevitable. He put out his hand in the dust. There was a dead cat—still caught in rigor mortis. *Oh God.* Amy Wylie had been right. He got up, stumbling forward—and pulled his robe around him.

"Amy?" he said. "Where are you? Are you...there?"

This time, he did not fall. Reason had prepared him and cautioned him accordingly. She was on the ground and thrashing—lying on her back, convulsing. Her hands had gone so deep into the earth that Marlow had to pull them out and lock them in place by gripping her wrists and holding them fast against her sides.

She was having a seizure—epileptic—alcoholic—drug-induced—he could not tell. But he knew, at least, that she was not dead.

Marlow wondered briefly why Lilah—who had been watching—did not appear. He decided that, given her own condition, the events in the laneway would be too alarming for her to bear.

It was Mrs Akhami who heard him call for help.

"Who is there, please?" she said from beyond the fence in her yard.

"Charlie Marlow. I live across the lane."

Mrs Akhami was standing behind her gate, refusing to open it.

"There has been a murdering?" she asked. "A dying of someone?"

Marlow explained that a woman had been taken ill. *Would Mrs Akhami telephone the police and ask them to send an ambulance?*

"The woman is alive?"

"Yes."

"Then ambulate her into your house."

"I can't do that," said Marlow. "She mustn't be moved until help arrives."

Mrs Akhami went up her walk and Marlow could hear her muttering. Then her door was opened—and closed.

While he waited, he realized that Amy must be kept as warm as possible. He removed his bathrobe and spread it over her—loosening her hands and making sure she was not in danger of swallowing her tongue. He also adjusted the angle of her head. It had been thrown back so far by the force of the convulsions that her forehead had made an imprint in the dust. He collected the scattered remnants of the bag of soup and the bag of cereals. He found the contents easily enough; the soup cans were like stones against his toes. He then hunkered down to wait beside Amy. His white pyjamas, once immaculate, were blotched with filth and the blood that Amy had drawn when her fingernails had found him during her spasms.

He wanted not to be there. It seemed a dreadful place, locked as it was in the falling darkness, streaked with shafts of window-light—and the dead, blank baffle of universal silence. Even the distant traffic noise was muffled—as drums were muffled in piles of lamb's wool.

Then he heard a sound that could only be one thing.

A cat jumped down from the roof of Mrs Akhami's garage.

It spoke. And Marlow answered.

"Wormwood?"

Yes.

A large red cat—with mangled ears and tangled fur—came out of the dark, lay down by Amy's side and began to purr.

In the end, Marlow had to lead the way on foot, while the ambulance that had finally arrived followed him into a half-dozen garbage cans, a hydro pole and someone's open gate. He fell so often and stumbled so often into things he couldn't see that he thought he was going to have to ask the ambulance attendants to take him with them to the emergency ward.

Nonetheless, he found the way back to where Mrs Akhami—her sari drawn up over her hair—waited for them with a lantern. She stood beside Amy, who by then had lapsed into a coma. Wormwood, too, stood guard and had to be forcibly removed. He bit Marlow twice. Marlow said: *damn you!* and put the cat back on his roof.

He told the driver to take Amy over to the Parkin Institute, where she would receive the care she needed. There was nothing else to be done for her until she had received some medical attention. She must be made to live.

Marlow gave his name as a reference and told the attendants that Amy had once been a patient at Queen Street. Her history would be there on file. He could not remember who her doctor had been. That was all too long ago—and now was immaterial.

They wrapped her in blankets and strapped her to the trolley and closed her inside and drove her away. They went with red lights flashing—a movable encephalograph. It was sad for Marlow—standing there with grudging Mrs Akhami—watching the lights fade away like that. The dark into which they passed was much like Amy's state of mind and Marlow wished its symbolism was not so blatant.

One of her poems ended:

and so we parted;
you to forget
and me
to be forgotten.

These lines had been addressed to her mind.

5

Kurtz's missing envelope was not unlike a lost mind. Its contents, if read, would make little sense to anyone but the man who had written them—and while Kurtz went one way in search of the envelope, it went another in search of him.

As happens with all missing objects, the owner's need for them increases as time goes by and anxiety grows. Kurtz, by the end of May, could no longer remember precisely what had been committed to paper. He was more and more alarmed by the thought of what might be written there.

No one would understand it, of course. But...

Everyone would understand it.

It was, after all, his personal response to various sources of research—and he knew his own methods of deduction well enough to realize that, in this instance especially, the annotations—if read by strangers—could be dangerous to him. And even more dangerous if read by the wrong acquaintances. Austin Purvis, for instance—or the Farjeon woman. Damn them.

The envelope and its contents—at first so casually missed—were turning, for Kurtz, into a booby trap waiting to explode. Even if held in someone else's hands, the messages, once read, would detonate under Kurtz. He—not the finder—would be the victim.

Manipulation of personality.

These words he recalled. He could see them set out onto the page and underlined. *Manipulation of intellect. Manipulation of perception. Manipulation of will...*

More. There was more.

But what?

Weeks, he had worked on it. Months. His project.

Docile and open to suggestion.

That he remembered.

Pages and pages of it.

What?

He went to the Metro Library. *Had anyone found an envelope?*

No.

(Someone had, but the Information Desk failed to notice it beneath everything else in the Lost and Found bin.)

He went to the Science Library.

Had anyone found an envelope?

No.

He went to the Robarts Library.

No.

Perhaps he should start the research again. Begin from scratch. After all, he knew now much of what he was looking for—and where it could be found. Which books—which periodicals—which files. But the doing of it, however strenuous, was not what concerned Kurtz. It was the finding of the envelope—the perusal of its contents—by someone else. By enemies.

Kurtz went down, as he seldom did, to the eighteenth floor. It was a deliberate descent. He was hoping to provoke a meeting with Marlow. The thing was, the meeting would have to be casual. He could not afford to draw the wrong kind of attention to what he was doing and, therefore, did not want Kilbride to send for Marlow through Bella Orenstein. He must bump him in the hall.

As things worked out, he bumped him in the Men's Room. Marlow was at the urinals. Kurtz, who could not bear to open his flies in the presence of another man, went into one of the cabinets. As Marlow finished and went across to the basins, Kurtz's sepulchral voice intruded into what, for Marlow, had been an empty room.

"I've been meaning to speak to you," the voice said.

Marlow froze.

The voice said: "that is you, isn't it?"

"Who?"

There was a slight delay. The cabinet door was allowed to swing open an inch or two. Marlow could see this in the mirror. Then the door closed. "Doctor Marlow," the voice said.

"Yes," said Marlow—suppressing a smile. "Is that you, Doctor Kurtz?"

Kurtz did not answer the question. Instead, he continued with his message. "I've been concerned about our friend Austin Purvis," he said. He was seated, fully clothed, on the toilet.

"Austin."

"Yes."

Marlow ran water into the sink. The soap dispenser had run out of soap. This was typical.

Kurtz said: "it's not the end of the world, of course, but—it seems to me he's going downhill—and I wondered what your opinion might be."

Marlow was careful. Clearly, Austin was in every kind of trouble a man can have. He was being eaten alive by his work—he had no private life—and now his boss was asking the kind of questions that often—too often—led to unemployment.

"I think there's no question Austin is overtired, Doctor Kurtz," he said.

Overtired was not the word Kurtz wanted to hear.

"Overextended, perhaps?" he said.

"It could be," said Marlow.

"Yes. Well," said Kurtz. "There you are, then."

"Where?" Marlow asked. He was not inclined to let Kurtz off the hook. Generalities were not good enough.

"Well..." Kurtz said, "...that was my reading of it. *Overextended.* Which is why I thought it would be best to relieve him of one or two more clients."

"Clients?"

"Patients."

"Of course."

"He's been a man of great value—Austin."

Oh, yes. Here it comes. The genteel dismissal.

"He still is," Marlow said.

"Yes. Yes. Of course. But..."

"Overextended..."

"Yes."

Marlow took down a paper towel and dried his hands.

Kurtz said: "I just thought you should know what I've been thinking. You're old friends. You work cheek by jowl with the man..."

"Not quite. More like wall to wall. I rarely see him."

"Oh?"

"Yes. The door stays closed, these days."

"I see."

Marlow thought he might as well say it. "He's afraid of robbers."

"Robbers?"

"That's right." Marlow kept a smile in his voice.

"Oh. I see. You mean me."

"Well—yes. You have, after all, made quite a dint in his practice."

"I'm only doing it for his own good, you know. It's only because I'm concerned..."

Marlow quietly crossed the room to the exit.

Kurtz went on: "...and, of course, we also have to think of the...patients. Don't we. We have to be sure they're being well served. After all, that's why we're here."

Bullshit.

"I had a mind, in fact, to relieve poor Austin of one or two others. I thought, perhaps it would be a good idea to cut his case load in half. And I was rather wondering if you could stand between us—act as a buffer. Coming from you, the news might be more welcome. Don't you think, Doctor Marlow?"

Kurtz felt a draft.

He opened the door again and scanned the room.

Marlow was gone.

On the marble wall of the cabinet, someone had written with a magic marker: *SAVE THE CHILDREN.*

That was interesting. Which children? Where?

Kurtz flushed the toilet and went his way.

After seeing Marlow in the washroom, Kurtz was to have a meeting with his research staff, but first he returned to his office in order to put on his lab coat. He wore it only to remind his people that Kurtz was one of them—that Kurtz, too, was involved in practical research and they could not pull the wool over his eyes by fudging issues or talking jargon.

In recent meetings, Doctor Shelley had spoken about the use of rats as test babies in her *Motivational Impulse Cross-Communication (MICC) research. Test babies* was a Shelley original. She had coined the phrase after having talked in a class about *using rats as guinea pigs* and everyone had laughed. Doctor Shelley did not enjoy laughter. Research was serious. *Research was life!* Now, she was making good progress. Her student Corben was also making progress with his monkey programme.

Doctor Sommerville's *White Mind Sleep* programme was proceeding apace, but the pace was slow. Perhaps necessarily slow. Sleep, after all, has its own sense of time—but Kurtz had hoped for swifter progress. He had in mind that a paper could be prepared for delivery at the Psychiatric Society of North America's AGM in September. Clearly, given Sommerville's continuing failure to provide conclusive evidence of success, no such paper would be ready. Kurtz, like all research scientists, lived in constant fear that someone else would produce results—and thus a paper—before him. To be first in science, one had to be first at the podium. All else was second-rate. Nonetheless, Ian Sommerville was doing his best and only Kurtz could have done better. But hands-on involvement was out of the question for Kurtz. His greatest value—and he knew it—lay in the work he was doing. Leading.

Doctor Nagata had positive things to say about the *apathon research*. Ten patients were currently being tested and the results were encouraging. So it had gone—good news, or mostly good news, until they got to Fuller and his bungling of the *orathon* project. A disaster. Fuller would have to be put onto something less important. He was talented enough, but his attitude was wrong. He was forever pulling back when he should have been pushing forward. He would take watching.

Then there was Marlow. Very interesting. Not involved in research, yet, but obviously keen—quick-witted—incisive—bright. Too bright, perhaps. But innovative. A valuable asset—*if he doesn't get carried away. Should have thought twice about pairing him with Purvis...* Still. It was the only spare office on a prestige floor—and Marlow was prestigious—not to be ignored. Most importantly, the groundwork had now been laid for solving the Purvis problem.

Kurtz put on his lab coat and glanced at his desk.

There was Fabiana Holbach's essay—the one he had asked for at Robert Ireland's dinner party.

Good.

He pulled it towards him.

Wasn't that odd, just now, catching sight of Olivia Price in the build-ing. Not odd, of course. She would be here about her sister. The poet with the red hair—not the other one, married to Webster...

Kurtz had seen Amy Wylie's name on the admissions sheet. Came in the night—comatose—*para-schiz* history. Marlow's purview.

Fabiana.

There were three typed pages. Single spaced.

Typed. Or word-processed.

Funny. He could not make the image of Fabiana seated before a machine. *Tippity-tap.* No. It simply wasn't like her.

Still, there it was.

He had time. He sat down—and read:

> You want to know who I am.
>
> It has always been my belief that people do not ask such questions. Mostly because such questions cannot be answered.
>
> Can they?
>
> Also—the question is impertinent. Isn't it, Rupert. (No question mark there—and you know why. Impertinence is as impertinence does.)
>
> Still. The question has been asked. *Who am I?*
>
> I sat here (office) and thought about it. Wrote down the words and looked at them. Should say WHO ARE YOU?—not WHO AM I? True, yes? Where do you stand when you ask that question—outside or inside? Ob- or sub- (jective).
>
> And why do you want to know, Rupert? Is it truly just a pro-fessional question—or is Rupert himself in there, lurking?
>
> Just asking.
>
> We have to face up to it, you and I. Here we are, after all these years.
>
> Dare I use the word *love?*
>
> Is that a word Rupert uses?
>
> Never.
>
> Is it a word Fabiana uses?
>
> Not any more.
>
> I have a friend. He writes. Novels. Stories—plays. He makes things up. He pokes and prods and listens and describes. After we've talked, he waltzes off with bits and pieces—a person's voice—a person's eyes—a person's fear...

This doesn't mean he knows who you are. Do you see what I'm saying. No one knows who you are. When Julian paints a naked man, he gives him one man's nipples—another man's hand and a penis from heaven. Then he makes up a face, and says: *here is a whole human being.* But part of that human being is *George* and part of it is *Arthur* and part of it is desire—and part of it is revulsion. Part of it is statement—and part of it is comment.

Who am I, Rupert?

Who is Fabiana Holbach?

Doesn't it depend on who is looking? And when?

And—this has just occurred to me—have you ever noticed how every artist paints a bit of himself—a part of herself—into every depicted figure? Yes?

Did you ever see a photograph of Modigliani? Find one. Look at it. What you will see is a man—a beautiful, never-smiling man—with attenuated limbs—and a kind of feminine languor (it was drunkenness) and a kind of all-consuming despair (it was suicide from inside out—not with a gun, but with a will.) There he is—the artist as art.

The whole damn world is a mirror. But no one sees anyone else. We only—all of us—see ourselves—AND TURN AWAY.

Yes?

My writing friend has looked in the mirror and what he sees is the whole world staring back. And he has the gall to say: *that is not me—it's you.* He claims he is looking for someone else. Just like Julian Slade. Just like Amedeo Modigliani. *Look at you!* these fellows say. *Look—I saw you! There you are!*

But it's really only themselves—in drag.

We're all in drag, Rupert. Me in black. You in grey. It's a drag act—men pretending to be men—women pretending to be women—but only the artists will tell us that. The rest of us cannot bear the revelation.

Who am I?

Who do you think is writing this?

I'll tell you.

It is my writing friend who saw me, once, in an unguarded moment. This was around the time Jimmy Holbach went off into the Amazon region—around the time I knew he wasn't coming back. And—somehow, in some way—he took a part of me with him. And I want it back.

All you have to remember is, the person who saw me was looking at me through a moment in his own life, too. Otherwise, I don't think he would have seen me at all. He would have seen someone else.

This is what he wrote:

"I know Jimmy went to the Amazon to escape me..." Fabiana says. *"He was like a drug you take at a party, for fun. And then you wonder what it was. And then you ask for more. And then you realize you're hooked. And you never stop to think they've hooked you on purpose. You only think what a lovely feeling it is..."* [I WOULD NOT HAVE SAID LOVELY] *"...and all you want is more. Until one day, they refuse.* There isn't any more. *Or, worse, there is*—but I'm not going to let you have it. *And then they hold it up and say to you:* no more, Fabiana. Never any more. *And then they shoot it into the air, they waste it before your eyes. And they walk away—and they leave you with this empty syringe—and nothing to fill it with. Nothing to fill your veins with. And it was theirs. It was unique. And then you get the message telling you they have disappeared forever."*

This is why I'm coming back to you, Rupert. Not as your lover, but as your patient. I can no longer see myself. I have vanished from view. I have been emptied. I am starving. And I do not want to die.

There.

Is that what you wanted?

If not, I will see what Julian Slade can say for me, in paint. Though, I must confess, I would rather be seen by Amedeo Modigliani.

Wouldn't you?

Kurtz had leaned forward over the pages as he read, and now he sat back.

What had she done to him?

He took his handkerchief from its pocket and held it, still folded, against his cheek. He was perspiring. It was hot. He had the unnerving impression that Fabiana Holbach had looked up off the pages and had seen him.

6

Olivia was not allowed to speak with Amy. She was, however, permitted to observe her and to speak with her principal care-giver, a nurse whose name was Alfred Tweedie.

"Have you been in such a place before, Mrs Price?" Tweedie asked.

"Not here—but yes. I've been to the Queen Street Mental Health Centre. My sister was a patient there some years ago."

"Okay," Tweedie said. "Then you can handle this."

Tweedie was relatively young—perhaps thirty-six or -seven. He had a bright, handsome face that suggested a happy man, with a sense of fun. Olivia suspected he was gay. He had the kind of energy she associated with gay men—he moved like a gymnast and you could tell he loved to dance. His voice had laughter in it—at a songlike pitch.

He led her through a series of locked doors, using a card for some of them, and pressing a buzzer to request the release of others. When they passed through the last of these doors, Tweedie and Olivia were in a wide, bright corridor where carpeting had been laid on the marble floor.

Tweedie explained the carpeting was to prevent the patients from harming themselves during seizures or other violent episodes. Olivia did not ask what these violent episodes might be. She could make them up.

A number of doors were ranged down either side of this corridor—and each of the doors had a window of glass and wire mesh. Some of the doors stood open—most were closed. Through the open doors, Olivia could see people sitting or lying on their beds—some of them asleep, some in a staring mode. Most of them wore bathrobes and pyjamas and a few of them wore clothing they might have worn at home—trousers, shirts and sweaters.

The rooms themselves were barren and blank—overlit with bulbs of an appalling brightness. Each room contained a table, chair and bed. A plain wooden dresser presumably held the patient's belongings. There were no pictures—no books—no radios—no television sets. Just the furniture and the figure of the patient.

A few of the patients appeared to be undergoing treatment that involved shaved heads—the heads painted yellow, perhaps some sort of antiseptic. None of them spoke. Not one.

Tweedie led Olivia along the corridor almost to the very end. He then looked through the window, there, of one of the closed doors.

He seemed content with what he saw and motioned Olivia forward and stepped aside.

Looking through, Olivia saw that Amy was seated, staring at the door—and even, apparently, straight at Olivia.

"Can she see me?"

"No."

"Is it one-way glass?"

"No," said Tweedie. "It's just that in this particular state, she is not seeing us—but one of her visions."

Whatever the vision was, it made Amy angry. Her face was twisted and distorted—as if she were going to yell.

"Is she drugged?"

"Yes, she is."

"Can you tell me what with?"

"No. You can discuss that with Doctor Marlow."

"It was Doctor Marlow who found her, wasn't it?"

"Yes. He committed her—and he will be providing her treatment."

"Does she ever lie down?"

"No. Most of the time, she sits like that."

"Oh, dear."

Tweedie said: "I kind of like your sister, Mrs Price. She's neat."

"Tidy?"

"No," Tweedie laughed. "*Neat.* You know. *Cool.*"

"Yes."

"I've read her poetry. Great stuff. Cogent."

"Good. I'm glad you like it."

"That room in there is full of birds," Tweedie said, nodding at Amy's door.

"Oh?"

"Yeah. Dozens of them. That's why she's angry. She says they're all dead."

"So it's bad," said Olivia. "I mean, this episode."

"Yes. But you can talk to Doctor Marlow. We'd better go now."

"Thank you."

Olivia took one last look at Amy before she took her leave. Amy was standing up, now, holding out her hands. To dead birds.

Marlow had said Olivia should meet him on Sub Two by eleven o'clock.

Now she travelled down in the elevator with a tall young man who was wearing bedroom slippers shaped like rabbits. Quite realistic. Fawn-coloured, with their ears lying back along the sides of the young man's feet. They sported glass eyes—one of which was dangling by a thread. Aside from the rabbits, the young man's attire was perfectly normal. T-shirt.

Dirty old cardigan. Blue jeans. Even one of those silver identification bracelets more and more people were wearing. Not that these bracelets told who you were. They told, instead, what you had: *STURNUSEMIA.* *LEUKEMIA. AIDS.* Disease—just another fashion accessory. Olivia wondered if Amy would be made to wear such a bracelet. *INSANE.* Or *MAD.* The young man's bracelet could not be read. His wrist was too endlessly in motion—turning, turning—caught in the embrace of his other hand.

Olivia needed to discuss with Doctor Marlow what might happen next if Amy did not recover. She had been ill before in this way—and other ways. Always a problem, never at rest—never making peace with reality. War was more like it. Amy with her arm raised—voice raised—flags raised over all lost causes, no matter what they were. Day care for terrorists—pensions for rapists—hospices for dying animals. Dead friends. And poetry.

Why does it make you so angry, Olivia?

Leave me alone.

Don't you love Amy?

Yes.

Poetry?

Yes.

Animals?

Yes.

Olivia waited to see if the voice would ask about her love of terrorists and rapists. No. Not a word. Good.

She had problems of her own. She was thirty-eight and pregnant—the first successful pregnancy of her life. But she was going to terminate it. Any day now, she would seek professional advice. Any day now, she would fall downstairs or step in front of a car. Any day now...

Stop that.

Silence.

Olivia never enjoyed an elevator ride. The idea of falling and rising did not appeal. She held onto the rail with one gloved hand, but tried to give the appearance of calmness. Tranquillity. In a madhouse—wasn't the Parkin a madhouse?—a person possessed of reason must appear at all times to be sane.

That's good, Olivia. Don't let them know you're hearing voices...

Be quiet.

Sub Two, so it had said on the index upstairs, was where the laboratories were and the lecture halls and also where they had the cafeteria—a magazine stand—a haircutting place—et cetera. Olivia wondered in which of these directions the rabbit man would turn once they arrived. His physical condition gave good reason to hope he would head for the cafeteria. His arms, his legs and his neck were painfully thin—reminis-cent of Amy at her worst—and his fingernails showed, by their yellow complexion and twisted shapes, a vitamin deficiency.

Olivia stood near the front of the car while the young man hung against the wall at the back. Olivia decided she was leaving too much space between them. The man would think she was afraid of him.

Olivia turned, still holding onto the rail, so he would see the calmness of her features—and she could get a better look at his.

Instantly, he looked away. His lips moved. Words—but silent.

Olivia stared at the ceiling. The Subsidiary floors seemed a great way off, and must be deeply underground. What did you call that? *The bunker mentality.* At last they arrived and the doors were opened with a soft, submissive moan. Olivia steadied herself but before she could dis-embark the young man spoke.

"Go on," he said, rather gently. Olivia turned. She was not completely sure he had spoken to her.

She waited.

The young man did not move.

"Go on," he said. "Get off," he said, still not looking at Olivia. She kept one hand on the doors so as not to be shut back in. "Get off..." He was whispering hoarsely now—the tone neither angry nor rude—but urgent. "...Please get off."

Olivia looked at him, curious to know why he spoke to her this way—wondering if, perhaps, he needed assistance.

"Are you all right?" she finally asked.

"Get off!"

Olivia had no choice. The doors were pressing at her hand. She stepped beyond the lip of the car and reluctantly let go. The doors shook a moment and shut. They were burnished brass and the young man was gone.

Sad.

You think so?

Yes. Don't you?

Not really. Disturbing—but not sad.

Why did he want me to get off? I mean, I was getting off anyway...

Who says he was talking to you?

To himself?

Think again.

Olivia made a picture of the tall young man in her mind. *Get off,* he had said, looking down. His...shoes?

Not his shoes, Olivia. His rabbits.

Oh.

With a hey-nonny-nonny
And his rabbits-o!

Olivia closed her eyes. You bugger. It's not his fault he's ill—and it isn't funny.

Oh yeah?

Olivia found herself in a large rotunda. A red-and-gold cavern. Very like the cavern in that painting upstairs—the one you could not avoid seeing. The one by Julian Slade with all the dogs and naked men.

Olivia could smell the cafeteria. It made her feel ill. She turned away from it towards a door marked *GLASS—BEWARE!* Beyond that door, she could see the distant vanishing point of a long marble hallway whose perspective seemed at odds with the rest of the building's geography. Surely no corridor could be so long as that. Perhaps it seemed so long only because she was seeing it through glass. The marble, like all the marble in the Parkin, was a variation of red—lit with lamps that were concealed in both the ceiling and the walls. An oncoming figure—dressed in green—passed in and out of these lights, which gave his approach a flickering, strobe-lit effect. Olivia had to close her eyes and turn away. She felt decidedly thrown off balance and stepped aside to find a chair.

There were none.

Olivia stood, in that case, leaning slightly back against a wall. A variety of people came and went—most of them silent, some of them clattering in heels. None of them spoke. It seemed, perhaps, that speech might be forbidden here—though nothing visible forbade it.

If only the doctor would come. Marlow might comfort her and calm her for her own sake, as well as Amy's. How appalling it was to think of Amy held like a prisoner in such a place.

Madhouse. Lunatic Asylum. Queen Street. The Parkin. Had it come to this?

They had been the Wylie Girls. *The Wylie Girls.* Three young women, shown in all the magazines—written about and photographed and courted for their wealth and rank and beauty. Even, on occasion, for their intelligence. *(Hah!)* The Wylie Girls. *The Wylie Girls.* Peggy, Olivia, Amy. Sitting on antique chairs, standing in flowered gardens—rooted in the grand old Wylie houses—graced with the grand old Wylie name—blessed with the grand old Wylie money—shown in John Dai Bowen's portrait, Peggy, Olivia, Amy—each gaze fixed on a different distance.

Comfort and catastrophe. These had been the conditions of childhood. Money, yes—stability, no. Eustace Wylie—floundering in grief—never to recover from the horrors he had seen at Dieppe. It took him eighteen years to die—long enough for Peggy and Olivia to have known him well—but Amy hardly at all. He had held her in his arms—she had spoken his name. They had all gone riding with him in his motorcar—sat with him on the grass behind Grandmother Wylie's house—knew that his work involved making roads—heard him sing off-key—listened to his recitals of poetry—clung to his pant legs—held his hands—smelled his hair—watched him embrace their mother, link his arm through hers and seemingly lean his weight against her. He never fell down in their presence, though often, they were later told, he would go to the ground on his knees and hide his head in his arms. They had seen him walk away and walk away and walk away. They had seen him come back, come back—and not come back. He died of despair in one of his absences. They had seen the coffin he had been returned in, though Amy had not seen it. *The young should not see such things.* Olivia had been seven years old.

She had worn his medals, once, on her tailored coat to church. Grandmother Wylie had nearly killed her. Olivia had then been ten. She had wanted to pay tribute to her father's torment—but Grandmother Wylie, who did not care for her son, had snatched the medals away and Olivia had never seen them since. It was Grandmother Wylie's opinion that men did not deserve sympathy. Men went to war because war was their job—their duty. And it should have been their joy. That Eustace Wylie had been destroyed by a war—and not a mark on him—was one of the family's deepest disgraces. No matter that Eustace had been brave—no matter the lives he had saved—no matter the decorations that had followed. Once home and haunted by the cries that had seemingly followed him there, he had ceased, in Grandmother Wylie's eyes, to be a "man." *Male, yes—man, no,* she had once said.

Olivia had practised silence early. Partly in deference to Grandmother Wylie's wishes, partly in respect of listening for her father's voice, or her mother's. But mostly in order to ward off commitment. She had noted that, when people spoke, there were often alarming consequences. Her father's having said *I am afraid* had cost him his mother's love.

As with all quiet people—people prone to extended silences—people given to listening—Olivia had become a watcher. It was only when teaching that she spoke at length. Her subject was history. She could recount the world of men and women because she had seen its minutest details—and she revelled in them. And yet, when she prepared the words in her mind that would tell the minutest details of her self—this child, for instance—*the Voice*—the words rarely reached her tongue.

The Wylie Girls.

Fifteen years since the John Dai Bowen portrait was taken. Olivia kept her copy of it hidden in a drawer with the dress she had worn that day—the dress in tissue paper and the portrait turned face down beneath it. Bowen, of course, had published the thing in his most recent book. Put it on the cover, damn him.

The Wylie Girls. The Wylie Girls. One of them a prisoner of fear. One of them mad. And the other...

Well. Alive, at least. You can't be more alive than when you're pregnant.

Yes. If you stay pregnant.

True.

She walked to the centre of the hallway.

Marlow was to meet her after attending the weekly seminar at which the doctors caught one another up on their work. He had apologized profusely, saying he had to attend, but if the session lasted beyond the hour, he would slip away and join her. Now—by Olivia's watch—he was already several minutes late.

The Info Board was written in Psychiatrese—which Olivia could not decipher. *AnPsychTheoPrac 1—LH—N2* and *PyPharmaNarcThera H—Red—S8* did not inform her of where she was meant to wait. And yet she couldn't just stand there. She hated waiting of any kind in public—not because she was impatient but because it meant being scrutinized by strangers.

She crossed to the *GLASS—BEWARE!* partition and, giving it a shove, went through. The smell of disinfectant increased and the sound of a motor, humming softly underground, caught her attention. It also became rather cold. This must be where they did whatever they did with animals. The Parkin was famous for that. It had been, at one time, a target for Amy's rantings. Kurtz had instituted several of these research experiments. Amy had thrown a stone at him once—but had missed.

Olivia began to pass a number of doors that were open.

Some of the rooms were dark and some were only dimly lit. One was very brightly lit with high, fluorescent lamps. She could see this room in the distance on the right-hand side of the corridor. In the meantime she could see that in all the rooms, there were cages—sometimes only one or two and sometimes five or six. Rabbits, rats and cats. No mice—no guinea pigs—and no people. Not a sign of anyone.

What was more disturbing was the absence of animal sounds. Not a peep—not a cry—not a squeak. In one room, however, a rhesus monkey stood up as Olivia passed and grasped the bars of its cage. The gesture was unnervingly human. She hurried further down the hall.

The fluorescent room was unique; not only because of its sizzling light—but because it was filled with stacks and stacks of cages—maybe

247

two hundred of them—all of them empty. In the centre of this room there was a large metallic table possibly made of lead or zinc. And in the centre of the table...

Keep on walking.

...there was the corpseless head of a rhesus monkey.

I can't move.

This head was in a little plastic tray. The monkey's eyes were closed but its mouth was open.

Olivia heard a muted sigh and then, inside the room, a tap was turned on.

Someone was there.

Beyond the table Olivia could see there were several garbage cans lined with green plastic bags and from one of these a paw was extended—dead—but clutching nonetheless to the edge. A perfect micromorphic hand.

The tap was turned off and a person almost appeared—an arm—a shoulder—white-coated—bleached—but then the door swung shut. Without a sound until the final click.

Olivia's palms began to sweat inside her gloves. But she could move, now—as if the clicking door had been a signal: release.

She began to walk, turning back the way she had come, feeling nauseated.

Doesn't anyone in this whole damn building ever sit down? There must be a chair somewhere... Looking either way, she discovered she was disconcertingly alone. Down by the elevators, off in the distance, there wasn't a breath of activity.

Humming vibrations underfoot.

Motor.

And her own irresolute reflection in the *GLASS—BEWARE!* partition.

From this side, the notice read: *!ERAWEB—SSALG*—something Amy might have said. It put Olivia in mind of a long-forgotten game their nanny, Glennie, had got the Wylie girls to play on rainy days when they were children. Rainy days, in fact, became another country where they spoke another language. Everything was backwards on a rainy day in childhood. *Doohdlihc ni yad yniar a no.* Backwards—or *in Welsh,* as Amy, aged ten, had pointed out. Amy both read and wrote the rainy-day language perfectly. Maybe that was where she lived. In a world reversed.

Or real.

Oh—please—shut up.

Olivia was about to push her way through the door when she felt a cold draught strike her back. Even through her coat, she could feel it.

Someone was coming.

She turned.

It was Kurtz.

He was flanked, as always in these professional situations, by interns and lieutenants. His grey suit was covered with a buttoned white lab coat. His dyed black hair was neatly brushed and had a peculiar shine to it, and his famous pallor was heightened by the hidden lights. Kurtz always seemed to be on parade—on show—when others were in his company. He rose above them all, not ever looking at one of them or the other, but straight ahead through his hooded eyes.

Olivia fell back. She felt both afraid and like a fool for losing her confidence so obviously in Kurtz's presence. She had known him for years. He had visited her house. He was a friend of Griff's. Griffin, she suspected, had made a donation to the Parkin—routing it through Kurtz— to offset the negative effect of Amy's campaign against the place. And the stone she had thrown. Olivia had never been intimidated by Kurtz before. Nervous of him, perhaps, but never intimidated. In this place, however—two storeys underground—it was like being an animal living in the earth and having a snake descend into your burrow, looking for something to kill. She had never thought this of Kurtz before. But then—she had never been trapped with him before in such a place.

Nothing happened. What could possibly happen? He was just a man, after all. He was not...

Yes, he was. He was everything she feared. Authority with an armed guard. Watching him approach with his people—all their clipboards and pencils poised to record his words—Olivia gave thanks to whatever gods protect the mad that Amy was not his patient.

About ten feet from where she stood, Kurtz paused. He turned away from her to speak with those who followed him. She heard his voice but not his words. Whatever he said, it was harsh. One of his lieutenants stood back as if he had been struck. His clipboard went to his side and he stood there with his head bowed. Kurtz could then be heard distinctly saying: "that kind of thinking will not be tolerated, Doctor Fuller."

In the room past Olivia's shoulder a cat tried to hide and, finding nowhere dark enough, it became as small as it could in the corner of its cage.

Kurtz turned back in her direction and started to walk again. The others followed. When he came abreast of Olivia, he looked at her and gave just the briefest nod of recognition—but made no comment and went his way. One of his lieutenants, however, stopped and said officiously: "is there something you want down here?"

Olivia said: "I'm waiting for Doctor Marlow."

The woman's eyes narrowed.

"Charles Marlow?"

"Yes."

"Are you a patient?"

"No. A relative."

"A relative of Doctor Marlow's?"

"No." Olivia tried to smile. She felt as if she had committed an offence. Perhaps, in this woman's eyes, she had. "One of Doctor Marlow's patients is my sister."

"I see. Well..." The woman nodded back down the corridor. "There he is. He's all yours."

"Thank you."

The woman turned and followed after Kurtz and the others. Olivia wondered why she had said of Marlow, *he's all yours*. It sounded both discourteous and derisive.

Marlow was hurrying towards her. He wore no lab coat and was smaller than Olivia had expected. Beyond him, a woman in a black suit was attempting to catch up with him.

Marlow was smiling as he approached. "Are you, by any chance, Mrs Price?" he said.

"Yes, I am," said Olivia. "But..." She nodded in the direction of the hurrying woman in black.

Marlow turned towards her.

"Charlie!" the woman said, out of breath, as she drew near. "I'm glad I caught you."

"Is something wrong, Eleanor?" He was frowning.

"No—not really. It's just..." And then she stopped and spoke to Olivia. "I'm sorry to interrupt. This will just take a second."

"Forgive me," Marlow said, turning to Olivia, his face still showing concern. "This is Doctor Farjeon, a colleague. And this..."—back to Eleanor Farjeon—"is Mrs Price."

There were brief smiles all around and then Eleanor said to Marlow: "there's nobody answering in your offices, Charlie..."—she paused for breath—"and I'm late for Queen Street—and desperate to reach Austin. Could you possibly leave a message for him when you go back up?"

Marlow looked relieved. "Of course," he said.

"He's bound to be there before he goes home," said Eleanor. "Just tell him, if you would—I can't possibly see him this evening but I'll definitely talk to him in the morning."

"No problem. If he's not there, I'll leave a note."

"Thanks, Charlie." Eleanor looked at her watch and grimaced. Then she turned to Olivia and said: "good to meet you..." And then, concerned: "are you okay...?"

Marlow saw that Olivia was decidedly pale, but before he could speak, Eleanor was moving off and calling back: "I think you'd better find Mrs Price some place to sit down, Charlie. She looks sort of faint!" And she disappeared from view.

Marlow looked around, spotted an open door across the hall—and guided Olivia towards it. "There's a stool in there, if you can make it."

Olivia—who was, in fact, feeling dizzy—nodded and let herself be gently propelled through the door and onto the stool that sat in front of a cluttered desk.

Marlow leaned in closer and peered at her. "Would you like a glass of water?"

"No, truly. I'm just fine, now. It was only..." Olivia managed a smile. "There's been a lot to do since the calls about Amy started last night."

"I'm sure there has been." Marlow crossed the dimly lit room and closed the door. "A few moments of quiet won't hurt either of us."

As Olivia looked around through the shadows, she realized, for the first time, they were not alone. There were several cages of rats set up on table tops. The rats made scurrying noises—but otherwise they were strangely silent.

"Why don't they have voices?" She nodded at the rats. "I don't understand," she said.

"Experimental animals, in a place like this, Mrs Price, all have their vocal cords removed. Or cut." He was leaning against the door.

"But...*why?*"

"Their voices get in the way of human sensibilities, that's why..." He peeled his back from the door and stepped towards her into more light. Olivia could see that he, too, was near exhaustion. She wondered if Amy was the cause.

Marlow went to the nearest cage—where a large male rat was enclosed with his droppings. "They tend to scream if they don't have their vocal cords removed," he said. "Or cut." He touched the bars lightly with his finger-ends—almost with a kind of sympathy for the bars themselves. "Not always screaming with *pain*," he said. He looked through the cage at Olivia. "The experiments here are not entirely physical, you understand. For instance, these rats are not in physical danger—aside from the loss of their voices. They have merely been separated from one another."

Olivia noted the distances between the cages, each distance gauged in centimetres and carefully marked with tape.

"A psychologist—Doctor Shelley—comes in here three times a day," said Marlow, "and measures the distances." He raised his eyes towards her. "Do you understand?"

"No. The distances are marked quite clearly now. Why do they have to be marked again...?"

Marlow looked at her a moment in silence. Then he said: "are you sure you're all right, now?"

"Absolutely."

"Then come over here."

Olivia went to where Marlow stood.

"Look carefully down at the tapes. And recall that a rat is a social animal."

She did so.

What she was looking for was not quite clear to her at first. The light was dim and the lines of the tape seemed to float in space. The markings themselves were nothing but a blur of tiny figures. Like the Tailor of Gloucester's stitches, they could only have been made by mice.

"I can't even begin to read them..." Olivia said.

"It isn't necessary to read them, Mrs Price. Only Doctor Shelley is interested in the figures. Look again."

Now Olivia saw what it was he wanted her to see. The edges of the cages were not all flush with the edges of the tapes. It took only seconds for her to grasp the meaning of what she saw—and when she had understood it, she stared at the separated rats. Each one was staring back at her with a sad and solemn madness.

Olivia stepped away.

"Dear God," she said.

"Precisely," said Marlow. "*Dear God,* indeed." He stood with his hands behind his back. "The larger rats, of course being stronger—are able to move their cages three or four inches in the course of a day. Every night Doctor Shelley destroys their advance by replacing the cages on the original demarcations. When a rat with a particular ingenuity or strength comes along, his cage will be suitably weighted with lead to counter his advantage." He paused. "I have never been present when one of the rats has moved his cage. But their techniques are most original and some— quite amusing. *Amusing* being Doctor Shelley's word. Not mine."

"They don't appear to have any water—or food."

"They don't." Marlow paused reflectively. "They are only fed in the dark."

"I don't understand."

"In the dark, they cannot see one another feeding. That is, they cannot see as well as they would in the light of day." He gestured at the dim yellow bulbs above, with a smile. "Doctor Shelley reasons a certain amount of paranoia can be fostered if they're fed in the dark. In fact, food is withheld altogether on some occasions and..." He sighed, embarrassed. "On these occasions, when a sound tape of feeding rats is played, some of the cages have been known to fall to the floor with the force of the shaking."

Olivia closed her eyes. "I thought you said something earlier about *human sensibilities*," she said.

"I did," said Marlow. "Human—not humane."

Olivia opened her eyes. "I see," she said.

Marlow continued: "Doctor Shelley's more recent innovations include the introduction of a female rat in heat. Her cage hangs there..."—he indicated a hook—"...*above* the others. You can speculate for yourself on the possible results. And finally, there's an experiment that even I cannot fathom—try as I will—bringing in rats whose vocal cords have *not* been severed—and..." He made a helpless gesture with his hands. "Shall we leave?" he said, looking down at the floor. "Just let me check the hallway, first."

He went across the room and very slightly opened the door. Olivia turned for one last look at the rats. They were silent, of course—not even moving against their bars. There was something desolate—perhaps resentful—about their gaze. For a moment, it seemed, they had sensed another kind of presence in their torture chamber—unlike the usual presence of Doctor Shelley. Clearly, they had hoped—unless all hope had been abandoned here—that something other than separation might be going to happen in their lives.

Olivia turned to Marlow. "Please," she said. "May we move the cages?"

Marlow smiled, for he understood her feeling. But: "no," he said. "I have often debated the same manoeuvre. However, if it were done, then Doctor Shelley would punish the rats for their...impertinence."

Olivia nodded. "I see," she said. And then: "may I ask you a favour?"

"Of course."

"Be certain not to introduce me to Doctor Shelley."

Marlow smiled again. "You have already met her, I'm afraid," he said. "That was the woman who spoke to you just outside this door before I caught up with you."

"The officious one with Doctor Kurtz?"

"That's right."

Olivia winced at the memory of it. "She was very rude about you," she said.

"I'm glad to hear it," said Marlow. "If I met with her approval, I should not be doing my job."

He ushered Olivia through the door and closed it without looking back.
They turned together and walked towards the elevators.

Olivia thought about what Doctor Shelley had said about Marlow:
he's all yours. She was glad of that—for her own sake, as well as Amy's.

7

Lilah was trying to do something constructive with her hair. In an hour,
she would walk into Marlow's drawing room and into the presence of
Nicholas Fagan. A woman called Fabiana Holbach would bring him.
Women, always—all those women. Lilah, long ago, had been one of them
herself. *Fagan's bevy—never a harem.* Just the pleasure of women's company—students, writers, actresses, sister academics. Fabiana Holbach
owned a gallery. She would be stylish, sophisticated, smart... She would
be glamorous. She would be thin.

It didn't matter. Why would it matter? How could it matter? Lilah
was going to be in Fagan's presence—that was what mattered—not who
he came with. Not all the other people in his life—only Lilah. She
prayed for one small moment alone with him. One small moment to tell
him *Kurtz is here. He got out under my hand and I can't get him back...*

He would know she was mad, of course. She had not been mad when
she met him first—not mad as she later became. There had been no
escapees, back then—no fugitives—only deliberate conjurings—only
chance encounters. But no defiant villains—not a sign of Heathcliff;
Otto, the arsonist; Jack the Ripper or Rosalind Bailey. Not a sign of
Kurtz, the headhunter. Now, Fagan would look at her and dismiss her
petition for his attention. *The woman is mad,* he would say. Unless she
could trick him into thinking she was sane.

I am sane!

Not with that hair, you're not.

Oh, to be Fabiana Holbach or The Surgeon's Wife or a Wylie Girl—
oh, to be someone in a magazine just this once.

Marlow had said: *you might be interested in joining us. Your old
friend, Nicholas Fagan, will be coming by for drinks the night before he
delivers the Appleby Lecture.*

She might be interested! The Marlow she had conjured did not know
the half of it. Otherwise, he would have been onto Kurtz before this and
would already have started—metaphysically speaking, of course—back
down the river with Kurtz. *He dead. The horror—the horror...*

Now, Lilah stood before the mirror in her tiny bathroom staring at the chaos rampant on her head. She wore, for the first time in years, a slip over her undergarments and its creamy colour made her want to weep for lost joys.

The colour and texture of clothing had once been one of Lilah's happiest preoccupations. She had loved the layering of shades and surfaces—building cream on shell and peach on cream—silks on cottons and wool on silks. Her modest income—when was that?—had forced her to choose her wardrobe with an eye for budget as well as taste. Her stipend went almost entirely to books, back then. Consequently, every piece of clothing was precious. The slip she wore today was always returned to its drawer in tissue paper when not in use. Cheesecloth ties of potpourri were folded in amongst her lingerie and blouses. One or two items had been kept in satin envelopes, with her monogram—stitched by her mother—raised on the face. *Oh, what times*—when hope was in the air—and she had dressed each day in its presence. Then, it could not have mattered less that her hair was uncontrollable, her make-up botched in the flurry of excited gestures. She had gone every morning into the world with such high expectations—everything performed with energy and interest. The bright unwritten faces of the young had turned with such enthusiasm in one's direction—how could a person not spill over with words? *Read! Read! Read!* Standing in behind the counter—caught in the morning light—beloved books on every side—a library of good companions waiting to be introduced...

And this damn hair.

It would not lie down. It refused to be disciplined. The most she could do was pin it here and there and tie brown velvet ribbons into its mess—perfect bows that would show at least that she had tried. When she was through with this, she seized a large blue-feathered puff and struck her face with it—once—twice—three times—causing explosions of powder to cloud the air—and to fall in drifts across her shoulders and breastbone.

Peering into the mirror, she saw her features staring back from a snow bank—two black, birdlike eyes and a mouth that was not defined until she opened it.

"There," she said aloud, and went along the hall into her bedroom.

Nicholas Fagan. His presence in Lilah's city was enough to make her think she was young again. *Dear God! And he is coming into this very house!* He would be there in half an hour. They would drink together—just like the pub crawls of old—and they would talk together. He would talk and she would listen. With Marlow. Nicholas Fagan had been an enthusiastic supporter from afar of Marlow's use of literature as a tool in psychiatric research. They had corresponded over many years and had met at Harvard, when Fagan had lectured there. That is why he was coming here tonight.

Lilah took down her brown wool dress and held it close, as she might a friend.

I would never not be I, she was thinking. *But I would gladly, this night, have been born some other I, not mad.*

Her eyes looked round the room until she found herself in the bureau mirror. There were her hands embracing the dress she would wear—and on her fingers, her mother's rings. They, like her mother's gifts of raising spirits and defying time, were gleaming lights that flashed in the fading day. *All my gifts to you,* her mother said in Lilah's mind, *are precious gifts for cutting through time. They are loving gifts—creative gifts and gifts of power. I brought you forth to be my gifted daughter...*

Lilah smiled.

...and to be no other.

Sarah Tudball's rings had spoken. Lilah was content. *This me,* she told the mirror, *is me enough.*

8

Fagan, with words, was mischievous and childlike. With ideas, he was anything but. His eyes, without his glasses, were a blue amalgam of fierce intelligence and sorrow. *The more one sees,* he had written to his late friend, Borges, *the more one prays for blindness.* It was a state that had not been accorded Fagan—but a curse that had blighted the life of the great Argentinian writer. Borges had responded to Fagan's despair by reminding him that *pulling down the shades does not shut out the world. It merely shuts out the light.* This way, Fagan had been reconciled to sight.

It was not for nothing that Nicholas Fagan's lectures had been attended by fifty-odd years of students crammed into the furthest corners of Trinity's draughty halls. He had a way of leaning forward confidentially in moments of suspense—whether standing behind a lectern, or sitting in Marlow's living-room—and when he whispered: *let me tell you a story*—breathing everywhere would stop. Stories were Fagan's medium—though he had never written fiction. What he did was create an imagined setting for truths, where they could be seen in ways that life did not present them. *This is the story of the trial of Socrates,* he would say—and he would tell the tale with all its facets in place. But Socrates would "corrupt" the youth of O'Connell Street, speak with a Dubliner's accent—and drink the hemlock in O'Malley's Bar.

"Tell us," Marlow said, "about your journey."

Fagan had only been once in an aeroplane. He was twenty-three and the thing had crashed, killing all others on board—including Isobelle Merton, his wife. It had been an excursion flight over Dublin Bay to Wicklow Head. The little plane—which carried only six—had lost its power and Fagan had seen the earth come up to bury them. *By some damned curse of fate, I walked away alive, but Isobelle and the others perished.* Fire had consumed them. *No one was there to see it but me,* he had said. *No one came running—just some cows—until I made the town and rang all the bells.*

This last was no exaggeration. Fagan, in shock, was delirious—and had gone from church to church and pulled all the bell ropes. Nothing of Isobelle Merton was ever recovered. *I came to believe she had never been,* he said. *In that part of her life she shared with me, I was convinced I had made her up. She was a fiction.* He had not remarried and all his encounters with women thereafter were nothing more than episodes of charm. He was adored, but he was beyond consoling.

So it was that all Fagan's journeys had since been made in trains and motorcars—and ships. He never went again by air.

The journey to Canada had been taken on board a Russian liner called the *Neva,* which Fagan had chosen because it docked at Montreal. He had boarded it at Tilbury on its way from St Petersburg. After Montreal, he told them, it returned to sea and down to New Orleans, after which it went on through the Panama Canal and across the Pacific to Japan, the Philippines and Australia—then on to India, Egypt, Italy, Spain, France and Sweden. *All that way, and finally through the Baltic, home,* he concluded.

When Fagan had finished ringing these names, there was a universal sigh of approval.

"The world is not enough with us in the age of flight," he said. "Imagine having the audacity to call yourself a traveller when all you pile up is jet-miles with nothing seen but sky."

"But I *love* a good flight," said Rena Appleby. She and Mason Appleby were Marlow's only other guests that evening—besides Fabiana and Lilah. They would all—but Lilah—go on to the O'Flahertys' dreaded dinner party. Lady Appleby lived on alcohol. She consequently spent her life in partial stupor—almost always smiling—whether lying down, standing up or sitting. She was currently seated. Her husband, whose bulk was immense, required an entire settee. Unlike his wife, he was alert and quick-witted. Trusting no one, he listened to all conversations as if every speaker might be a spy.

Fagan went on to describe the journey upstream to Montreal—past a *landscape still and grey along the dead shore.* He pointed out the fetid colours of the water and the rivers, frothing with chemicals, running down from the mined interior and the boarded-up towns giving way to the cities pouring yellow waste into the wake of the ship and the sick, dying whales that rose from the deep. He said there were many wonders, too—the Saguenay—the Citadel of Quebec—*and farms where actual cows could be seen in actual fields...* And then to Montreal, where he debarked and the Neva turned back towards its ocean voyage.

"You make the landscape sound horrific," said Fabiana.

"I mean to," said Fagan. And then: "it was not for nothing that I came that way."

"What does that mean?" said Appleby.

"It means that I was not the first to come. It means I followed where others had gone before me."

"Immigrants?" said Fabiana.

"All of us are immigrants," said Fagan. "Even the so-called aboriginal peoples of this continent came from somewhere else. I believe it was across an ice bridge, now the Bering Sea."

"We don't call them aboriginals," said Appleby. "We call them Indians."

"Oh, yes." Fagan smiled. "I had forgotten where I was."

"Well, they aren't Chinese," said Appleby.

"One name I recall is *Cree,*" said Fagan. "Another is *Ojibway.* And what are you, my lord?"

"English," said Appleby. "What difference does it make?"

"Order of arrival," said Fagan, still smiling. "Order of arrival, you see, equals order of perception. I only mean to say—this place was once perceived as nothing more or less than a place in which to survive. A place to live."

"Still is," said Appleby.

"You think so?"

"What else could it be?"

"A place to buy. A place to alter. A place to destroy."

"Are you a communist, Fagan?"

"Well, now. I've never thought about it."

"People like you," said Appleby. "You hate everything, don't you."

"Now, Mace—don't start in on that," said Rena, waking up from a snooze.

"Couldn't agree more," said Marlow, fearing that politics were going to wreck the evening.

"You see," said Fagan, "my journey up the river made me think about what it was those others who came before us had in mind. They might be greatly surprised by what they found here today. And greatly dismayed, I fear."

"How do you mean?" said Fabiana.

"I mean there is nothing here of what anyone proposed. There is little beauty left—but much ugliness. Little wilderness—but much emptiness. No explorers—but many exploiters. There is no art—no music—no literature—but only entertainment. And there is no philosophy. This that was once a living place for humankind has become their killing ground."

There was a brief pause.

"So," said Appleby, "I seem to have brought a viper into our midst. I hope your lecture has something more positive than that to say about the state of things."

Fagan waved a hand.

When it came time for Marlow to lead his visitors to their cars, Fagan said he would first like to use the washroom. Lilah had been prepared for this moment, and at once she offered to help the old man find his way. "It's a treacherous house," she said. "A person can get lost so easily."

Fagan was delighted with his tour guide and said to Lilah: "I was your tour guide more than once, in your Dublin days. Now, you can exchange the honour."

As they left the room, Rena Appleby stirred from her sleep just long enough to ask: "are we there yet?"

Mason Appleby hunched his shoulders and gave a belly laugh. "She thinks we live in the back of a limousine."

Lilah did not lead Fagan to the washroom off Marlow's kitchen. Instead, she led him into her own apartment and indicated the tiny bathroom there.

Fagan remarked: "I shouldn't send Lord Appleby in here. He wouldn't be able to turn around." And shut the door.

Lilah heard the running of taps. She was thinking: *now. Now. I have him here and must keep him here until he understands what I have done.* She waited across the hall in her bedroom, where Fam was asleep on the window-sill.

At last, the bathroom door was opened and Fagan stepped forward. His hair, with light behind it, was a cap of white feathers. *He must be very old,* Lilah thought. *A man who doesn't know how to die.*

"So this is where you live, then," he said.

"Yes."

"Your cat?"

"Fam—the house cat. She lives all over us."

"I see."

"Doctor Fagan?"

"Yes, my dear?" He was looking at her books, his hands behind his back for balance as he leaned forward.

"I must tell you something that will seem at odds with reality," Lilah said. This was the sentence she had prepared in her mind when first imagining this meeting. "I must tell you that…"

Fagan turned towards her as if perhaps he had not heard her speak. He was preoccupied with the titles of her books and he said: "has it struck you as being remarkably coincidental that Marlow, our host, is working with a man called Kurtz?"

Lilah blinked.

"I have just seen the title of the book they share under Conrad's aegis—*Heart of Darkness*. There it sits, with Marlow in the next room—and Kurtz on his way to join us. The chance encounters life provides—wonderful, wouldn't you say."

"Yes, sir."

"Kurtz and Marlow. Marlow and Kurtz. My, my…"

"If you opened up that copy of *Heart of Darkness*, Doctor Fagan," Lilah said, "you would find some words of your own in there."

"Really, now?"

"Yes."

Lilah stepped forward and handed him the book—opening the cover to reveal Fagan's words from long ago. *If I were to propose a text,* he had written, *for the twentieth century, it would be Joseph Conrad's* Heart of Darkness…

Fagan read his words to the end, where he had said: *the human race has found its destiny in self-destruction.* Being reunited with the text appeared to move him, and he lifted the book up higher into the light where he could see the words more clearly.

Lilah said: "do you still believe what it says?"

Fagan said: "yes—to my regret, I do."

"I think it is the saddest sentence in all the world," said Lilah. "And I wish you had not written it."

"The sentence is sad, Miss Kemp—but not the sentiment it contains. I think it is a very angry thought."

"Yes. Angry, too. And sad."

"I'm flattered that you've kept it as a memento. And I see that I have signed it."

"Yes."

"When was that?"

"Before I left Dublin to return to Canada. That time in Ireland was the best in all my life. Studying with you—and those lovely walks we had."

"The pub crawls. Yes."

"Doctor Fagan..."

"Yes?"

Lilah touched the book in Fagan's hand. "Kurtz has got out of this book, from page 92, and..." She faltered. "I let him out. I didn't mean to, but...he got out. And now..."

Fagan smiled.

"Kurtz is with us always," he said. "I don't think you can blame yourself for that. The human race cannot take a single step, but it produces another Kurtz. He is the darkness in us all."

"Yes. But this Kurtz..."

"Has a Marlow, like all the rest. Is that not so?"

Lilah was silent. She did not want to blame Marlow for his inaction, seeing he was known to Fagan and liked by him.

"You are deeply troubled, Miss Kemp. I can see that."

Troubled? I'm a madwoman. Can you see that, too?

"It's just that I feel responsible," she said out loud. "I did it—and I cannot get him to go back in."

"Are you speaking of Doctor Kurtz? Doctor Rupert Kurtz?"

"Yes."

Fagan turned away and riffled the pages of *Heart of Darkness.* "All books are a conjuring, Miss Kemp," he said. "That is the most precise description I can give. They are all a conjuring of humankind and the world that we inhabit. Conrad was not the first to conjure Kurtz—and not the last. He was merely the first to give him that name."

"Yes, sir." Lilah had fallen into sadness and disappointment, and could barely be heard as she spoke. Even Nicholas Fagan, it seemed, did not understand the danger they were in, so long as Kurtz was out there off the page.

Fagan put the book on its shelf. "I must go," he said. "We have this dinner to attend." He stepped towards the door. "You are joining us, aren't you?"

"No," Lilah said. And then: "Doctor Fagan?"

"Yes?" He turned.

"It has been good to see you."

"Thank you. And I say the same, with pleasure."

Lilah could not bear to let him go, though she knew she must.

"May I have a memento of our visit?" she said.

Fagan was not too certain what she meant by this. Did she want to kiss him?

"It depends," he said—smiling. "Do you want my money, or my life?"

"Neither," said Lilah. "I wondered if I could have your initials."

"My initials?"

"Yes." Lilah was removing the largest of her mother's diamond rings. "Do you remember Esther Johnson?"

"Esther Johnson?"

"Stella—on the window pane."

"Ah, yes. *That* Esther Johnson. Of course. Her little verse cut into the glass."

"Could you, before you go, cut your initials into my mirror, where I shall see them every day?" She held out the ring.

"Which mirror? Where, my dear?"

"Here above my bureau."

Fagan took the ring and cut *N.F.* into the glass near the top. "Shall I cut yours, too?" he asked.

"Yes. Please."

L.K.

Then, on a whim, he added: *In Memory of Swift and Stella.*

Having done this, he took Lilah's hand and placed the ring on her finger.

"Goodbye, Miss Kemp," he said.

"Goodbye, Doctor Fagan."

He began to disappear in the darkened hall. Lilah would never stand in his presence again.

9

There was a fine mist hanging over the rolling grasslands north of the city. Earlier it had rained and the air, being somewhat cooler, brought the heat up out of the ground. Once, the whole area had been a forest—and after that, until the 1940s, the most productive farmland in the province. Now it was covered with housing developments and winding roads.

The rich lived here. The very rich. They had chosen it because it was a place where they could all be together—a community founded on wealth that had been generated by two world wars. There was nothing of Rosedale here or of long-standing family compacts. These were the people whom Rosedale had shunned, as they emerged—but who now had surpassed that other bastion of wealth in riches.

On the night of Marlow's reception, the roads winding through the mists of this place were invaded by convoys of limousines and foreign cars coming up out of the city and converging on the residence of Michael and Patti O'Flaherty—she who had danced on Gatz's pool. This was to be the site of a dinner party given in Fagan's honour. It would be attended by more than eighty people whose wealth was the fount of the city's charity funding—from cancer research to the proposed raising of the Titanic. Somewhere in between these causes, room had been made for this night of culture.

The source of the O'Flahertys' wealth was the construction industry. They had built the head offices for half a dozen banks and trust companies. The Baycorp Building, where the Beaumorris Corporation was housed—the Gardner Building, home to Gardner Trust, and the Bank of Ontario Building—these were among O'Flaherty accomplishments. It was said—with the usual caustic sneer of jealousy—that each new O'Flaherty tower was erected only in order to give the O'Flahertys somewhere else to keep their money. Michael and Patti O'Flaherty were numbered among the top twenty wealthiest people in the country and *MIPAT,* their construction firm, was among the top ten corporations.

When Fagan was told the names of his host and hostess, he said: "oh, my God! A real, live Pat and Mike!"

The house, made five years before of stone, gave all the appearances of having been found in the vicinity of Versailles. But the Versailles south of Paris and the "Versailles" north of Toronto were not true reflections of one another. The latter—for all its mansard roofs and French doors—was entirely without character. It was a film set of a house—behind whose façade the courtiers awaited their cue with TicTac on their breath and autograph books in their hands.

Patti O'Flaherty wore a lacquered wig that looked as if she had borrowed it from a Kabuki actor. *Gale-force winds would not have disturbed an hair of it,* Fagan would say. She wore a red dress and—he was certain—*Ann Miller's tap shoes.* She seemed incapable of producing speech that did not require her to search the distance for cue cards. There was also the problem of her false eyelashes, which kept falling off through the evening. Fagan, at one point, found one of these on his sleeve and thought it was a centipede. "That's mine!" said Patti O'Flaherty—snatching it from him, as if he had wanted to steal it from her.

Michael O'Flaherty was less spectacular than his wife—though a good deal taller. He wore his hair in a pompadour, having been a youth in the days of rolled-up sleeves and Elvis Presley. His suit was what he called, when asked, *electric blue,* and was made of raw silk. He wore white shoes and, through the evening, kept lifting his trouser legs to show them off. "You like these?" he would say. "You like these? Hey? Palm Beach specials!" He had just come back and was black with tan.

Catherine, their daughter, was shy—which came as something of a shock. She was big, like her father, and blonde and pale and clothed in grey wool. Everything about her made a statement: *I am an orphan—I do not live in this house—I have never met these people before.* She hung back, most of the night, in whatever shadows she could find.

The guests were an eclectic lot, and their varied modes of dress suggested a varied understanding of why they were there. Some unquestionably recognized the nature of the company they were to keep, and these were turned out in business suits and evening wear. A good many others, however, seemed to be under the impression they were about to dine with film stars—or gangsters. As if they had mistaken Fagan for Reagan. There were seventy-five-year-old women wearing miniskirts and one of these had pulled on stardust stockings. The make-up above the gowns had the effect of having been applied to men in drag.

Kurtz was there, returned from Chicago in a new grey suit and hovering endlessly in the vicinity of the Applebys. At one point, Marlow looked across the room and noted that Mason Appleby was keeping Rena Appleby upright by holding onto the back of her dress.

The dining-room contained a half-dozen circular tables, each one set with yellow cloths, dyed green flowers and stark white china: the colours of Ireland, whence the honoured guest and the forebears of his hosts had come. A mass of small gilt chairs surrounded each of these tables, which Fagan said *were like little children in party dresses waiting to be seated...* Other dinner guests were to sit in the adjoining solarium, which was large enough to accommodate another four tables.

Fagan was seated with Patti O'Flaherty on his right and Fabiana on his left. Privately, he thanked his gods for Fabiana's presence. She restrained him from time to time by engaging him in conversations whose subjects ranged from sturnusemia to the war in New Zealand, where the South Island had just declared its independence from the North. Anything, to keep him from laughing out loud.

Marlow was seated on Patti O'Flaherty's right and throughout the meal was pestered by her constant interrogations concerning her guest of honour. "You're a psychiatrist, Doctor Marlow," she would whisper in his ear, seizing his wrist in an iron grip. "Do you think Professor Fagan is enjoying his soup?" And: "what should I say to him about his last book?" To which Marlow replied: "that you've read it." "But I haven't," she said, as if offended.

Between her bouts of anxiety at the table, Patti O'Flaherty was excessively gay and expansive—calling out to her husband beyond the dyed green flowers or telling jokes whose punch lines she invariably forgot. Marlow found her almost endearing, she was so obviously ill at ease at her own dinner party. He could imagine her as being an entertaining guest in someone else's house, if a musicale was to follow the meal. He was never unaware of her wide, red mouth—and the tap shoes lurking beneath the table. The words: *why don't you sing for us?* rose to his lips—but he could not bring himself to say them. *What if she did...?*

When the soup, the salad and the entrée had been consumed, Michæl O'Flaherty rose to propose a toast to Nicholas Fagan, meaning to say of him: *he is one of Ireland's favourite sons!* For whatever reason—drink or nerves—what he actually said was *one of Ireland's favourite sods!* Fagan—at last—was able to laugh out loud.

Marlow had noted earlier that a curious library was housed in one of the smaller rooms through which he had wandered. The panelling here was of pale yellow oak and all the books were uniformly bound in green leather. When he took down *Moby Dick,* he discovered the leather bindings contained a paperback version of the novel. *Abridged,* he noted, and put the book back in its place.

Only to verify his suspicion, he then took down *The Picture of Dorian Gray—Frankenstein—The Great Gatsby—*and found that these, too, were paperback versions, but unabridged. He smiled. He wondered if any of them had been read. Catherine, perhaps, had read them—but he doubted Michael O'Flaherty or his wife had done so. The green leather bindings, however, were both attractive to see and lovely to hold. Better that such books were present than none.

Marlow sat in a circle of personalities so eclectic as to have no sensible cohesion. He could not help thinking that fame brings the strangest people together. And the strangest thing of all was the universal sense of curiosity that had brought them all to this place. It could not have mattered less what Fagan was famous for. It only mattered that he was. Marlow thought: *does it matter that Patti O'Flaherty has not read books? Does it matter that Michael O'Flaherty has not? We all have but one chance at life, and must find our own way to survive it. Any book will tell you this, simply by setting out to describe the human condition.*

Why, then, read books at all, if they can tell us nothing more than what we can glean from any neighbour's life?

Books were just cultural artifacts and, if found in some vault a thousand years hence, could probably not be deciphered. The code would be lost by then—locked in the workings of some machine that had rusted and broken down. Current technology would fare no better than books in that coming time. What was it someone had said about *The Dead Sea Disks?* That they would be found in a cave by descendants of our computer society—by people who would have no means of retrieving the information recorded there because the means of retrieval would be locked in the disks themselves. *The Dead Sea Disks* would be used then as skipping stones—spun out over the waters, where they would float for one glorious moment before they sank forever out of sight. As books would already have done.

Marlow looked at his fellow guests—at his hosts—at the room at large. *We are lost,* he was thinking, *because we savour too keenly the brightness of the moment as it reflects upon our selves.*

He disliked it here in this place. It made him feel deeply uncomfortable—and he knew that part of that discomfort stemmed from the fact that he was a snob, an élitist and—against his wishes—a believer in that most dangerous of concepts, the concept of men and women who were superior.

He wondered what it was that drove him to think so badly of people who had found a way, as both the O'Flahertys had done—and many of their guests—to live without the support of books. To live, in their way, entirely without the support of culture. What could Fagan possibly mean to such people—and why was he at their table?

It was perplexing.

A wind had risen out beyond the windows. Marlow could hear it riding through the trees. A waiter came and poured more wine into his glass. Red. At another table, someone threw back his head and laughed. A sweet was served. Candles flickered. A woman with fanciful jewels was shaking her bracelets as if in time to music. But there was no music. Only voices. Patti O'Flaherty spoke his name.

"Doctor Marlow?

He stared at her.

"Are you still with us?" she said.

Marlow smiled as best he could.

"Yes, ma'am," he said. "I am here."

"You went a great way off," she said. "*Miles!*"

"Yes," said Marlow. "I apologize."

The room, all at once, was hot beyond endurance.

"Listen to the wind," said Fabiana.

"Yes," said Fagan. "A storm. Just what we need."

In *Harper's* magazine, six months later, one of Nicholas Fagan's "stories" appeared: *a fable*. When Marlow read it, he knew it had been engendered by Fagan's visit to North America and, more than likely, by what had transpired at the O'Flahertys' table. Fagan was used to being feted—but he never got used to being feted out of context. The great world of literature in which he had moved through his long life was failing and falling apart around him. In the years to come after Nicholas Fagan had died, he knew he would be forgotten as surely as what he had been about would be ignored. The failure of context would have won the day.

But, unlike Marlow, Fagan did not resort to pessimism. He resorted instead to the stabilizing influence of his anger. He fought back. He drew a bead with his aging eyes and fired at human pride and wilful ignorance—not with a fusillade, but with a single bullet. Thus:

The Assassination of Jean-Paul Sartre

By the time the century ended, it was thought to be common knowledge that Jean-Paul Sartre had died in his bed of a heart condition. This, I happen to know, was not the case at all and I will tell you now what occurred.

This story takes place in a house in Dublin—a fine old eighteenth-century house that had been rented by a motion picture company. It was the company's intention to shoot the interiors there for a film about Sigmund Freud. Jean-Paul Sartre had been hired to write the script for this film.

On the occasion of which I write, a dinner party was being given in honour of Sartre and his companion, Simone de Beauvoir. Having completed his scripting task—Sartre was about to return to Paris. Because of my place at the university, I was asked to attend this event.

Of course, under normal circumstances, Sartre and de Beauvoir would have been seated at different ends of their table, in order to extend the benefit of their presence as far as possible. But given Sartre's near total blindness, de Beauvoir had requested they not be separated. Consequently, they were seated side by side. Others at that table included

myself—John Huston, the director of *Freud: The Movie*—
the Dean of St Patrick's, Dublin—the Editor of the *Irish
Times* and his wife—an actor, a psychiatrist and a famous
transsexual. There were others I do not recall, but ten in all.

Before the entrée, a pause was taken in honour of Sartre's
devotion to cigarettes. He and de Beauvoir lighted up their
Gauloises—the blue smoke rising around the departing fish
plates and the intrusion of the waiters' arms.

Three men in short white jackets had been assigned to
each of the tables and one of these was exclusively devoted to
the pouring of wine. The waiter in charge of drink at the
Sartre/de Beauvoir table was more than somewhat nervous—
perhaps because Sartre was seated there—or perhaps
because he seemed, unlike the other waiters, to be performing an unfamiliar role. His movements were quick and studied, a little too precise, a little too rapid—as if he had been
rehearsed. The bottles from which he poured and the nap-
kins in which he wrapped them seemed more like props than
the familiar tools of the waiter's trade. Was he then an actor?

The ashes from Sartre's cigarette were scattered all about
but not inside the provided ashtray. Others cascaded over his
person until it seemed entirely possible he might be going to
set himself on fire. In the meantime, he expounded—with
some amusement—on the subject of *existence*. He did all this
in order to entertain his neighbours—gracefully realizing
Sartre was expected to sing for his supper.

As the first of the red wines was poured, Sartre was saying
that, after many years, he had finally been freed from his
oppressive awareness of others. And, especially, of their awareness of himself as *object*. His blindness had been the catalyst of
this new-found freedom—*my blessed, blessed blindness*, he
called it. *I see nothing, now*, he said, *but what I want to see.
Whether it is actually there or not is of no importance.*

The waiter's arm intruded. The tip of the bottle touched
the lip of Sartre's glass. The sound of the pouring was muted.

"We pay attention to one another in accordance with our
functions in one another's lives," Sartre said, as the wine was
poured. "I desire wine—I call the waiter. The waiter, at first,
is nowhere to be seen. I call again. I conjure him—according
to my needs. *Poof!* He appears—and my glass is filled. And
once my glass is filled, then—*poof!*—he is gone. The waiter

no longer exists. He has, you see, an obligation—from my point of view—to exist only in terms of my need for his services. This obligation is not in any way different from the obligation imposed on us all. When you good people want Sartre, then—*poof!*—I am here. Our condition is entirely one of ceremony. We dance our lives to the piper's tune. There is the dance of the grocer, the dance of the tailor, the dance of the waiter—and the dance of Sartre..."

Simone de Beauvoir removed the stub of the cigarette from his fingers and placed it for him in the ashtray.

Sartre blinked and drank wine. He seemed, all at once, to have tired. The glass at his lips was shaking and he had to set it down. Looking up, he made a rounded motion with his hand, embracing the other guests at the table. "It is only through you that Jean-Paul Sartre exists," he said. "Because you see me, I am here."

This was followed by applause, as if the master had performed a trick.

The famous actor was not impressed. He straightened his back and rested both his hands on the table top.

"But, *maître,* you are blind," he said. "And if you cannot see me—then who am I?"

"No," said Sartre. "You have failed to understand. It is not *who are* you?—but *are* you?"

Someone laughed.

Sartre gave a yellow smile.

"There," he said. "You have received your existence through that laughter."

As we moved through the entrée—which was pheasant—the conversation turned in other directions—films and plays and books—and Sartre, all at once, out of nowhere, said: "I have long been fascinated by the subject of *pornographie*—and I should like to hear what the rest of you have to say about it. So," he said. "Who will begin?"

"I will," said the famous actor.

But he got no further. A fountain of blood had sprung, all at once, from the forehead of Jean-Paul Sartre.

"What?" someone asked.

Sartre turned, amazed, to his left—to Simone de Beauvoir. She was staring at him—blank-faced—and putting out her hand in his direction, as if to shield herself from what she saw.

Sartre—still gazing sideways at her—batted now at his glasses, thinking they had somehow been smeared with the darkness that had begun to envelop him.

De Beauvoir reached in his direction—but he was sagging—falling beneath the table—sliding from his chair and pulling at the tablecloth with both his hands. Already dead, he disappeared...

There was a hush.

It was only then that I heard the gun go off—a noise so loud that I closed my eyes and raised my hands to my ears before I knew what I was doing.

When I looked again at where Jean-Paul Sartre had been, he was utterly gone and Simone de Beauvoir was falling to her knees. Only one other figure in the whole room moved.

It was the waiter who, till then, had been pouring the wine, and he went around behind me and away to the other side of the table. He stood there for a moment looking down at the figures on the floor. And then he fired—and fired again. And again—until he knew that both of them were dead. The slaughtering was over.

My own gaze was fixed on the void before Sartre's chair. His wine glass, pulled by the cloth still clutched in the dead man's hands, was balanced right on the lip of the table's edge. Emptied by Sartre only moments before—it was now full of blood—and someone, at last, had started to scream...

This is my fable.

Now it is over.

What have I told you?

How a man and his lover might die in their bed of a nightmare?

No.

I have told you what happened, in truth, to Jean-Paul Sartre and Simone de Beauvoir. I have told you this truth in much the same fashion as I would tell you the story of how, one day, a man with a box of matches walked into Chartres Cathedral and burned it to the ground. Or of how, in the midst of his life, a man called Michelangelo pulled out his eyes, in order to punish them for what they had seen. I have told you the dangerous consequence of failing to pay attention—and the savage consequence of ignorance.

Marlow, having read at midnight, let the magazine fall to the floor at the side of his bed and turned out the lamp. Rolling onto his stomach, he embraced his pillows. *Sleep.*

But he did not sleep. He thought about Fagan's words and he thought about darkness. Twins. The darkness he was in and the darkness Fagan described—the darkness where assassins move and arsonists provide the only light.

Beyond the windows, the sky was yellow, showing where the D-Squads had been at work. Marlow closed his eyes—and opened them. What was the point of pretending sleep would come?

He tried to imagine the burning down of Chartres—and a world that had not been seen by Michelangelo—a world where intellectual speculation and feminist determination were blown away by men with guns. It got worse, this imagined world, which is why Fagan was urging his readers to see beyond the examples he offered, all the way to a bonfire of human yearning and a void where art did not exist. He was urging them to conjure the mass grave of all philosophies. And yet...

He is also telling us where we are. He is saying: *all we have is this. Less light. More darkness.*

Marlow rolled to his side—away from the view through the window.

Sturnusemia and AIDS were not the only plagues. Civilization—sickened—had itself become a plague. And its course, in Marlow's world, could be followed by tracing the patterns of mental breakdown. The Parkin Institute was not alone in being overcrowded, overworked, overextended. Psychiatric case loads, everywhere, carried alarming numbers. Broken dreamers, their minds in ruin. This was the human race.

Marlow faced the ceiling, lit with the faintest streaks of yellow. Cries could be heard out there in the dark. Cats, dogs, Moonmen.

Don't.

There was a great, long cry that Marlow could not identify—out there beyond him—but in him, also. At last, he closed his eyes. The darkness in his mind was preferable to what he saw beyond the windows. At least in his mind, there was no one devising new ways to kill all the birds. In there, the living were granted life. He also caught a glimpse of Chartres still standing, and of Michelangelo bending forward, the tip of his brush on the hand of God. And just before he finally slept, he saw a round, small man in a rumpled suit, still sitting upright and smiling as the woman beside him reached out to dust the ashes from his lapel.

Not over yet, was Marlow's last thought before he finally slept. *Not gone forever. Yet.*

271

SEVEN

There is a weird power in a
spoken word... And a word carries
far—very far—deals destruction
through time as the bullets go
flying through space.

Joseph Conrad
Lord Jim

1

All morning long, Bella Orenstein had listened to Austin Purvis talking to himself in behind the closed door of his office. She was certain he was talking to himself because none of his patients had passed her desk. And Marlow had told her he would not be in today, so she knew it was not him in there.

It was also unlikely that Austin was dictating notes into his tape recorder, because whenever he did that, his voice flattened out and became monotonic. The voice Bella heard all morning was argumentative—even alarming. The man seemed to be castigating himself for some misdeed: an oversight, perhaps, or a failure. Bella heard the words: *I should have stopped it....*

What?

Had one of the patients harmed himself? Or died? Or broken free of his nurses—escaped his guardians? Surely Bella would have been informed if such were the case. An escape was always registered with bells, and a death with immediate phone calls to all concerned.

Her buzzer rang.

Bella gave a little cough of surprise. She had not fully realized how tense she was.

"Yes, Doctor Purvis?"

"Is anyone there, Mrs O.?" The doctor's voice was hoarse, as if he had been making a speech—which, of course, in a way, he had.

"No, Doctor Purvis. Are you expecting someone? There's no one on my calendar until tomorrow."

"Where is Doctor Marlow?"

"He's working at home today and tomorrow, Doctor Purvis."

"What time is it now?"

"Eleven forty-five."

"Go to lunch, Mrs Orenstein." This was given as an order—quite unlike Doctor Purvis's usual manner.

"I'm not hungry, Doctor Purvis."

"GO TO LUNCH, BELLA!"

"Yes, sir." She paused in place, then pressed the button and spoke again. "Are you all right in there, Doctor Purvis?"

"Perfectly. In fact, since Marlow won't be in," his tone softened—slightly, "why don't you take the rest of the day off."

"But, Doctor Purvis..."

The voice sharpened again. "Goodbye, Mrs Orenstein!"

"Yes, Doctor Purvis. Very well." She heard him hang up. "I'll see you in the morning."

Bella took up her handbag from its place in the bottom drawer and crossed the room to where her coat was hiding in the closet. Automatically, when she opened the closet door, she waited for someone to come out. No one ever had, but in a place like this it was best to be prepared.

The corridors would be filled with students and interns, potential nurses, social workers, doctors—always unnerving. There was something about the young that Bella, even when young herself, had never been able to tolerate. The weight of their collective energies had always seemed, somehow, to intimidate her. This is why she had said: *I'm not hungry, Doctor Purvis.* She preferred to wait and take her leave of the building when all the students and interns were safely ensconced in the Sub Two cafeteria. Then, unseen in her unremarkable coat, she would make her way on rubber soles through the marble halls, descend alone in the first vacant elevator, pass through the foyer, go down its steps, swing through the wide front doors, pass down the ramp and hurry along the walk to College Street, where sanity prevailed.

All this she did today, in her straw-bowl hat and her shapeless mack-intosh—stepping over guttered sparrows and turning away from the pigeon corpses brushed in tight to the Refuse Zones marked in yellow. The streets, now summer was promised, were open graves—or so it seemed—through which a person had to move with caution for fear of stepping on something dead. On days such as this, when the D-Squads had been at work in the night and the fugitive victims were lying by the dozen on the sidewalks, Motley's Bar and Grill on Spadina Avenue seemed a hundred miles away.

He yelled at me, she said to herself through her tears. *Oh, what is wrong? Why, oh why won't he let me help? I love him...*

There was a pigeon struggling at her feet. Without even thinking, Bella stooped to move it to safety. It pulled its wings in tight as she lifted it—and died, with a shudder, in her hands.

Someone passing looked at her and said: "you're crazy, lady." Stur-nusemia must be rampant in every feather.

Bella set the dead pigeon down in the Refuse Zone with its fellows. At Motley's, having ordered the first of her double martinis, she went to the

washroom and held her hands beneath the hottest water she could tolerate. She did this for fifteen minutes and then returned to her table, where
she proceeded to get as drunk as she had ever been since widowhood
struck ten years before. Was this what freedom from love was going to be
like—dead pigeons, vodka martinis and a table in the window?

Oh, Doctor Purvis, do not leave me here like this, she thought. *I
cannot bear it.*

Thank heavens this was not a day when Oona Kilbride would be joining her for lunch. When Bella drank too much, Oona tended to become
high-handed and she would moralize. Not that she was blindly devoted
to moralizing—but she was passing good at it. Bella took another swallow of her current drink. *Nobody,* she thought, *should be blindly devoted
to anything. Excepting, of course, to Austin Purvis.*

And to vodka martinis.

2

Austin had telephoned to Marlow at noon and had said: "come at once.
I need you."

"I can't come at once," Marlow told him. "I've got to finish this paper.
The printer has to have it by tomorrow night."

"Don't hang up on me." As if Marlow would. "Listen," Austin said,
"I've done something terrible. I'm in trouble."

Marlow thought it best to play his role lightly—not to let Austin get
too serious. He laughed and said: "you cheated at cards and they found
you out?"

"Don't laugh at me, Charlie," said Austin. "I'm deadly earnest, here."

"All right," said Marlow. "What have you done that you think is so
terrible?"

There was a pause. When Austin spoke again, he lowered his voice.
"I can't discuss it over the telephone, Charlie. Please, just come."

But Marlow could not give up his paper. A printer is a printer. They
kill for a deadline. Marlow had a deadline. He said he would come as
soon as possible.

Now, he was in the corridor of the Parkin's eighteenth floor. It was
just after one-thirty. A dozen student social workers slouched in
Marlow's direction, making for the elevators. None of them spoke.
Something had silenced them—perhaps their first encounter with the
Terminally Mad, a group of professional performers hired once a week

to harass the students and push them to their limits. In the first semester they had been mentally tortured by another group, the Head Set.

Marlow had not encountered the Head Set. They had been before his time at the Parkin. But he had been present for one of the sessions involving the Terminally Mad. Three young men and three young women, presumably actors, had locked themselves in a lecture hall with a dozen incipient social workers and had proceeded to taunt them, badger them and to physically abuse them—though not, in the latter case, with any degree of harm. The point of the exercise had been to defy, at every turn, the authority of the students—to "madden" them with mad responses to every trick in the social workers' bag.

Marlow had been impressed with the group—but glad he had not been asked to suffer the Terminally Mad in his own student days. Their technique, however abrasive, was brilliantly conceived. Above all, he thought, because they seemed to understand the logic of madness in ways that social workers had not been taught to imagine. Social workers were not allowed to believe in imagination. Imagination was their enemy. It reeked of anarchy. The logic of madness was central to Marlow's own technique with his patients. Never to draw the patient towards reality for reality's sake alone, but only for its place in the madman's sense of logic. It was Marlow's opinion—shared for the most part by Austin—that modern psychiatry depended far too much on placating the mad by stressing the comforts of reality—ignoring almost entirely the madman's fear of it. This way, drugs had played too large a role in the lives of too many patients. Drugs could be fashioned to be dictatorial—which is why they had champions such as Kurtz and Shelley.

Something of this had been the subject of the paper Marlow had just completed, and now that the paper was done—even in spite of Austin and his trouble—Marlow felt rather light-headed and delighted with his accomplishment. Beyond the building, the sun was shining—following a beneficent fall of rain. Marlow stepped like a dancer along the marble squares. A tune was playing in his mind. It had no name and no composer other than himself—a tune for a cello that took up singing inside his head whenever he veered from focused thought. He didn't want to think, just now. He didn't want to know why he was there. Austin's crisis was obviously coming to a head, but Marlow had no desire to second-guess the cause.

Now, at some distance before him, he saw the beckoning doorway of the Purvis/Marlow offices throwing an arm of daylight out in his direction. All the other doors he passed were closed.

Where was Bella? Still at lunch. Her coat was gone.

Marlow spoke: "Austin?"

There was no reply.

"Are you going to let me in? It's Charlie."

Still no reply.

"Please, Austin. Don't play games."

After a moment, the lock turned over and the door stood open.

Austin Purvis was standing there, shirtless. His suspenders hung down over his hips, accentuating his tallness and his tendency to deny himself those foods that created flesh. In the whiteness of his singlet, he looked like a fading photograph.

"Come in," he said. But that was all.

There was an automatic pistol in his hand. A Smith and Wesson. Marlow looked at it and heaved a sigh. He had been in the presence of guns before, but never a gun wielded by a friend.

"I see," he said. "All right. Let us talk."

The door became a barricade again. The lock was turned and the bolt was shot. All the venetian blinds had been lowered and the light in the room was dim. Pale, louvred streams of dust left their traces on every surface. As Austin positioned himself behind his desk, the flickering air between them fragmented Marlow's view of his friend. The effect was not unlike the effect of strobe lights.

Marlow dabbed at his eyes with his handkerchief. He did this partly to clear them of grit—but mostly to play for time. He wanted to know what he was seeing. *Vandalism* was the word that first occurred to him. A marauder must have come into the room and tipped the contents of all the filing cabinets onto the floor. Not only onto the floor, but into the seat of every chair and across the surface of the desk. Text books and pieces of paper littered the carpet. Only a supplementary table dragged into the centre of the room had any sense of order about it. Piled on its surface were a dozen files or more whose contents were still intact. On top of these—as if to further set them apart—was Austin's shirt, neatly folded— cobalt blue with stripes of white. Marlow coughed. He glanced for the briefest of seconds at Austin's hands. He wanted to know what had become of the Smith and Wesson. It was lying on the desk, already collecting dust. Beneath it, there was a notebook bound in leather—a notebook Marlow recognized as the one that Austin carried with him everywhere he went. It was even rumoured—by Bella Orenstein—that he carried it into the washroom, for fear some other glance than his own would fall upon its pages. Now, it lay there under the protection of a loaded gun.

That the gun was loaded, Marlow had no doubt. Everything, it might be said, about Austin Purvis was loaded though not in the drunken sense.

He had a loaded mind and a loaded imagination and an arsenal of disciplines to keep himself in check. Even the gentle, twilight-loving part of him was held in place by daily acts of will. Marlow thought of his friend as being on a self-restraining leash. Elegant but harsh. Thus, when Doctor Shelley had broken his nose with her clipboard, Austin had not struck back at her. Not because he was afraid of her—and certainly not because he was a gentleman. He had not struck back because, in part, he had believed in the integrity of Doctor Shelley's anger. It was her right to be angry. But if she could not control her anger, that was not his problem—it was Doctor Shelley's problem. For himself—Austin did not believe in physical violence. The noticeable muscles in his forearms and shoulders were the proof of this. He got them from holding himself at bay.

Marlow looked at the ruined room, took off his gloves and said to Austin: "who has done this? One of your patients?"

"No." Austin gave a pull at the waistband of his trousers, as if he were afraid of losing them. He stared at Marlow openly, without expression and without blinking. But *no* was all he said.

Marlow nodded—already guessing the answer to his question. Austin had given over and vandalized the room himself. That much was clear. His hands, Marlow now could see, were bleeding. A gash ran round from thumb to palm on one of them—the right—and some of his fingernails had been torn.

"You said, on the telephone, you were in trouble. Is this what you meant?" Marlow gestured at the scattered books and papers and the chaos on the floor.

Austin said: "no," as if it was his only word. Marlow began to realize that his friend, to some degree, was in shock. This would explain the vitreous, almost frightening stare. Austin would not relinquish Marlow from his gaze.

"You also said you wanted to talk..." Marlow left the sentence dangling. He looked away and took another step into the room.

Austin did not reply.

Marlow looked down towards his feet. There was a photograph there—8 x 10—with a glossy, glaring finish.

"What's this?" he said—and stooped to pick it up. Behind his back, he heard Austin sigh, and sit down.

Marlow looked at what was in his hand. He had never seen such a photograph before, though he knew such things existed. It showed a naked boy—fourteen, perhaps, or less. And he was dead. Someone had killed him.

The word *snuff* floated into Marlow's mind and out again.

What to say next?

Well.

"Was one of your patients responsible for this boy's death?" Marlow knew that Austin had dealt, over time, with psychopaths of every kind. But Austin did not respond.

Marlow turned, now, and saw that his friend's bleeding hand was resting near the gun. His fingers were spread on top of the desk—as if he were considering what might be done with them.

"Austin," Marlow said—dead quiet—almost whispering. "Tell me why I'm here." The dead boy hung between his fingers.

Austin leaned forward—lifted his hands and used them to push himself, still seated, away from the desk. He opened a drawer and took out a bottle, as yet untapped, of brandy. He removed the cork and filled a cup that was amidst the scattered papers before him. He drank without comment and pushed the bottle in Marlow's direction. "Please don't speak," he said. "Let me."

Marlow drew a stiff-backed leather chair towards the desk, removed his raincoat, pushed the mess of books and papers from the seat, sat down and lighted a cigarette. Looking at the floor, he spied Austin's tie that had been drawn off over his head—knotted still and nooselike.

He waited.

The cigarette tasted bitter.

He drank some brandy—two short pulls directly from the bottle. Then he set it back on the desk. Austin was staring at the photograph Marlow had laid before him.

"This boy here," he said, in a flat, inflexible voice, "he's been dead...I don't know. His name was George."

Austin stood up. His tall, lank body tilted slightly forward when he walked. His arms were covered with short, black hair—the same black hair that covered what could be seen of his chest beneath his singlet. Watching him, Marlow thought: *he was once a boy, himself, like the boy in the photograph. That young—that innocent.* Austin picked up the gun and moved across the littered carpet to the table where his discarded shirt protected the stack of files.

"These will tell you the story of George," he said—throwing his shirt aside and laying his bloodied hand on the pile. "These—and my notebook there on the desk... In my notebook, look for Kurtz."

"Doctor Kurtz?" said Marlow.

"Kurtz is everywhere, Charlie," Austin said. "You will find him everywhere."

"Are you saying that Kurtz killed the boy?"

"No, Charlie. No. Only that...he is everywhere."

Austin had been looking down at the back of his bloodied hand, but when Marlow turned to watch him, he walked away towards the windows.

Out there, beyond the blinds, were what he had once described for Bella as the great, good houses of learning. Also, the pale green tops of trees. Twilight would commence out there at six o'clock. Austin imagined the chiming of the hour.

It was now about fifteen minutes past two.

Austin fingered the cord that would lift the nearest blind—but he resisted its appeal. He knew, somehow, that what was out there to be seen would look no better than what he conjured of it in his mind. It was like the photograph of young dead George. There comes a moment when the image of what one knows takes the place of the reality. There would be no more lifting up of blinds; no more looking down from windows. The present louvred twilight of this room would have to do.

He turned back to Marlow and it seemed for a moment he was going to fall. He pushed a dampened strand of hair from his forehead. He blinked.

"I'm fifty-two years old," he said. "Can that really be?"

"Yes," said Marlow. And waited.

"I've never killed a thing in my life," Austin said. He was staring at the gun. His voice was dead and breathless—the voice of someone exhausted by a long climb.

"I know," said Marlow. They had once gone fishing together and Austin had thrown every fish he caught back into the river. A wide, cold river with a deep current.

Austin said: "the man who killed that boy—he's there in those files on the table. I want you to read them all."

"Why?" said Marlow. "What about the police...?"

"You don't understand," said Austin. "I haven't made any contact with the police. I...couldn't. And now, I'm handing this man—and those others on the table—over to you."

"But...why?" Marlow repeated. "What's going on here?"

He was trying to maintain a lightness of tone, hoping it would bring Austin down from the heights to which he had so obviously climbed.

"If you don't take them, Charlie," Austin said, "I cannot answer for the consequences." He took three steps in the direction of the table and put out his hand. His fingers brushed the sides of the files. At first, this was almost a loving gesture. Gentle. In his mind were the words *save the children*. Somewhere, he knew, he had written them down. It barely mattered where they were—*Charlie will find them. SAVE THE CHILDREN. Charlie will deal with it. Charlie will...*

282

Suddenly, Austin lifted his hand and made a fist of it, banging it down on top of the files. "Someone has to make this stop!" he shouted. "You, Charlie! *Please!*"

Then he withdrew his fist and stood—a recalcitrant child—with a gun in its hand.

"I've no one else to turn to," he whispered, on the verge of tears. "I've failed all these people. That boy. I'm so ashamed. That's why it has to be you who settles it. You're strong, Charlie. I'm weak. I gave in. I didn't fight back."

Marlow said: "what are you talking about, Austin? I don't understand what you're saying. I don't know what you're telling me."

Austin said: "it's all in here." The files.

For Austin, the subject was closed. He went across the room and stood again behind his desk. He picked up the cup and drank. Marlow became more alarmed. The gun, of course, was the major cause of his concern—but the brandy was also troubling. Austin had never been one to gulp down liquor. He was hardly a drinker at all.

A shudder passed across Austin's shoulders and drew his chin down briefly towards his chest. Then he looked up and spoke. "Give me one of your cigarettes," he said. His voice was now so hoarse he could barely speak.

Marlow opened his packet of Matinées and held it out in Austin's direction. Austin's fingers seemed, for a moment, not to be able to function. He fumbled a cigarette and placed it carefully between his lips, where it hung till Marlow rose from his chair and lighted it.

"Thank you."

Marlow waved his hand and sat back down.

Austin took the cigarette from his mouth and stood there wavering heel to toe. He wanted stillness. He was so very—so appallingly tired. *I'm tired, Charlie*, he thought. But he said nothing. His skin was so pale it seemed it might have never seen the sun. He looked up briefly through the dusty light—gazed at Marlow boylike—almost beautiful— and smiled. There were tears in his eyes.

"I'm sorry, Charlie," he said. "I'm sorry to do this to you. But you're the only one who can bring the horror to an end."

After that, he lifted the Smith and Wesson to his face and fired.

Marlow was already thinking, before he saw the gun go up, that no one should kill himself on the first of June.

No sooner had Austin fired than Marlow began to fall to one side. His body did not fall, but his mind did. It went over all the way to the floor, leaving Marlow sitting upright without the power to move. Words wouldn't come. How could they? There was no one there to speak to. Austin had dropped with his arms in the air as if his hands had wanted to catch the bits of his head that blew back onto the wall behind him. Marlow's first awareness of what had happened was the sound of brain tissue hitting the floor like rain.

Movement seemed impossible. His hands were gripping the arms of the chair in which he sat so forcefully he could not, at first, unlock them. His heart and his lungs were convulsing. *Stand up,* he said to himself. *Stand up.*

He wondered if he was going to walk away; go to the door without turning back and pass through the building all the way to the street. He wanted a place in which he could run and the street would take him all the way home. *Get up. Get out.*

As his senses returned to him, one by one—he knew that he could not get out.

Could not. Would not. His affection and respect for Austin would not allow him to leave him lying there unattended to.

Standing up at last, Marlow went to the other end of the desk and switched on a lamp. Austin had turned on none, in deference to his beloved twilight.

Don't look down, Marlow said to himself, in the way he would say it on a mountain top. But the view, as on a mountain top, was irresistible. *My friend has fallen,* he thought.

Go down.

Holding onto the lip of the desk, Marlow squatted by Austin's flung-out arms. One of the man's legs was caught up against his chest and the other had thrown itself forward, kicking the chair aside. A pool of blood, more black than red, was spreading out from the shattered head, but it seemed somehow benign and tranquil. The quiet was so pervasive that Marlow could hear that his own wrist-watch was out of sync with Austin's.

Marlow got up then and went back over to the table with its stack of files and picked up Austin's shirt from the floor where Austin had thrown it. Cobalt blue with thin white stripes. He held it—why?—to his nose. It was an animal gesture—cued by some atavistic impulse. The smell of the shirt was of peppermint candies, cologne and tobacco—the body smells of a man obsessed with oral pleasures. Marlow noted that all the buttons were missing but one. The one at the bottom, hanging by a single thread, was still in place. The rest, presumably, were scattered over the Turkey carpet and the parquet floor—*pop! pop! pop!*—when the shirt was torn open in Austin's rage. Rage or, possibly, contrition. Lamentation. What in another age was called "distraction."

Marlow himself was distracted—lost in the time lapse of shock—only able to function in slow motion. He took off his suit jacket and loosened his tie. Then he removed his tie altogether, folded it into a pocket and laid the jacket aside in the farthest corner of the room.

Go over, he thought. *And do what must be done.*

Carrying the shirt, he went in behind the desk and laid the shirt like a shroud over Austin's head. That accomplished, he picked up the brandy bottle and, lighting a cigarette, he retreated to the windows on the north side of the room.

Sitting on the window-sill, turning sideways, raising the blinds and noting Bella's African violets potted, already mourning beside him, he gazed out through the glass and took three pulls on the bottle—feeling nothing—no relief from his dreamlike state; and then—with the fourth pull, deeper and longer—he felt the pit of his stomach flare at last with the heat.

Austin.

Austin Purvis.

The words—no longer a name—had taken on meanings they had never been intended to convey. Key words, suddenly turning the lock on those files on the table in the centre of the room.

This boy has been dead...I don't know...his name was George. Somebody killed him.

Marlow stood up and retrieved the photograph of George from the desk. He carried it back to the window and switched on a lamp beside the bookcase at his back. He sat again and the lamp shone over his shoulder. If only the bloody windows could be opened. But they were hermetically sealed. The room was stifling.

Marlow could feel the brandy moving up into his throat as he looked at the shameless photograph in his hand.

George's nakedness was more intense than any other Marlow could remember. Not being a connoisseur of pornography, he had never seen the mass of naked flesh revealed this way in magazines and films, where human nakedness has no currency unless it brutalizes the eye. George's shackled legs and manacled arms were displayed in ways that had to do with jeopardy; nothing to do with desire. *No one we trust would ask us to expose ourselves this way,* Marlow thought. *There would be no need. We are only exposed this way if we are helpless to prevent the worst of what we fear.*

He noted that George had not been gagged. His cries, therefore, and his pleading had been intrinsic to his killer's pleasure. Also, the placement of the boy's body—curved over backwards across the arms of a comfortable chair, bent in such a way that George could not see but only guess what was going to be done. Apparently, a razor had been used. Certainly, a razor lay on the floor by George's feet. Death itself had been achieved with a gun.

A gun.

Marlow got up.

He went to the door and opened it—but only wide enough so he could see if Bella had returned. She had not.

The door to the corridor was closed.

Someone must be out there, Marlow surmised, and in time the cleaners would arrive. Discovery of Austin's body and the disarray of his office was unavoidable. He closed the door and turned back into the room. The humming of a string quartet—formal, precise and unmelodic—started in his head. Before he could abscond with the files, Marlow must obliterate all signs of his having been there when Austin killed himself.

Is this what someone did when George was killed?

As he went about the business of removing all the evidence he could find that would speak his name, Marlow wondered if the killer would be someone whose name he would recognize. People who killed for pleasure were not so numerous that one of them could pass unnoticed into custody. Austin, obviously, had treated this man—but whether that had been before or after the man's arrest, Marlow would only know when he had read the files.

George Anonymous and Austin Purvis, dead.

And Marlow, caught in the wake of their passing.

3

When the telephone rang, Lilah thought: *don't answer.*

It rang ten times and stopped.

Lilah was sitting at her own kitchen table with Mary Shelley's *Frankenstein* unopened beside her. She was drinking some of Marlow's Lapsang Souchong tea—*petty theft, but he won't mind. It was me who went over to Wong's and got it for him.* The dark, smoky flavour was almost like a drug.

The telephone began to ring again. The door between the houses was open and Lilah could hear the ringing out in the hallway beyond Marlow's kitchen. *One—two—three—four...*

Grendel came and lay down where Lilah could see him—spattered with sunlight on the floor.

Lilah was wondering whether or not she dared open *Frankenstein*. What if the man got out, bringing his monster with him?

More books were lying there, too. As others make a tea by setting out plates of sandwiches and scones, Lilah's table was set with *David Copperfield, Pride and Prejudice, Tess of the D'Urbervilles* and *Frankenstein*.

The telephone rang.

Lilah's hand had been on Shelley's gothic novel. She knew the story by heart. *I saw the dull yellow eye of the creature open; it breathed hard, and a convulsive motion agitated its limbs...*

Grendel was watching her from the floor. His tail thumped in time to the telephone.

After the tenth ring, the thing in Marlow's hallway went on screaming. *Eleven...twelve...thirteen...*

Lilah said: "oh, for pity's sake," and went out to answer it.

It was Marlow himself.

What he had to say was electrifying. *Please come. Can't explain. It's about someone else in the building. Urgent.*

Lilah listened—agreed to comply with Marlow's requests—and hung up.

It's about someone else in the building.

Her heart thumped.

Kurtz.

Finally, Marlow was taking on the role he had been destined for. That must be why he had sounded so odd. Tense. Almost distressed—but controlled. Even when he said he wanted her to bring...it was the strangest request. He wanted her to bring...

But why?

He wanted her to go to him at the Parkin Institute. The eighteenth floor. And bring...

Well, Lilah thought. *Maybe someone has left a baby on the doorstep. But goodness knows what that has to do with Kurtz... Still...*

She had now returned to her own kitchen table, where *Frankenstein* lay open, waiting for her return. *Did I do that?* she wondered. She did not remember looking inside... The book was displaying its final page. *He was soon borne away by the waves, and lost in darkness and distance.* Lilah closed the covers and went to collect her coat and her tam.

She locked all the doors and said goodbye to Grendel and to Fam— *wherever you may be*—and pushed the baby carriage out to the lanes. The carriage was empty of everything but its blankets and its pillow. As requested.

Lilah knew no other way into the Parkin than through the front door. This meant dragging the buggy up the ramp and backwards into the building. Consequently, her first view of *The Golden Chamber of the White Dogs* took her completely by surprise. There it was, staring down at her when she turned around.

"What are you?" she said.

A painting.

Not a very pleasant painting.

Not my fault.

I guess. But still... Who are your people?

Men. Twelve of them.

Naked.

Yes. And six dogs.

White.

Lilah squinted. She stood back as far as she was able without tumbling over the railing.

What are they doing in there?

That's for them to know and you to guess.

Anyone can see they're killing one another.

If you say so.

Why are there no women?

Women are not allowed.

Seeing what's going on, I'm just as glad. I don't think I like you.

It is not required that you like me.

Lilah stared. There was something disturbingly familiar about what she saw. Moonmen without their silver suits—Leatherheads without their leather...

The lights, which Kurtz had programmed to accommodate various times of day, adjusted to the lengthening shadows.

The Golden Chamber of the White Dogs revealed new images.

For the first time, Lilah saw the four human heads stuck up on their poles.

She did not speak.

The painting, too, was silent.

One of the heads appeared to be grinning—its lips pulled back in a wide grimace.

Who did this to you?

Guess.

I can't. You frighten me.

Think where you are.

The Parkin Institute of Psychiatric Research.

So?

Lilah's chin went up.

Kurtz. The horror-meister.

Kurtz, the headhunter.

Silence.

Lilah felt faint.

The head's eyes were closed—as if it dreamt.

In the distance outside, a D-Squad siren wailed.

The painting was now entirely mute.

The siren moved closer.

A cloud of birds had risen beyond the windows. The lobby darkened.

Lilah started towards the inner building. Marlow would be waiting. And somewhere in there, Kurtz would be waiting, too.

When Lilah reached the eighteenth floor, Marlow was standing by the elevator. He was tieless. His shirt was open at the collar. There was blood.

"Thank you for coming," he said.

Lilah said: "you're bleeding."

Marlow said: "there has been an accident..."

"Kurtz?"

Marlow had already started to lead Lilah forward into the labyrinth of corridors. He stopped and looked at her, taken aback by her assumption.

"What makes you think it is Doctor Kurtz?"

Lilah's face reddened beneath its white powder. She bit her lip. "Nothing," she said. "I just wondered."

Marlow started forward again. On their journey, they saw no other people—but there was evidence someone else was up there with them—shut into one of the offices. A woman's voice could be heard. She was singing.

Marlow pushed open the door to Bella's office. And closed it after them. The singing faded.

Lilah stood balanced behind the baby carriage in front of Bella's desk. A note had been taped to one of the inner doors.

DO NOT DISTURB. THANKYOU.

There's someone dead in there, Lilah thought.

Marlow had lighted a cigarette. She could also smell the brandy on his breath. She looked at the bloodstains that marred his beautiful shirt. And his trousers, too. She could see his necktie looping out of his pocket.

Have you killed someone?

She did not say this.

What she said was: "why did you want me to bring the buggy?"

Marlow went behind Bella's desk and laid his hand on top of a cardboard box that was sitting there. It was brown and on the side, she read: *NAVEL ORANGES*—which was not, Lilah knew, what it contained. What it contained was voices. Muffled—indistinct as the singing down the hall—but voices. That was certain.

Marlow said: "I told you there had been an accident, Miss Kemp."

"Yes."

Was it the accident's victim in the box? A baby? A part of the victim? A human head?

Marlow said: "a friend has died..."

Lilah held on very tight to the buggy handle. She waited—silent.

Marlow said: "before he died, my friend entrusted me with what is in this box..."

Voices.

"...and I must be honest with you..."

Please.

"...there are things in here which should not, strictly speaking, be taken from this building. Files," Marlow said, "that belong to the Parkin."

Files. Lilah sighed with relief.

Marlow was still speaking. "In effect, I am asking you to help me break the law," he said. "Do you trust me? Are you willing?"

Lilah looked away before she spoke. If the law must be broken in pursuit of Kurtz, she would break it. "Yes," she said. Her hopes were rising again.

"Thank you." Marlow gave a nod. And then: "I thought we could put the box in the baby buggy. If we cover it with the blankets, you could walk out with it..."

"It's bigger than a baby."

"Yes, but..."

"If we laid it on its side, it might be more babylike."

"All right."

They did so.

Lilah unfolded the blankets and spread them over the box. As she did so, her eye caught the letter *L* at the end of *NAVEL*.

Linton.

My baby. Missing.

It was a sign.

Lilah reached down and set the pillow in place beneath the box's head.

"It's all right," she whispered. "It's all right." This is what she used to say to Linton. *Everything's all right, now. I am here.*

She turned.

Marlow was still in his shirt sleeves.

"Aren't you coming with me?" she asked.

"I can't," said Marlow. She could see that he was wasted. He looked appalling. He was leaning over the desk, resting all his weight on his fingers, his iron-grey hair almost white in the glare of the overhead lights.

"When will you come, then?"

"Sometime. After dark, most likely."

Lilah looked at the door with the note taped onto its surface. Somehow, it seemed very sad. *DO NOT DISTURB. THANKYOU.* Lilah wanted Marlow to know she trusted him.

"There's someone dead in there, isn't there," she said.

"Yes," said Marlow.

"Is it your friend?"

"Yes."

"I'm sorry."

Marlow waved a hand, unable to speak. Her acquiescence to this reality moved him. She looked almost beautiful, standing there with her crazy hair and her black stone eyes in her masklike face. *The mad, sometimes,* he thought, *are wonderful to behold.*

"I'll leave the box in your study," Lilah said.

"Thank you."

"And something in the fridge for you to eat."

"Thank you."

Marlow walked around and opened the door. Lilah pushed the buggy past him and said: "good-night, Doctor Marlow."

"Good-night, Miss Kemp."

Lilah heard the door close behind her.

In the corridor, the only sound was the sound of her own footsteps and the turning of the buggy wheels. Whoever had been singing had stopped—or perhaps had gone home. Lilah could not remember a single lullaby—but that was what she wanted. And a Linton to sing it to. But he was gone and she was alone, now.

Sing us your favourite favourite! a voice said in memory. *Sing us your favourite favourite favourite!*

So it was that Lilah got all the way home with "Dublin in My Eye."

Marlow did not return till morning.

$$\underline{4}$$

When Bella Orenstein arrived at the Parkin the following day, she discovered the piece of paper taped to Austin's door: *DO NOT DISTURB. THANKYOU.*

Marlow knew that Austin's spelling had been eccentric and that one of his most persistent mistakes was in making *thank you* a single word. Wearing his gloves, Marlow had typed up the note on Bella's semi-retired IBM Selectric, which she could not bear to part with and kept in the corner of her office on a table of its own. Beside the table there was a small ornate chair. She had brought this from home in the way that others bring photographs and calendars with which to decorate their offices. The chair had been meant to give Austin Purvis some indication of Bella's good taste, but he had failed to see it. Certainly, he never mentioned it.

This morning, though distressed, Bella did not suspect a thing. She knew that Marlow would still be working at home today, and she was hoping that Austin would ring at any moment to call her into his office. *Come in! Come in!* Or perhaps he, too, might be at home and would ring from there, wholly recovered from yesterday's aberrant behaviour. The note on his door—he would tell her—did not apply to her but only to the cleaning staff. *Oh, please let him call,* she prayed as she hung up her coat in the empty closet and returned to her desk.

As soon as she was seated, Bella's fingers were itching to pick up the telephone. *But I'll wait another five minutes,* she decided. *Then, it will be ten o'clock and he will either have announced his presence beyond the door or he will walk into the office from the hall.*

What a lovely day, Bella! he will say. *I've just come all the way from Cluny Drive on foot!* The tension would have faded from his lips, his eyes would be unclouded.

The telephone rang.

Bella leaned forward, cleared her throat and picked up the receiver.

"Doctor Purvis's office. Good-morning. Can I help you?"

"Is he there, Bella? It's Charlie Marlow speaking."

"Oh, Doctor Marlow—I'm so glad you called. He has a notice posted on his door: *DO NOT DISTURB*—and I haven't seen him since yesterday before noon..."

Marlow said: "well—he's not at home. I've just been ringing there. Have you knocked on the door, or tried to ring through?"

"No, I haven't, Doctor Marlow. He seemed so determined...."

"Determined?"

"Yesterday. He locked the door and wouldn't let me in."

Marlow said: "go and knock on the door, Bella, while I'm still on the line."

Bella said: "yes, sir," and set the telephone aside and rose and smoothed her skirt along her thighs and walked across, afraid, to the door.

She "knocked" the same way she had as a child on her parents' bed-room door—with her fingernails. *Click. Click. Click.* "Doctor Purvis?"

There was no reply.

She used her knuckles.

Still no reply.

She used her fist.

Nothing.

She rattled the knob and pushed with her shoulders against the wood. Still, the silence was adamant. Nothing.

"There isn't any answer," she said to Marlow when she returned to her desk. She was breathless now and verging on panic. "I tried and I cannot get in. Oh, please," she said, "I cannot bear it. Something is wrong. I know it."

"Hang up, Bella," Marlow told her. "I'll come right over and we'll have the door broken down."

"Thank you," said Bella. She put the receiver back in its cradle and went and sat in her ornate chair beside the IBM Selectric. She could smell his peppermint candies in her mind. She could hear his clothing as he moved. She could see the back of his head as he left her office to go into his own. Light sprang up all around him—the kind of light that comes from being seen as you pass through someone else's eyes.

Marlow arrived. He gave the appearance of calmness—but she could see that he was tired. *All that writing...* Others came with him, some of whom she recognized as Parkin janitors. One of them carried a crowbar. Another carried an axe.

All the time they battered through the door, Bella did not move. But: "let me go in," she said, rising as soon as they were done. She wanted to be there first in order to protect him from their astonishment. She had guessed already that he must be dead—but she didn't want to hear the words from someone else's lips.

5

Marlow was running a bath. He stood on the threshold of his study lis-tening to the water pouring from the taps behind him down the hall. It was a comforting sound and among his favourites—soothing, reassuring, full of restful promise. Any moment, he would sink into the depths and be at peace. Water was his element.

The whole abhorrent episode of breaking down the door and of "finding" Austin's body had ruined him. Till then, he had kept himself alert to the danger he was in—silent lest some word or phrase slip out that would betray him. Poor Bella Orenstein had completely broken down. She had tried so hard to maintain her poise, but in the final moments when they came to take Austin's body away, she had failed. A great unearthly wail had issued from her mouth and she had thrown her head back, baying like a stricken animal. The sound of it was filled with the pain of all that would never now be said or consummated: Austin Purvis was dead and she had never told him how she loved him.

Marlow had to look away before her cry was done. *There is pain,* he thought, *that no one should be made to witness.* For a moment he hated Bella for the nakedness of what she was betraying. When Charlotte, his wife, had died, he had not cried aloud at all. It was a relief when one of the other doctors came and put Bella out of her misery with an injected sedative. Oona Kilbride arrived and stood watch with her and, later, took her home and stayed the night.

Marlow had waited long enough to surmise that, for those who were investigating the case, nothing was found that did not confirm the fact of Austin's suicide. Plainly, the man had killed himself and nothing remained but to verify that fact with the mandatory autopsy. If an inquest was required, it would be a mere formality. Nothing bore witness to Marlow's having been present—nothing, that is, *in situ.* He had removed the shirt—Austin's own—with which he had covered the damaged head and laid it in the pool of blood the head exuded. Wearing his gloves, he had wiped the bottle of Hennessey clean with his handkerchief and tipped it over on its side on top of the desk, so it would be assumed that whatever part of the contents were not in Austin's stomach had poured out onto the floor. He had taken up his own cigarette butts and placed them in his pocket. What else?

Nothing.

Before leaving the office, he had gone to stand at the window. His face had hovered there in the glass, under its cap of hair. The wide, solemn mouth was thinner now than it would be after sleep and the shadows under the eyes would pass. But the expression in the eyes would not. They were filled with the same alarm that had flared when they had first seen the gun go up to Austin's mouth. It would not go away. It stayed there, incongruous and slightly mad, locked in an otherwise placid expression all the way through that day. And through the next.

Now, the box of files and notebooks was safely ensconced in Marlow's study in the house on Lowther Avenue. Having maintained a cool demeanour all the way to his staging of the discovery of Austin's body, he was now beginning to lose his way.

The water in the bathtub was deepening.

He leaned in against the door-jamb and closed his eyes.

He tried for music, but it wouldn't come. He was losing focus. Too long upright, he wanted only to slide down into the bath and soak himself into a stupor. He would crawl into his bed and let the answering machine do all the talking.

Way downstairs, the back-yard door to Lilah's apartment opened and shut. For a moment, there was silence—and then: "I'm here!" she called from the bottom of the stairs.

That was good. Marlow had not been aware till then that he was afraid to be alone.

"I went out to get those things on your list," Lilah said. "That tea you like. And the cream you wanted. Also a dozen lilies."

Marlow made an image of Lilah in her tam-o'-shanter, standing before Mrs Wong at Wong's Groceteria and asking for *that Chinese tea Doctor Marlow likes—the one whose name I can never remember.* Mrs Wong would have handed it over to her in its magenta tin without a trace of comment. She had given the very same tea to this very same woman only the day before. Mrs Wong had a face carved in stone and behind it, she had withstood the genteel bigotry of her customers for over forty years.

Marlow went along to the landing and looked down. He could see Lilah's hand on the newel post.

"Do you think you could bear to eat some breakfast?" she asked. "I'm sure you're famished and you really should eat before you sleep."

Marlow did not know how to answer.

"Two poached eggs?" she tempted him. "Some bacon. Toast. And marmalade. Tea."

"Thank you, Miss Kemp," Marlow said. "I would be delighted to accept."

"I will bring it," Lilah said, "on a tray."

She was gone. Her neat, small feet in their slippers whispered along the lower hallway until she reached his kitchen. Marlow knew she was there because he could hear the bumping of the water tap as she drew a kettleful. When she plugged the kettle in, the lights on the landing briefly dimmed. Marlow went into the bathroom—stripped—and stepped into the tub. On the marble shelf beside him he had already placed a glass of red wine. Côtes du Rhône and a room of steam — the two best ways to relax in all the world.

He sank into the water—sliding down so that only his knees and his head were visible. Reaching for the wine glass, he knocked a blue plastic nail brush shaped like a duck into the water, where it floated towards his chin. One of his patients had given it to him—a concert pianist whose hands had voices of their own. *They want you to have this duck,* she had said, with that formal earnestness schizophrenics are forced to adopt when they're having to push each word across the space that separates their world from yours.

Marlow took a long, deep draught of the wine. The pianist's name had been Rosalind Joyce. Like many young schizophrenics, she had been destined for suicide. When she first came into Marlow's purview—this had been years ago—all the others who had been treating her had given up. *You try,* they had said. Marlow was always the agent of last resort. As with Austin Purvis...

He fingered the duck. Its yellow eyes had faded clear away and its blue was worn and bleached with soap. A small child's friendly toy—in Marlow's bath. He smiled, and flicked it so that it spun away into the steam and disappeared beyond his knees—and was gone. Just like Rosalind Joyce. Marlow had not been able to save her.

He drew an *X* on the dampened wall. *Rosalind Joyce.*

Like Austin, she had apologized before her death. But not to Marlow. It was to someone else in whose behalf she could not win her wars. *If I could just be deaf to the voices in my hands,* she had said, holding them up between herself and Marlow like strangers. *If I could just be deaf, I could win.* She had started covering her hands in multiple layers of gauze and gloves, as if somehow to muffle their complaints. *I'm sorry,* she had said. *I'm just so sorry.* Two months later, Rosalind Joyce was dead of starvation. Her mother claimed the child had become a kind of saint. But Marlow did not believe that. He knew it was just the mother's way of explaining the inexplicable nature of her daughter's madness: *God must have something to do with it.*

Austin had shouted at him: *someone has to make this stop! You, Charlie! Please!*

He made a second *X* on the wall. *Austin Purvis.*

"I'm tired," said Marlow out loud. "Tired."

Would he put another *X* on the wall? *Charlie Marlow?*

No.

When Lilah had taken the breakfast tray away and he was left alone with Grendel in the bright tall room that served as his study, Marlow half-closed the door to the hall.

Grendel accepted and ate the piece of buttered toast that Marlow had kept aside for him and settled down to stare at the street. To do this, he perched in a chair that sat in the sun towards one side of a triptych of windows facing south.

Marlow stood beside the box of files, fingering their curling edges and Austin's blood-stained handprint. It didn't matter which file he chose. They were all in there together—one whole world of people in a cardboard box. Marlow took out the notebook. It was black and on its leather cover Austin's initials were impressed—*A.R.P.* The *R*—if Marlow remembered correctly—stood for Rankin or Ranklin—a family name. Inside, Austin had written: *PRIVATE AND PERSONAL.*

Not any more, Marlow thought as he thumbed through the pages. They were covered with sentences written out exclusively in black ink, each word made in a tiny, perfect script that, in places, became so small that a magnifying glass would be required to read it.

> Monday, December 9th: it snows again and F. tells me she has P-Secunda on her roster now. The third to turn up c'tonic. This means it has started to fill in from both ends....

Marlow flipped through a few more pages, hoping to spot a name he might recognize—but none was anywhere in evidence. About two-thirds of the way through the book, he came upon an entry that seemed to reflect the spirit of the first one he'd read.

> The F-group burgeons. She attempts to convince me some of them are mine. I tell her to stop this.

Very unnerving.

The date of this entry was relatively recent.

Marlow wavered. He was too tired to read more. He would have to start at the beginning, but he could not start anything without some rest. Sleep was imperative. It was now 1:00 P.M.

Still, he could not resist the thought of George, the dead boy. He wanted to see the photograph one more time before he slept. He needed to verify what had begun all this.

He rummaged in the box until a large manila envelope was in his hand. He had noted its presence while preparing the files for transport in Lilah's buggy. Now, Marlow moved away to the window, carrying the envelope into the light. He gave Grendel an absent-minded scratch on the head and booted him from the chair. The dog wagged his tail and went on looking out the window from the floor.

The envelope—9 x 12—contained more photographs. They were all of George undergoing his final ordeal. In the last one, he was already on his way to death—bound, but still alive. Wooden-faced—feeling nothing—Marlow leafed through them all. Perhaps they had lost their currency in the face of Austin's death. Or perhaps they were just too grim to seem real. He could not tell.

Who could have held the camera during such a happening?

It had to be the person who had done the killing. Otherwise, it meant the boy had been tortured to death in front of others. How many? Who? It was unthinkable. Who could have watched such a thing?

Marlow stood up and crossed the room and put the envelope back in the box and closed it. Calling to Grendel, he left the study and went down the hall towards his bedroom. Grendel followed after him.

Marlow went to his bed and climbed underneath the duvet. Grendel watched—confused. Why were they going to sleep in broad daylight? After a moment, the dog padded out of the room and lay down in one of his favourite places—on the landing halfway down the stairs.

Above him, as he carefully laid his muzzle down on his paws, Marlow's collection of pictures hung—silent and, to Grendel, unreadable. Photographs mostly of people deep in the past. Marlow with colleagues (Austin was one of them)—school chums—his dead wife. One showed a girl no more than sixteen years old standing up on a stage beside a piano. There was an orchestra seated behind her. The girl was holding flowers. She was wearing a floor-length dress. This was her moment of triumph and yet she was not smiling.

In the feathered comfort of his bed that afternoon, Marlow had the first of his dreams about Austin Purvis.

In this one, Marlow was precisely where he was in fact, lying under his duvet, wearing a pair of white pyjamas. All around him, filtered through the whiteness, the light was the colour of membrane—a pale orange shade of red full of florid movement just as living tissue would have been. Suddenly, there in the dream, knives came plunging through the covers—one knife or several, Marlow could not tell—and he was pulled from the bed, his arms extended, trying to hold the duvet around him for protection. Austin bent down over him, breaking through the lights—and rolling Marlow over onto his back. Marlow wanted to stand up, but he could not gain his balance. Austin was naked, young and like a boy with no body hair—his long arms reaching to gather Marlow in and hold him so that someone else could stab him with the knives. This way, Marlow knew for the first time ever what it was like to die in a dream—not to be saved by the usual jolt of gravity, but to fall entirely into the dark and to know in there that he was dead.

Wake up.

The room was silent.

No. A clock was ticking.

Marlow's body inside the white pyjamas was soaking wet.

He threw the duvet away from his face and opened his eyes as wide as he could get them so the dream would go away.

Dear God, he thought. *I died.*

He raised himself onto his elbows.

"Grendel?"

Marlow could hear the dog's tail thumping against the wall as he entered the bedroom. "Come onto the bed, Gren," he said.

Grendel hopped up over the side of the mattress and lay down facing Marlow—looking at him wistfully, wondering still what they were doing on the bed in the middle of the afternoon. It passed through the comprehending part of his brain that Marlow might be ill. He smelled funny. Wet, of man-piss; not at all right. Grendel shifted his gaze from side to side and frowned, piling wrinkles up between his eyes.

Marlow sighed and fell back onto the pillows. His chest felt cold because of the chilled sweat and he pulled the duvet up to his chin. He focused on the ceiling—taking refuge in its blankness—its wilderness—its wonderful whiteness. Like a snowfield. Safe. A person could get properly lost up there and disappear. That would be nice—to leave, now, without a trace and not come back until Austin's ashes had been scattered on the wind and all the awkward, devastating questions had been asked and answered.

There are no dead children, Marlow said, inside. *No Rosalind Joyce; no naked boys; no velvet armchairs; no shackles and no manacles. No dead children. None.*

Austin is dead. He killed himself. You were there. He was insane—a madman for just one moment—the moment when he raised the gun to his mouth.

Suddenly, Marlow remembered the sound that Austin had made in his throat as the gun went off—a gagging sound like a man about to choke on phlegm or food.

Went in there and died in the dark.

What made him do it? Pain, perhaps. Cancer. An inoperable cancer. Surely that was what it really was. Not dead children. Not a dead boy.

AIDS, even. Why not? Anyone is prone. We all are, now that it's every-where. AIDS or cancer or sturnusemia. It could have been that. Not dead children.

Wake up.

He was drifting.

Grendel had closed his eyes, but the frown was still there. Marlow looked at him and smiled. *I'm not alone,* he thought. *I have a dog.*

He began to head for the dark again. Swimming. It was not unpleas-ant. A few easy strokes and the water parting—the water itself a liquid kind of darkness. Then he floated. His legs made one extended slow-motion scissor kick—sideways—and Marlow dropped his chin and rolled his shoulders, dipping them down into the duvet—drowning in feathers.

People do not kill their own children.

Who said that?

I didn't say a word.

He slept.

Wake up.

"I brought tea," said Lilah Kemp.

Marlow, under the duvet, heard her thump a tray with dishes on it down onto the bureau.

"It's 4:30 now," she said. "And you wanted me to wake you, Doctor Marlow." She whooshed the curtains open, one and then the other.

Grendel got up and walked around on top of Marlow.

"Could you get him down, Miss Kemp," he said. "He's walking on my kidneys."

"That's what I call *the bladder-dance,*" said Lilah, scooping Grendel onto the floor. "An animal's way of making sure you get up. You can't lie under the bladder-dance for long, first thing in the morning. Fam does that to me. Animals are smart. They know where to get you."

"Thank you," said Marlow. "I'll include that information in my next paper."

"You're awake now, are you, Doctor Marlow? No going back to sleep?"

"I'm awake, I promise."

"I'll see you later, then."

He heard her on the stairs and he heard her cross the lower hall and then he heard her walking underneath him through his kitchen to her own.

He got out of bed and poured himself a cup of tea. The image of Mrs Wong rose up in his mind and sank in all her stony glory.

He saw himself in the mirror.

The look on his face was extraordinary. For one whole second, he caught himself not knowing who he was. Then—what made him do it? Marlow put down the cup and slowly raised his hand to his lips—parted them and stuck two fingers into his mouth.

"Bang," he whispered. "Bang." Out loud.

Then, for the first time since Austin had shot himself, Marlow wept. He sat on the bed and sobbed.

<u>6</u>

What Marlow wanted right now was a drink. On the way, he had better just check that the files were safe.

As if anyone would steal them.

You stole them.

True.

He went down the hall and Grendel went with him. "In you go," he said to the dog—and they both went into the study with its bright summer light.

The box still sat where Marlow had left it—with Austin's handprint in blood on the top file. Grendel went to the window and sat in his chair. Marlow stood by the box, looking down. There was no need to look again at the photographs. He knew what they showed.

Who was George? A prostitute?

How did Austin know his name?

Marlow opened the box and lifted out one of the files.

It was thick with papers. Marlow recognized them instantly as transcripts—transcripts always being printed, at the Parkin, on bright yellow paper. These were numbered from one to twelve and each of them, stapled in the upper left-hand corner, was approximately ten pages long. Marlow wondered where the tapes might be that had been the source of these transcripts—and he also wondered who had typed them. Had Bella done it, with her impeccable discretion? What if one of the stenographers down in the deadly Subs had been the typist?

Marlow had not been too often to the archives on Sub Four, the deepest of all the Subs. It was a dreadful place—overlit and overguarded. The woman in charge of the archives was particularly unpleasant—officious, suspicious and vain. Her staff was of both sexes, but she treated them all with contempt. As a consequence, they were in a constant state of seething rebellion and prone to loose talk and gossip.

Marlow's reaction had been to be fearful of entrusting any of them with his patients' dossiers.

He brushed his fingers over the pages. Like all archival material, they gave off a musty smell. How many eyes, he wondered, had gazed upon these files? Dozens? Hundreds? *If secrecy corrupts—absolute secrecy corrupts absolutely*. Governments had proved that over and over.

Governments—corporations—scientific institutions...

Kurtz.

Marlow's fingers froze above the name.

It was appended to one of the files—written by hand on a yellow Post-it and the Post-it stuck on the folder.

Kurtz is everywhere, Charlie...

Marlow withdrew his finger from the name.

You will find him everywhere...

He lifted the cover of the file, turning it slowly to the left.

Nothing.

The patient inside did not even have a name.

And yet, the Post-it said *Kurtz.*

Kurtz's patient, perhaps. Or Kurtz had requested the file. Or Kurtz had returned it. Certainly, he did not appear to be its subject, and a flip-through of its pages did not reveal Kurtz's name.

Still. Marlow would be watching for Kurtz like a hawk when the time came to read through the files from beginning to end.

Now, he gazed—still burning with fatigue—away from the box, at the shelves of his books and his watercolours and drawings set against the dark blue walls and he listened to Grendel snoring and the gentle wheezing of the traffic—and then the clock struck six and he turned, leaving Grendel behind him, and moved to his bedroom, put on his clothes and went downstairs to the kitchen.

He located the Ricard at the very back of the crowd of bottles pushed in helter-skelter under the china cabinets that hung above the cutting board and the sinks.

In honour of his exhaustion, Marlow poured an extra-large drink and took his first mouthful without diluting it. The taste of aniseed was especially pleasant to him—even though, without water, the Ricard burned his tongue and the back of his throat.

The doorbell rang.

Oh, please, Marlow thought. *Whoever you are—not now.*

It rang again.

By the time Marlow reached the vestibule, Grendel had reached the bottom of the stairs. And Lilah had reached Marlow's kitchen.

Marlow pulled the door open, impatient to be rid of whoever might be there.

It was The Surgeon's Wife. Emma. She was standing on the walk, just beyond the porch steps.

"Hello, Charlie."

What was the matter with her? She looked at him as if he might not know who she was. Tentative. Wavering.

"Hello, Emma."

"I'm not here to stay," she said. "I was just..." she made a vague gesture over her shoulder.

Out by the curb, a uniformed chauffeur was standing by the Great White Whale. He was looking the other way—as Emma's chauffeurs were trained to do. For all he knew, Marlow was one of Emma's customers.

"I was just passing by," Emma said. "The sight of your door was irresistible."

"Will you..?" Marlow jerked his head at the vestibule behind him.

"I never go into houses, Charlie. Bad things happen." She pulled her collar closer around her neck.

"How have you been?"

"I'm here," Emma said. "I'm alive." This was not diffidence. It was a simple statement of fact—voiced as one would voice it after an accident.

"You look wonderful," he lied.

"No, I don't," she said. "I look awful. Not that it matters. Inside the Whale, I do look wonderful. It's all done with lights, Charlie. You know that. Lights and make-up and surgeon's knives."

Marlow shrugged.

"So," Emma said, "how are you?"

"I'm here." Marlow smiled. "And alive."

Emma was wearing a slim white dress. He had seen it before. A Spanish shawl was draped around her shoulders. Marlow still held the glass of Ricard in his hand. Grendel was standing behind him.

"You look like Carmen," he said. He wanted to make her laugh.

Emma said: "you look like Charlie Marlow—with his dog." She, too, smiled.

There was a pause in which Emma stared so hard at Marlow, he had to look away.

Then she said: "Charlie? May I kiss you?"

Marlow took a step towards her.

"Yes," he said. "Of course."

Emma leaned upward and took his hand. She looked into his face. *How tiny she is*, he thought. *And thin and breakable.*

"Thank you, Charlie," she said. And then she drew him down and kissed him on the cheek.

"I'll see you," she said. And turned around and went down the walk to the gate.

He watched her, afraid.

She went to the limousine and allowed the chauffeur to shut her inside. Marlow was unable to see her, now, because of the tinted glass. But he knew she would be watching him.

He waved.

He waved again.

The Surgeon's Wife was driven away. Dusk was in the streets. Against all expectation one bird, somewhere nearby, was singing.

Marlow thought: *I could lose her, now—and must not. There have been too many losses.*

For a moment he hovered, drink in hand, in the yard before his house—barely aware of its flowers. *That bird singing will give itself away*, he thought, *and bring the D-Squads.*

He wanted to throw a net around the bird in order to protect it. Just as he wanted, now, to throw a net around Emma, in order to protect her. Her loss would be appalling. *Why are all bright creatures doomed?* he wondered.

Plumage. Song. Intolerance.

Show me your feathers. Let me hear you sing. I will use you, then I will destroy you. Yes? I will wear you. Yes? I will dine on your flesh. Yes? Wipe you from my lips. Yes? In the dark I will love you. Yes? In the light, I will laugh at you.

Brilliant birds and gaudy women—all despicable. Yes?

It was true.

Everyone had used her, just as he had used the bird to lift his spirits. But no one had said to Emma or the bird: *is there nothing I can do for you?*

Marlow would try. He had resisted loving her—now he must resist despairing of her future.

He looked at the sky. It was brighter, now, in that way that brightness flares before the sun dips down below the horizon. No more bird song. Nothing but the sound of traffic—and the thought of the Great White Whale with its cargo of lost souls, moving through the twilight into darkness.

Emma would have to be deferred. Marlow was too caught up in the present to think creatively about her future. She was a creature, in his mind, to whom he had attached a tracking device. He would follow her, but from a distance. He was an expert tracker. In the long run, he was certain, she would not elude him.

Seeing that the moon was rising, Marlow turned from the fading garden and went, with Grendel, back into the house.

Sitting in the drawing-room, Marlow had spent the whole evening drinking. Now, he got all the way upstairs and all the way to the bathroom—carrying his last glass of Ricard before he remembered the lights in the kitchen. *Oh,* he thought. *No. I can't.* But he did. He went all the way down and turned them out—noting that Lilah had closed the door between their houses. Moments later, just as he was stepping back onto the stairs, he turned to look over his shoulder into the dark and saw, by the glow of the dying fire in the drawing-room grate, the shape and shadow of a cat.

It was sitting absolutely still in the middle of the carpet—only its shadow moving in the moving light. And it was staring up directly into Marlow's eyes. When he turned away—and back again—the cat was gone.

"Fam...?"

There was a thud as the cat achieved a favoured sleeping place, perhaps on top of a radiator cover—and Marlow returned to the bathroom.

Staring, now, directly at himself in the mirror as the cat had done, Marlow saw the tension in his face. He also saw the pale ruby imprint of Emma's lips.

Oh, he thought—reaching up to touch where she had kissed him. *No, he thought. Don't.*

7

AP: ...they asked her if she knew you and she said yes.

P: She was lying.

AP: I'm only telling you what they told me. They didn't say she knew you by name—but she had seen you before. And you had spoken to her before.

P: She's lying. I didn't. I never...

AP: This is what they told me.

P: (Shouting) Well, they were lying!

Marlow was sitting up in bed with the transcripts. It was Sunday morning, now, and he had slept and wakened and slept again before he had gone downstairs. The door was still closed between the kitchens—but he knew it would not be locked. Lilah had simply been wary of him while he got drunk. He had fed Grendel and put food down for Fam, poured juice and made tea—and had brought the latter back to his bedroom. He had decided to treat the day as a day of convalescence. He had, after all, still to recover from the shock of what he'd seen and the lack of sleep he'd endured sitting up with Austin's body. And bed, besides its other amenities, held out the promise of absolute privacy. At his age, he thought, it wasn't likely anyone was going to break down the door to join him there.

The passage he had just re-read in one of the files had disturbed him the first time he'd encountered it and, now, it disturbed him even more. The image it made of a dissolute middle-aged man in a motorcar, talking through an open window to a thirteen-year-old girl—or twelve, as the case might be—who claimed to know him—was charged, to say the least, with alarming possibilities. Whoever the man was, he had been so violent in his denial of what the girl had said that Marlow thought at once he must be lying. There was no earthly reason why the girl should claim she knew the man, unless she did. To deny it would not have been to her advantage. It would have put her in jeopardy of prostitution charges: the soliciting of strangers. Austin, too, had apparently thought so. *I hope she was telling the truth,* he was quoted as saying, *because what she said is part of what saved you...*

Part of what saved him. And what might the other part have been? His phone call to Austin? *I'm not well,* Marlow could hear the man saying to the policeman who wanted to arrest him. *I'm not well, and you must let me talk to my doctor...*

It was nonsense, of course, for the man to think this ploy would work. Your psychiatrist could not save you from the police. He could only ease the process. Unless there was something else—a name to be reckoned with. The man might have been well known—might have used his position of power to persuade the police they should not press charges.

Marlow thought about the man sitting in his car. Where might all this have taken place? Why had the two policemen been so conveniently standing by?

Surely there was something to be had from the answer to this question.

Perhaps, for some reason, they had been following him.

Or perhaps he had parked his car in a zone already marked for observation—a corner notorious for paedophilic activity, for instance. There had, after all, been an increase of assaults on children over the past few years.

Since AIDS had become so widespread, more and more men were turning to children as the only "safe" sex partners. Though *partners* was hardly the word for it....

The girl was wearing what sounded like the uniform of a private school. Marlow flipped back a page. *Something blue...* it said.

Something blue—but, of course, both the Anglican schools for girls and the Catholic schools had blue uniforms. And this girl had been wearing something over the uniform—a raincoat, perhaps.

Accepting the girl's story, how would she have known the man?

Who was he? Why had Austin filed him incognito?

Marlow drank tea and flipped pages.

AP: Why weren't you at work, then?

P: I'd been to one of those lunches at Vermeer's. You know the kind...

AP: No, I don't, as a matter of fact. I never eat at Vermeer's. It's beyond my budget.

There, Marlow thought. *The man is rich. Feeds at Vermeer's.*

His picture of Austin's patient began to shift. He saw, now, a pinstripe suit—a dark overcoat—and a car that was definitely not North American or Japanese. German, perhaps, or English.

P: I didn't leave the table until after two-thirty.

AP: Who was with you?

P: People.

AP: I suppose who they were makes no difference...

P: Some friends were there. On their way out, they stopped and we ordered another bottle of wine.

AP: You aren't going to tell me who they were?

P: Why should I? They were just friends.

AP: The police picked you up at four o'clock.

P: So?

AP: So you must have had quite a bit to drink. Is that why you tried to pick this girl up, David? You'd had a little too much to drink?

P: (Yelling) I didn't try to pick her up! I wanted to buy her fucking underwear!

AP: Had you talked about this with your friends after lunch?

P: (Does not answer)

AP: Well?

P: (Ditto)

AP: This is important. Was your conversation with your friends about sex?

P: For Christ's sake, Austin. Everyone talks about sex.

AP: With twelve-year-old girls?

P: (No answer)

AP: All right, then.

P: What?

AP: I'm going to tell you something.

P: (Laughter) What? You fuck dogs?

AP: No. I'm going to tell you that you are not alone.

P: What the hell does that mean?

AP: It means there are others who turn up here, who have similar interests.

P: In crotch-wear?

AP: No. In children.

P: (Something falls over—he yells) She wasn't a fucking child! The dirty little cunt had been sent there to wait for me! She'd been sent!

Marlow held his breath.

His eyes itched. He couldn't see.

Austin's reply was on the next page and Marlow couldn't get the page to turn. Finally, he dipped his finger in his tea—because his mouth was dry—and he scrabbled the edges of the paper, top and bottom, until at last they co-operated and he read:

AP: I thought as much.

P: You thought as much... You did, did you? You bastard. What is this? Some kind of trap?

AP: No, it is not. It is just that I happen to know one or two things about other aspects of this situation and, because I know these things, I believe you are telling the truth about the girl being sent.

God, Marlow prayed. *Don't let Austin say he's involved in some way...*

P: What other aspects? Jesus, what other aspects? How much do you know?

AP: Nothing said in this room will ever go beyond it. Never.

P: I'm supposed to believe that? Oh—Jesus Christ—what have I said and done? What have I said and done—Jesus Christ? Oh, fuck...

AP: Blow your nose. Come on. Pull yourself together.

P: I can't. Oh, Jesus—what have I said and done?

AP: You have to understand the law in such cases. No one can force me to reveal what is said here, unless there has been a killing. And even then...

P: You wouldn't lie to me?

AP: Why would I lie to you?

P: (Partly unintelligible) ...trap.

AP: No.

P: Who are they, then—these other people who turn up here...?

AP: I'm not about to give you names, for heaven's sake. Any more than I would give your name to one of them.

P: Why not? It could prove to be interesting... (Laughter)

AP: I'm sorry you think it's funny.

P: Tough.

AP: Thing is, you have to understand that your interest in children is something we can deal with, as long as you're perfectly open about it. That's why I told you there were others...

P: Perfectly open? You mean I should take out an ad in the papers?

AP: Am I boring you—or do you really want me to help you?

P: I want you to help me.

AP: Then stop making infantile jokes.

P: Paedophilic jokes. (Laughter)

AP: Okay, maybe I'd better just call the police...

P: No. Don't. Please.

AP: I haven't time for this. Or the patience.

P: (Unintelligible)

AP: *Perfectly open* simply means telling me what's on your mind. If we talk about it—if we deal with it—then we stand a chance of preventing anything serious.

P: (Unintelligible)

AP: Actual contact with a child.

P: (Partly unintelligible) ...nothing serious...underwear...

AP: Tell me what you do with the underwear.

P: I can't. It's too embarrassing.

AP: Try. Don't forget—I've heard worse. I've heard everything.

P: I...no.

AP: Try, will you?

P: I touch it.

AP: Well, there's nothing greatly strange about that. Is that all you do?

P: I smell it. That's why it has to be used.

AP: Do you masturbate with it?

P: (Does not reply)

AP: Well?

P: What?

AP: Do you masturbate with it?

P: No.

AP: All right, then...

P: What I do is take a shit and wipe my behind with it. (Shouts) So I can muck your fucking face with it! (Sound of banging)

AP: All right. Calm down. (Sound of banging)

P: (Shouts) How dare you ask me such a thing! (Sound of banging) How dare you ask me such a thing! (Banging) How dare you ask me such a thing, you fucking goddamn asshole...!

BO: (Interview interrupted) Do you want me to call Security, Doctor Purvis?

AP: Thank you, Mrs Orenstein. (Pause) Well?

P: Well-fucking-what?

AP: Do I want Mrs Orenstein to call Security?

P: (Does not reply)

AP: Good. Thanks, Mrs Orenstein. There's no need.

BO: Very well, doctor. Buzz if you need me. And may I remind you—you have another patient waiting.

AP: Yes. Thank you. (Sound of movement)

P: Is that what you call us?

AP: What do you mean?

P: Is that what you call us? Patients?

AP: Yes.

P: Where's the bed? (Laughter)

AP: You're in trouble.

P: Oh?

AP: Yes.

P: How? What way?

AP: You are riding too close to the edge.

P: What does that mean?

AP: It means you need help.

P: So. I need help. What kind of help?

AP: You need to stop for a while.

P: Stop what? Buying kids' underwear? (Laughter)

AP: I want you to take some time off. You need to stop—and you need to rest.

P: Who the hell has time to rest? You must be crazy.

AP: No. I'm perfectly serious. If you don't stop—then I can't take responsibility for you any more.

P: Are you saying I'm having a breakdown?

AP: I'm saying you need a rest. I'm going to prescribe medication.

P: (Unintelligible)

AP: All right?

P: Yes. (Sound of movement) Thank you.

(Tape ends)

8

Eleanor Farjeon was being buffeted on all sides. Her brood was not responding to treatment and the Medical Director was attempting to intervene in behalf of the hospital. He had called her into his office earlier that day and given her a dressing down that was doubly distressing—first, because of its bullying tone and second, because it was given in front of witnesses. Clearly, he wanted to demoralize her in the hopes that she would find the Queen Street Mental Health Centre an intolerable venue for her therapy experiments. His name was Stern. Eleanor had to smile when she thought of it, in spite of herself.

Doctor Stern had not been receptive in the first place when Eleanor had requested the special dispensation necessary to house her group of troubled children in his facility. There were other facilities in the city given over wholly or in part to troubled children—centres that had been designated to treat the mental disorders of the young. Queen Street was not such a facility, but the Psychiatrist-in-Chief, Doctor Farrell, had been persuaded by Kurtz to make an exception in his behalf. If it had not been for Kurtz's great reputation—*and his goddamn charming ways,* as Stern put it—the brood would never have been allowed through the door.

Stern had been Eleanor's enemy from the moment she arrived, insisting on extraordinary precautions and strictures—none of which was called for in behalf of the children, but all of which made it possible

311

for Stern to wash his hands of Eleanor and the brood if anything went wrong. He insisted on more locked doors than you could shake a stick at—and, because of his own fears, far more discomforts than were really called for. These latter had included nightwatch lights that made it next to impossible to sleep or to achieve any sense of privacy—and a paucity of comforts such as pillows and stuffed toys *for fear the children would use them to murder one another.*

From Eleanor's point of view, Queen Street was a means of separating her child-wards from other children. For this was an absolute necessity. Early on, when she had had the first of the brood at a youth-oriented centre, the confrontations with other children had been violent and terrifying. The sight of another child with long hair, for instance, would send the brood into a frenzy. A sort of gang-war situation had developed that was dangerous for everyone. The facility had been glad to be rid of them.

This morning, Stern had called in the head nurse and the hospital's dieticians and had threatened Eleanor's charges with force-feeding *by whatever means* if she did not gain control of their weight loss. Eleanor knew that force-feeding could be achieved only by intravenous means—which would necessarily call for drugging her children in order to make them compliant. It was Eleanor's belief—and she had good evidence to support it—that her brood were already suffering the effects of over-drugging and she was determined that chemotherapy would not be a part of their treatment.

"And if they starve to death?"

"They will not starve to death, Doctor Stern. I will not allow that to happen."

"How can you prevent it, if you won't allow them to be fed intravenously?"

"I will feed them with spoons by hand. They will let me. To them, I am their mother. I will feed them with my fingers, if I have to. But they will not be drugged into submission."

The head nurse had then reported an incident of violence to Doctor Stern that had involved one of her staff. Eleanor was flabbergasted. It had been her understanding that all such incidents were for her alone to deal with.

This one had been minor. A male nurse had been bitten on the neck by the girl called Sandra. Eleanor could have shown them ten thousand bites of which she never complained. It was heartbreaking. She had no allies—no one *in situ* to consult with—no one to back up her decisions.

Well, she had chosen this route herself and must stay with it, or perish.

Later that afternoon, following her disastrous session with Stern and the head nurse, Eleanor had received further proof that the brood was in a state of deterioration. The boy Adam, who had no previous medical record of seizures, had gone into a convulsive state and had broken a blood vessel in his forehead. The sight of him bleeding had caused a panic, both amongst the children and amongst their keepers.

Eleanor, who was present when this happened, went down on her knees and attempted to soothe the boy by holding his head in her lap while she cleaned away the blood. Aaron, who had always been particularly close to Adam, apparently thought that Eleanor was trying to harm his friend and he threw himself onto her back and locked her in a stranglehold.

The sight of this caused the other children also to come to Adam's "defence" and Eleanor was suddenly swarmed by all of them, excepting William. William stood watching from a distance and, finally, sat on the floor and covered his eyes.

This uproar lasted no longer than a minute, but Eleanor had thought she was going to be torn to pieces. The strength in the children's fingers was literally terrifying. She had seen it being exercised in previous out-bursts, but had never felt it concentrated on her own person. In the past, the children had bitten, hit and scratched her—but they had never torn at her before this afternoon.

The orderlies on duty saved her, pulling the children away and dis-abling them with hammerlocks. A nurse, whose name was Denise, helped Eleanor to her feet and took her to the infirmary for treatment of minor cuts. The boy Adam had been removed to his room and, within half an hour, the incident was closed.

When Eleanor returned from the infirmary, she thought it best not to let the children see her and, thinking to avoid them, she went into their ward through an auxiliary door which led directly from the observation room. None of the children was visible to her—all of them presumably now in their individual cubicles. But she had not accounted for William.

William was standing in a corner of the room that could not be seen from the observation window unless you stood up close to the glass. He was trembling, as though in the throes of a chill. Eleanor, when she saw him, froze in her tracks. She was alone in the room with him.

William looked at her, his body still shaking—both hands at his sides and fisted.

Eleanor said: "hello, William."

He did not answer. But he did unclench his hands.

Eleanor walked across the floor in his direction. Her knees were sore. And her elbows. There was a bandage on her neck and she covered it with her collar, uncertain as to how William might respond if he saw it. Nearing him, she saw that he was in a state of terrible distress. His eyes were focused on a vision of violence that was beyond her perception.

This was the boy whose suffering had been so profound that it seemed a miracle he had survived it. Clearly, nothing had ever been good for William, though Eleanor had no access to the details. As with most other members of the brood, William's history could not be traced. Though in two or three cases, Eleanor had been able to identify individual children—even to locate their families—in William's case there had been no reports of a missing boy whose description he matched. And because he did not speak or write, there was absolutely no way of discovering where he had come from. He had been unable to tell his own name—but all the other children recognized him and many had called him *William*. Whatever horrors they had endured in their shared past, William was like a beacon to them—lighting their faces with his presence. All he now had was the support of the brood and of Eleanor's love, which she feared he could not comprehend. Clearly, and for whatever reason, William believed that love was a trick and something of which to be wary.

"Let me help you, William. Please," said Eleanor quietly.

He stared at her—or tried to. He could not achieve focus—his gaze still locked on the vision that tormented him.

Eleanor bit her lip and closed her eyes. She was fearful that William would see she was afraid of him.

"William," she said, "come here." Her voice was barely audible.

She opened her arms and waited.

After what seemed an eternity, she felt him come forward and, her eyes still closed, she enfolded him in her embrace.

He was cold and wet and his heart was racing.

"Please don't be afraid of me," she said. And she stood there holding him for twenty minutes, until two orderlies came and took him off to his room.

Now it was midnight. After. She had left the children with their night keepers and had driven away from the hospital, heading through the rain to Lake Shore Boulevard and speeding then to the west. Eleanor drove like a demon. It was her only vice. She would open all the car windows, no matter what the weather, and take off at a hundred, a hundred and twenty-five, a hundred and forty kilometres an hour and dare all the gods in heaven to kill her. She would drive this way for an hour—hurtling over the Burlington Skyway all the way to Hamilton and back.

Then she would park somewhere at the side of the road and listen to the radio—mostly to country-and-western music. Songs that told of tragedies she could hope were worse than her own. But all the runaway lovers and all the honky-tonk infidelity in the world could not make her weep. Only her brood of children could make her weep—and she had given up on that so long ago she could not remember when it had been. But they themselves had tragedies no one could articulate. Only their faces told you. Only their eyes.

At six o'clock, with the sun about to rise, Eleanor parked in the lot of a doughnut shop—bought a *Globe and Mail* and went inside to end her day. She would eat two dutchies, drink four cups of coffee, smoke ten cigarettes, read the paper, leave, go home and sleep for two hours. At ten, she would return to Queen Street. This was standard. This was her life.

Today, she flashed the pages open, read her way through one whole section and, turning to another, was caught by news that she was utterly unprepared to receive. Her purse fell to the floor. Her hand tipped over her coffee cup. Coffee scalded her wrist.

Austin Purvis was dead.

She was now entirely alone.

9

Marlow had come down into the kitchen and was preparing to boil an egg and make some toast. He had been down earlier to make the coffee he had taken back upstairs to drink while he got shaved, showered and dressed. It was nearly nine o'clock. Grendel was in the garden digging up or burying another giant's glove. Lilah sat at her own kitchen table, drinking tea and reading. She had given in to Frankenstein and, so far as she knew, the monster was still contained in the story. Fam was on her window-sill, looking out at Grendel.

Spread on Marlow's table were the sodden pages of *The Globe and Mail*, which had been rained on in the dark. The paper had wilted on the doorstep while Marlow was involved in the file of the unknown man. He had thought of putting it into the oven to dry it out, but remembered that similar circumstances had left other papers curled and crispy and unreadable.

Having scanned the ruin of the front page, he saw that *Births and Deaths* were to be found in the *Classified* section buried deep in the mushy overlay of sections dealing with *Arts and Culture—Sports and Fashion—Business and Real Estate.* Cars for sale, employment wanted and several columns of professional services and personals preceded the obituaries.

O'BRIEN...OSSINGTON...PACKER...PRICE...
PURVIS.

There it was.

Marlow was so nervous of reading it, he shut off the gas beneath the pot and poured himself a glass of Merlot before he sat down and faced it. He also lighted a cigarette.

> *PURVIS, Austin Rankin, M.D., F.R.C.P. (C), at Toronto on June 22...et cetera...son of the late...et cetera...brother of the late Harold Purvis, Sackville, New Brunswick and the late Mary Wells, Portland, Maine...et cetera.*

Marlow had forgotten all these details of his friend's life. He read on.

> *Austin Purvis, late of the Parkin Institute of Psychiatric Research, University of Toronto, received his M.D. from McMaster University, and his Ph.D. in Psychology at the University of Toronto. Private cremation. Donations to the Heart Foundation would be welcome...et cetera.*

The Heart Foundation.

So that was it. They were going to pass it off as a heart attack.

But *private cremation*. Who had authorized that? Marlow cursed the delivery boy and the rain for having conspired to rot the front section of the paper, where—if anything had been written about the death at all— an item would have appeared.

Funny that Marlow had so completely forgotten the existence of Austin's brother and sister. He had met them once—he could not remember how or why, but perhaps it had been when their father had died. They had been older—and were dead, now, too. Marlow had been Austin's friend for so long, he had a vivid memory of the father—the Reverend Curtis Purvis—a name that had always made Marlow smile. What a war that had been, father and son going at it like Michael and Lucifer—the defender of the faith and the humanist psychiatrist. Marlow could still hear the Reverend father spitting out: *you're nothing but a cold, unemotional scientist!* at his son when Austin had, yet again, denied the existence of God.

That must have been it—the meeting he could remember with brother Hal and sister Mary. A concerted sigh of relief, as the old man—at last—was lowered into the earth and the stone set in place to keep him there.

Now the last of the Purvis children was dead—and not yet sixty.

Well. It was done. There was nothing left of Austin Purvis but the transcripts spread on Marlow's bed—and a box filled with horrors.

10

High up over the city, on the twenty-fifth floor of The Citadel, Kurtz sat in his conservatory beneath the arching green of a bougainvillaea vine. He was fielding telephone calls and warding off the press, using one of his many talents—an ability to silence others politely.

Yes, he had said ten times or more, *a promising career cut short. I warned him. I warned him. The pressures can become intolerable. But he wouldn't listen. I'm so very sorry...*

Kurtz had arranged the cremation. Paid for it. Accepted the condolences of colleagues. Stood alone in the chapel while some words were read. Drove away. Composed the obituary. Informed the newspapers. Done.

Now, he must deal with the consequences. *A cinch.* Was that the right word? No.

A pleasure.

EIGHT

But hope has faded from my heart—and joy
Lies buried in thy grave, my darling boy!

Susanna Moodie
Life in the Clearings
versus the Bush

1

Eloise Wylie hurried through the lobby of the Parkin Institute. She had no interest in the painting of the Golden Chamber. All she wanted was to survive the crisis with Amy and get back home to Nella and her Scotch. The known would save her.

Peggy Webster, who accompanied her mother, had seen the painting at the Fabiana Gallery and, though she had no affection for it, she recognized its brilliance and paused long enough to acknowledge its presence.

"Interesting that such a painting greets you in such a place," she said.

"Why interesting?" said Eloise, moving relentlessly towards the distant elevators.

"It's a depiction of hell," said Peggy. "I should have thought a depiction of heaven might be more helpful, given where it's hanging."

"Who would you expect to recognize heaven in an insane asylum?" said Eloise. "I dare say the images in that painting are something of a comfort around here."

"Oh?"

"A bunch of naked men dismembering one another—feeding each other to ravenous dogs—can you think of anything worse? In light of that painting, Peg, mere insanity is nothing."

Walking behind Eloise, Peggy smiled. "Yes, Mother," she said.

Both Eloise and Peggy were dressed as they might have been if their destination had been a tea party or an outing for cocktails. Eloise did not believe in hats and simply wore a veil that covered her hair. It was speckled with tiny black sequins and held in place with a velvet bow. The dark eyes in her hawk's face were accentuated by this veil and the white hair beneath it. She was trim, if slightly bent, in a grey linen suit and she might have stepped from a magazine—were it not for the fact that magazines rarely showed anyone over the age of twenty-two.

Peggy wore a tailored cloth coat and a hat she had found in Rome, where she had gone on an organized tour of museums. The hat was not unlike a shallow velvet box. It was hexagonal, sitting towards the back of the head, and it gave her the appearance of a Renaissance attorney—a Portia with no brief. The only client Peggy had to defend was herself against Ben. She wished that Olivia had been able to come with them, today. Of all the sisters, Olivia had the greatest authority, and was the most practical. Peggy was inwardly battered and exhausted. Olivia's energy would also have been appreciated.

Eloise went first into the elevator and stood four-square at its centre, like a captain on a ship. When others got in, she did not budge an inch. Both mother and daughter adhered to the protocol of silence in public vehicles. If either had ridden on a bus or a streetcar—which was unlikely—their rectitude would have been the same. The best way to hide from others is to ignore them—say nothing and see nothing. That way, no one can possibly know who you are.

They were met at their destination by Amy's nurse, Tweedie, who had been warned of their coming. He informed them that Amy was at lunch but they would be welcome to view the dining area if it would interest them. *Yes,* Eloise told him. *It would interest us.* Peggy wished she had not said this, but did not complain. Tweedie led them through the corridors and into the locked wards.

All at once, Peggy was stopped in her tracks.

Tweedie turned and waited.

"Is something wrong?" he said.

Peggy was staring at one of the closed doors.

"Mrs Webster?"

Suddenly, Peggy burst out laughing.

"Peggy?" said Eloise. "What is it, dear?"

"Come and look, Mother. You have to see this."

Eloise turned back to where Peggy stood. Inquisitive, Tweedie joined them.

"That sign," said Peggy.

"*THERAPIST,*" said Eloise, reading.

"Yes. I can see that now, mother. But when I saw it first, I thought it said *THE RAPIST.*"

Ben.

Tweedie did not say so, but he was intrigued by the fact that Peggy Webster had construed the sign that way. Only one other person had made the same mistake, and she was now sedated in one of the cubicles along this very corridor. The patient in question had thrown herself repeatedly against the therapist's door, vowing to kill whoever stood beyond it. Tweedie could not help but wonder if something like this had been in Peggy Webster's mind when she misread the sign. He had caught her expression just before she burst out laughing. It had been angry—and alarming. Sad.

At the Parkin, the patients on the trauma floor ate in a communal dining-room where the atmosphere was not unlike a boarding school. Monitors were assigned to each of the tables—where the behaviour was often on a par with the behaviour of quite young children. Minor wars broke out from time to time concerning the disposition of cereal boxes and milk jugs—and major wars were staged when one patient coveted the hallucinations of another.

It was a decent room so far as size and light were concerned. Wide wooden chairs with slung leather seats and backs were ranged either side of oak refectory tables. The curtains at the windows were made of orange hessian which gave the room a pleasant hue—neither too bright nor too dim. Two-thirds of the way up the walls, beneath a fourteen-foot ceiling, a balcony ran round three sides of the room, with doors that led back into the labyrinth of corridors. Tweedie ushered Eloise and Peggy onto this balcony, so they could look down without being seen.

When Amy Wylie had been deemed sufficiently stabilized to eat with others, she was still living in a private version of the world. But this was true of nearly everyone with whom she came in contact. The thing was—not to let the multiplicity of private worlds collide. Room must be made for each one to exist side by side with the others. Frontiers had to be established and, sometimes, border guards had to be posted.

Amy, for instance, required a certain amount of space for her birds. This was not much different than other forms of social accommodation—elbow room at the table—don't kick your neighbours—et cetera.

Looking down, Eloise and Peggy could see that Amy was seated at a table where only two other patients were seated—both of them across from her, rather than beside her. A monitor—male—was seated at one end. Amy's birds, as a consequence, were spread out along her side of the table, many of them perched on the arms and backs of the otherwise vacant chairs. No one else, of course, was aware of their presence.

When the woman opposite Amy was made aware of the birds, her response was: "just so long as they don't interfere with my quilting things." Then she had leaned across to Amy and whispered: "any magpies?"

Amy shook her head. No magpies.

"I don't see any birds," the third diner had said. He was small, quite young and balding. His name was Norman.

The quilting woman had given him a scathing look and proclaimed: "you don't see anything. You sat on my sister Mary the other night—and you still haven't apologized." Then she had smiled at Amy and lowered her voice. "Men," she had said, "will sit on anything—including your relatives. You can't be too careful."

A hot meal was served at noon. As Eloise and Peggy could see, it was plain, but substantial. There were meatballs, mashed potatoes and peas on everyone's plate. All the food had to be edible with spoons. Knives and forks were too convenient as weapons—and since para-noid-schizophrenia was almost universal in the ward, such utensils had been dispensed with. Also items made of glass. Liquids were drunk from plastic cups.

Bibs were worn.

Almost at once, the man across the table from Amy began to talk to his food.

"Make up your mind," he said to the contents of his spoon, having raised the spoon to his mouth. "Are you going in here, or not?"

Apparently not.

The spoon was let back down to the plate and Norman said: "don't tell me your troubles! If your mother ended up on someone else's plate, that's not my fault."

Amy watched, rigid. Her hands were under the table.

Norman said: "I can't do that. I can't possibly ask her to let me inspect her peas." There was a pause. "No. I can't," he said into his plate. "And I won't. It's not done!"

After this, he heaved a great sigh and looked at the quilter, shyly.

"Madge," he said, "I am sorry, but may I have your peas?"

Madge said: "you aren't going to sit on them, are you?"

Norman shook his head and crossed his heart.

Madge slid her plate along the table. "Help yourself," she said.

"Thank you."

He scooped Madge's peas out over the rim of her dish and let them rain down on top of his own. When Madge's plate had been returned to her, Norman pushed all the peas around until they were separated and said: "well? Is she there?"

No.

"Oh, for pity's sake!"

Norman looked at Amy.

Amy did not even wait to be asked. She pushed her plate—so far com-pletely ignored—across the table, where her peas were duly scraped off to join the others. As he handed the plate back to Amy, Norman said to her: "these peas have lost their mother. They want me to try to find her."

"Eat them," said Madge, "then they'll find her soon enough."

She should not have said this.

"I'll mash your potatoes, if you don't watch out," Norman said—his voice rising.

Madge was calm. "They're already mashed," she said.

Norman stood up.

Eloise, watching, stepped back from the edge of the balcony railing. Norman's monitor rose and took a step forward.

Amy's birds shuffled closer to her.

"Pea-mother! Pea-mother! Help!" Norman cried. "They're going to eat your children and only you can save them!"

Everyone in the room began to mutter *pea-mother, pea-mother* until it became a kind of low-voiced chant.

Amy watched apprehensively.

Madge paid no attention. She was eating her meatballs.

"Pea-mother! Pea-mother! Help!" Norman shouted.

"Now, now," the monitor said, "settle down. Settle down." He put his hands on Norman's shoulders. Norman sat down and stared at his plate.

"I tried," he said. "I tried—but I failed."

"No you didn't," said Amy. These were the first words she had uttered since reaching the table. "Here she is." She handed over a single pea.

Looking down, Peggy held her breath.

"She was hiding in my mashed potatoes," Amy said.

The man burst into tears.

"All that yelling frightened her," said Amy. Then she smiled at Madge. "You have to humour him, that's all," she said, quietly.

"He's crazy," said Madge, out loud.

"I know," said Amy. "But that's not his fault."

"Whose fault is it, then?" Madge was deeply suspicious.

Amy said: "no one's."

Madge said: "if you want to know my opinion, I think it's because he's a man." And she jabbed the last of her meatballs with her spoon and swallowed it. Whole.

"You'd think they'd learn not to serve that man peas," said Eloise, as Tweedie led them away.

"It wouldn't work," Tweedie said. "Every day it's something different. Last week, he was trying to find all the parts of a single chicken."

"Oh, dear," said Eloise. "I hope he doesn't ever try that with roast beef."

They were walking again in the corridor.

"Why were so many of them bald, with yellow dye on their heads?" Peggy asked, referring to a number of patients she had seen in the dining-room.

"Those are the manic-depressives," said Tweedie. "They're in a programme involving scanners."

"I see." Peggy did not see, but she did not want to express her ignorance.

"There are three scanning programmes at the Parkin," Tweedie told them. "Only the manic-depressive programme requires head-shaving."

"Thank heavens my daughter is safe from that," said Eloise.

Peggy said: "does one of these other scanning programmes apply to schizophrenia, Mister Tweedie?"

"Yes, ma'am. One of them does. That would be the PET scanner."

"Pet scanner?" said Eloise.

"P—E—T. Positron Emission Tomography. They use it to study the biological and cellular functions of the brain..."

"Will my daughter be subjected to this?"

"I can't say, Mrs Wylie. That's entirely up to her doctors."

"Is it a good idea, Mister Tweedie?"

"It can certainly help, in some cases."

"Does it hurt?" said Peggy.

"No, ma'am. The experience can be alarming to some patients, but I can promise you, there is not an iota of pain."

"In my daughter's case, Mister Tweedie, would we be informed before such a procedure was undertaken?"

"Yes, ma'am. You would be informed."

They turned a final corner and went along the last of the corridors.

"Your daughter should have returned to her room by now," Tweedie said.

Amy's was the last door on the right in a sequence of ten. Peggy had been counting, not knowing why. Somehow, the numbering in order had been a comfort. She was not enjoying this experience. It made her feel disoriented, claustrophobic and slightly panic-stricken.

When Tweedie opened the door, Eloise entered fearlessly. Peggy hung back. Tweedie hovered discreetly in the corridor.

Amy was seated on her bed, with her feet pressed together and her hands folded in her lap. Peggy's first impression was that Amy's hair had been cut off—but this was not true. It was simply lank—drawn back and held in place with a wide elastic band.

"Amy?" This was Eloise. "Dear? It's Mother."

Amy did not move.

"We've come to see if there's anything you need," said Peggy, still standing in the open doorway.

"What I need is to go home. I have to feed the birds."

This was said in a monotone. Amy had still not looked at them.

Eloise crossed the room and pulled the only chair provided forward.

"Don't do that," said Amy.

Eloise paused, with her hand still resting on the chair back. "I would like to sit down," she said.

"You can't sit there," said Amy. "If you must sit down sit here."

Amy stood up. Clearly, Eloise was being offered the place where Amy had been sitting, and no other. She accepted. Amy went and stood with her back to the wall, her arms at her side.

"You look thin," said Eloise.

Peggy said nothing.

Amy said: "I'm not hungry. I never was."

Eloise said: "you have to eat, my darling. The body requires it."

"Not my body."

"But, dear child..."

"Stop telling me what to do," Amy said. All of this was said without inflection.

Peggy said: "she isn't starving, Mother. Why not talk about something else?"

Eloise looked at Amy and said: "are you comfortable here?" *What a ridiculous question*, she thought, even as she put it.

"Yes."

An equally ridiculous answer, Eloise thought. *But the one I would have given, myself.* "How are your clothes holding up?" she asked. "Would you like a new pair of shoes? A bathrobe? A blouse?"

"No thank you, Mother."

"What about a pair of nice new slippers?"

"I DON'T WANT ANYTHING, MOTHER!" This, all at once, was a shout and it came so suddenly that Peggy stepped backwards and hit the door-jamb with her shoulder.

Eloise sat frozen. She was bewildered—but accepting. Amy's temper tantrums had begun when she was in her mid-teens. The usual practice then had been to ignore them.

This was before it was understood that Amy was ill, when she had seemed nothing more than extremely wilful—and had gone her own way, for the most part, unless she was clearly putting herself in some sort of jeopardy. In that case, she was monitored. Glennie had still been around in those days, thank heaven, and was already practised in keeping an eye on Amy. Amy was discouraged from taking walks at night, for instance, unless someone else was with her. Not for fear of molesters and rapists—but because it could not be told how far away or where Amy might go. Her predilection for disappearing had been truly alarming—and when the answer to *where have you been?* became *I don't know* instead of some familiar destination, Eloise—at last—had accepted the truth. Her daughter was crazy.

Over the years, Eloise Wylie had suffered all her family nightmares in a state of calm—the disastrous results of giving birth—jar babies, Amy—the disintegration of her husband's will to live. It was only afterwards that she took up despair and made of it a way of life. Now, she sat on Amy's bed and set her gaze on her own arthritic hands.

"Have you anything to say to her, Peg?" she said. "Otherwise, I think we might as well go."

Peggy felt trapped. Her mother always put the onus on someone else to get her out of embarrassing situations—social cul-de-sacs—her own drunkenness—Amy's illness.

Amy, as a child, had always been the one who brought home dying squirrels and run-over dogs and there had been an almost constant infirmary of sick animals which she nursed. Peggy, then, had thought her sister's animal alliances were just plain silly—sentimental nonsense—though, later, she had softened when it became clear that her sister was a poet. Not a pretend-poet. Not a schoolgirl-poet, but a real one.

Peggy had always looked on both her sisters with a certain wistful envy. Olivia was strong and definite. Amy appeared, above all other things, to have freedom and a total lack of fear. Peggy had none of these qualities, and, even now in middle age, she had failed to gain them. This was why she looked on Amy's present situation as bitterly ironic. Fate—or whatever it was that arranged these things—had been a proper bastard where Amy was concerned—and all Peggy felt was pity.

She looked across at her sister, now, and wanted desperately to hold her. Not that holding her would do any good. Amy had no sense at all of her own tragedy. She would probably wonder why she was being held and why Peggy was so upset. Peggy said: "if you want me to, I will feed your birds while you're in here."

Amy looked up. Her expression was extraordinary. A light might have shone on her. "Tell them I will come back," she said.

Two minutes later, Eloise and Peggy were walking to the elevators.

"What is all this about birds—and you feeding them?" Eloise asked.

Peggy said: "one of us had to say something she wanted to hear, Mother. So I did."

"But how many birds are there?"

"I haven't the foggiest notion."

"Then how are you going to feed them?"

Peggy said: "I'm not going to feed them, Mother. Don't be ridiculous. I don't even know where they are."

"But you said..."

"Yes," said Peggy. "I said it to make her feel better."

Eloise looked at her eldest daughter and tilted her head to one side. "I wouldn't have thought you could be so thoughtless," she said.

"I'm not thoughtless, mother. I'm a realist."

"That's right, Peggy. Just what we all need—a good dose of reality." Eloise was brisk and cold. "You told her you would feed her birds. Not to do so is simply cold-hearted."

Peggy did not answer.

In the car, however, driving Eloise back to 39 South Drive, she said: "all right, Mother. I will do what I can about the birds."

"Thank you," said Eloise. "I'll drink to that."

Peggy smiled. *I'll bet you will*, she thought.

2

Marlow headed for bed shortly after midnight. Grendel went with him. They were both depressed—the dog because he had not been outside for almost three days and also because of Marlow's depression, which made him apprehensive. He sighed a lot in Marlow's company. The man hardly spoke and the tension in him was palpable. Grendel sensed that something was going to break or be broken. He was right.

A plate cracked top to bottom in the kitchen, making a sharp, sudden noise—like a stick being snapped underpaw when you're halfway over to a squirrel and the squirrel bolts up a tree. The plate sat upright on a shelf—a round, decorative plate from Brittany. Grendel, of course, knew nothing of that. For him, the plate was just another brittle reflector poised above him against the wall. It rattled from time to time but had not seemed threatening till now. The crack appeared to have happened in response to the burden of Marlow's depression. The plate had split as Marlow came through the door. Grendel hid under the table.

Once Marlow had gone upstairs to his bed, the cat—in the way it always did—went into another room and became invisible. Grendel was no longer surprised by this procedure. The house was filled with other beings he could just perceive—creatures Marlow could not see at all. Even when they moved through the very rooms he was in, Marlow had no awareness of their presence.

A century of dead mice inhabited the walls. An earth-spirit dwelt beneath the floorboards in the drawing-room and it came out and danced in the light of the street lamps every night when Marlow had retired. There was also a woman in residence who had died almost a hundred years before. And a human child. And something in the cellar that could not be described. That it once had been alive was all the dog or Lilah could tell of this creature. Its voice was sibilant and soft and when it moved, it got no further than the bottom of the stairs. Lilah had spoken to it once—late at night in the dark. She had opened the cellar door and, looking down where nothing could be seen, had said: *don't cry. Don't cry. There's nothing can be done about it, now.*

She had been talking and walking in her sleep when this happened. But, later, she remembered the incident and said to Grendel: *don't go into the cellar. Something down there has lost its wits.* Grendel was not inclined to go to the cellar anyway. He feared its depths, having once been caught in such a place when a storm had slammed all the doors and shut off all the lights. That had been in Cambridge, Massachusetts.

Now, there was Grendel's mother. How she might have found him if she had remained alive cannot be told. But the dead can always find their children and Grendel's mother had tracked him down. She was out beyond the high board fence in the lane and, every evening as the sun descended, she called his name. Twilight had been the time of her death. She and the brood that preceded Grendel had all been beheaded in order to determine if they were rabid. They were not, but had been trained to kill by their owner, McCarthy, who had given them up to the authorities on demand. This way, they were doomed.

Grendel was afraid of the headless dog, not knowing at first who she was. Calling his name, she would come to the gate and scratch with her paws and, many spring evenings, she would lie out there in the lane and whimper. Grendel could hear her from inside the house if he happened to be in the kitchen. But he would never answer. And if he was near her out in the yard when she called to him, he would creep to the door and shout for Marlow or Lilah to let him in.

Not even Lilah understood his predicament. She was more concerned with the spirits dwelling in the house. Marlow was only a little concerned. He would say to Lilah: *do you think there is something wrong with Grendel, Miss Kemp? His nose seems dry—and he's off his food...* If only Grendel could explain—but, of course, he could not. His greatest fear was that one of the humans would open the gate to the lane and let the headless dog through.

This night—which was hot with early summer—Marlow finally got into his bed very late with Grendel at his feet. A visit from Olivia Price had caused some pain. Her sister was not improving with treatment. Amy, in fact, was resisting all Marlow's efforts in her behalf. On occasion, she had to be restrained and this was always distressing. Olivia, whose intelligence could not be questioned, was nonetheless obtuse about the fact that progress could not be made. She refused to believe that nothing could be done to relieve her sister's condition. Medication had always worked in the past and Amy had never resisted treatment before. In the long run, it was clear that Olivia was afraid of Amy's illness and Marlow had a suspicion as to why this might be so. She had asked so many questions about hereditary mental illness—*madness in the blood,* she called it—that he suspected she was pregnant.

"Everything about you, Mrs Price, informs me that you are some months into a pregnancy, and yet you have never once mentioned it. Why?"

That it might not be any of his business had, of course, occurred to Marlow, but he was somewhat taken aback by Olivia's vehemence when she said: "I don't intend to discuss it with anyone. I must ask you not to mention it again."

"Not to mention it, Mrs Price, would be extremely unprofessional, given the circumstances."

"What circumstances?"

"The circumstances of your attitude."

"I have no *attitude.* Don't be ridiculous."

Marlow laughed. "That line wouldn't even play well in a theatre, Mrs Price. Why don't you tell me the truth. The truth is what we both need, here. Not obfuscation. I will absolutely guarantee confidentiality. Your tension over this matter—and your inability to cope with Amy's condition—make it very difficult for me to discover how I might help her. I need your co-operation."

Olivia picked at her skirts and finally was still and said: "I'm not sure I want this baby, Doctor Marlow."

Marlow said: "what does Mister Price have to say about it?"

"Nothing," said Olivia. "I haven't told him."

"He must be blind."

"No. He is not at home. He's abroad. He goes abroad a good deal in behalf of his business concerns."

"Where is he, now?"

"Prague. He's bought a glass factory there."

"I see." Marlow waited a moment. Then he said: "will you tell him when he returns?"

"I don't know. I'm hoping to have it resolved by then."

"You're considering an abortion?"

"Yes."

"How far along are you?"

Olivia lied. "Three months," she said.

"I see." He knew she was lying, but did not press it. Instead, he said: "so—one of your worries has to do with whether or not Amy's condition is hereditary."

"Yes."

"I would be less than honest," said Marlow, "if I told you it was not. There is, I'm afraid, some evidence that a genetic link does exist from case to case of schizophrenia. But the evidence is haphazard. There is no guarantee, thank heaven, that inheritance is inevitable. The disease peters out. Or it skips generations—sometimes several generations. Other times, it skips sideways and moves into distant cousins, nephews, nieces. In your case—concerning this child of yours—I must avoid speculation until I know more about Amy's background. Which is why it is so important that we talk."

To date, there were not enough facts to go on and Olivia could not—or would not—provide any answers beyond those already written into Amy's long-standing file. These had been given to another psychiatrist, during an earlier episode, by their mother. Something about an uncle with epilepsy. Something about a great-grandparent who had tried to kill his wife. Something else about a psychoneurotic disorder in one of Eloise Wylie's sisters. *Somnambulism* was noted. But there was nothing more. Certainly nothing more about paranoid schizophrenia. And nothing whatsoever about a baby in a jar.

Olivia mentioned a cousin who was homosexual.

"Homosexuality is not a disease, Mrs Price."

"I know that," said Olivia. "But other people think it is."

"Well—other people are wrong."

"I wish you could tell my cousin that."

"I would happily see him."

"I think not. He's dead."

Marlow said: "I'm sorry."

"It was quite spectacular. His death."

"Oh?"

"Yes."

This was followed by a silence in which Olivia searched through her purse for something she could not find.

"Are you going to tell me what you mean by *quite spectacular?*" Marlow finally asked.

"I will—if I must."

"I'm not here to intimidate you, Mrs Price."

"I know that. I'm sorry. Have you got a cigarette? I've given them up because of the pregnancy—but I want one now, if you could..."

He provided both cigarette and lighter and watched as she inhaled. It seemed the very opposite of what it was—as if she were inhaling air after suffocation. He also wondered if she was aware of the irony of trying not to smoke in order to protect the health of a foetus she wanted to abort. He did not, however, mention this.

"What happened?" Marlow asked. "To your cousin."

"He courted death. He wanted it. *Death,* he said, *with bells on.*" She waved her hand.

"I see."

"You may say *you see,* Doctor Marlow—but you don't."

Marlow made a deprecating gesture. "I apologize," he said.

Olivia removed her gloves and slapped them down into her lap. Marlow wondered what it was that made her seem so contrary—eager to help her sister, but withholding information; longing to unburden herself, but obviously fighting off the words that might relieve her.

"What makes you say your cousin courted death, Mrs Price?"

"Because he did. He was always putting himself in jeopardy. Free-falling out of aeroplanes. Speed-driving. Bungee-jumping. All that. But, more than that, he courted it through people. His friends were danger-ous. Most of them. I can't remember that my cousin ever had a gentle relationship with anyone. Except his dog. He loved his dog."

Marlow thought, unavoidably, of Grendel.

"Tell me what happened," he said. It seemed this cousin's death—his homosexuality—his apartness—were of singular importance to Mrs Price, and Marlow was now in pursuit of the answer, if only for her sister's sake.

"Free-falling out of aeroplanes. That was his favourite. And that was how it happened. He went up one day alone. I mean—he piloted the plane himself. He took off from Buttonville and flew down towards the lake..."

Marlow watched her make a picture of it in her mind. It was very much as if the aeroplane hung there between them in his office—silent like a movie with the sound turned off.

"He had a sort of crazy conversation with the people in the tower at the Island Airport," Olivia said. "Afterwards, they told us he might have been drunk. I doubt it. He would never have gone on such a great adventure under the influence of anything but adrenalin. To begin with, he didn't need to be drunk. He would not have wanted the sensation to be blunted. I only ever saw him drink when he was trapped on terra firma..."

Olivia dropped one hand into her lap and lifted the fingers of her gloves.

"He threw down all his clothes onto the runway," she said. "Even his handkerchief. Piece by piece. One by one. Including his underwear. He was laughing when he did this. Not like a crazy man, but...joyously. As if he was shedding his woes. He was flying dangerously low. One man thought he was going to hit the tower—and said so—and everyone fell down onto the floor. It's lovely, isn't it—the image of that. Of everyone falling down. He would have called that *paying attention.* At last."

She paused for a moment—lost, perhaps, inside the control tower with all the fallen people. Or, perhaps, inside the aeroplane with her cousin. Marlow could not tell. When she began to speak again, her voice had taken on the tone of its engine.

"He began to climb, after that. In circles. Someone said there was not a cloud in the sky. Clear—clean space—and nothing else. At twelve hundred feet, he made a wider circle and levelled off. He flew back in towards the city. This was to be the last of all his manoeuvres—a slow, banking circle—skimming past the office towers. And then, out over the lake—the plane on automatic pilot, now—and my cousin stepping onto the wing. Naked. Waving. Falling." She paused. "With his dog."

Marlow sat back.

Olivia leaned forward and took a final drag. She was looking for somewhere to stub the cigarette. Marlow pushed an ashtray in her direction. When all this was done, they were both silent.

Olivia began to put on her gloves.

Marlow said: "I hope you understand, Mrs Price. He wasn't crazy."

"Wasn't he?"

"No, ma'am. Crazy people don't kill themselves." He thought of Austin Purvis. "Sane people kill themselves because they are cornered."

"In the sky?" Olivia said—and smiled.

Marlow liked her for that—very much. And it came as a relief to him—the smile. Because it meant she would be all right, for the time being.

"Why didn't someone tell him he wasn't crazy?" she said.

"I'm sure they did. There must have been someone in his life who was kind enough to do that."

"Not anyone in our family. No."

"Didn't you tell him?"

"Oh, yes..." Olivia's voice drifted. Her gaze followed it. "But who ever listens to me?" Then she shrugged and stood up. "I'm sorry," she said. "I've taken a lot of your time."

"Not at all," said Marlow—rising. "I'm glad you did."

At the door, Olivia turned back.

"Does this mean," she asked, "that Amy is not in danger? I mean—of suicide?"

Marlow said: "yes." But that was all he said. Some lies—for everyone's sake—must be maintained. Others, like this one, must be established and given credence—in order to get someone through to the other side. Intact.

Suddenly, Olivia said: "my cousin was like those rats we saw the other week, wasn't he. Whoever told him being a homosexual was a mental illness put him in a cage and took away his voice. I never really understood that before."

Marlow waited. She would say something more.

"You won't allow that to happen to Amy. Will you, Doctor Marlow."

It was not a question.

"No," he said.

And she had gone.

Now, in his bed, with Grendel at his feet, he regretted not having asked the identity of the cousin. It seemed, somehow, the final discourtesy, not to have given him his name. In the morning, he would write to Olivia and offer his apology. In the meantime, he had come upon the young man's identity in one of Amy's poems—and that was the last conscious thing he was aware of before he finally slept.

He had said:
*If I climb up
into heaven,
they will see
who I am.*

And so he
went up climbing.

This last is
what no one
understood: the thing he
feared the most was

falling from the
sky. Wouldn't
you know it?

The poem was called *Icarus*—and all through the night they fell
together—Marlow and Icarus. And two dogs.

3

Lilah heard sighing.

It was long past midnight, now, and there was an aura of expectation.
Something was going to happen.

She waited—seated primly right at the edge of her bed. She had
thrown a red bandana handkerchief over the shade of the lamp on her
table. She was wearing a flannel nightgown under her bathrobe—the
nightgown reaching to her toes. She was determined not to speak until
she was spoken to. A medium always waits to be summoned.

The sighing came again. She could not tell where it originated—
which room or hallway. It was seemingly everywhere—behind her,
above and below her. Also—beyond the door.

Perhaps it was that creature in the cellar.

See.

Lilah rose—without slippers—and made her way to the bedroom
door. She opened it and looked along the corridor. A light was shining
beyond her kitchen. Perhaps it was just the doctor, come down to make
a sandwich or to get another glass of wine. He was drinking a lot of wine
these days. Wine, and that Ricard he loved. Maybe it was only him. But
she would not speak until she was spoken to. That was a rule.

Partway along the hall, she stopped and pressed her ear to the
cellar door.

The sighing was not there.

She pattered on—small steps, never long ones. She came to her
kitchen entrance and listened as she had above the cellar.

Nothing.

She moved on through towards Marlow's kitchen, where she pushed
the half-closed door wide open.

The light was not as bright as she had thought. It came from the
farthest side of the room, obscured in part by the shelves above
Marlow's stove.

Go in, she told herself. *Go on.*

She stepped forward. Once. Twice.

To her left, the shelf where the cracked plate stood. To her right, the view of the sinks. A tap was dripping and she went to turn it off.

The sighing came again. Behind her.

The air was frozen. She could barely move.

Someone was at the kitchen table.

It was not Marlow. It was one of Them. A woman. She was turned away from Lilah, bending forward over the table top, moving rhythmically back and forth—back and forth. Lilah knew at once what it was the woman was doing. She was scrubbing the surface of the wood. There would be a brush in her hand—a spirit brush.

Lilah still did not speak. The rule still held.

For the briefest moment, she stood there watching—thinking the woman perhaps should not be disturbed. If she had been sitting, that would be different. An activity, however, must not be interrupted.

The sighs continued—induced, it seemed, as much by the scrubbing as by the woman's torment. It took on the tone of a song one might hum while doing something repetitive—a way of getting oxygen into the bloodstream. But this woman had no bloodstream. She needed no oxygen. She was dead—long dead—a century, almost.

Lilah decided the scrubbing might go on forever if she did not intercede. The appearance of it was mechanical, as though the poor woman had no means of stopping it. Lilah made her way forward—blessing the silence of her bare feet—and stood where the woman could see her.

The scrubbing stopped mid-motion—the woman leaning forward, bearing down on the wooden brush whose bristles had almost been worn away. Her dark eyes turned towards Lilah.

Kemp, isn't it.

That's right.

The woman stood up straight—one hand pressed into the small of her back and the other, still with the brush, using it to push aside the hair that had fallen sideways across her face. When she spoke, her voice was full of damp and darkness.

I give up, she said. *I can't do this.*

She brushed at her hair again.

She sat down.

This is where he died, she said. *And I can't make it clean. The table.*

Lilah ventured forward.

Who, she said, died?

My boy.

337

Oh, yes.

He died on the table right here.

I'm sorry.

A doctor came.

Lilah waited.

There was a tumour in his brain, the woman said. *The doctor wanted to operate.*

Yes.

My boy Stuart. The woman's hands went out above the table, as if to find him there. *He was eleven.* Her hands drew back.

Yes.

Have you dead children, Kemp?

One. My only.

I had others died. Two others. But neither one long enough alive to be mourned for what they lost. Babes—that's all they were. Breath was lost. Light was lost. Warmth. The smell of me. My hands. Breasts. Hair. They lost all this—but nothing of being alive in the world out there was lost. That they never knew.

Lilah conjured Linton. Gone entirely.

My boy died living. Full of life. He was eleven.

Lilah said: my boy was just a baby.

Yes. Well.

His name was Linton. His father was Heathcliff.

This meant nothing to the woman. Lilah did not pursue it. Instead, she said: were you with him?

Yes. Must I die? he said. And I said: no. I don't want to die, he said. And I said: everyone must die. Not now, he said. And I said: no—not now. I said: you will not die now. And then he died.

Lilah waited.

The woman had dark brown hair with streaks of grey in it. Her dress was black and her apron white. Her sleeves were all unbuttoned, pulled and rolled above the elbow. She had not been old when she died. The grey had come from labour and grief.

Lilah wondered where the dead boy was. He had appeared before with his mother. Lilah had seen them two or three times together—but now there was no sign of him. The woman was alone.

I have never heard your name, Lilah said—closing her eyes to say it.

The woman was smiling now. *I was Martha. But I cannot make this table clean, no matter what my name was. I couldn't then—I cannot now. This is where he died.*

Lilah looked across the table at the mourning woman—exhausted even after death. The table, of course, could not be the one on which the boy, Stuart, had died—but the woman seemed unaware of this.

How long ago did he die? Your Stuart.

I can't tell that. I don't know when this is.

Lilah told her the date.

That means he died one hundred years ago—and ten, said Martha. *It was a Sunday. In the morning.*

Here in this very room, Lilah thought. *One hundred years ago. And ten.*

He hides, this day, Martha continued. *Somewhere. He hides, because he still does not want to die. He hides from me because I broke my promise.*

You cannot be blamed for that.

I would like to find him.

I have only ever seen him in the passageway with you, said Lilah. And sometimes on the stairs.

He is not there, now. I have looked.

All at once, Fam was sitting in the centre of the table.

Fam.

Yes.

Fam leaned out towards Martha and touched the woman's hand with her paw, as if at play.

She sees.

Yes.

Fam stood up and jumped down onto the floor. She walked to the door—the door that led to the front of the house. Then she stopped and looked back up at the women—one of them dead, the other living.

Come, she said—saying this with her tail and with her back. *Come.*

Neither woman spoke. Instead, they followed.

They went up the stairs—Fam first and Martha second. Lilah, who endured real fatigue, could not climb up so fast as they did. Martha did not touch down. She seemed, as Lilah watched, to flow. She leaned out over the stairs and swam upstream.

At the top, in the dimly lit hall, they all turned together to the right and moved towards the study. Who had left the lights on for this journey? Certainly Lilah had not. And Marlow was not in the habit of lighting the rooms he was not inhabiting. Someone else must have done it.

In the study, there were noises. A sort of distant clamouring.

Fam went over to the box that said *NAVEL ORANGES.*

Martha went with her. Lilah did not. To her, the box was forbidden territory—though perhaps it was not forbidden to cats and spirit visitors.

339

Martha stood over the box. Fam sat down beside it. Lilah stood back beside the door.

Fam made a chirping noise—the kind cats make when they come to where their young are hidden.

Martha was still not grounded. She lay out over the box and stayed there a moment, listening intently. Then she went back towards the floor with her feet.

Missing children, she said.

Lilah stepped forward.

Fam jumped down.

Lilah stood so close to Martha, they merged. The skirts of Lilah's dressing-gown and nightdress mingled with Martha's apron. Each put out a hand above the box.

Lilah removed the tape, yellow and squealing.

She did all this in a trance, knowing it was forbidden, but Martha led her and she could not resist.

As the flaps were pulled open, a rush of whispers escaped and Stuart—from the air—said: *Mother—here I am.*

Lilah could not see him. Nor could Martha.

Stuart said: *I have found some others.*

Lilah said: he means in the box.

Yes.

But Martha was looking for Stuart, not for others. She had no interest in the box once it had released her son. She spoke back into the room. *Where,* she said, *are you?*

He did not answer.

Martha went about the room, searching.

Lilah leaned in closer and stared down into the box. Because of her height, she had to tip it towards her.

"Stop that!" she said, aloud.

Someone was pushing from inside.

The box fell over and all the files cascaded to the floor.

"Oh, dear," said Lilah. "Now I'll never get them right." She bent down quickly over the chaos.

In his bedroom, Marlow heard none of this. He turned to sleep on his other side. Grendel, however, was awakened. He raised his head to listen. Far off, down the hall, he could see a light and hear scrabbling. The mice, perhaps, were back. He did not like mice—whether dead or alive—and he lowered his head accordingly. Nothing would induce him to leave Marlow's feet for a pack of mice. Nothing, except his breakfast—and he knew it was not yet time for that.

In the study, Martha had begun to look for Stuart by the windows. She was searching up around the ceiling.

Lilah was down on her hands and knees—panic-stricken but attempting calm. She knew that panic might cause her to fumble. The thing was, she had to put things back in order. She righted the box and lifted the files up one by one. Some of their contents had slipped beyond the covers—spilling like milk across the carpet. Lilah tried to align them without disturbing their sequence.

I will help you, Stuart said.

He's here with me, said Lilah.

Martha floated overhead.

Lilah's hands were struck, all at once, by a force so harsh and sudden she withdrew them in surprise and almost called out.

Let me, Stuart said.

She offered her hands to the air.

The force returned, but this time she was prepared for it. The shapes of other hands were fitted over her own—cold as any cold she had ever known. She could feel them drawing on like gloves.

Let me, said Stuart again. His voice was still the voice of a child—unbroken, but verging on hoarseness.

Lilah closed her eyes.

Yes, she said.

Martha hovered above her—agitated but silent. Stuart was not yet visible, even to her.

Lilah's hands were pressed down over the papers. At once, they began to shuffle the pages with a cardmaster's speed. As each of the files was filled, her hands put it back in the box. *One, two, three*—all the way to ten. With that, the ordering stopped. The eleventh file would not go back. Her hands became rigid. One of them made a fist.

Oh, Lilah thought. *Don't...*

The fist struck the file three times. A sign—a signal.

One. Two. Three.

I am here, said Stuart.

Martha descended—lying out over the eleventh file with her feet still elevated. Lilah crouched beside her. She let the hands do their work.

A wide brown envelope.

There was a sigh. A scurrying sound. Fingers scrabbled inside against the paper. There were voices. *Help us,* they said.

Help us.

I am here, said Stuart.

Lilah's hands undid the flap.

She brought forth... Photographs.

And voices.

Me and *Me* and *Me* and *Me*...

Each voice had its own image.

"Oh," said Lilah. "Oh." And she fell down over them, so as not to see.

Me. Me. Me and *Me.*

Eight of them. Naked.

Martha said: *more missing children...*

Mother? Stuart said.

Yes?

I want to leave here, now.

Lilah could feel his hands withdrawing finger by finger from her own. She raised herself and sat back onto her heels. Her eyes were closed.

Open them, said Martha.

Lilah looked. The light was altering—wavering. The voices were silent—but every eye in the photographs was watching her, waiting.

Martha said: *I have my Stuart now. He's here.*

Lilah turned towards her.

Martha was standing on the carpet. She had started towards the door, but now she was still. Stuart was beside her.

Lilah squinted. She had never seen him so close. He wore short brown pants and long black stockings. Boots. His suspenders were blue. His shirt was grey. He had a solemn, pinched expression—as if he had always been in pain. His head had been shaved against the impending surgery that would kill him. He held his mother's hand. That alone was reassuring. He had forgiven her—for another year. *Would this go on forever?* Lilah wondered. Would he never be reconciled to his death?

Martha looked down at him, smiling.

We will go now, she said.

Lilah nodded.

Martha started to leave. She began to disappear.

Stuart, however, did not go with her. He stood very still, with his gaze on Lilah.

He spoke. But Lilah could not tell what he said. Not quite precisely.

Please, she said. Again.

His lips moved.

Curse, he said. Or seemed to say.

Curse.

Lilah closed her eyes.

Speak again, she said.

Curse.

That was all.

Lilah felt him going, just as Martha had gone before him. When, at last, she opened her eyes, the boy had disappeared. And his voice had gone with him.

The sighing stopped.

Beyond the windows, it was replaced by the sound of a rising wind.

Fam jumped up where the fallen box had been. She began to clean herself.

Lilah looked down at the floor.

There were the photographs and the file from which they had tipped. Their envelope rested beside them. Nothing else remained of the mess that had been so daunting. With Stuart's help, the other files had been set in perfect order and rested now in their box.

Lilah forced herself to see the pictures.

More missing children, Martha had said of them.

Some of the faces were vaguely familiar—but Lilah could not tell why. She could not remember where it was she might have seen these children. On a bus somewhere? The street? In the Metro Library? At Queen Street?

They were all in their altogether...

She winced. The expression seemed so trivial in the face of what she saw. Eight naked children, whose childhood in everything but name was over. What it was they were doing could not, in every case, be named. Some of it was not in Lilah's vocabulary, in spite of all her reading. Clearly, what they were doing was sexual, though why it should be considered "sexual" was beyond Lilah's comprehension. In all that she had read and seen, there were nowhere words or images to give these gestures meaning. Nor could she devise the uses, in her mind, for the paraphernalia shown. Though ropes and gags and handcuffs were clear enough, what was the meaning of razors, rubber gloves and scissors? Pillows. Blindfolds. Truncheons. Tubes.

There were no voices now. Just the children—mute and shining in their photographic gloss. Some had beautiful faces. Yes—and bodies, if you could see them past the poses. Long-legged girls with breasts like tender, burnished apples; boys—broad-shouldered and slim. None of them smiling. Not a trace of youth remaining, only the catalogue of youthful assets.

Me and *Me* and *Me* and *Me.*

Me. Me. Me and *Me.*

Missing children. Dead or dying.

No.

Not now.

Stuart had said that. *No. Not now.* To his mother.

Where were the mothers, Lilah wondered, and the fathers who would let this happen?

The surgeon came. He wanted to operate.

Razors. Rubber gloves. And scissors.

Not now. No.

Lilah gathered up the beautiful faces. She refused to see the rest. She began to slip the pictures, one by one, into their envelope. *But I have seen them before,* she kept thinking. *Where?*

Fam stepped up and away, and sat on Marlow's desk while Lilah replaced the box that had fallen to the floor. Not that it had truly "fallen," of course. It had been pushed by Stuart. But if Marlow were to discover the files had been tampered with, there was no way Lilah could claim a dead boy had done it.

Curse, Stuart had said. What did that mean? *Curse.*

If only she could discuss these things with Marlow. But he was distracted enough already with the contents of the box. He would not take kindly to opinions offered up by her madness. Lilah Kemp was dear to him and he was kind to her—but he wanted her company, not her advice.

She wound the yellow tape back in place and pulled against it to make it stick. She flattened it down with the palms of her hands and gave the box—and Fam—a little pat.

She turned to go.

It was time to sleep.

The wind was singing.

By the window, Grendel's chair looked bleak and lonely.

The trees in the lamplight beyond the glass were thrashing back and forth. The sparrows, in the morning, would all be driven to the ground.

Oh, why is everything so cold and bleak and sad in here in the Heart of Darkness? *Riding up along the river in search of...*

Curse.

Lilah felt the night itself rise up her back and cross her shoulders.

She spoke the word out into the air. To the dark and silent room.

"Kurtz."

Fam jumped down—and ran.

4

Austin Purvis's death weighed heavily on Marlow. All his attempts to drag himself out of mourning failed. Added to which, he was baffled by what the obituary notice had said. In the context of the stolen files, the obit took on added weight—and the words *Kurtz is everywhere* took on new meaning.

Eleanor Farjeon, too, was in mourning—though not exclusively for Austin Purvis. She had been fond enough of him, and for a while he had been her ally. But he had withdrawn from her in the last weeks of his life and, by the time he died, he had started to refuse her phone calls. But the shadows of what was in Austin's files fell increasingly upon Eleanor's brood of damaged children. She had not yet made the full connection—but there were ties and threads in what Austin had told her that continued to intrigue and worry her. With Austin gone, she wanted someone else with whom to share her suspicions. She therefore thought of Marlow, because he had been Austin's friend. So far, however, there had been no opportunity to broach the subject with him. And now, she had lost the lad she had called *William*—the sweet one, all smiles and bruises—the gentlest one of all her brood. He lay down, one day, in the observation room and stayed for so long, so quietly, that Eleanor, at last, had gone through to rouse him. He was dead.

Just dead. No struggle—not a sound. To all appearances, William had lain down deliberately to die—and that was the end of him.

The autopsy report was no more edifying. It said what it had to say in medical terms that were properly cool and objective. But the gist of it was that William's nervous system had failed to respond to an episode of apnea. In other words, he just stopped breathing.

The brood had lost its centrepiece.

Eleanor went even deeper into mourning—and, like William, nothing could rouse her.

This way, the vital conjunction of what she guessed and what Marlow was discovering was thwarted yet again.

On the twelfth of June it rained. It rained all morning and all afternoon. At two o'clock or thereabouts, Lilah returned from Wong's with the baby carriage filled with groceries. There had been several sirens in the night and she had thought it would be best to do her shopping in the rain, since falling rain precluded any further spraying.

Off at the other end of Lapin Lanes, she had seen the usual D-Squad patrol advancing towards her in a Land Rover. They came along at a snail's pace, one man driving and two others searching for the residue of bird corpses from the night before. This was standard procedure on a rainy day. The D-Squads used non-spraying hours to clean up the streets and laneways of dead and dying pigeons and starlings—and whatever else had succumbed or was succumbing to the previous night's activities. Quite often, birds that had received a lethal dose of ABS-482 would escape from the spray sites, and they would clutter up the public thoroughfares with their disease-ridden remains. From time to time, during these mop-up operations, gun shots would be heard—informing the public that a stray dog or cat had been dispensed with. This was called *species-cleansing*—always a secondary aim of the D-Squads. The killing was done on the grounds that cats and dogs were natural hunter/scavengers and therefore were apt to have sanguinary contact with the diseased birds. Blood for blood.

Amy Wylie had been an outspoken opponent of this practice and had been arrested on two occasions when she had tried to prevent a canine or a feline slaughter. She had also posted bills—an act which was forbidden—at many locations as part of her protest. These bills reminded the authorities that, during the great bubonic plague of 1665, their London counterparts had massacred all the dogs and cats that might have saved them from the plague itself, since dogs and cats—*being natural hunter/scavengers*—could have rid the great city of the very rats that carried its death warrant.

On the 12th of June, having entered the yard of 38-A from the lane, Lilah made a grievous mistake. It was nothing more than failing to wait until she had heard the gate click shut behind her, but it was enough to assure that, when Grendel went into the yard five minutes later, the gate stood open.

Marlow had just finished a frustrating session with Amy Wylie when a call came through from Lilah.

Grendel had been shot by the local D-Squad and could Marlow come at once?

All the way home, he cursed the rain, which piled up traffic in his path—and, as so often happens in emergencies, caused him to lose much time.

When, at last, he burst through the door at Lowther Avenue, the house that greeted him was silent.

"Grendel! Miss Kemp! Grendel!"

He went on through to the kitchen, yelling one name and then the other.

They were both there waiting for him.

Grendel was lying on a blanket beneath the table. Lilah was on her knees beside him.

"Dead?"

Lilah shook her head. "No—but dying," she said.

"Why did they do it?" Marlow asked. "What had he done?"

"Nothing," said Lilah. "All they saw was Grendel in the lane with a bird in his mouth—a starling—and they shot him. I heard it happen and went out, running."

Marlow fell down by the dog and lay on the floor beside him.

"I stood between them," said Lilah. "I wouldn't let them shoot again." This she had done, but later she would tell herself that one of her reasons was the fact that she had left the gate undone. She never told Marlow this, but she also never left Grendel's side in her mind.

Marlow thanked her—but his whole attention was on the dog.

"Gren," he said—and touched the dog's head. "Don't," he said.

Grendel opened his eyes. He made an attempt at uttering, but nothing came. Beyond the gate, his mother was calling, but only he could hear her.

"Did you ring the vet?"

"Yes," said Lilah. "She came right away. The bullet passed through his shoulder. She cleansed and dressed the wound. Her name was Natasha. It was not the vet you expected. That vet died on Friday of sturnusemia."

"Jesus," said Marlow.

They were both silent.

Finally, Marlow said: "what did Natasha say?"

"She said we are to love him—and pray—and give him these." She held out a box of prepackaged shots in pink syringes.

"Should they be in the fridge?"

"Yes," Lilah mumbled. She stood up and went to the other side of the room, where Marlow could hear her putting the medicines into the refrigerator. Both of them were numb.

Marlow lay out flat and stared into Grendel's face.

"You aren't going to die," he said. "We aren't going to let you."

He stayed that way with the dog until, an hour later, both he and Grendel slept.

Lilah went back to her room and returned with her rabbit shoes.

She sat at the table and placed the shoes at its centre.

All she said was: *please.*

5

The reading of the files continued. The folders sat in their box on their table—and every night, long after midnight had struck, Marlow sat there with them—much as some Victorian counterpart might have done in this very room with a coffin containing the corpse of a dead child.

The process of mourning had lost its formal edge and Marlow regretted that. The wearing of armbands—the donning of black—the funeral wreaths that hung from the door—the callers who came and left their cards and departed—black-bordered stationery—flags at half-mast. He remembered period photographs that showed an undertaker standing beside a hearse—the hearse made of glass and drawn by horses the colour of ink. *'Tis not alone my inky cloak, good mother, nor customary suits of black...*

He should have worn black for Austin. He should, at least, have worn an armband. *Why not wear black for everyone in here?* he thought one night as he stared at the box. He reached out and touched it. *I am the undertaker of these dead. This is my morgue.* Wasn't that what they called a place for dead files?

He had made himself two sandwiches, and he began to eat as he opened the box.

Grendel lay on the floor by his favourite chair in the window and snored and snuffled. The shot had gone into his left front shoulder and had torn away some flesh—a wound from which he had bled profusely. Marlow could not bear to leave him, and carried him up and down the stairs and into his bedroom. Grendel ate—as convalescents will—a little soup. And steak.

Marlow's sandwiches were made of thinly sliced onions dipped in sugar and lemon juice, laid out on lettuce leaves between thick cuts of caraway rye bread. Marlow adored them. They had become his midnight vice and he took them with a bottle of Merlot.

He removed one of the files from the box and flipped through stapled pages and paper-clipped notes—the pages neatly typed, the notes in Austin's handwriting.

Who was this?

Meeting with F. distressing.

Accuses me now of more than mere complicity. Says I have "conspired" with these to bring about her tragedies...

Undated.

Maddening. Who was F.? The file was labelled simply *PHALEN*.

Says I have conspired with these...

What were these—or who?

...to bring about her tragedies.

What tragedies? Which particular tragedies?

Marlow stood up and flipped through the files in the boxes. *F.* Any file that bore a name beginning with *F.*

FIRSTBROOK—Norman

FULLERTON—Mark

That was all. Both male. But Austin's note referred to her tragedies.

Marlow returned the Firstbrook and Fullerton folders to the box and continued to read from the file that lay open before him. Then he saw the full name.

PHALEN—Frances.

Frances.

F.

He pulled himself closer to the light. He had finished the sandwiches and was drinking the wine. Grendel was having a dream. A headless dog was pursuing him. Marlow repaired the half-torn tab with Scotch tape, opened the file and began to read.

Frances Phalen was an unknown quantity. She had become a patient of Austin's two years ago. She was then severely depressed and suicidal. Something had happened to her children. One of them had disappeared and the other had become catatonic and was hospitalized. These were her tragedies. But what they had to do with Austin was not made clear. Yet Frances Phalen had accused him of complicity.

Who was Frances Phalen?

She appeared to be a woman of wealth. There were references to San Moritz and extended voyages on passenger ships. Some of these journeys had been organized by museums and art galleries—cruises through the Mediterranean with stops in Egypt, Greece and Italy. Frances Phalen took these journeys alone. Neither her husband nor her children were mentioned as having accompanied her. Once, however, she made a point of telling Austin she had gone to Rome with Peggy Webster. But this was the only name mentioned in all the accounts of touring. The excursions, at first, had been entirely for pleasure. Frances appeared to be an enthusiastic connoisseur of art. Then, however, the travel took on a new and more revealing nature. She was avoiding her children and escaping from her husband.

The words *distressed, upset* and *troubled* began to be replaced by words like *frightened, alarmed* and *desperate.*

Frances Phalen was married to Peter Phalen—a man whose name was vaguely familiar to Marlow. But nothing was mentioned in the file of what he did. He moved, it was obvious, in the male counterpart of his wife's circle—the York Club was mentioned—a schooner was mentioned—some horses. A man named David was often mentioned in conjunction with the notes regarding Peter Phalen. *David was there again... David was with him...I am getting mighty sick of David...* unquote. Then the emphasis was switched to the Phalen children and David disappeared.

The Phalen children were both girls. Their ages, while not precisely given, were clearly in the teens. Schools were mentioned. Boys were mentioned. Waywardness was mentioned. A distressing *romance* was mentioned—followed by an abortion.

One girl was Paula, the other was Prue—though which was the senior was not made clear. Maddeningly, Austin's references to them were often in a kind of shorthand—*Pa* and *Pr.* The problem with this lay in Austin's writing—where *a*'s and *r*'s were interchangeable in form. Consequently, Marlow could not make out whether Paula or Prue had endured the distressing romance and its attendant abortion, nor which of them had disappeared. It would have been interesting to know which of those events had preceded the catatonia.

Then—a notation.

David is back!!!

Austin had appended the exclamation points to the transcript—but it was not immediately obvious why he should do so. David had clearly not returned with the missing girl. Nor to sweep Frances Phalen off her feet in a roaring affair of the heart. Nor to quit his nerve-wracking association with Peter.

Marlow pushed his chair away from the desk and stood up to stretch. He went across the room and gave Grendel's ears a scratch and watched, for a moment, through the window. A clock struck somewhere, telling him it was half past one. He wanted desperately to go to bed and dream his way out of the mess that Austin had left behind. The mess—the mystery—the madness. Whatever it was, it was indecipherable. Marlow could not bear that. He wanted just to get through the door and then he could pause. But the door stood closed and there seemed, so far, to be no key. The only evidence that all was not well on the other side lay in the shouts and cries that rose from the files. Those—and the image of George, who was dead. And Austin—bloodied, shirtless—also dead. Both deaths acts of mayhem.

All at once, Marlow returned to the desk where he shuffled the latter pages of Frances Phalen's file. Her story, which seemed a *non sequitur,* was nonetheless in with all the others Austin had chosen. There must be some connection: *George, Frances Phalen, David, P...the file with no name.*

Marlow sat down.

He lifted the Phalen file and looked again at the notes that had started his search for *F.*

Meeting with F. distressing...

Meeting.

Accuses me now of more than mere complicity...

Accuses.

Why would a patient accuse her doctor? Unless he had abused her—unless she was paranoid. But nothing in Frances Phalen's documents indicated paranoia, and Marlow was certain that Austin had never been abusive.

He referred to the notes again.

Complicity.

What did that mean—refer to? And then: *says I have conspired with these to bring about her tragedies.*

Missing children. Catatonic children. Dead children.

Paula. Prue. And George.

There must be some connection.

Children.

Well—not children, precisely. Some of them old enough to be looking forward to university. But children, legally.

Please, Marlow thought. And he rubbed his eyes. *Please don't tell me Austin was part of this. Dead George. Missing Paula. Catatonic Prue. Please don't tell me that.*

But there it was in black and white—in Austin's unmistakable hand. *F. accuses me now...*

He threw down the notes and brushed them to one side.

He was too tired for this. He could not follow any more tonight. He would have to stop.

He closed Frances Phalen inside her file and crossed the room to Grendel.

"Come on, my friend," he said. "The troops are retiring from the field till tomorrow." Then he bent down and, groaning with the effort, lifted the dog and carried him down the hall to Valhalla.

Well, Marlow thought, as he began to undress. *It certainly feels like Valhalla, what with that battlefield out there.*

6

"I'm missing some files," Kurtz said one morning to Oona Kilbride.

"Which ones are those, Doctor Kurtz?"

"I'm afraid I can't say. I only know they're missing."

"Can you give me a hint, Doctor Kurtz? Even one name would be a help. Things that are lost tend to cluster. One name could lead to others."

"Frances Phalen," said Kurtz.

Oona was standing, as always in Kurtz's presence. Now, she looked down at her desk and pushed a pencil back into place. She knew perfectly well that Frances Phalen was not one of Kurtz's patients. How could she phrase this?

"Oh, yes," she said. "Mrs Phalen is on your monitor list."

"Quite correct." Kurtz was slightly flustered that she should know such a thing concerning a file like Frances Phalen's. Phalen, after all, was a very minor figure...a woman who had no importance in herself but only through her connection to other matters. Had his secretary kept lists of the files he had monitored? Every last one of them?

Yes. Apparently.

"Mrs Phalen was Doctor Purvis's patient," said Oona. "I would assume that is why the file is missing. It will have been returned to Mrs Orenstein's system."

Kurtz was now in a quandary. He knew too well—because he himself had done the gleaning—that every file in which he was interested had already been removed from Bella's cabinets. Or from Sub Four. The thing was—when he had looked just now in his own filing cabinet for Frances Phalen's file and some others—they were all gone.

"Well," he said. "Good for you, Kilbride. Would you go down, then, to Mrs Orenstein and ask her if the Phalen file has turned up yet?"

"Certainly, Doctor Kurtz."

Oona went downstairs to Bella's office and asked her if she had any notion of a patient called Phalen.

"Oh, yes. Doctor Purvis treated her."

Bella was finally able to say Austin's name without tears.

"Would she still be in your system?" Oona asked, "or has she already been assigned to another doctor?"

"No. Not assigned to anyone else. I'm sure of that, because no one has been reassigned yet." Then Bella said: "that I'm aware of."

The telephone rang.

It was for Oona.

Kurtz.

He wanted her, while she was there in Bella's office, to inquire about another file.

"Yes, Doctor Kurtz. And whose file would that be?" Oona stood with pencil poised and a sheet of Bella's paper, and then she wrote down the name that came through the receiver. "Yes, sir," she said. And hung up.

Another missing patient. Someone called Smith Jones.

But neither one in Bella's files.

Somewhat later that morning, Oona came back empty-handed to Bella's office from Sub Four and found her sitting at the Selectric in her ornate chair. The door to Austin Purvis's office was open, now, and sunlight poured through. Marlow's door was shut.

It was Oona's intention to ask Bella if she would like to have lunch at Motley's Bar and Grill. She wanted to talk about the mysterious files. But before she could issue the invitation, she was stopped in her tracks by the sight of Bella's hands on the typewriter keys. They were gloved. In white cotton.

Oona's heart sank.

There had always been the hat. And the rubber-soled, flat-heeled shoes. But...gloves? To type in?

She said nothing.

When Bella saw who it was, she said: "I'll be right with you. I'm just typing out this list."

"List?"

"Yes. Of all the missing files."

Oona could not refrain from smiling. At lunch, she would make certain that Bella would have her full complement of double vodka martinis.

Missing files. Doctor Kurtz's missing envelope. Patients being transferred. Austin Purvis's suicide—and now Bella's gloved distress. Something, Oona thought, *is rotten in the state of Parkin...*

7

Myra Cherniak had worked the Information Desk at the Metro Library since the building opened in 1974. She was now in her fifties and had gone through three different sizes of the staff blazer. She was largely self-educated and most of that education had taken place inside the library's walls.

Myra was an avid reader—and there was barely a subject represented in the system with which she was not conversant. *Quest? See Don Quixote. Gerhard Berger? See Auto Racing. Wessex: See Maps*—England; *Novels*—Hardy and *Mysteries*—Rendell. *Inflorescence? See Plants*—Flowering.

One morning in June, just before leaving to take her lunch break, Myra was sorting through the message centre and came across an envelope that must have been in there for weeks. It was lying within the folds of some gift-wrap one of the clerks had left there after opening a birthday present.

"Dear, dear, dear," she said. "Oh, this is too bad..."

Antony Savage was just coming into the carousel to relieve her when she found it. "Look at this," she said.

"Isn't that a scream!"

Myra held the envelope out to Antony Savage, who saw that it had no address and just one name on the back. "What is so funny?" he asked in his formal English.

"Well, look whose it is!" said Myra, laughing. "It's wonderful!"

Antony stared at the name.

Kurtz.

"So? Who is Kurtz?"

"Oh, pu-lease!" Myra said. "You've got to be kidding."

"Uhm..." said Antony. "No."

Myra had no patience with this. No patience and no time. Her girl friends would be waiting for her at Dinty Moore's and she didn't want to be late.

"Look it up," she said.

"But where?" said Antony Savage.

"In there, of course. See you later."

She was already on her way to the outer door.

Myra had a way with her hands. Her gestures were large and all-inclusive. She might have been telling Antony to search for Kurtz in almost any book in the library. The book she had intended was lying on a shelf of reference books in the carousel. *The Reader's Encyclopedia.* A useful volume when answering questions concerning literature. There, Myra knew, Antony Savage would be sure to find *Kurtz—Heart of Darkness—Joseph Conrad.*

That is not what happened.

Instead, Antony seized the book lying next to *The Reader's Encyclopedia*—which happened to be a copy of *Who's Who in Canada.*

Kurtz? Kurtz?

Kurtz?

Rupert Kurtz—M.D., F.R.C.P. (C).

There he was.

Antony Savage read through the given data—birth—parentage—education, et cetera, until he came to: *currently Director and Psychiatrist-in-Chief, Parkin Institute of Psychiatric Research, Toronto.*

Now what? Antony wondered.

Pass it on.

So it was that Antony Savage retrieved the Toronto Directory and copied the appropriate address onto the face of the envelope. After which, he sealed it and wrote in the lower left-hand corner: *ATT'N: R. KURTZ* and dropped it into the Out basket.

Done.

As for the birthday-present wrapping in which the envelope had hidden since that snowy day in March, Antony folded it carefully into his pocket and took it home. It was covered with silver birds in a blue sky.

8

When Lilah descended from the streetcar one day at the corner of Queen and Shaw streets, she stepped into the heart of a summer windstorm. The traffic could barely move, the force of the gale was so great. Flying dust and gutter debris made a nonsense of trying to see. Litter was a chronic problem, these days, as city refuse control fell behind because of all the dead birds the garbage collectors had to deal with. Now, windblown dirt and paper were creating a blizzard of trash. And yet the motorcars and streetcars kept on moving doggedly forward. Few enough people were about and those who were leaned forward into the wind at an absurd angle—almost lying flat out against the storm. This was why Lilah had not brought the baby carriage. She did not want it blown away. The wind itself was hot—and might have come in from a desert.

Lilah made straight for the nearest doors of the Queen Street Mental Health Centre. As she came near the entrance, she saw a most curious sight. Ten ragged scarecrows—men with brooms—were attempting to clean the sidewalks in front of the Centre. They were hatless—wearing baggy shorts and torn sweaters. Some of the sweaters were so ill-fitting they fell away from their wearers' shoulders, creating a new but grotesque male fashion. Lilah had seen this crew before. They were mostly alcoholic out-patients at the Centre who received an allowance for clearing the walks and raking the lawns. They were not unlike a chain-gang—always in a row and always going about their work in a unison that indicated only one of them knew what he was doing—while the rest made an imitation of it. Most of these men were so far gone in their drink, their brains had been damaged by years of rot-gut wine, vanilla extract, rubbing alcohol. A few of them were relatively young—but most of them were old.

They were a peaceful, harmless lot—benign and somehow sad. In good weather, they dozed beneath the trees on the grounds, standing up against their rakes and brooms. They seemed, to the eye, to be a band of brothers. Their features all bore the same deep marks of acid wear—and their eyes all had the same dazed expression. They were uniformly thin almost to the point of emaciation. But it was alcohol, not food, for which they were starved. Whoever paid them knew there was not much hope of having their wages spent at Loblaws. On the other hand, they received a steady diet of soup and sandwiches at one of the nearby missions. Sadly, from their point of view, the amount of alcohol their wages could buy would do no more than keep them alive. All these men would be found, in their time, curled up dead in a Queen Street doorway, wearing their ragged sweaters as shrouds.

"Why don't you stop!" Lilah shouted at them as she passed. "You can't sweep dust in a tornado!"

They did not want to hear her. Perhaps it was in their minds that if they gave up sweeping, they would be blown away. As it was, they were pushed back endlessly against the walls of the building—moving forward again to fan their sweepings into the air.

Lilah was almost killed by the doors as she fought to open them against the wind. Just as she was passing through, a woman came rushing towards her shouting: "you're letting in the storm! We'll all be killed!"

Lilah paid no attention. "Silly coot," she said—and began to sing—and kept on walking.

She had learned that in these corridors a person singing was seldom interfered with. The mad will not interrupt the madness of others. Solitude is precious, and the solitude of madness is like no other—a commodity, not a condition. You earn it only by a ruthless pursuit of privacy. The reticent, in madness, will never earn their solitude. They will constantly be pestered. A person has to shout back—strike out—sing songs to win her solitude—and songs were what Lilah had chosen.

Today, she was to have her Modecate injection and she dreaded it. It had occurred to her in the night that if she were to go on placing herself in the drug's protection, she would lose her ability to follow Kurtz to the end. She might lose sight of him and that would be a disaster. It was her mission, now, to save the children in the photographs. She could not afford to have her contact with them broken, even though she did not yet know who they were.

On the other hand, if she did not regain control of her condition, Marlow might become wary of her. And not fulfil his destiny. Then what would happen? Kurtz would triumph.

Having turned the corner, she gave up her song and fell silent. She must decide now what to do—accept the Modecate or reject it. Mavis Delaney would be expecting her—all her disposable needles lined up in rows. And the fridge and the shelves full of sleep and peace. All those bottles and vials and pills—ways to pull yourself into the dark and wrap yourself in normalcy. Or what the sane called normalcy. *Little did they know,* Lilah thought. *Little all the way to nothing.*

Lilah could not remember being sane. It had been too long ago. Now, whatever normalcy was gained from the Modecate was ruined by the tension of waiting to be called back over. Better to let yourself go over and have done with it. Stop all this to-ing and fro-ing. Like a journey made on a tall, narrow bridge—that's what it was. Tightrope walking. A high-wire balancing act, with your sanity perched on top of your head. Walking—arms out—heel to toe. *Don't fall down. Don't fall.* As if a person had a choice.

She came to the sign.

MODECATE CLINIC

The door was closed. Mavis would not see her standing there.

You have a duty to be sane, said one voice.

Save the children, said another.

Lilah stepped back.

She would wait. There was no harm in that. Half an hour would make no difference. First, she would seek out her mentor in the cellar—ask her advice. That was the ticket—see what Mrs Moodie had to say.

Lilah ignored the elevators. She had always used the stairs in the past when she went down into the tunnels to visit Susanna Moodie.

A beehive humming greeted her as she pushed her way through the door at the bottom of the steps. There was no one there to prevent her, though she knew there were others besides Susanna who toiled down here or were hidden in the shadows. Long black strings of yellow bulbs spread out above the tunnels like a spider web of light.

There was also a single track that ran down the centre of the floor and, sometimes without warning, a service trolley would hurtle through the passageway and knock you down, if you didn't watch out.

Lilah wondered if she ought to call out. Sometimes it was necessary to summon Susanna forth. She slept a good deal of the time and was deaf. Awake, she was sad and in constant mourning—though, because she hated clothes of black, she refused to wear them. The mourning was all in her face and her voice.

Because Susanna Moodie was a writer, she and Lilah had talked a good deal about books. She was partial to the novels of Charles Dickens, whom she had glimpsed in her lifetime on the streets of Toronto. *When was that?* Lilah had wanted to know. *1842,* Susanna told her. *He had a fine tall hat, which he tipped in my direction....*

Lilah had found this fascinating—to speak with one who had actually been in the great man's presence. *What was he doing here?* she had asked. *He came here to read to us. My husband, Dunbar, was Sheriff then of Victoria district and we lived in the town of Belleville on the Moira River. Moodie could not come up, so I came with my daughter Betsy on the steamer and there he was, Mister Dickens, on the very street I was walking...* This had been a spectacular highlight in her life.

Susanna's passion for Dickens had its focus mostly on what he wrote of children. Fagin's brood in *Oliver Twist*—the cruelties endured by David Copperfield when Murdstone became his stepfather—the horrors of Squeers and his dreadful school in *Nicholas Nickleby*—these were all like salvos for Susanna Moodie, driving her to begin a personal crusade to better the lives of children in her own time and place. Because she had endured the loss of her youngest child, the deaths of all children were poignant to her—and the worst of tragedies. This was why Lilah required her counsel in this moment. Susanna might know how to solve her present dilemma regarding the children in the photographs. She might even know how to find them.

Lilah had reached the darkest corner of the cellars—the darkest and perhaps the oldest corner—where the earth had broken through the stonework of the building that had preceded this current structure. A room of some kind had been here—perhaps a root cellar or a cooling larder. The old asylum had grown its own produce—and even had its own dairy cows. Winter vegetables would have been kept down here besides the cheese and butter, the salt beef and the pork.

"Susanna Moodie?" she said aloud. "It is Lilah Kemp. Are you here?"

There was a groan—a sigh—and the sound of a body turning.

Kemp?

Yes.

You have been long enough in coming.

Yes—forgive me.

All this was spoken—silently—spirit to spirit. Susanna rose in the corner and pulled at her shawl.

Well! Don't shilly-shally. Tell why you're here.

Susanna sat down on a wooden kitchen chair she had brought from the dark—and offered Lilah the same. They drew together, facing one another, almost knee to knee.

Children, said Lilah.

Dead children?

Some of them. Others dying.

Drowned? Drowning?

Maybe.

A picture came into Lilah's mind of a swimming pool.

I had a drowned child, said Susanna. *I have been searching for him a hundred years and more.*

Yes, I know, said Lilah. Johnny.

Susanna sat back in her chair. She sighed and adjusted her fingerless gloves and looked at her wedding band and her heirloom sapphire.

He loved these rings, she said. *He used to play with them. He was not quite six—but on the verge of it when he died...*

This was what Lilah Kemp and Susanna Moodie had in common— what Lilah called *the death by disappearance* of their children.

You said you had been searching for him a hundred years and more. Was the body not recovered?

It is not the body you lose, Kemp. You must know that, being one of us.

Yes—but...

Do you call yourself a spiritualist—or are you just a medium, Kemp?

Lilah did not know how to answer this. Like so many of Susanna's questions, it was overlaid with what appeared to be contempt. The one thing Lilah dreaded in these confrontations with her dead friend was Susanna Moodie's cantankerous Christianity. Cantankerous, because it was based so thoroughly on a sentimental view of Jesus Christ.

I suppose I'm a medium with spiritualist overtones, Lilah said. I never think of myself as anything more than one who can summon forth.

Do you believe in Jesus Christ?

I believe in Christian virtue.

And?

I believe that Jesus Christ was a wise and compassionate teacher.

And?

And...

That He died on the Cross, was taken down and rose from the dead?

Lilah wanted only to get back to the subject of children. But she was not about to tell Susanna a lie.

No, she said. I do not believe those things.

Then you are not a child of Christ.

I was taught he had no children.

He had ten trillion children, Kemp. And my son Johnny was one of them. Susanna removed a handkerchief from her bosom and wiped her eyes. *And now, I have lost them both.*

She blew her nose.

Lilah said: I'm not too sure I understand what you mean by *lost them both.*

Jesus Christ and Johnny!

Lilah sat back and waited.

Susanna was folding her handkerchief into a triangle, using her lap as an ironing board.

I am telling you, Kemp, she said, *that Jesus Christ went off with my boy and the two have not been seen since 1844.*

Lilah sat frozen with apprehension.

These, surely were the words of a madwoman—not of her hitherto intelligent, down-to-earth mentor.

I see, she said, evenly. She wondered when Susanna might have stopped taking her medicine—whatever it was that was given for madness in the nineteenth century.

Are you not well? she asked, putting it gently as she could—hoping the question's freight would not be clear to Susanna.

Not well?

Is there nothing you could take to relieve your anxiety? Was nothing prescribed?

Laudanum.

Oh. Well—we don't have that any more.

Hot baths.

Those we have.

Susanna considered a moment and then said: *they once bored holes into your head to relieve the pressure. Did you know that, Kemp?*

No.

I saw that, once. Here.

Good Heavens.

These were the prescriptions of my day. Either you were drugged with laudanum and tied into a bath—or you submitted to violence.

That has not changed.

No?

360

No.

Nothing changes.

Just the methods.

You and I are sisters in time, said Susanna.

Lilah smiled.

If you were offered the chance to abandon your search for Johnny, she said, would you?

No.

You would never give it up?

Never.

Good, said Lilah. You have told me what I must do.

How?

They have offered me a way of giving up, Lilah said. Sanity—which is very tempting. More relaxing. Peaceful. But I must refuse it. I know that, now.

How do you get this sanity—what is it?

A drug. Called Modecate.

I've never heard of it.

It was invented after you were alive.

Fascinating. Are you sane at once?

Not quite. But quick enough. It takes four hours to work its way into your system. Then, a day or two more to calm you.

Since you have access to such help, do you think you can find my boy, Kemp?

I can try, Lilah said. She doubted she could locate Jesus Christ—with or without Modecate—but Johnny might turn up—especially if she allowed the full force of her spiritualism to take over. She would add him to her list of missing children.

You had better go, now, said Susanna. *The trolley cars have started to roll.*

Lilah could hear them out in the tunnel, rattling their metal sides. It must be getting on to suppertime. The trolleys smelled of food. Macaroni and cheese. Tomato sauce.

She stood up and handed over her chair to Susanna, who had also risen.

Don't be so long coming back, this time, the old woman said. *You will know my son by his lisp, which is due to missing teeth. And ask him, if you find him, how he spells his name. If he spells it J-O-H-N-Y, it is him. He always left out the second N.* Susanna almost wept again. *He was my darling boy,* she said. *Bring him back for me, Kemp. If you can.*

Yes, said Lilah. I will try. Before she could say goodbye, Susanna had turned back into the dark and was gone.

Lilah made her way carefully through the tunnel—stepping aside only to let the silver trolleys pass—seeing children's coffins in their shapes.

Now it was decided. She would not take the Modecate. Mavis would have to cross her off the list. Lilah must abandon herself to a future she could not predict—but in it, she might find the missing children. Including Johny.

Emerging from the tunnels, Lilah discovered the exit was not where she had entered. She was somewhere out on the lawns behind the buildings, where the wind was less aggressive. She hurried beneath the trees. This was her trial break for total freedom. Modecate had been her prison.

She now wished devoutly that she had brought the baby buggy. It gave her something real to hold onto. But she would reach it soon enough. And the safety of her kitchen and the open door to Marlow...

Something moved at her feet.

It was Susanna Moodie's groundhog.

Lilah bent forward.

Can I help you? she asked.

The groundhog stared at her.

I'm not going to hurt you, Lilah said.

The groundhog sat up and whistled for her young.

Lilah could see them coming forward, moving through the sandy air across the already withered grass. They were larger now than when she had seen them last. Somehow, this was a comfort to Lilah. Here in this wilderness of trampled earth and cement, of dangerous roads and madmen—something small and wild and seemingly defenceless had survived. By their wits—and by their will.

Leaving them, Lilah turned back for one last look. The three had gathered together and were moving into the falling darkness. Alive.

NINE

...it was written I should be loyal to the nightmare of my choice.

Joseph Conrad
Heart of Darkness

There were occasions—mostly when he was troubled—when Marlow walked to work. There was a choice of routes, each of which had some pleasant aspect. One of these took him through the St George campus—a route with many trees and open spaces—playing fields and parks. This way, he approached the Parkin from the rear and did not have to pass the dreaded painting—dreaded because it had come to reflect more and more the stories emerging from Austin's files. Surely Julian Slade had got his images in the same dark place where George had been murdered and Frances Phalen had lost her children.

Marlow walked down Avenue Road to Bloor and cut across to the west, where he passed through the gates and down the steps to Philosopher's Walk—so inaptly named, since there was no philosophy taught on the campus any longer. Still, it was a beautiful passage—winding, as it did, through a shallow ravine of trees and rolling lawns that in summer were a favoured tanning spot for students unafraid of the disappearing ozone layer.

The path's slight curving gave a pleasant effect of being in a park. In the old days, this place had been a haven for birds and squirrels—though it was less so now. Today, the squirrels were thought to be dangerous vermin, and every bird that moved, a liability. Nonetheless, pigeons continued to haunt the ledges of the Royal Ontario Museum, the Edward Johnson Music Centre and the slated roofs of Trinity College. Sparrows of three or four kinds still chattered where someone had thrown down forbidden breadcrumbs—an offence against the public health for which, as of last September, you could be charged, fined or sent to jail.

Starlings, too, were in evidence on occasion. They gathered in more abundance than the other species, as if in response to their increasing victimization. Or was it defiance? Starlings were given to massive proliferation because they mated two or three times a season. It was this devotion to procreation that would doom them in the long run. *KILL A STARLING—SAVE A LIFE!* was a popular slogan—emblazoned on the sides of buses and in subway cars. *LIFE,* presumably, was a human possession only.

It was ostensibly because of a starling that Grendel had been shot. One of the birds escaping from a spraying area had got as far as Lapin Lanes, where Grendel had found it. It was doubtful the dog had intended to eat the starling. Dogs very rarely eat feathered birds. They prefer the meat of Thanksgiving turkeys and Christmas geese—plucked and roasted. A cat can deal with feathers—but a dog cannot.

It was more than likely that Grendel was going to bury the bird. He had, already, a well-stocked larder in the back yard of buried soup bones and other savouries—a shoe—the giant's gloves—a frog. But before he could reach his destination, the passing D-Squad had seen him and shot him.

Thank God for Lilah Kemp, Marlow thought—looking at the trees. If she had not been there, Grendel would have died—and more than likely been carted off to the crematoria, where cats and squirrels and other contaminated creatures were incinerated.

Sometimes, Marlow drew a blank on such information. It was meaningless and out of mind—not to be dwelt on any more urgently than people dwell on where shoe leather comes from, or what goes on in slaughter-houses. But every once in a while, the thought of the proliferating immolation of birds, cats, dogs and squirrels was troubling. Marlow would stumble in these moments over the fact that he had never encountered a purely scientific rendering of sturnusemia. Every level of government, from federal to civic, had endorsed the analysis of the plague provided by the Ministry of Health and Welfare. A vaccine appeared. The D-Squads were everywhere. Propaganda jumped at you from every medium — visual and aural horror stories about the dangers of lice-infested birds and the cats who ate them and the squirrels who cohabited their trees.

Cohabited.

That was the word that had been used.

Cohabited.

A squirrel ran across the path at that very moment.

Marlow recoiled.

Then he stepped forward, ashamed. *Propaganda works...even as you repel it.*

Marlow, in his student days, had thought of Philosopher's Walk as *the place of singing trees.* Hundreds of birds would gather in the elm and maple trees and sing Italian street songs. At least, it seemed to Marlow's ears the starlings had done this. He would conduct them in his head—

where his mind-music played—adding mandolins and trumpets when the birds were particularly numerous. Vivaldi. Whole choirs of feathered singers—mostly starlings—would sit in separate groves and try to drown out one another's voices. Robins and blackbirds sang occasional arias against this background. Doves and pigeons murmured approval high in the eaves or from the "cheap seats" down on the ground. Marlow, then, could have whole concerts, if he took the time to sit them out. Sometimes, he did so—resting on one of the benches, watching and listening. It was—or it had been once—an entertaining and amusing practice. Whatever had troubled him, whether then or now, had faded in this pleasant place. It had been his sanctuary.

This morning, that would end.

Just as Marlow reached the tip of the path at Hoskins Avenue, the Bloor Street gates were closed and all the windows of the adjoining buildings shut. The sirens wailed and railed. The now too-familiar yellow metal barriers were raised and the yellow tanker trucks with their yellow-suited crews drove into the short ravine and did their worst. Marlow paused unwillingly. Too many citizens refused to witness these events. But to see is to remember, Marlow believed. And so, with his handkerchief pressed to his nose and mouth, he stayed.

The efficiency of the slaughter was alarming. Two thousand birds were sprayed and removed in less than an hour. Marlow, standing there, prayed for them—though not to God—and when it was over, he turned aside.

Long ago, the giant elms had died from a plague of their own. More recently, the maples and the oaks had begun to perish from the effects of acid rain—though the government, as always, denied it. Now—the birds and squirrels. He would come this way no more.

2

Amy Wylie was adrift on her bed. Her gaze—half-masted—was focused on the shadows of several new birds which had entered the room while she slept. They were gathered—shuffling over on the bureau where she kept her food bag. Also a plastic mirror. Also the *Globe and Mail* obituary of a woman named Augusta Ward, whose manner of death had seemed intriguing—*lost at sea with Pearl, her cat...* Also—nothing else. A blunted spoon, perhaps.

It was hard for Amy to perceive which birds there were. Certainly a bittern—with its feathers shagging down across the corner of the bureau; and a pair of cormorants whose wings were spread out to dry; and a walking bird that might have been a sandhill crane, except that Amy had never seen a sandhill crane and couldn't think why this one might have taken up with her. Perhaps she had seen it in the papers—or in one of those *National Geographic* magazines out in the common room. No—she could not remember. Anyway, there it was—but only a shadow—merely a silhouette and very, very still. It stood on one foot.

The smaller birds were just the ordinary birds that Amy was used to now—the tiny saw-whet owls, seven inches high; the shrikes, like bandits in their masks; and the red-eyed, whiskered whippoorwill. All these latter birds had followed her ever since the farmlands north of the city had been sprayed—*however long ago had that been?*—and now they were sitting, some of them shifting along the edges of the bureau, others of them perching perfectly still—watching and waiting for the dawn to be complete.

They made such a lovely gentle sound as they sat there, safe in the protection of her mind—the sound of feathers, turning—being turned—for comfort. A rustling, whispering, secret sibilance.

Until she slept again.

Dreams now. The dreaming.

A dry, dead road with buffalo being herded along before her. Someone—her father—driving them, but the drovers he had hired, unseen and unidentified. This was the wilderness where Eustace Wylie had died—a wilderness—a war zone—a no man's land in a dream about a nightmare. Clouds of red and yellow dust rose up into the air and hung there, drifting slowly back to earth like a shroud and covering the buffalo backs and Amy's arms and hands and hair with a fine gold patina. Red. Gold. Trucks convoyed past in the opposite direction, as if the world was being evacuated from some disaster up ahead. Except—there was no one in the trucks but the men who drove them and all of these men wore sand-stained neckerchiefs pulled up across their mouths and noses. In the backs of the trucks, there were giant machines—yellow but unidentifiable—all with great arms and buckets—chains and pulleys.

The buffalo calves kept falling back because of the pace of the drive and many cows fell back as well in order to find them. None of these beasts was running. All were walking, dying of drought and exhaustion.

Amy could see herself in this dream—but she also saw through the eyes of the self that was down there trying to move forward. She was afraid of falling back like the buffalo calves, but the fear of this was numbed by the weight of her body and the feed-bags she carried as she tried to lift both them and herself from the earth.

The destination in this dream—which she had dreamt many times—was never gained. The dry, dead road went on, it seemed, forever. The only variation in the landscape through which they passed came when, every so often, Amy would spy through the churning dust the image of a high board fence—*along the top of which, perfectly balanced, a male orange cat was running in an attempt, apparently, to keep in the sights of Amy's gaze.* Wormwood. In the dream, however, she could not remember his name.

Cat-a-cat-cat! she would cry. *But no sound came from her mouth. Just the feel of sound—and the shape of it. And the hurt of it having been wrenched from her throat.*

Always, at the end of this dream, Tweedie would come and wake her up. *You've been yelling again, Miss Wylie,* he would say.

Sometimes—especially after the starlings began to arrive—Amy would panic whenever Tweedie opened the door. She would shout at him on these occasions, but the words were unintelligible and McCabe, the orderly, was called and shots of lithium were administered.

When Marlow was told of these yelling episodes, he came from the eighteenth floor and sat with her.

This time, the moment he was through the door, Amy looked over at him from her place by the tiny window.

"Doctor Marlow," she said. "I thought you had abandoned me."

"No," Marlow said. "I saw you yesterday."

"You'll have to stand," said Amy. "There's nowhere left to sit." She waved her hand at the empty chair and the bed. "Unless you want me to move them..."

"No. I can stand."

Amy said: "more arrive every day."

"I see," said Marlow.

"Someone is killing them. That's why they come here. It's safe here. For them."

Marlow waited a moment and then he said: "tell me how many there are."

"More than a person can count. Over a hundred. Most of them are starlings."

"Starlings?"

"Yes."

First, exotic birds. Now, plain.

"I want to leave here, Doctor Marlow," Amy said—not looking at him. "I hate it."

"Because of the birds?"

"No. Because no one believes me. I have to save them."

Silence. Marlow watched her. She was playing with the rubber-banded pony-tail at the nape of her neck—twisting it round and round. She was dreadfully thin. She must have given up eating altogether. Marlow made a mental note to request a power diet for her. Liquids might be easier for her body to accept.

She said: "you believe me, don't you?"

"Yes."

"Can you see them? The birds?"

"Yes." A lie—but a necessary lie.

"We have to stop the killing."

"Yes."

"Will you help me? Please, Doctor Marlow. Please." She was like a child who believed that, if you built an ark, you could save the world. "The birds need someone who will help," she said.

"Yes."

Marlow could not wipe away his first comprehensive picture of Amy, lost in the lanes with her bags of food. And Wormwood—in whom no one else had been willing to invest belief. Her madness was benign—excepting that it held her in its thrall. There was little outright violence to it. None that was harmful. Only the yelling—and it was always defensive. The fact was, Amy Wylie suffered, Marlow conceded, from a madness called *benevolence*. And it was killing her.

"I will see what I can do," he said.

She looked at him accusingly. "I know what that means," she said.

"Oh?"

"Yes. It means that nothing will be done."

Marlow said: "no. It means that I will do whatever *can* be done. I promise you."

He was forced, however, to lie to her when she asked about the recent activities of the D-Squads. He said, having witnessed a slaughter only that morning, there had been no spraying for a week.

Later, Marlow reflected on his complicity in Amy Wylie's madness. *I told her I saw what I did not see—her birds,* he thought, *and I told her I did not see what I saw—the yellow tankers.* Then he thought: *I am like her medication. We both promote a world of lies.*

When Marlow returned to his office on the eighteenth floor, an unexpected visitor was waiting for him.

Bella said: "this is Mister Griffin Price, Doctor Marlow. I told him you would not have time to spare him—but..."

"Thank you, Mrs Orenstein."

Griffin Price was taller than Marlow had imagined, but not as intense as Olivia had led him to believe. The man who stood before him was smiling and cordial and perfectly relaxed.

"I've come to visit my sister-in-law Amy Wylie," he said. "And I thought I might as well drop in just to have a word with you, Doctor Marlow."

"Certainly."

They went to the inner office, but Marlow let the door stand open. He wanted to reinforce the fact that another patient was expected.

"Oddly enough," he told Griffin, "I've just come from seeing Amy, Mister Price. Do sit down for a moment."

"Thank you."

Griffin was carrying a small, square package done up in blue paper with a yellow bow. He set it to one side and sat down opposite Marlow.

"Your wife tells me you've been in Prague, Mister Price."

"That's right."

"I trust it was a pleasant visit."

"Quite exciting, actually. My factory there has just begun making a new line of souvenirs. As a matter of fact, I've brought one for Amy." He held up the package by its ribbon.

Marlow said: "that's very good of you, Mister Price. I'm afraid I should warn you, however..."

"Yes?"

"Mrs Price may already have told you this—but, Amy is in extremely bad shape right now. We have not been able to settle on effective medication. Her contact with reality is at low ebb."

"I'm sorry to hear it."

"I'm not too sure, to be perfectly frank, that seeing her would be a good idea—at the moment."

"That bad?"

"Well..." Marlow opened his hands and shrugged. "Have you had much experience of Amy's illness, Mister Price?"

"Some. Nothing like Olivia's experience, of course. But..." Griffin crossed his legs and removed a piece of lint from his trousers. "...I guess the worst was having to rescue her from the police after one of her hunger strikes. You know about those, I presume."

Marlow nodded.

"This one," said Griffin, "was in protest against the first sturnusemia spraying—however long ago that was. I don't remember. More than a year or two..." Griffin gave a light laugh. "She hit me."

"Yes. I've been hit, too," said Marlow. "I sympathize."

"Oh, it wasn't serious. It was just a shock. You don't expect to be hit when you've just got a person out of jail."

"No."

There was a somewhat awkward silence. Griffin uncrossed his legs and sat forward, looking at his hands. Marlow thought how handsome he was—in spite of his thinning hair. His blondness was quite remarkable. Almost Scandinavian.

"Doctor Marlow, it is not, perhaps, my place to interfere in Amy's treatment. Believe me, I have no qualms whatsoever about her being here. But..."

"Yes?"

"You should know that I'm saying this in behalf of my mother-in-law. Of Amy's mother. I don't believe you've met."

"No. Although I have read some of Amy's background that was provided by Mrs Wylie. What does she want you to say, Mister Price?"

"She had some literature which I suppose was provided by someone here at the Parkin. It was about a scanner. Does that mean anything to you?"

"Yes. That would be the PET scanner. Positron Emission Tomography."

"That's it. Well. Eloise—my mother-in-law—has got it into her head that this PET scanner might do Amy some good. Is that possible?"

"It's not a treatment, Mister Price. It's only a means of making an assessment."

"Oh, yes. I realize that. It shows, I take it, some indication of how the brain responds to medication. Is that correct?"

"More or less, yes."

"Has Amy had such a scan, Doctor Marlow?"

"No."

"May I ask why not?"

"Of course. But you may not like my answer. The thing is, in Amy's case—especially given the severity of recent episodes—having the scan could be extremely distressing."

"Painful?"

"Not in the least. But frightening to her."

"I see."

Griffin Price stood up and went to the window, where he turned his back on Marlow.

"Is it possible to get a second opinion on that?" he said. "I mean—you see—my mother-in-law would like a scanning to take place."

"Nonetheless, I advise against it."

"Yes. But a second opinion..."

"Well—I certainly can't prevent you from getting a second opinion, Mister Price. But I have been your sister-in-law's doctor during this entire episode, and I..."

"It would be appreciated." Griffin turned. Marlow could now see, by the coldness in his visitor's eyes and by the set of his mouth, what it was that cautioned Olivia against revealing her pregnancy to him. His expression was almost military in its adamant refusal to hear the word *no*. Price was obviously a man who never made concessions. He had come to Marlow with "orders" from Eloise Wylie—and the "orders" were going to be carried out.

Marlow decided that, for Amy's sake, an argument about second opinions would only be detrimental. Price would have the PET scan whether Marlow approved of it or not.

"I will accede to your request on one condition," he said.

"Which is?"

"That you leave the timing of this procedure up to me."

Griffin smiled. "That suits me," he said. "Just so long as we know it will be done."

"It will be done," said Marlow.

Griffin prepared to leave.

"If you think I should not go down to see her today, Doctor Marlow, would you be kind enough to take this package to her?"

"Of course."

The small blue parcel was handed over.

"Thank you. It's somewhat delicate, by the way. Glass."

"Glass?"

"Yes. A glass bird. I'm very proud of it."

"Patients in Amy's condition are not allowed to have glass in their possession, Mister Price. I'm sorry."

"What a pity. Well—perhaps you would set it aside for her until she can receive it."

Marlow nodded.

Griffin shook his hand and departed. All very businesslike. Mission accomplished.

When Price was gone, Marlow held the package up and inspected it. The blue wrapping covered only three sides. On the fourth side, a cellophane window allowed the customer to see what he was buying—in this case, a small crystal owl of a size that could easily be held in the palm of the hand. The owl's tail was fanned and its wings were partially spread. Its head, turning upwards, was angled to the left. The whole effect was charming and yet rather sad.

Marlow thought: *how curious,* and placed the package on his desk. A glass bird—caged. Not unlike its prospective owner.

3

Peggy Webster had been parked on Boswell for more than half an hour before she got out of her car. Her problem was that she was about to break the law and she was not certain how she would deal with that if she got caught. Of course, the thing was *not* to get caught—but Peggy had never learned to think that way. If you broke the law, you were already "caught." You caught yourself with your conscience and paid the penalty in lost sleep.

What she was going to do was feed Amy's birds. Nothing could be simpler—or more mundane. And yet the fine for bird-feeding was one thousand dollars—more than you would pay if you threw your garbage into the street or defaced a public building. More than you would pay for having shop-lifted or for spreading a false alarm or for beating your dog or for striking a neighbour. It was ridiculous. But it was the law.

Peggy had gone into several shops and had bought such things as unshelled peanuts, sunflower seeds, cracked corn and millet. All grains and seeds that were displayed for human consumption. Also, two loaves of whole wheat bread. Bird seed itself was unavailable—a thing entirely of the past. Her "contraband" was relatively bulky—awkward, but not heavy. She took it to Amy's front door and, using her sister's key, went inside.

Amy's house was small, but pleasant. It was sparsely furnished with old wooden tables and chairs of the simplest kind, mostly unfinished, but some of it painted blue. Blue and white and cedar—these were the colours of Amy's life.

Peggy went through to the kitchen and opened the back door. She would spread the seed and the bread in the yard, where a minimum of people would see it. Or see her.

When Peggy stepped out into the shade of a honey-locust, the first thing she saw was a large red cat with a torn ear. It was lying half asleep in a flower bed by the fence. When it heard the door open, it came completely awake and ran to greet her. This was Wormwood—but Peggy had no notion of the name.

Spreading the peanuts and corn and millet, Peggy thought: *I feel wonderful.* How odd it was to break the law. With only a cat as a witness—and perhaps some curious neighbours watching from behind a curtained window. There were, of course, no birds. Not one. But, in time, per- haps—one bird would come and, feeding, tell others.

Surely they would imagine Amy had returned. Surely they would imagine she was free and that all was well.

Peggy stopped mid-gesture.

She let the hand fall to her side.

She smiled.

And then, in ever-widening circles, she spread the rest of the corn and the peanuts and all the bread. If anyone had seen her, they would have assumed that Peggy Webster was a dancer. But she was simply imagining freedom—for her sister, Amy, and for herself—a thought that had never occurred to her. To be free, after all, one must break the law.

4

Ben Webster was lying in the bathtub with the door locked. Having already done three lines of cocaine, he was feeling warmly contented— ambitious—eager. His penis lay against his thigh, the focus of idle atten- tion. He knew that if he watched it long enough, it would stiffen and lie against his belly. He looked at it through half-closed eyes, his arms laid out along the sides of the tub. To touch it was to cheat. He had played this game since puberty. When he was seventeen he could make himself ejaculate at will. *Look, Ma—no hands!* Those days were long gone—but the memory of them was tantalizing. Seventeen was also the year of his first seductions. Rosemary Wright—Bonnie Franks—Jennifer Bonnycas- tle... Girls, not women. Virgins. *Cherries Jubilee.* He wanted that back. Nothing since had equalled it.

The tub was deep enough and long enough to contain Ben entirely— allowing him to stretch his legs and press his toes beneath the taps—the taps both seeping, the sounds of water falling drop by drop and the smell of some dark herbal essence rising in the steam around him. He lifted his wrist with its silver chain and let it down gently onto the ledge so the noise of its descent was unobtrusive—muffled by moisture and heat and the buzz of cocaine that spread through his brain and made him wince with anticipation.

Tonight. This evening. The phone calls had paid off. In two hours' time, he would be standing with others—the Club of Men. Watching with them—urging them to go that one last bit of distance that haunted him because he dared not trespass there alone. Tonight, he would be inducted into their company. He wanted their approval. He wanted to see. And be seen. Sex was meaningless without a witness. He knew that now from having seen the Shapiro boy. *A person must be watched, or there can be no satisfaction.*

Allison and Carol.

One and then the other.

John, his brother, need never know. Why should he know? Who would tell him?

We must mould—he thought—*the children to our needs.*

His penis stirred. He raised his knees, creating a harbour for it in his groin. He reached down and touched it tenderly with his finger-ends. To hell with the game. Its patience had come to an end. The word *reward* occurred to him. It would dine that night on caviar. And he would drink champagne.

5

Emma and Barbara Berry were seated at the dining-room table. As usual, Maynard's place was set—but his chair was empty.

Orley hovered in the doorway. The telephone had rung and, having answered it, she was coming to tell Emma the call was for her. Before she could speak, however, Barbara cut her off.

"Mother is not taking calls tonight."

"No?" said Orley.

"No," said Barbara.

Emma had not turned, but leaned above her plate as if in a state of euphoria. She had drunk too much before dinner and was now somewhat lost.

"That so, Mrs B.?"

"What?"

"You not going out tonight?"

"Depends."

"Well, there's a call here for you."

"Who?"

"Man."

"Which?"

"I never ask, Mrs B. Not after six o'clock—the way you told me."

"All right. I'll come."

"You said you weren't going," said Barbara. "Tonight is my hair night."

"We can do your hair tomorrow." Emma pushed her chair back and stood up. She was not so much unsteady on her feet as in her mind. She did not seem to know which way to turn.

"Come back this way," said Orley. She led Emma into the darkened hallway.

Barbara got down off her chair. She went along to the head of the table and took three cigarettes from the packet resting there beside her mother's wine glass. She then returned to her place. *Wuthering Heights* lay open on the seat. She had been sitting on it. Now, she knelt on the chair and reached for the wine bottle. By the time Orley had returned to clear the plates, Barbara, cigarettes, bottle and *Wuthering Heights* had disappeared.

"You in here?" said Orley.

There was no reply.

Orley put plates and glasses on her tray and went back into the kitchen. In the hallway, Emma concluded her conversation and came to the dining-room door. "I will be going out," she said. "I'm sorry. But this is someone..."

Barbara was not there.

Emma went to the sideboard and opened another bottle of red. Then, having poured a full glass of it, she called out: "Orley—call up John Bolton and get him to bring the limo." John Bolton had taken over Billy Lydon's job, but not his place. Billy had been sweet and silent. Bolton talked incessantly. Emma went upstairs fuming. *To hell with everyone,* she was thinking. *Maynard. Barbara. Orley. Everyone. You turn your back two minutes and they all disappear.*

Barbara could hear Orley talking to Bolton on the house phone—not the words of what she said, but the sound of it beyond the swinging door. Orley's voice was reassuring. It seemed to be anchored so deep in her body. Men had voices like that, but not many women. The only other woman Barbara knew who could also sing basso was Mrs Fitch at school. Mrs Fitch played the organ in chapel and also conducted the choir. She loved to sing out over all the others—even over the booming chords from the organ—and she sounded like an opera singer. Orley's voice was not so deep—but it was never raised, the way Mrs Fitch raised hers. *Never shout in daily life,* Orley said. *A shout should be saved for emergencies.*

The only black children Barbara knew were a girl from Ethiopia at school and the son of one of the doctors at Sunnybrook Hospital where her father seemed to spend his entire life. This black boy had come to

377

dinner, once, with his parents and had sat across the table from Barbara, staring at her. He was nine. And English—or, as he said, a *Brit*. Barbara hated him. Not just because he stared at her, but because he was a snob and had been rude to Orley.

Orley was taking away his plate between courses and the boy said to her: "why are you a maid?"

Orley thought he must be joking, so she laughed and said: "you haven't been here long, have you?"

The black boy—whose name Barbara had stricken from her memory—did not think this was funny and said: "no black person should be a servant." He spoke in a stilted, formal fashion—no matter what he was saying. He seemed, Barbara thought, to be reading from a book of grammar.

Orley had moved on by then and was facing him from the other side of the table, standing behind Barbara. Her voice did not betray what she might have been feeling. It was still its deep, calm self—with an edge of laughter. "You, child," she said, "I suppose you have a white maid at home."

"Of course we do," the boy replied. "White people make the best servants."

"Oh?" Orley said, still smiling. "And why is that?"

"Because," the boy replied, "they're afraid of us."

"I see," said Orley. "I hadn't noticed that."

She backed, then, into the kitchen with her tray—fanning the air with the swinging door.

The four parents seated at the table—even Maynard had been there—sat without speaking and the silence was not broken until some-one asked for another slice of beef. It was the boy.

When Orley came back to serve the meringues and chocolate sauce, she did not say a word. In fact, she did not say another word until the guests had departed. Then she said: "bang!" Barbara, who was seven at the time—did not know what this meant. She only knew it made her want to hide.

Now, she was hiding again—beneath the table.

Orley came in with fresh fruit salad in a cut-glass bowl. She set it on the sideboard and poured herself a glass of wine. Then she sat down. She was tired all the time, these days, partly because of Emma's erratic behaviour since the deaths of Mister Gatz and Billy Lydon. There had been a lot more drinking since that event and it was not just Emma who was doing it. Emma was doing her share—but so was Orley and so was Barbara. The only abstemious person in the house was Maynard—and he was rarely there to exert his influence.

Orley was drinking more, but she was never drunk. The drink—mostly beer—made her feel she could bear what must be borne. That was the extent of it. She did not, on the other hand, know what to make of Barbara's drinking. That a child should be drinking to excess was not a situation Orley had encountered before. Not that Barbara drank all the time. But she drank every day. God knows where she was right now—but one thing was certain. There would be a bottle nearby.

Orley opened the lab coat she wore over her skirt and blouse and gave a long sigh. Looking around her, she thought: *this is a pretty room. Pity there's not more happiness in it...* Then she smelled smoke—and saw it curling up above the lip of the table.

"I see," she said. "We're under there, are we?"

"Don't call me *we*, Orley. I hate it," said Barbara.

"What're you doing with that cigarette I smell? Burning the house down?"

"No, ma'am."

Orley watched as a puff of smoke emerged and formed a perfect circle.

"Very clever," she said. "Can you do that twice?"

Barbara blew three more smoke rings in a row.

Orley applauded.

The sound of a wine glass being filled came next, and a low, unsatisfactory belch.

"I heard that," said Orley.

"What?" said Barbara.

"Somebody belching. Sounded like a pig, to me."

"I'm not a pig. I'm a person."

"*Persons* say *excuse me*," said Orley.

"All right. Excuse me."

"Thank you."

Orley searched for one of her man-size tissues and wiped her forehead.

"You want your dessert?" she said. "I have a nice cold fruit salad here."

"No, thank you."

They both fell silent. Another smoke ring appeared.

"You're good at that," said Orley.

"Practice makes perfect."

"Bobby Hawkins used to blow smoke rings. I never could."

"Do you miss him, Orley?" Barbara asked.

"Of course I do. Just about every minute of every day."

After a moment, Barbara said: "everyone keeps leaving."

"Unh-hunh..." Orley drank wine.

"Bobby Hawkins—Billy Lydon—Mister Gatz—Mother—Father—Isabel Holtz—everyone."

"I guess so," Orley said. "On the other hand, Bobby Hawkins and Billy Lydon both got shot. That's not exactly choosing to go away." And then: "who's Isabel Holtz?"

"I told you before. You've just forgotten. She's my friend Ruth Holtz's sister. And she disappeared off the face of the earth. Just like the others. All gone—every one."

"Yep."

"I'm sick of it."

"Yes. Well."

"Why don't we go away? We could go off somewhere together."

"I think not."

"Why?"

"They call that kidnapping."

"I'm not a kid."

"Yes you are."

Emma could be heard above them, opening and closing her bureau drawers.

Orley said: "you thinking of coming out from under there sometime, maybe?"

"No."

"Okay, then. Suit yourself."

There was a pause. Finally, Barbara said: "Orley?"

"Yes?"

"You know what I think?"

"Not until you tell me, I don't. What's it about this time?"

"Why people kill themselves."

"Good Lord! What brought that on?"

"Different ways of dying. You know—like we were saying? Bobby Hawkins—Billy Lydon—Mister Gatz."

"And?"

"So, I know why people kill themselves."

"Okay." Orley tried to be diffident. "Tell me why, then."

"They do it because there's nowhere else to hide."

Orley put down her wine glass.

Dear God in heaven, she thought. *Children.*

Out loud, she said nothing.

Emma came down the stairs in black chiffon and left without a word.

The door closed.

Orley said: "you can come out now. She's gone."

Barbara did not appear, however. She stayed down under the table and poured another glass of wine.

6

Grendel, at last, was able to walk. Or rather, to hobble. His off-rhythm gait could be heard in all parts of the house. The stairs, however, were still his enemy and—though he would try them—he often failed and would sit in the lower hall and wail. On these occasions, Marlow would lift him up and get him to the top, where a bout of face licking was the carrier's reward.

Lilah's method of transporting Grendel was now passé. During the time when the dog could not walk at all, she had rolled him onto a blanket and pulled him to his destination as though by toboggan. He came to rather enjoy this and Lilah could sometimes still be tricked into dragging him here and there when his behaviour insisted he was *lame today and cannot possibly do anything for myself.*

The vet, whose name was Natasha Reynolds, was pleased with Grendel's progress and finally confessed to Marlow that she had been fairly certain the dog would die. The loss of blood had been severe and the general shock to his system had made her doubtful of his recovery. For the first while, Natasha had come every day. It had been agreed that Grendel should be treated at home. Separation from Marlow in the midst of his trauma would have killed him outright. Natasha said: "we have to remember that some of us really do live for others. I don't mean unselfishly—only that others are often at the centre of our own well-being. Dogs are like that."

Marlow wanted to know more about sturnusemia. Grendel, after all, had been shot because of it.

"You know—it's interesting, Doctor Marlow," Natasha said. "We have a fair number of beasts brought into the clinic who, one way or another, have made contact with dead birds. Cats in particular. Hysterical owners bring them in and beg us to save them. But—unless they've been shot, like Grendel, or victimized in some other way—not one of these animals has ever had a single sign of *anything* being wrong with them. Now—it is possible," she went on, "that the starling Grendel had in his mouth was not itself diseased. But my colleagues and I are coming to the conclusion that sturnusemia has not been seen to be—and therefore *is* not—as transmittable as it's supposed to be. This is mere observation," she warned. "But that has been our conclusion. Of

381

course, I mean transmittable to animals through blood-contact or by contact with bird lice. So I wouldn't worry about it. On the other hand, the minute you see any sign of it in Grendel, let me know. A sudden rise in fever—lack of interest in food—blood in the stool..."

"But the disease does exist," said Marlow.

"Yes," said Natasha. "It exists. My husband is one of its victims."

"I'm sorry."

"He's not dead yet—but he's in the latter stages. His skin has begun to speckle."

"I have to ask you this. Forgive me—but is your husband also a vet?"

"No. He's a chartered accountant."

"So he didn't get it through contact with birds or cats?"

"We have a cat," she looked at Marlow—and he wondered if she was lying, when she added: "and the cat is perfectly fit."

"May I ask you one other question?"

"Of course."

"When Grendel was shot, Miss Kemp began by trying to locate your partner, Susie Boyle. Susie had given Grendel his shots and had taken care of him when he was still a puppy. But Miss Kemp said Susie Boyle had died of sturnusemia. Is that true?"

Natasha said yes and looked away. She was putting things back into her black bag.

"Please forgive me, Doctor Reynolds, but is it even remotely possible there could be some connection between..."

"Yes," said Natasha—cutting Marlow short. "That also occurred to me. Susie was our best friend. We spent a lot of time together."

Nothing more was said, but it got Marlow thinking.

In reading Austin's files, Marlow found that two things were now coming clear. One of these was that Austin himself had not been involved directly either with George or with the latter-day histories of many of the patients whose stories Marlow was exploring. They had either left psychiatric therapy behind them—or had been moved into Kurtz's sphere of influence. The other certainty was that a number of the files had never been in Austin's purview to begin with—but had been lifted either from Sub Four or from Kurtz's own filing system.

One of these latter was a file so thin and sparsely papered that it seemed the patient in question must either have died or been whisked away into another venue altogether—not the Parkin and not the Queen Street Mental Health Centre. The patient had, to put it bluntly, vanished—and Marlow was deeply concerned about his case.

The man's name was given as *Smith Jones*, which put Marlow on alert the moment he saw it. Smith Jones could not be anyone's real name. Unless, of course, his parents were confirmed sadists. Marlow—unable to bear the name any longer, began—as he read—to think of the man as *The Paranoid Civil Servant*.

The Paranoid Civil Servant's file had only twenty sheets of paper in it. The first three of these contained an example of what Marlow had become accustomed to calling *Kurtz's essays*. Like everything else in the file, the essay was undated. And the lack of dates was not an oversight. They had once existed, but had, at some point, been excised—with scissors, or a razor blade.

> The first thing you must understand *[Marlow read]*—is that I am perfectly sane. Others will want you to think I am not, but their denial of my sanity is a part of the conspiracy I have uncovered. What the conspiracy is, and who the "others" are, is easily made clear.
>
> All you need to know of my personal history is that I have worked as an immunologist for over twenty years. For the past decade of that time, I have been Chief Research Officer at the *[excised]* branch of one of this continent's largest government-sponsored medical research institutions. The name of the organization does not matter. In fact, I deliberately do not include it here because whenever I mention it in tandem with the story I have to tell, people invariably bring up the institution's "impeccable" reputation—and then, however they phrase it, they call me a liar. They rarely come right out with the word itself, but the gist of their accusation, however tactfully worded, is just that: *I am a liar.*
>
> I am not a liar. *[This had been underlined.]*
>
> I grant you, what I have uncovered is not so easy to believe. It calls into doubt the integrity not only of Canadian governments, past and present, but of science itself. And although I have frequently had my misgivings about the former, I have spent my entire professional life devoted to the latter. It is a terrible thing to discover that your most fervent beliefs have been betrayed. It is a form of infidelity far, far worse than religious or marital unfaithfulness.
>
> Simply put, what I have stumbled on is a ministerial stratagem to dupe the public over a vitally important issue—namely, the origin and nature of the disease which has

laughably been called *sturnusemia*. It is laughable because the name, based on the starling genus, *Sturnus,* represents a complete fiction. The disease in question has nothing whatsoever to do with starlings. Or with birds of any kind. At the risk of presenting a mixed metaphor, birds, in this context, are nothing more than scapegoats.

You have asked that I be brief. I will therefore not encumber my story with the details of how I made this discovery. In a nutshell, my encounter with this deception has less to do with science than with sloppy bureaucracy. A set of papers marked *CONFIDENTIAL/TOP SECRET*—were mistakenly delivered by an inexperienced office clerk to my desk. Before the error was realized, I had read enough to know the truth about so-called *sturnusemia.*

I still have the greatest difficulty believing my scientific colleagues would be capable of such duplicity. Some of these men and women have been my research partners and my closest friends. I simply cannot comprehend their motives. I have not been able to bring the subject up with anyone directly involved. You will say this means I am a coward. Perhaps I am. But, given the reaction of my family and the few carefully chosen colleagues to whom I first revealed this ghastly situation, it is plain that I cannot expect rationality from anyone who has actually been party to deception on the scale of this intrigue. Even if they believe they are doing "the right thing"—even if they have somehow been convinced it is in the public good to conceal the truth about the plague that is presently upon us—how can I expect to penetrate to whatever core of integrity may still reside in them? How can I hope to reach the *humanity* in them that could convince them they are doing *A TERRIBLE WRONG. [This had been underlined twice.]*

It is less difficult to deal with the scientific truth of the situation. That, at least—as all things scientific *should* be—is pure. Pure in the sense that scientific truth is not burdened with moral issues; it is *knowledge.* You, Doctor Kurtz, will already understand this, since you yourself are a scientist. And so, the *science* of the situation is this:

The plague that is currently spreading across the face of this continent—and, presumably, will shortly launch its deadly invasion elsewhere—is the *direct* consequence of human activities. Perhaps, if only one of these byproducts of our careless treatment of the planet had appeared, we might not today be facing the dire menace that confronts us. But of what use is speculation at this point?

What has happened is this: as a result of an unpublicized experiment with genetic engineering, a new virus strain escaped from an allegedly "safe" trial station and entered the world at large. It was a virus intended to have a benign and useful effect on skin pigmentation—a biological prevention of sunburn, to replace the old-fashioned sun screens and tanning agents already on the market. And perhaps it might have remained "benign and useful," if its creation and release had not coincided with another far more widespread and potentially hazardous situation—the nearly complete depletion of the ozone layer. As everyone knows, this latter is the result of the irresponsibly continued use of fluorocarbons. Thus, we have the combination of two agents—a deliberately altered virus capable of affecting the body's production of the brown pigment, melanin, and a highly increased intensity of ultra violet rays coming from the sun. The result of this disastrous combination is the disease we have been told is spread by birds: *sturnusemia.*

The one truthful aspect of the information governments have disseminated about the disease is its symptomatology. It does, indeed—as reported—include the production of multiple melanomas—the "speckling" of the skin that, ridiculously enough, has been explained as having something to do with the speckled pattern of colours on a starling. *[An exclamation point had been bracketed here—and crossed out.]* These particular skin cancers—potentially lethal in themselves—have, in this new disease, been joined by a meningitislike condition—a "brain fever," so-called—which is usually fatal.

At the moment, of course, there is no known cure for sturnusemia. And little is being done to find a cure. This, in spite of the fact that a totally neutral vaccine has been offered to the public under the government's imprimatur. *[Underlined.]* (I speak as one whose professional life is deeply involved in the kind of work that should be underway in order to combat the new plague. Yet nothing of genuine potential has been activated.) What *has* been activated is one of modern history's

greatest hoaxes—a propaganda programme aimed at conceal-
ing the truth about the genetic engineering industry's—and
government's—role in bringing about the conditions in which
this disease could arise. D-Gas (ABS-482)—D-Squads, the
campaign to rid our cities of birds—these are all subterfuges.
Distractions. Camouflage. To allow the great corporations and
their protective partners, the duly elected governments of our
nation, our provinces, our cities...to continue their profit-
making and their exploitation...unhindered and unhampered
by conscience, by adverse publicity, by an informed electorate,
by... It's terrible. Dreadful. I cannot understand it. I can't....

*At this point, Smith Jones apparently found himself unable to
continue. Classic case—p-s—vivid construction of hallucinatory "scientific data"—total conviction, total lucidity. Will
refer to [excised] Suggest [excised].*

R.K.

Marlow folded The Paranoid Civil Servant's file and pushed it to one
side. He thought about what Natasha Reynolds might think if she were
to read it.

But who else would believe it? No one. And where could one go for
confirmation? Nowhere. Was there anyone a person could trust with
such information? No—there was not.

What, then, was paranoia?

One thing might be done. Marlow would ask Bella Orenstein for a
list of reputable science reporters. He would telephone one or two—
make enquiries—ask them if, over the past two years or so, there had
been any speculation—from whatever source—regarding the *bona fides*
of sturnusemia. This way, he might discover who one's fellow paranoiacs
might be. And what had become of their speculation. And of them.

Oddly, Marlow smiled in that moment. He was considering the word
speculation. Even as his mind was thinking it, his brain was giving the
word a new and—in the light of sturnusemia—a very interesting
spelling:

Speckulation.

The phrase *speckled with doubt* also occurred.

And *specktator—specktacle—specktacular*. And *specktral.*

And *specktre.*

7

"Gentlemen, be seated."

The speaker was John Dai Bowen.

The Club of Men had convened and all twelve members were in attendance.

"This night," said John Dai—facing the others with a nervous smile— "we have a special attraction."

There was applause.

"We have waited some time for this young lady to appear. Our selection committee has attempted and failed in the past to secure her acquiescence. But—persistence is the mistress of rewards..." There was laughter.

Ben crossed his legs and smoothed his trousers. He was seated— masked—in a yellow chair. His heart was beating in his ears. *After all, he was thinking, this is the night of my initiation into these affairs. Perhaps they have read my mind and the girl who walks through that curtain will be Allison...*

Who else could it be?

Why else had he been invited?

The Club of Men had begun as an élite group of faggots. Models were hired—all men. And then it became the fashion for non-models to be enticed to appear—that sports announcer among them. Always good for a laugh, that one. And, gradually, strangers—young boys, younger and younger. Then girls—young girls—younger and younger, with their budding tits and hairless cunts. *And then—then—then—*Ben's mind went stumbling—*who was it?*—that Fullerton man. He had walked in one night with his daughter. Nothing had been the same since. It only took the one occasion—then they were on their way. Which is why Ben Webster had consented to join.

He had not mentioned names. It wasn't done. No one mentioned names. Assumptions were made—that was all. Sons—daughters— nieces—nephews—the children of friends and neighbours. The selection committee simply made assumptions. Connections. *Bingo!*

Ben and Peggy had no children. That was well known. Ben was straight as a die—that was well known. They were not going to bring him some dumb boy. They would bring him Allison. Carol. Moira—one day.

Kids were the safest fuck in town. If you knew where they'd been—if you knew what they'd done, then you pretty well knew you were safe. If the kids were your own or your brother's kids, then it followed that they had to be clean. Long, long ago, there had once been a song that talked about *sweet sixteen*. The kid in the song was a kid that you met when you went to the village green. Ben was thinking the song could be updated, now. It would be about *fucking green-teens*. He began, in his mind, to hum the tune...

John Dai had spoken for so long now, Ben wanted to yell, *get the hell on with it!* But that would be unacceptable behaviour. Decorum was required. Patience. Tact. Discipline. Dress code. Everyone wore a jacket and tie. Nobody wore a condom. Not with your own kids.

Finally, John Dai went to the bedroom door. The moment had arrived. Ben closed his eyes.

"You may come out, now," he heard John Dai simpering. This was followed by an intake of breath on all sides. Approval.

It must be Allison...

He opened his eyes.

It was not.

It was young Kim Firstbrook.

She was twelve.

And she had no breasts at all.

The picture-taking bored him. If the girl was there—you ought, at least, to be able to fondle her. But no. It was all for the eyes. She was so inexperienced she could not even perform the crudest forms of masturbation. She was dull-witted, too. A drugged-out stupid girl. Only half-pretty—not the least bit beautiful. Except her skin, maybe. But if you couldn't touch it—what the hell good was it?

The Club of Men was a complete bust. Ben did not even stay for copies of the pictures.

Instead, he went out on the street and drove around the Track until he saw what he wanted. A fifteen-year-old in a miniskirt that looked as if he could have it off in two seconds flat. Over it, the girl wore something white that Ben could see through. She also wore a pair of short-wristed leather gloves. This was of interest.

She was with him in the car for thirty minutes. He paid her what she asked. Why not? He barely heard what she said. He went home enraged. She had lied about her age. She was just a tart dressing down from twenty—not the kid he had wanted, at all.

When he went inside the house on his return, he went directly to his stash of coke and did some lines before he called for Peggy.

Where the hell was she?

Gone.

And would not come back.
The note was curt.
She had left him.
He was finally alone.

8

Marlow had been won over to Eloise Wylie's side in advocating a PET scan for Amy. After Griffin's visit with the glass bird—and following another week of yet one more trial medication—Marlow had come to see the efficacy of letting the scan into the process. The least it could do would have to be positive in the long run—since, one way or another, it would show the effect of medication on Amy's brain. Marlow had come to realize that his concern about the procedure had been more in his own behalf than in Amy's. The fear of it was his. Something all along had informed him that Amy's case was unique in more ways than one. Every schizophrenic is unique—but Amy was doubly unique (*interesting phrase*, he thought) because she actively resisted being released from her demons. She wanted them. And the fact was, she wanted them more than they wanted her.

The process of achieving a PET scan begins with the making of a mask—a procedure that requires its own time. This can prove to be difficult for the patient, depending on the extent of paranoia and the level of claustrophobia. In Amy's case, there was no one alive who could not be read as being a potential enemy, and any procedure of confinement was necessarily traumatic, since it involved—from Amy's point of view—the possibility of being prevented from having contact with her birds. Therefore, a sedative was given in the hope that it would calm her. She also requested that Marlow, whom she more or less trusted, be present through the whole process.

The purpose of the mask is to provide attachment points to facilitate the immobilization of the patient's head during the scanning process. Standard plastic masks are available, but each one has to be reshaped to fit the patient's head and face. This is accomplished by using a softening agent to render the plastic malleable and expandable. The material is then laid onto the face and the moulding process begun.

The technician in Amy's case was a Chinese woman who hummed all the time she was working. Marlow held Amy's hand as the mask began to shape itself to her features beneath the plastic. The Chinese technician's hands were small and wet and they moved over Amy's face the way an artist's fingers move over clay—cajoling, smoothing, shaping—all with a gentle exertion of pressure that fluctuated as bone was raised and flesh was flattened. And all the while, a song was being evoked—no words, just melody—a lullaby, as Amy's fears were soothed.

"Hot," Amy said through clenched teeth. Hot, but not alarming. Her lips had been greased with Vaseline and her eyes had been shrouded with round pads of cotton batting. When she spoke, her hand held more tightly to Marlow's.

When at last the mask was complete it had hardened into a tough, almost leathery version of basic human features—not unlike a mask that might be worn by an actor in a play. It buckled on at the back of the head, and had fasteners built into it that could be attached to the scanner in order to achieve the desired immobility.

The following day, Tweedie took Amy to the PET Centre, where Marlow was already waiting with the technologists and the radiologist who would conduct the scan. The latter was a man called Menges, who seemed to Marlow to be quite alarmingly young for someone in charge of such a new and expensive set-up. Still, he was more than competent and certainly had an admirable way with patients. Having discussed Amy's hallucinatory version of the world with Marlow, Menges greeted her with the news that room had been made in the scanning room for her birds. There was no elaboration on this. It was simply said. Marlow was grateful. Amy said nothing.

There was one bad moment as Tweedie and one of the technologists were taking Amy through the antechamber that led to the preparation room. This antechamber had a viewing window, giving onto the mask lab. Twenty or more masks lined up in ranks on black display bars stared out at Amy like an audience of skulls suspended mid-air.

Amy said: "don't!" and threw her arms across her face.

Tweedie said: *it's all right. They can't get through the glass,* and he moved Amy on past the window and into the room where she would be prepared to undergo her scan. This was where Marlow had waited for her and she said to him: *am I dying, Doctor? Is this death?* and he said: *no,* and he told her he was hoping it would turn out to be a way of setting her free and she said that, in that case, it could not be death because *death is not freedom, but just another form of detention.*

Marlow smiled. There was something wonderfully wilful about her attitude this morning—as if she were certain she was about to be released. When the mask was placed over her face and her eyes and mouth were the only living features to be seen in its contours, she looked at Marlow so directly that he had to look away. If she had been a witch with magical powers, Marlow would have been certain in that moment that Amy Wylie was about to vanish—snap her fingers, invoke her powers and disappear.

Doctor Menges came through at that moment and said: *are you ready?* and Marlow said: *yes, we are.*

In the scan room, Marlow stood to one side for a moment while Menges and the technologist discussed the procedure. Menges reminded the technologist of Amy's birds. In the meantime, Amy was being injected with the mildly radioactive solution that would allow the scanner to read whether or not her brain was utilizing the medication.

To date, Marlow had attempted to bring Amy's illness under control with a number of neuroleptics. He had not prescribed any of the injected drugs, being fearful of the length of time they stayed in the system. He prescribed only drugs that were taken orally. Amy's condition had been alleviated by none of them. Mellaril (thioridazine), Largactil (chlorpromazine), Orap (pimozide) and, most recently, the strongest of them all, Haldol (haloperidol). As usual, because Haldol had relatively severe Parkinsonian side effects, Marlow had also been giving Amy a drug called Cogentin (benztropine).

The radioactive solution Amy was receiving was prepared with the help of the PET Centre's own cyclotron. The scanner, sensitive to the radiation emitted by the injected solution, would be able to show the location and nature of chemical activity in Amy's brain. This process would consequently indicate how the brain cells were responding to the tagged medication.

Masked, Amy was brought through into the scan room. Her reaction to the scanner itself was one of horror. It seemed to be an enormous target, with a hollow bull's-eye. She was to be the arrow.

"I won't," she said when she saw where her head was to go.

Marlow stepped forward.

"I will show you," he said, and bent down with his head partially in the bull's-eye.

"You see?" he said. "All is well."

Amy, lying on a gurney, was persuaded to be wheeled into position, and her head was settled between the restrainers. She folded her arms across her breasts and Marlow at once thought of medieval effigies.

"My birds," Amy said.

"All is well," Marlow repeated.

Menges retired to the control room which could be seen through its observation window. The technologist said that Marlow must also withdraw before the scanner could be started. But Marlow said that he had promised Amy he would stay with her until the process was completed. Menges said through the intercom that this was permissible so long as Marlow stood sufficiently to one side.

In a moment, the scanner came alive. Amy's head was held stationary by the mask—now firmly anchored—and her body kept rigid by her own muscles. Suddenly, her voice emerged from the nose-and-mouth aperture of the mask. "*Charlie,*" she said, "I am learning to fly."

Marlow closed his eyes. Not because she had called him *Charlie,* as only Emma of all his patients had before. But because the image of Amy flying was attached too vividly to the image of Icarus, her cousin. Both, now, went climbing in his mind and one of them would fall. He wondered why she went with Icarus and if, like him, she was afraid.

All at once, Marlow was overwhelmed with the certainty that she was going to escape him. He opened his eyes to confirm her presence.

She had raised her arms and now she dropped them.

Not falling. Flying.

Wouldn't you know it.

9

Emma increasingly gave the appearance of walking in her sleep. As she left the house each evening, she rarely spoke. She never said how long she would be gone—and never said *goodbye.* Ironically, she was increasingly beautiful—in the way people are with a wasting disease. Pared to basics, she had the look of a Japanese drawing—black eyes, red mouth within a frame of black hair. Nothing more. The face itself dead white—mime-like—with the features drawn there in ink. An occidental geisha.

Orley would stand at the bottom of the stairs and turn her in the direction of the door. Emma acknowledged this by raising her hand in farewell as she walked towards the limousine. But there were never words.

Barbara had given up watching. She now ate almost exclusively alone—sitting halfway between her father's and her mother's empty chairs. Their place settings were always accoutred with silver and crystal—with Emma's enamelled blue ashtray off to the left of her napkin, the napkin ringed and white and crisp. Wine bottles, candlesticks and a Waterford vase with a complement of flowers filled in the rest. Orley would come and go and bring the various courses in silver dishes, some with lids and some without. Barbara now drank more than half a litre of wine at these solo meals—a glass of white, two glasses of red. Orley insisted the glass not ever be filled to the brim. *If you're going to drink this stuff,* she said, *you're going to drink it as prescribed. A person's glass is never over two-thirds filled...*

Barbara also smoked a mid-meal cigarette, and two when the meal was finished—the cigarettes provided by her friend, Cynthia Stern. She had commandeered a Crown Derby demitasse saucer for her ashtray and took great pride in the fact that she had learned to roll the ashes from the end of the cigarette—not to flick them. Emma flicked them and half her ashes ended up on the mahogany.

One night towards the end of June, Barbara was shocked to discover her father would join her for dinner. Part of her was elated—part of her was furious. This meant she would have to forgo both wine and cigarettes. That was the negative. But the positive lay in the fact that she would get to hear Maynard's voice and to see his beautiful hands.

"What are you reading now?" he said to her.

"*Wuthering Heights.*"

"I thought you'd finished it."

"No. I gave it up to read *A Member of the Wedding.*"

"Why?"

"Because it's about a twelve-year-old girl—and I'm a twelve-year-old girl."

"I see. And now you're back to *Wuthering Heights.*"

"Yes."

"Is she dead yet?"

"Who?"

"Catherine what's her name?"

"Earnshaw."

"So. Is she dead yet?"

"Thank you, Father, for ruining the entire book. I didn't know she died."

"Of course you did."

"No. As a matter of fact, I didn't."

"Then you should have guessed it."

"Why?"

"Characters like Catherine Earnshaw are only created so they can die. Same as Heathcliff."

"Oh, Father! Damn you!"

"I beg your pardon?"

"Now you've told me *he* dies."

"You didn't guess that either?"

"No." She had, however, suspected it. She simply did not want to know it until she got there.

"Others live," said Maynard—waving his knife. "That is the nature of tragedy. People die, but death is never the winner. At the end of every good tragedy, life is left standing. Catherine Earnshaw has a daughter— Cathy, I think—and Cathy lives."

"Sounds familiar," said Barbara.

"Oh? How?"

Barbara said: "Mother."

Maynard set his utensils down. He poured himself a glass of wine. Barbara noted it was exactly two-thirds full. She also noted that her father's hands were shaking.

"Why don't you ever talk about her?" Barbara asked.

Maynard considered briefly and then said: "because I don't know what to say." Then he looked along at Barbara and gave a crooked smile.

How pale he is, she thought.

Maynard said: "there is nothing I can do to help her, Barbara. Nothing. Please don't imagine I haven't tried."

"Do you love her?"

"I did. Yes. Very much." Maynard pushed his plate away and drank some wine.

"Did Mother love you?"

"I can't answer that."

"Why not?"

"Because. I would never answer such a question for someone else. Only your mother can answer that. But..." he raised his glass. "I can tell you this. We both loved you."

"Loved? Past tense?"

"You know I didn't mean it that way, Barbara. I meant we loved you when you were born. We wanted you. Both of us."

Barbara looked askance. She yearned for a glass of wine. She longed for a cigarette.

"You wanted Mother, too," she said, "but you didn't want her the way she was."

"What does that mean?"

"Her face, Father. You changed her face."

"Only because we thought it would make her unhappy the way it was. She'd been in an accident. It was a face she didn't have to live with. After all, it's my business to solve that kind of problem."

"It wasn't a problem."

"Well..." Maynard shrugged.

"It was a problem for you—but not a problem for Mommy."

"You have no right to say that."

"Yes, I have. There are photographs of her before the accident. She wasn't beautiful. She was never beautiful. She was only ever pretty. Pretty—and *herself*. After the accident, you made her completely different. *Completely*."

"I don't understand why this makes you so angry, Barbara. I made her better—not just different. It was an improvement."

Barbara watched him. She did not believe a word he had said. Maynard looked away—but she wouldn't let go.

"You wiped out who she really was when all you had to do was restore her. But you made her someone else, instead. Someone for you to look at."

Maynard said: "it's not as if I wanted to harm her."

"Would you make Orley white?"

"Dear God, Barbara. Don't be ridiculous." He was getting angry.

"Well, then," said Barbara. "Don't you be ridiculous about Mother's face."

Maynard shook his head. Where had all this come from? She was only twelve. She frightened him. Once, she had run to him. Now, she hated him.

Barbara said: "would you have tried to save Catherine Earnshaw? I mean—if you'd been there?"

"If I'd been there," he said, "and saved her, there wouldn't be any story."

Barbara folded her napkin.

"That's what I thought," she said. "As long as it makes a good story, you don't care what happens to anyone."

"You have no right to say that, Barbara. No right at all. It isn't true."

"It's why you save people, isn't it? Isn't that why you save them? So you'll have a good story?"

Barbara lifted her fork as if to eat—and dropped it. "Mother made a good story," she said. "Until she began to make it up herself—to get back at you."

There was a a terrible silence. Then Barbara said: "I'm going to have a glass of wine."

She got down from her chair and went along to where Emma should have been sitting. She picked up the wine bottle there and filled two-thirds of Emma's glass. Then she sat down. In Emma's place.

"What are you doing?" said Maynard. He was now alarmed.

Barbara adjusted her glasses—pushing them up against her face so that her eyes were all at once enormous. She stared at him and said: "I just wanted to see you from this end of the table, Father. That's all."

Then she drank some wine. And lighted a cigarette.

10

Kurtz had already prepared to retire for the night and was standing in his solarium wearing white pyjamas when the telephone rang.

A man whose name was Cawthra and who claimed to be a police detective was calling from the Queen Street Mental Health Centre.

Kurtz informed him immediately—and not without irritation—that he had no patients there and was not the appropriate person to be calling with his problem. "You want Doctor Farrell," he said.

Cawthra politely contradicted him and told Kurtz that, given what had happened, he had definitely called the right man.

As Kurtz listened, he grew pale. And as he hung up, he dropped the telephone to the floor, where it shattered a pot of cyclamen.

"Damn," he said. But, inside, he was saying something else.

Good.

Then he went and changed back into his suit. Twenty minutes later, he was driving down University Avenue.

The cyclamen were red. Which was appropriate.

TEN

*"The wilderness had found him out early,
and taken on him a terrible vengeance
...it had whispered to him things about
himself which he did not know, things
of which he had no conception till he
took counsel with this great solitude—
and the whisper had proved irresistibly
fascinating. It echoed loudly within
him because he was hollow at the core..."*

Joseph Conrad
Heart of Darkness

1

At Queen Street, Kurtz drove into the Emergency area and left his car in the section reserved for staff. All the way down, he had been aware of the yellow sky above the city—a hot, roiling sky filled with muddy clouds. Some of what he saw was smoke from chemical fires that had been lit by the D-Squads. A major clean-up of birds was taking place somewhere to the southwest and the sky had barely any night in it at all. Having stepped from his car and locked it, Kurtz paused long enough to see that the sky was now orange. He then hurried over to the Emergency entrance. Three police cars were parked there. And a hearse.

All at once, it began to rain.

Inside, a tall, expressionless man with a drooping moustache stepped into Kurtz's path and said: "if you're Doctor Kurtz, I'm Sergeant Cawthra."

A crazy response leapt into Kurtz's mouth: "and if I'm not Doctor Kurtz—who are you then?" But it did not get out. Nothing got out. He only nodded.

"Come with me, please," Cawthra said, and he took Kurtz down a long, familiar hallway towards the elevators. There were two uniformed policemen in the corridor. Neither spoke. There were official keys that had to be turned, but Cawthra had somehow acquired them and he got the doors of the elevator opened, pressed the appropriate button and got the elevator moving without a word.

Cawthra looked away from Kurtz and spoke to the metal walls in front of him.

"This is not going to be pleasant, I'm afraid," he said.

"All right," said Kurtz. He was beginning to steel himself. There would be blood, he guessed—but he had dealt with that before.

The elevator arrived and the doors opened. They were on the third floor—and the hallway was only dimly lit. Windows faced them, covered with thick wire mesh and hammered shut. The orange sky flickered in the rain.

"We go this way," said Cawthra—and he moved off in front of Kurtz, turning to the right.

Kurtz was glad of his practised poise. It would not have done him any harm, he supposed, if he had shown some signs of the discomfort he felt—but he preferred to move in marching order. Ramrod straight. Hat in hand. Tie impeccable. Not a drop of perspiration.

Cawthra's shoes squeaked. He moved like a boy, with a lope that had something of an animal quality. He might have been moving through a forest or a jungle. His head was rather small, considering the size of the rest of him—huge, knobby hands and enormous feet. His hair had been cut that day and the razor-sharp edge of it was outlined in chalk-white, unweathered skin. The rest of him was ruddy-coloured—possibly the result of being so taciturn—of holding so much in. Kurtz could have given him lessons in how to present such a front without raising the blood pressure.

They were making for a windowed door, beyond which—through more wire mesh—there was obviously an abundance of light and a view of other people.

"Here we are," said Cawthra—and he rang a bell to one side of the door. Kurtz had the dimmest memory of where they were.

Once through, with the door securely locked behind them, Kurtz began to sicken against his will. He could not prevent it. There were people there covered with blood—one of them stark naked—others with torn clothing. These were patients—all of them young. All of them—male and female—had pale, bald heads. All of them maintained the same eerie silence. Kurtz had seen more than one of these patients before—but he could not name them. That had been excised from memory. The names. Four or five nurses—most of them men—moved amongst the patients, soothing them—cleaning them—holding them. There were also one or two orderlies and several police of both sexes and a couple of doctors Kurtz did not know by name, but whom he recognized from having seen them during earlier visits to Queen Street.

Cawthra walked right past all of this—expecting Kurtz to follow him—setting a pace that demanded obedience. Kurtz could not see wounds but only blood on the patients—none of whom turned to see him—all of them seemingly blind.

At last, they came to another door, and the lights beyond its window glass had been lowered and Kurtz instinctively knew that this was where the body would be. Given the dimness of the light, he also knew that what he was about to see would be dreadful.

And it was.

Eleanor Farjeon was lying on the floor.
Someone had torn off her head.

2

Marlow did not hear of it until the following day. In the light of what he had been reading in the files and in the light of Austin's suicide, Eleanor's death was doubly shocking.

An accident had occurred, so he read. There was a squib on page one of *The Globe and Mail*, which did not even mention Eleanor's name. It simply said: *DOCTOR BEHEADED* and where it had happened and when. It then added: *please see page 8.*

On page 8 there was a photograph which showed that Eleanor had once been young and exuberant. *How wonderfully full of life she was,* Marlow thought. Then he read what was written there.

> ### DOCTOR KILLED IN BIZARRE ACCIDENT
> *The body of a well-known psychiatrist was found last night at the Mental Health Centre on Queen Street West in Toronto. Doctor Eleanor Farjeon had been working late with a group of patients on the third floor. "Apparently overtired and some-what disoriented, Doctor Farjeon became trapped between the doors of an elevator," said a spokeswoman for the hospital. "It can only be assumed that no one heard her cries for help, and she was consequently killed," said Doctor Leona McGreevey, a colleague. "It is a tragedy for all of us. Doctor Farjeon was a pioneer in treating traumatized and autistic children."*
>
> *The Queen Street Mental Health Centre was not Doctor Farjeon's normal venue. She had been, for some years, on the staff of The Parkin Institute for Psychiatric Research and had been working at Queen Street only for the past six months on a special project.*
>
> *An investigation of her death is underway.*

That was the extent of it. Nothing whatsoever was said about decapitation. And yet, the front-page teaser had been *DOCTOR BEHEADED.* Why?

The death notice was no more helpful—or truthful. It simply stated that Eleanor Farjeon had died *as the result of an accident.*

She had no survivors, the death notice told him—her children having predeceased her. They, too, had been the victims of an accident—the car crash in which Eleanor's husband, Alastair Farjeon, had also been killed five years ago. This was the tragedy of which she never spoke. *So now,* he thought, *the book has closed on them all.*

Marlow cursed himself for not having paid more attention. As a colleague, he would have enjoyed both her company and her ideas. She had always been so poised and self-assured. Never pushy. Simply there. It was quite unlike her to give way to self-interest. For her charges, yes—but not for herself. She gave no sense of self-importance. She was a passionate defender of her brood—but she never lost control. And now what? Now what? Death by decapitation? Certainly death by misadventure. *What did it mean?*

Walking home that evening, Marlow could see the orange glow of D-Squad lights—caught in the mist of their spraying. A D-Squad tanker lumbered up Avenue Road and made the turn away from him, heading for the lights. If they had called in more than one tanker, they were more than likely spraying in a ravine—somewhere with lots of trees.

The colour yellow now made Marlow feel ill. It reinforced his sense of paranoia. *I want my bed,* he thought, the way a child reaches for safety. He thought of his mother. *How ridiculous. I'm a grown man.*

But the thought of Edwina Marlow, with her arms held out towards him, was irresistible. She had been the safest place in the world. The house could fall down and she would stand there holding up the roof. *How do we lose that? When do we lose that? The sense that other people are safety personified. Our parents. Our lovers. Our friends.*

It hardly mattered that people had ceased to be the repository of safety. It was the illusion that had mattered. *Safety is just an idea,* he thought. *There is nowhere truly safe. There never was.*

Eleanor had wanted to talk to Austin. Austin had been her safety—but he had turned away from her.

Now she was dead.

3

Marlow had requested a meeting with Olivia Price.

This occurred on a Thursday morning, two days after Amy's PET scan—and after Eleanor's death. His case load was beginning to distract him from constantly thinking of how she had died—and why she had died. The shock remained—but Marlow shut it out. He would not listen when it raised its voice.

On arrival, Olivia was wearing a Liberty scarf at her neck which, she confessed, was her *anti-D-mask*. In the street, she pulled it up over her nose and mouth to protect her against the proliferating chemicals in the air. "They may be spraying to kill the birds," she said, "but they're doing their damnedest to kill the rest of us, too."

Marlow had wanted to see Olivia to tell her he had come to the conclusion that her sister Amy should be released from the Parkin.

"I've seen the PET scan results, and discussed them with Doctor Menges, who supervised the procedure."

Olivia said nothing. When Marlow showed her the colour prints of the scan, with Amy's brain depicted in bright colours, she stared at it numbly. All she could think at first was *Jar babies—Jar babies, go away...*

Marlow said: "we can see by these colour concentrations here that your sister's medication is not being utilized by the brain, Mrs Price. Certainly not by the area that should be able to benefit from it."

Olivia held the map of the brain scan in both hands and turned it on its side and upside down and finally right-side up again. She traced the colour pattern with her finger. "It looks like a Rorschach test," she said.

"Yes, it does."

Olivia held the map out to Marlow.

"Do you see what I see, Doctor?"

Marlow glanced at it. "Good Lord," he said.

"Wonderful, isn't it," said Olivia, taking the paper back. Watching it, she smiled. "It looks like a bird in flight."

Which it did.

Finally, Olivia said: "can you change her medication?"

Marlow shrugged. "We could try—but my advice remains that Miss Wylie should go home."

Olivia who had been faithful in her visits—and had seen Amy twice a week—said: "but she hasn't been cured."

Marlow said: "she will never be cured, Mrs Price. Never. As a consequence, we have two choices. We can opt for one Amy or another."

"One or another?"

"One of them—assuming we can adjust her medication successfully—would spend the rest of her life in a drugged condition that would amount, in effect, to sedation. This Amy would have no poems, no birds, no Wormwood, no other world but the dead world out there now—and she would be incapable of responding to it. It would simply be a landscape through which she moved—deadened, uncaring and uninvolved."

"And the other Amy?"

"The other Amy would have a minimum of medication. Only enough to reduce the extremities of her anxiety. She would be a slightly less tense version of the Amy we have now."

Olivia looked from the window. "What would become of her?" she said.

"She could go home to her house—and be with her birds."

"But—dear God. Doesn't freedom put her in jeopardy?"

"Not in my view, no," said Marlow. "It would give Amy back the only life in which she can function—in which she is happy."

"What about her writing?"

"There is every chance this Amy would continue to produce poetry. After all, the Amy who wrote in the past was very nearly the Amy we have."

Olivia thought about it.

All of a sudden, she laughed.

"Something amuses you, Mrs Price?"

"Well—yes," said Olivia. "The word *freedom*." She sat back and looked at Marlow. "I believe you know my sister, Peggy? Mrs Benedict Webster?"

"Not actually, no. But you have spoken of her and I believe she came to visit Amy with your mother—though I was not present."

Olivia said: "she has left her husband."

"I'm sorry to hear that."

"Oh, no—don't be," said Olivia, still on the verge of laughter. "It's the best thing that's ever happened to her—and the most courageous thing she's ever done. She turned up at my door one night, Doctor, and simply said: *here I am.* She didn't have to say another word."

"What made you laugh, just now? Was it that?"

"In a way, yes. You see—my mother once said that my sister Peggy was *born dead.* She meant, of course, that she was incapable of making things happen. Peggy was fearful, Doctor Marlow—locked into always doing *the right thing.* Now, she's free—you see. *Born alive,* at last. And now, you want to set my sister Amy free..."

"I wish it could please you, Mrs Price."

"It does," said Olivia. But she was looking rather sad as she said this. She did not explain that, of the Wylie girls, she was the only one still a prisoner.

You still a prisoner! What about me?

Yes. And you, too.

Marlow said: "I need your permission to proceed with Amy's release, Mrs Price. Yours—or your mother's."

"You have it."

"Thank you."

Olivia?
Yes.
I need your permission, too. To proceed...
This, Olivia did not answer.

4

*I came upon him, and if he had not heard me coming, I
would have fallen over him, too, but he got up in time...*

Lilah was reading page 93 of *Heart of Darkness*. She was seated at her
kitchen table, early—very early—in the morning following a sleepless,
drugless night. She wore her long white cotton nightie, her blue cotton
wrapper and her carpet slippers. A teapot—emptied—sat on a trivet. A
cup by her elbow. Peter Rabbit's shoes were lying close at hand, in their
opened tissue wrapping paper—touched, from time to time, by Lilah's
fingers seeking magic.

Page ninety-three. Oh, page ninety-three, she chanted. *Deliver Kurtz
to Marlow and to me...*

Nothing.

Nothing, that is, but the dead blue world of her kitchen at dawn and
the mice who bellowed in the wall. Grendel's mother, out in the lane,
gave a wild, long cry from beyond the gate for her injured son... Sarah
Tudball sat with her back to Lilah in the only other kitchen chair available. She wore still the tall brown hat and the overcoat in which she had
died. Her neck was knotted with all her scarves—each scarf a favoured
colour—purple—violet—burgundy—rose—magenta. Sarah had come
in the night and would not leave. And what if Mister Hyde had pursued
her—rising from the Rosedale ravine where they had struggled all those
years ago? Certainly, the kitchen had a damp, dark, leafy smell and
someone's boots had imprinted mud marks across the floor...

*Page ninety-three. Oh, page ninety-three. Deliver Kurtz to Marlow
and to me.*

Nothing.

Lilah read:

> *He rose, unsteady, long, pale, indistinct, like a
> vapour exhaled by the earth, and swayed slightly, misty
> and silent before me...*

405

The sun was rising in the world beyond the windows. Its light was spreading through the tree-tops—kissing aerials and chimneys—running its fingers along the hydro wires—singing.

Lilah covered her ears with her hands.

The sun does not sing. It has no voice.

Lilah forced her gaze back to the page.

> *...at my back the fires loomed between the trees, and the murmur of many voices issued from the forest...*

Someone was whispering.

Lilah looked across at her mother's back, but Sarah was silent and still.

The whispering was somewhere in the book.

Lilah touched the pages with her fingers. She dabbled in them—fishing—riffling.

Speak.

Nothing.

And then a sigh.

Lilah's right-hand index finger pushed against what seemed to be a tide of words—a wall of words in water—spraying letters back across her hand as she pushed up farther over the pages. She could hear, besides the whispers, water and paper splashing and tearing...*stop.*

Here.

> *The wilderness had found him out, and had taken on him a terrible vengeance...*

Lilah closed her eyes.

She raised her hand and made a fist and struck the page.

Come forth!

And then, aloud:

"COME FORTH!"

Marlow found her half an hour later, lying on the floor sound asleep.

She was smiling.

The first indications that Kurtz was not well were presented in a somewhat surprising manner—several days after the death of Eleanor Farjeon. One of the people who witnessed what happened was Bella Orenstein, who was making her way towards Sub Two. She was standing in the foyer at the top of the stairs when she saw Kurtz.

He was passing through from the street on his way to a Board meeting. All at once he stopped in front of the Slade triptych, took off his hat and held it down at his side. Staring up at *The Golden Chamber of the White Dogs*, he began slowly banging the Homburg against his thigh. This banging—or, as Bella described it to Oona, this "batting"—became more and more severe until it seemed that Kurtz might bruise himself. As a gesture, it also had the look to it of someone beating time to music as the music—perhaps *The Rite of Spring*—became more and more violent.

Two or three people who had intended to cross the foyer in order to depart the building later said they had been so intimidated by Kurtz's agitation, they had fallen back and chosen another route.

The painting gave off its own peculiar light—the gold shining down over Kurtz's face and shoulders, the white dogs gleaming, almost phosphorescent. Kurtz passed the Homburg into his left hand and, with his right hand, began to undo the buttons of his summer-weight topcoat until it stood open. He did this seemingly entranced—never taking his eyes from the figures hanging above him—never once pausing between buttons—everything done as if in time to the music inside him.

Pulling the overcoat back, Kurtz reached into an inner pocket and withdrew a handkerchief. One of his father's handkerchiefs—though only Kurtz, of course, was aware of this.

Very slowly, he flicked it open and brought it up to his face, where he used it as a swabbing cotton, drying his chin—his cheeks—his forehead—the back of his neck.

Black dye was running down one side of his face—almost as if an invisible make-up artist was creating a sideburn there. Kurtz, not looking, wiped the dye away. He was not aware of the running colour, only of the perspiration that had now begun to bud in such profusion, it seemed that he was melting.

The Homburg fell to the floor.

Kurtz did not retrieve it. The painting held him enthralled.

At last, the tension eased—or gave at least the appearance of easing. Kurtz sagged a little through the shoulders. He let the handkerchief rest just under his chin, like a bib, and his lips began to move.

None of the witnesses could hear what he was saying, if indeed he was actually saying anything. But they caught the sound of something vocal—a mouth-music sort of sound—almost a keening, but very, very faint.

After that, Kurtz began to walk away, and did so without referring in any fashion to his hat. The hat did not exist; it was no longer his; it had disappeared from view and was gone.

In making his turn to enter the building proper, Kurtz almost fell—a loss of control which Bella described as terrifying. Some may fall—but not Kurtz.

He righted himself and walked into the darkness. The hat remained on the marble—abandoned.

A patient came to the foyer next—someone who had not been present during the episode just ended. She was wearing a long pink housecoat and looked entirely out of place. Her head had been shaved and painted with a yellow antiseptic solution.

"Hey—a hat!" this woman said, and picked it up. And then: "anybody lose a hat?" But none of those watching answered. The fear of Kurtz had increased by virtue of his visible loss of control.

"You want a hat, lady?" the yellow-headed patient said—holding out the Homburg after giving it a quick brush with her pink sleeve.

"No, thank you," said Bella. "I already have a hat." And she continued on down the stairs.

The woman shrugged at that point, and walked with the hat to a marble-topped table that held a large bouquet of flowers.

"One hat," she said—and laid the Homburg in the shadow of some lilies. "One hat—headless."

Then she took a lily from the vase and, eating it, walked away into the same darkness where Kurtz had gone. The woman, yellow-headed—Kurtz, bleeding dye and running the first of the fevers that would bring him down.

6

Amy Wylie stood on the grass in Queen's Park, north of the Legislature. There were benches and trees and walkways. Summer students in twos or threes—piles of debris. Half-dead peonies. Edward VII on his horse. A man with balloons. Another with a popcorn cart. But no children. None.

A wheel of pigeons rolled through the sky. There were hardly any left, now. Perhaps these were someone's personal flight of homers—illegal these past few years—but a few remained. A very few. Secrets—except in the sky.

Amy was carrying a shopping bag made of canvas. She was—like the pigeons—going home. Marlow had said she might. *If I can find it.*

She could make an image of it in her mind—of its blue door with the green trim and its narrow, pointed roof and the bird graves marked with arching lilies and bleeding heart—red and white.

Amy sat down.

Her calves itched.

They made you wear these terrible socks. She pushed them down. She remembered, doing this, being a girl—coming out of the Royal Conservatory of Music and pushing down your socks. Hiking up your skirt, and running. They had wanted her to play Schumann. She could not. She had wanted another kind of music.

A squirrel had come out into the sun. She was alone. Everything was decreasing. Carried off or killed. Ants, mice, aphids, worms... Squirrels.

Hello.

Amy watched.

The squirrel was sitting up, gauging the dangers that surrounded it. She seemed very old. Her grey coat was worn and ratty and her eyes had a dull, aged look to them. Her ears were tattered like a cat's from too much fighting. Her paws were raw from digging.

Amy reached down into her bag.

She had managed to pilfer a loaf of bread and four cans of Campbell's tomato soup on the way out.

You want this?

She held out bread.

The squirrel lifted her snout and tasted the air. She looked at Amy critically.

It's me, Amy said, with her eyes averted—lowering her head—dropping her chin—letting the bread fall down from her hand. *It's only me.*

The squirrel came forward.

Amy was perfectly still.

The squirrel ate.

Amy scratched her leg.

The squirrel scratched her own cheeks. Sympathy. Then she disappeared up a tree. To safety. To what had always been safety. Once.

Goodbye, said Amy. *Goodbye.*

The popcorn vendor blew his whistle. But still no children appeared. Amy walked away.

On Boswell Avenue, an hour later, there was more than a little neighbourhood interest when Amy returned—as the homers returned—to her house with the blue-and-green door. She had been missed as much for her entertainment value—her madness—as for any other reason.

Amy went up to the door and gave it a push.

It opened into a view of welcoming tables and chairs. And one old sofa. And one new visitor.

"Greetings," said Marlow. "I got the message you were on your way, so I came around to open the windows."

In the kitchen, there were bags of sunflower seed and millet left behind by Peggy. There were also—set out by Marlow—four bottles of red wine, a bowl of oranges and six cans of cat food.

Amy's home, she said to the sink.

"Thank you, Doctor Marlow," she said out loud. The voice, unmedicated now, had fallen back into fragments. Only half of each word got all the way out. The rest was swallowed. "Look," she said—and she took him to the back door, already standing open—screened. "My friends."

Amy had been smiling—and Marlow smiled back. Now, Amy clouded.

"Tree," she said. "Oh. Gone."

"Yes," said Marlow. "I'm sorry. It had to be cut down. They mustn't have any excuse to come and spray you out."

"Oh, well," she said. "there are still the fences to sit on. And all the hydro wires."

"I guess."

You go up there, now, she said, and made a sweeping gesture with her arms.

The birds went up. Except the sandhill crane. Except the herons. They stayed down on what was left of the grass.

"See them all?" Amy said to Marlow.

He looked.

Of course, there was nothing there.

Not that it mattered. The birds were everywhere in her mind. She had saved them.

In half an hour, having made sure that Amy remembered where everything was, and that Wormwood had put in an appearance, Marlow took his leave and started home down the lanes. This was the route that Amy took in search of Wormwood when he wandered. The last he saw of her, she was spreading forbidden seed on the grass. *Well,* he thought. *She's alive.*

Twenty yards farther on, Marlow heard a flock of starlings arrive. Their Italianate chatter was the same as it had been, long ago, on

Philosopher's Walk. Looking back, he saw to his astonishment not a sign of birds. But he heard their voices.

He smiled.

Amy Wylie was back at work.

7

The next day, Kurtz did not go in to the office. He telephoned to cancel his appointments and gave as his reason for doing so *a slight fever, nothing serious.*

He remained in his apartment and showered three times. When he towelled his hair in front of the mirror, he was shocked to discover that a quantity of scalp was revealed. Taking up a comb, he carefully eased his hair forward—using the wide-spaced end of the comb to do so. Several strands of hair came away with each pass.

This was shocking to him. In spite of many years of hair dye, there had never—in the past—been any hair loss, except in the normal course of shedding whatever amounts of hair a human male gives up in a year.

His first thought was: *I'm dying.* But even Kurtz had to smile at such a ridiculous leap between a few missing strands of hair and imminent death.

The one appointment he regretted was a scheduled lunch that day with Maynard Berry. They had intended to meet at Arlequino's—still the only restaurant where Kurtz felt comfortable. The lighting was so helpful—neither dim nor overbright—and the clientele, as Kurtz described it, was always *safe.* Fabiana often took her artists there to introduce them to potential buyers and it remained one of his greatest aesthetic pleasures to sit across the room from her and focus from time to time on the wonder of her appearance.

Fabiana had been his client now for just over a month and they had seen each other on that basis only twice. He had put her on a fortnightly schedule because he wanted to draw the process out as long as possible. Knowing Fabiana's propensity for procrastination when it came to self-reflection, he did not want her to feel she was being pushed into a situation that forced her to confront herself too profoundly...

Did he mean that?

No.

In truth, he wanted to back her into every corner he could find. In truth, he wanted her to become so deeply self-involved that she could not avoid coming face to face with him, wherever she might have kept him hidden in her ego. In truth, he wanted her to turn that corner and fall at his feet. But none of this could be said—none of it could be forced.

Kurtz had been so long out of practice that he no longer knew how to be in love. His private expression of it—his mode of focus—was entirely based on being loved—not loving. Fabiana must discover that she loved him— reveal that she loved him—panic that she might lose him. Panic in the sense that she had faltered in the sudden absence of Jimmy Holbach. Whatever it was that had been written of her in that moment—even though she denied it—was true. She had lost her centre. The core of her life had been struck down—blown away—devastated by Jimmy's desertion.

But none of this had been forthcoming in Kurtz's behalf. Not yet, at any rate. Fabiana was still resisting him. Their sessions had been fruitless.

Kurtz had loved her so completely, once. But Holbach's entry into her life had routed him.

No. That was not true. He had turned away from her as an act of revenge.

When Jimmy had gone off to the Amazon region and disappeared, Kurtz's first reaction had been to pick up the telephone and console Fabiana. But when he saw her abroad in the world of receptions and exhibitions, she had seemed so aloof in her sorrow that Kurtz could not approach her. For six years, now, they had played the game of climbing to the tops of ladders and down again—each one apart from the other—each one watching to see what the other would do. Kurtz had been stymied. Stopped. The fact was, Fabiana had more capacity for growth than Kurtz.

She had told him the other day that in the years since he had first expressed his interest in her—and she had *so coolly turned him down*— (she had smiled, saying this)—she had come to see more in him than a man of mere ambition. *I opened my eyes to your other qualities, Rupert*—she said. *Your sense of dedication—your interest in art and artists—your willingness to explore the limits of creativity...*that was all.

What Fabiana had not yet told him was that she also recognized his loneliness—and sensed, as he did not, the seat of that loneliness, which lay in his essential fear of human contact. Over time, his aloofness had grown harsher. He was anchored in it—and as Fabiana softened, Kurtz's attitudes began to freeze around him, locking him in place. Emotionally—Fabiana knew—Kurtz had ceased to grow. He was fixed as firmly in his apartness now as he was in his determination to rule from the top of the Parkin Institute.

He stared at the telephone, willing it to ring—but it did not. He wanted someone. Someone. Anyone. Not to be alone. On the other hand...

Anyone would not do. People are troublesome. They carry baggage everywhere they go. Not everyone—but most. Maynard, for instance, had no baggage. You could sit with Maynard Berry and what you got was the stuff of your meeting with him—nothing more. Nothing of Emma. Nothing of Barbara. Nothing of his life as a surgeon. Business, plus a cursory acknowledgement that the rest of the world was still there, was what you got. The weather—minor gossip—the dead birds...

Dead birds.

Sturnusemia.

No.

Yes. Why else would he be feverish? Losing his hair? And blood in his stool...

No.

STURNUSEMIA KILLS! HAVE YOU BEEN VACCINATED?

Everything we have been told about sturnusemia is a lie... Kurtz knew that from The Paranoid Civil Servant. He had already known it when Smith Jones first appeared.

Everywhere you turned, the posters stared back at you from billboards and buses, television and newspapers. Nothing would stop it. The vaccinations were a hoax—the government holding out false hope, claiming it was doing something—*THE TIDE WILL TURN—BUT ONLY YOU CAN TURN IT!* Images of speckled children holding out dead birds. Starlings lying in the gutter—claws pulled tight in death—*DO NOT TOUCH!* And perhaps the most sinister of all, the poster displaying a leaf-barren tree, its branches covered with starlings, and the legend: *IF YOU SEE THIS, CALL FOR THE D-SQUAD!*

And underneath: *BIRDS OF PREY.*

Kurtz had begun to perspire again. He glanced in the mirror, afraid of what he might see. But there was—as yet—no speckling. Nothing but sweat.

He decided to call Maynard Berry. He could not imagine eating lunch with anyone, today. They could postpone their meeting. Tomorrow, perhaps—or the day after, when Kurtz felt better.

He wanted desperately to talk to Maynard about his project—bring him up to date on Doctor Shelley's most recent findings—see if Maynard was interested. Surely, he would be. Then, a meeting with Shelley to tell her the good news—*Maynard Berry wants to be part of it. We can go even farther...*

He picked up the telephone and dialled the appropriate number. This was the way to survive. This was the way to stop sturnusemia—keep yourself busy—focus on something else. Stay on your feet—don't lie down. Don't let the mirror catch your eye. Fight for what you want to achieve. Get Maynard to commit. Make him say *yes.* For, the truth was—Maynard Berry was still not on side. Their alliance was all in Kurtz's mind. But Kurtz did not know this. He refused to know it.

8
—

Orley Hawkins was sitting in the Berry kitchen drinking a Coors. This was the peaceful part of the day, when Emma slept and Barbara was at her art class. *Two P.M. and all's well...*

The sky beyond the windows was a pale, benign blue—not a cloud in sight and way high up, there were gulls—or something white—wheeling on the updrafts, no wings moving, just the endless circling, higher and higher.

Orley had been leafing through a magazine. *Life*. She enjoyed its mix of prose and photo essays—stuff about politicians—stuff about movie stars—stuff about places she had never been—stuff about places she had lived, but did not remember being the way they were portrayed. Stuff about "stuff"—gimmicks—inventions—new things to eat—new kinds of pantyhose to wear. Funny, she thought, how all the black people in the advertisements look like white people dipped in milk chocolate, wearing stuff they got out of Bloomingdales. None of it bargain basement, neither. Most of the models with thin white noses and prissy white lips...

And Barbara saying: *Orley, you want to be white?*

I think not, said I.

There in *Life* magazine there was a picture sequence all about Baltimore. The city where Orley Hawkins had been born under the name of Johnson. And grew up with all her brothers until she was nineteen. Then ran off to Washington D.C. Baltimore was pure white, almost, and from the look of it in these pictures, still was. Nearly a southern town—not quite—where every highfalutin house had a black cook and chauffeur. All those streets you never got to see unless you were a servant. Streets with brick mansions and oak trees leafing out over the sidewalks. All that shade. Black nannies walking the white kids—pushing white baby buggies—burping white babies—nursing white patients—digging white graves. That was Baltimore as it was. And is.

And Toronto, too—come to think of it. Except there's hardly any American black people here. Most of them from the Caribbean—Trinidad, St Lucia, Jamaica, Barbados. Housekeepers, maids, cooks, nurses. Cab drivers, car washers, factory hands. Not that middle-class blacks did not exist. But...

414

Here I am. Cook and nursemaid.

Had my own store once. Almost middle class.

Good education. Finished high school.

Sitting in a kitchen, north Rosedale, Toronto.

Just like all those maids in the movies. Even Whoopi Goldberg played a maid.

Whoopi Goldberg. There was class—nothing to do with lower—middle—upper. A woman of class. Period.

And Toni Morrison. Alice Walker.

Heroes.

Why?

Because they are themselves. Entirely.

That was it. To be yourself—entirely.

As if I'm not.

You are.

Yes.

Orley took a sip of Coors and fingered a few more pages.

There was an article there called *Monuments of Dust*. It had a text by a man called Lemmly. Carl Lemmly. White. The pictures were by a man called Aaron Tait. Black. You knew this because it showed them standing side by side on a summer street—both of them looking dusty, as if—because of the title of their article—someone had rolled them in dust. Black and white men in a black and white photo. Dusty.

The monuments in the title were all in Washington, D.C. Orley's other city. The one where she had met Bobby Hawkins—the city from which they had fled in the Vietnam war.

Orley ran her fingers under the text as she read—a habit she had got from doing the accounts at Mac's Milk. It was as though she couldn't focus without her finger end to guide her.

It seemed that Carl Lemmly and Aaron Tait were sad and angry. The gist of Lemmly's text was that every national monument in Washington, D.C. had been rendered meaningless. While millions of Americans came each year, for instance, to be photographed standing at Lincoln's feet, nothing of Lincoln remained in American culture. This cut Orley two ways.

One way was unavoidably nostalgic—and the other was acquiescence. Who could not agree with what this man Lemmly said? Who could fail to see the absence of dreaming in all the faces shown in Aaron Tait's photographs.

Orley stared at the Lincoln Memorial. It still took her breath away. So much had happened there.

Looking at Abraham Lincoln himself, brooding in his chair, made Orley homesick. What a good idea this Lincoln had been, with his sad, exhausted body and his mournful face. But he was just another lie. Turned into one by death and time.

She remembered going there with Bobby. Young. They had been so young. She remembered climbing up the endless rows of steps—each flight growing steeper—and Mister Lincoln looming over them.

Nigger-lover.

That's what someone had said as they stood there. Someone right beside them—looking up at Abraham Lincoln and saying out loud: *nigger-lover...*

That did not make her feel homesick. But the certainty that it was home made her want it again. To turn again and gaze off down the placid waters to the Washington Monument—to stand with other people there and to think: *this is mine.* Or it was.

Right on this very place here—Orley thought, looking down and placing her finger on the spot itself in the photograph—stood Martin Luther King. Right on this very spot. And I stood there—her finger moved—right there. And Bobby beside me. What a hot, blue day that was, with its merciless heat—and all those tens of thousands. That was just about two seconds, maybe, she was thinking, before all those monuments turned to dust.

All that marching. All those dead.

And the ringing words.

And, afterwards, the gunfire.

As if to stand at Mister Lincoln's feet was to invite his fate upon your own head. Reverend King went down to bullets—Reverend King—Mister Lincoln—Bobby Hawkins...

Bobby Hawkins—dead while living—dead while young.

The war was hot then, too—hot and getting hotter—sort of like that day Reverend King made that speech. But the March on Washington was nothing compared to the March on Vietnam.

Orley stood up and went to the fridge for another Coors.

Those steps, she was thinking—the ones climbing up to Mister Lincoln—they used those steps to enslave us all again. Even in spite of Reverend King's *dream*—even in spite of fourscore and seven years ago—even in spite of all this, they drew us back inside the circle and shot us down.

Orley returned to the table and pulled the tab on her beer. She readdressed her attention to the picture.

Now—you stand there at Mister Lincoln's feet and look out over all the dead of Vietnam. All the American dead.

Not Bobby Hawkins, though. He is not there. He came to Canada—just so as not to be there. Bobby caught his bullet in sanctuary. So-called.

Orley turned the page and gazed at the Vietnam War Memorial—all that black marble, since refuted in *Desert Storm*—just as Lincoln had been refuted in Ford's Theatre.

All those names. Thousands of them.

Orley bent in closer over a photograph of a single panel.

Panel W 30, she read.

Theodore C. Hall—William E.L. Hart—Clarence M. Holland—Robert Jackson, Jr—Daniel M. Noeldner.

Others.

Endless, so it seemed.

She thought: Bobby might just as well have joined them on that wall, for all the good it did him.

Down at the bottom of the page, Carl Lemmly had written: *where are the monuments to Watts and Birmingham, Selma, Wounded Knee? They are,* he wrote, *buried here in the dust of these others...of Lincoln, Washington, Jefferson, Vietnam. America.*

Orley lifted her head. She thought of Bobby Hawkins. She was his monument. He was buried in her heart where no one else could see him. Somehow, she had kept him dead—instead of giving him *life everlasting.* Isn't that the phrase? The dead can only be alive again if the living allow them to be. If the living call them forth.

She sat back and drank beer.

Here I sit in a white man's kitchen, she thought, playing the black servant. Just the way I would in a white man's book.

Who was that one that Barbara was reading about? The one the other week in *The Member of the Wedding.* Berenice. *Berenice had been the cook since Frankie could remember. She was very black and broad-shouldered...*

And that Dilsey. Everybody knew about her. The servant of servants. Cook of cooks. Mammy of mammies. Coloured of the coloured. Negro of Negroes. Black of black.

But written white. William Faulkner.

Black—with a white hand hovering over the page. All the pages of her life written by a white hand. *Dilsey. They endured.*

Damn right they did.

But only in a white man's imagination.

I'll do my own enduring, thank you. I'll do my own damn enduring.

Orley flipped over the pages until the magazine was closed and the back of it stared up at her. *The United Colours of Benetton,* it said. And it showed a lot of black children. Africa. Somewhere.

Except that one of them was an albino. White.

From now on, Orley decided, *I will write myself.*

9

Eleanor Farjeon could not yet be buried. There had to be an autopsy—and they would take their time with it. The investigation was continuing, with too many unanswerable questions.

Sergeant Cawthra, who was still trying to unravel the events leading up to the death at Queen Street, paid a visit to Marlow.

Marlow was told for the first time how Eleanor had died. It left him numb with horror.

As they talked, Marlow remembered something Eleanor had told him. It was about the boy who had tried to tear off his own penis. And had almost succeeded. The mad could possess appalling strength. In such a state—when you are driven to violence—you hardly need instruments of death. Whatever possesses you makes instruments of your hands. Your feet. Your teeth.

But none of this got said.

When Cawthra asked him how Eleanor had seemed during the weeks before her death, Marlow answered painfully, but truthfully: "I don't know."

"Was she agitated?"

"Tense, perhaps. But she was always under control."

"Did you know what Doctor Farjeon was doing at Queen Street?"

"Oh, yes. We all did. Or many of us did." This was a lie.

"Her patients were all kids," said Cawthra.

"Mid to late teens. Yes. That's why she had to be given the special dispensation to be at Queen Street. Normally, no one under eighteen years of age is treated there. There are other venues for that."

"Why would she have wanted them to be there?"

"The facilities. More equipment—more space. Also, to separate them from other children. I don't know why. But that was definitely part of it."

"Who do you think killed her, Doctor Marlow?"

Marlow could hazard a guess—but did not yet want to voice it.

"I haven't the foggiest notion," he said.

"What is the nature of the problem shared by these children? Do you know that?"

"In part. They have all been similarly traumatized, Sergeant. That's what Doctor Farjeon was trying to discover—why they shared so many traits and symptoms—why they all appeared to recognize one another." He continued to be extremely cautious. Whatever suspicions he had himself about the nature of their shared traumas, he was not going to tell that to Cawthra. Mostly because he was unhappy with his own guesses. He wanted to leave a way open to finding the answers—and he knew too well from past experience how a police investigation can close doors instantly, instead of opening them.

Marlow wanted to know—and did not want to know—how Eleanor's death had occurred. It was such a forlorn and dreadful death. As if Eleanor had been written into the wrong book. That, of course, is the nature of most violence. It happens where least expected to the least likely people.

"Did the children kill her, Doctor?" Cawthra said.

Marlow made a helpless gesture with his hands. "She trusted them," was all he said.

"But they were troubled."

"Deeply."

"Our problem is," said Cawthra, "we can't get any one of them to speak."

Marlow considered telling Cawthra about the boy who had tried to mutilate himself, but he said nothing. It would be, he was thinking, unbearable if the brood had killed her. And so he said: "she loved them. That is all I can tell you."

10

Tell her to put it in her mouth.

Put it in her mouth.

The evening was drawing to its close. The finale was being performed on top of the piano.

Each man had chosen, as was usual, a footstool, a chair or a place to lean back against the wall as his vantage point. The fathers—in this case, Shapiro and Bentley—were sitting side by side on John Dai Bowen's prize Victorian sofa.

Bentley's daughter and Shapiro's son were well matched. The Shapiro boy was not tall—but he was thick and stocky. Strong. The Bentley girl was of equal height and her breasts, in spite of her age, were sizeable. She was lying splayed on the Steinway, with her head hanging back. Neither child spoke—or made any other vocal sound. They performed as if by rote—their eyes wide open—the girl's expression lost in the boy's groin—the boy's expression absolutely blank.

All at once, Shapiro stood up. A sound was strangled in his throat. He then made his way to the piano.

No, said John Dai.

But, *yes,* someone whispered.

Yes, someone muttered.

Yes, said another, distinctly.

All these voices had no faces—only masks.

And then, Robert Ireland's voice.

Yes!

John Dai looked helplessly at Shapiro, who had reached the piano. John Dai was frightened. This must not be a repeat of that other time—the after-hours session with just the four of them: John Dai, Robert Ireland, David Shapiro. And Shapiro's younger son. George. The membership must never know what happened that night. It must remain a secret—from everyone. But how could that be, if it happened again?

Shapiro had now moved around until he stood before the girl's splayed legs. He began to ease himself up across the piano keyboard—sounding a clumsy chord as he did so.

The watching men were electrified. For them, none of this had ever happened before. It was a rebellion.

Shapiro looked out across Tom Bentley's girl at the others. *Well?* he said. His face was scarlet. Blotched.

There was a pause of mere seconds.

John Dai closed his eyes. The photo image of young George Shapiro—mutilated—dying and dead—rose up.

And then the answer came.

It was a shout.

Yes.

11

Marlow woke up.

His pyjamas were twisted on his body.

Someone had shouted. A name.

He swung his legs out over the side of the bed. He could not find his slippers. Grendel was lying on them. Marlow made his way along the hallway, barefoot, turning on lights as he went.

The cardboard box stood open, its yellow tapes hanging down.

Who had done that?

Perhaps he had. He was getting careless. Overtired.

Downstairs, someone was moving about. Grendel? No. Grendel was back in the bedroom; Marlow had left him there only seconds ago. Lilah, then. But why? It was dead of night and Lilah... Perhaps she was walking in her sleep again. It would not be the first time. Marlow had found her sitting blank-eyed in his kitchen, once. Midnight. Also, he had looked out and seen her in the yard by moonlight. But never upstairs—never in his study. And yet—someone had shouted. *Shouted a name.* Lilah's?

He switched on the nearest lamp—and pulled the box flaps aside.

David.

In Frances Phalen's file, there had been those exclamation marks after *David is back!!* But hadn't there been another mention of a David? Where?

Marlow's fingers flashed through the folders—and stopped when he reached the nameless file. A.P.'s patient, noted simply as *P.* Yes.

When the eye knows what it wants to see, it sees it.

There it was. Austin had said it: *David.*

Is that why you tried to pick this girl up, David? You'd had a little too much to drink?

It took only moments to leaf through the name tags of the remaining files—and to find the name David Shapiro. But the name of the psychiatrist on the case was not Austin Purvis. It was Rupert Kurtz.

Marlow started to read. About the Club of Men and John Dai Bowen's photographs—Club and photography both already familiar to Marlow from the Robert Ireland file. And George Shapiro. Suddenly, poor dead George—*in an after-hours session, with his father and Robert Ireland. The boy heavily drugged—the men out of control.*

Kurtz had known? All along, Kurtz had known about George and how he had died? Shapiro had given him the photographs.

Marlow, all at once, sat down.

He made a prayer that he was dreaming still.

George had been this man Shapiro's son.

Jesus.

People do not kill their own children.

Jesus.

People do not do that.

Marlow slumped. His mind buzzed.

You mean, they don't kill their own children the same way they don't screw their own children? Or was there something else you had in mind?

No.

Do something, Charlie. Do something. Save the children.

Someone had shouted. Deep in Marlow's subconscious, the word *David* had taken up residence and had waited for Marlow to recall it. The shout had been Marlow's own. A shout of recognition. The brain will do that. He knew it was so. The brain sets things aside, until a person is ready for them. The words of seemingly forgotten poems—the tunes of songs—the names of strangers.

David.

Marlow bowed his head.

12

Olivia and Griffin Price were walking through the Far Eastern Gallery of the Royal Ontario Museum. This was on July 5th. Olivia's appointment with the staircase was on the 6th, in the morning. She could wait no longer.

Olivia had a wide summer coat which offered some visual protection. It was cut very like an opera cloak, but without the length—grey, with a cerise silk lining and accents. Olivia adored it—it reminded her of warm, rainy days.

Tomorrow, Griffin would fly to Bucharest to discuss a new factory there. Or rather, an old factory newly purchased where he wanted to begin an "Oriental" gift line. This was why they were touring the Far Eastern collection. Griff wanted one last look at what had inspired him. He now had two such factories in operation—the glass factory in Prague, where the Inuit art was imitated, and a plaster factory in Warsaw where Aztec and Inca imitations were manufactured. Both operations were doing a roaring trade—and soon Griffin would have the Romanians thrown into gear.

Olivia had been fighting off the Voice all morning—turning down the volume—covering her ears. Now, all at once, it was there again.

Why don't you tell my father? Creep up behind him and call him Daddy.

He doesn't want you. That's why.

Why the hell did you get me in the first place?

Because I wanted you.

Then—but not now? Not any more?

You wouldn't understand.

Try me.

I'm afraid.

Of me?

Of course not. Of what will become of you. Of this appalling world.

You're out there. What's so special about you?

When I was born, the world wasn't like this.

Wasn't it?

No.

I suspect the world was always like this.

That's the problem.

Nothing changes?

No. It all gets worse.

C'est la vie, eh?

Very funny.

Olivia paused before a display of ivory monkeys. Some of them were as small as fingernails.

Mother?

What?

I want to be born.

Olivia raised her hand and laid it against the glass. One of the monkeys was making a face at her.

Rage.

"Olivia?"

Griffin was standing over on the other side—looking through at her.

"Are you all right?" he said.

"Yes."

Had he heard?

Mother?

"Can we leave, Griff. I'm feeling... I don't feel right."

She was not quite certain what it was. Not faintness. Not nausea. No kind of pain. But a pang of something. Almost arterial. Something like a bell-pull—the feel of it and the sound of it ringing through her body from top to bottom.

Mother?

"Olivia?"

There must be somewhere to sit down. Or somewhere to hide. Or somewhere to run to. Or somewhere to fall. She did not know what her body wanted of her. It just kept pulling at her. Ringing.

She began to walk.

Griffin caught up with her.

She began to hurry.

Griffin hurried after.

She began to run.

Mother?

She began to race.

"Olivia?"

Several people stepped aside. Was there a fire?

A commissionaire came and stood in front of her, but she brushed him away.

"Madame, please. No running allowed..."

Olivia ran a gauntlet of displays. Shoes. Dolls. Chairs. Tables. Mandarin hats and robes. Fans. Knives. Japanese armour. Masks. Bowls. And parasols...

Her coat flew open.

Mother?

Out.

The steps.

The railings.

Doors.

Air.

Mother?

There was a traffic jam. The whole of the street from Bloor to Queen's Park was filled with cars and yellow trucks and limousines. A siren wailed. A dozen horns were jammed. Two men were fighting. A school bus was emptying. A hundred children suddenly ran up around her into the past. Their teacher came after, throwing up his arms in despair. A band started playing down by the Legislative Building. *The Maple Leaf Forever.* Someone must be arriving. Or departing—bringing or taking good wishes—a trade deal—a lost cause—an old complaint—or a new one.

Griffin said: "what in the name of hell is going on, Olivia? Why are you running?"

Olivia paid no attention. She was looking skyward.

Up above them, making circles, an old-fashioned aeroplane with wings and a propeller was dragging a message through what old books had once called heaven:

YELLOW-DAY SALE AT K-MART!

"Griff?" Olivia looked at him, shading her eyes.

"What is it?" he asked.

Olivia was smiling.

"We are going to have a baby."

Yes.

13

Kurtz, increasingly, did not come to the Parkin. There were phone calls to Oona Kilbride—anxious inquiries about the state of the Appleby project. The proposed new wing. *Had a letter come? Anything from Appleby's lawyers? Requests of more information? A cheque...?* The answer to all these questions was *no.* Lord Appleby had not been in touch and it was Oona's understanding he had returned to London.

There were also calls to Doctor Shelley.

Had she made any progress with her Amelion *research? In-patients? Out-patients? Had there been any increase in docility?* The answer to all these questions was *yes.*

When asked the state of his health, he was evasive. *Did he need anything? Did he want anyone to come and see him? Was there any hope of his returning soon?*

The answer to all these questions was *I will call you back.*

One day, a curious envelope turned up on Oona's desk. It had been forwarded from the Metropolitan Toronto Reference Library.

Oona had been opening all the mail, as she normally did, and dealing with most of it herself. To one side, she kept an open file of letters that would require consultation with Kurtz before she could answer them. It was into this file that she was about to tip the curious envelope and its contents when she turned it over and saw the single word *Kurtz* in large black print—somewhat old-fashioned. It was not, however, stationery she had ever seen. A relative, perhaps.

She opened it. It had already been so long delayed, there might be good reason to telephone Kurtz immediately—a family death—a birth announcement—a wedding invitation...

No.

The pages inside were written in Kurtz's own hand. *A letter to himself?* Intriguing.

With no sense of guilt—Oona, after all, was the man's secretary and read more than ninety percent of his mail—she turned the pages onto her desk, flattened them—counted them—and began to scan them, one by one. There were seventeen pages in all.

We psychiatrists—she read—*must necessarily appear to the mentally ill as being in the nature of gods. We approach them with miracles up our sleeves. "Save us!" they cry—and we do...*

And: *...with a simple pill, we can exert a power for good that is practically unbounded...*

Here, the words *for good* had been excised with a single stroke, leaving the sentence bereft of decency.

Oona thought this odd—the writing of it—leaving such a sinister string of words on the page to be seen. And yet, the thought it contained was in keeping with the Kurtz she knew. The idea of exerting a kind of power *that is practically unbounded* was pretty well the way he functioned in other areas outside of science. It was certainly not the least bit at odds with the way he thought of himself as Director of the Parkin—its spokesman—its leader. But to write it down was to speak it aloud—to say: *I am God.*

Then she read—on another page:

I began this journey when I was young. All these many years, I have been on my way upstream—the stream of human endeavour. A man must go against the current until he reaches that point where the river rises—the point of absolute power. It is only by arriving at this point that one can then begin to place one's theories in the mix of things and float them back downstream to the mouth of the river, where others have been assembled to obey one's orders—to fulfil one's dreams.

Oona re-read this. *Absolute power?*

Now, she continued reading down the page and over onto the next.

This document will show the route by which I have risen through my profession to my current position, which gives me access to others with greater power...

Oona blinked. There was more, then, on the theme of access.

Access to the personal obsessions of the élite equals access to the pockets of the élite.

And then:

...psychiatry is my mode, psychiatric research is my delivery system...

Followed by the phrase:

Give them whatever they need.

The word *need* deleted. The word *desire* imposed. The whole sentence underlined.

And:

Under my guidance, they will soon enough become the willing addicts of desire.

Oona laid the document down. She could read no more of it. She sat back and folded the pages into their envelope—and set it farther off across her desk. A pariah.

Looking at it, she decided she could not have understood what she had read. If she did understand it, then Kurtz had penetrated farther up his *stream of human endeavour* than he himself had realized—and was lost very deep in the wilderness there. This, Oona could not yet bear to admit.

She would not return it to him. However unethical that decision might be, she could not countenance the prospect of Kurtz expanding on the content of these pages. They were gone from him. Let them stay gone. He was ill. He was incoherent. He was obsessive enough as it was. He was...

The word *dangerous* crossed her mind.

Or did she mean *endangered*?

She got up and went into the corridor. She took the letter with her.

She would show it to Bella Orenstein. She would see what Bella made of it. Maybe Oona was over-reacting. She hoped so. She wanted that to be the case. Perhaps it was all just day-dreaming *done up in notes and doodles*. That could be it. Kurtz was just speculating. Everyone does that. The words: *what if...?* It could be as simple as that. *What if I had a million dollars? What if I was a movie star? What if I ruled the world...?* Nothing more than that.

She descended two storeys in the elevator and went along over the marble already feeling better. Of course she had been wrong. Bella would prove it.

That, however, is not what happened.

When Bella had read the entire document—which took the whole morning—she met with Oona at Motley's Bar and Grill on Spadina Avenue and said to her: "did you read the bit about that pharmaceutical company offering him access to new drugs before experimentation and testing were complete?"

Oona shook her head. *Dear God.*

"Stuff he was passing on to Doctor Shelley? Her patients, in other words, unwittingly becoming the recipients of..."

"Don't tell me. Don't. I don't want to know that."

"Doctor Purvis did not kill himself for nothing, Oona."

Oona looked to one side and locked her mind against what she was hearing.

Bella said: "there's something in these notes you have to verify, Oona."

Oona turned. "All right," she said. "What is it?"

"He mentions someone here—a man named Smith Jones—who claims that sturnusemia is a hoax. Did Doctor Kurtz ever treat such a man?"

Oona sighed. At Kurtz's request, she had typed the transcript herself, instead of sending it down to *Sub Four*, as was normal.

"Yes," she said. "Only Smith Jones didn't say sturnusemia was a hoax. He said that what we had been told about it was a hoax."

"What happened to him?"

"Doctor Kurtz had him committed."

"Where?"

"Penetanguishene."

"But that's for the criminally insane," said Bella.

Oona shrugged. "That's where he is," she said. "And that's all I can tell you."

They drank their martinis.

"What will we do about it?" Oona finally asked—pushing at the envelope that sat between them.

"Leave it to me," said Bella. "I will think of something."

Returning from Motley's Bar and Grill, Bella hung up her summer coat in its hiding place in the otherwise empty closet and set her handbag down on top of her desk. She still, as always, wore her straw bowl hat and her white cotton gloves. Her small, round face was serene—the result not just of an extra double martini, but of having set her mind at peace with what she was about to do. She felt as kamikaze pilots must have felt when, drugged with zeal, they fell towards their enemies—or assassins—when they raise their guns and draw a bead on tyranny. *I will do this calmly,* she thought. *I won't even raise my voice.*

Not that she often raised her voice—but she had felt the urge increasingly as, page by page, she had read her way through what Kurtz had in mind for himself and for the Parkin.

She turned first to Austin Purvis's empty office. The door, as always now, stood open. No new tenant had yet been assigned—and the only things alive in its spacious emptiness were three of her African violets and the memory of Austin Purvis. *I will do this for you,* Bella vowed. And then she turned to her desk and picked up her handbag. Holding it by its handle tight in against her chest, she walked to Marlow's door and knocked.

"Come in."

He was with a patient Bella had forgotten was on the day-chart. This threw her—but only for a moment.

"I can wait," she said. "I beg your pardon."

The patient was a man named O'Hare, a large pale soul who had killed his mother when he was ten years old and had only recently been discharged from custody. Now forty-two, he was entirely apologetic—every

428

gesture self-deprecating: little bows and downcast eyes, his voice a mere whisper.

"Mr O'Hare is just leaving, Mrs Orenstein."

Bella stood to one side, allowing O'Hare to pass. He did so, turning to flatten himself in order not to brush her with so much as a draft. She heard him mutter: *good day,* and, when he had gone, she stepped all the way inside and closed the door behind her.

"Doctor Marlow," she said, "I have come upon a document which I believe you should read. In my opinion, it reveals a situation of life-and-death proportions..."

Marlow was watching her, amused.

"Mrs Orenstein," he said to her, "you are radiant."

It was true. She was shining with determination—and might have risen from the dead.

"Tell me what you have there," said Marlow.

Bella opened her handbag and withdrew the document in its envelope. "This," she said—and handed it over into Marlow's outstretched hand. Then she sat down and watched him as he read.

When he was finished, Marlow turned down the final page and closed his eyes.

At last, the tension broke.

"You believe these things?" he said.

"Yes, sir. I do."

Marlow said: "yes. And so do I."

Bella, barely aware of what she did, lowered her head and wept.

As Marlow passed her, making for the outer door, he paused just long enough to say: "you must take the rest of the afternoon off, Mrs Orenstein. In the morning, we will talk again. In the meantime, thank you for what you have done. You are very brave."

She heard him depart. She could even hear him walking away down the corridor. *Oh,* she thought. *It is almost over.*

She wiped her eyes and looked from the window. She felt, all at once, the relief an ant must feel in the shadow of a departing foot. The world might shake—but it would not end.

She stood up, after that, and went into Austin's office, where she watered the violets and closed the door.

14

Marlow left the Parkin and drove to The Citadel on Avenue Road. This gave him a good excuse to bring his rage to heel. He was basically fearful of driving—and needed to be calm in order to manage it. He put his car in the basement and rode up to Kurtz's floor.

What he found there was shocking. Shocking because it was Kurtz's palace—that fastidious, pristine world in which a person had once been able to see himself in every shining surface—all the glass cases lit from invisible sources—the famous ivory collection—the paintings—the grey-walled splendour—the black leather richness. Now—all this was a chaos of dust and disorder. Kurtz had pulled his world apart and was lying in the wreckage. Papers, notebooks, photographs, scientific journals, plates of uneaten food, glasses of undrunk wine, cups of tea and coffee, bowls of soup and silver spoons were strewn over every table and across the floor.

"Is it really you, Marlow?" Kurtz asked from his place on a sofa—propped up with linen pillows, his skin discoloured. He was now completely bald, and had not been able to shave for days. Speckles showed on the backs of his hands and his forehead. If they had spread to his chest Marlow could not tell. Kurtz was holding his high-necked robe shut tight, which gave an ecclesiastical impression—the look of a priest gone native in a nineteenth-century outpost of empire. He was also feverish, and smelled of stale breath and medicine. The doctor in Marlow surfaced at once.

"Why the hell aren't you in a hospital?" he said. "How long has this been going on?"

"I haven't any idea," said Kurtz. "And I couldn't care less. I'm dying. That's what's happening here."

Marlow crossed over and laid his hand above Kurtz's forehead. The heat could be felt a foot away.

He went into the kitchen and came back with water.

"I don't want water. I don't want anything. I want to talk."

"You're dehydrated," Marlow told him. "I insist."

Grudgingly, Kurtz allowed the glass to be held to his lips. Marlow, bare-handed, lifted the dying man's head from the pillow.

"There," he said. His fingers tingled—the skin beneath them was hot. He had not before touched a victim of the plague and a strange exhilaration took him, as it would if he were tempting fate by reaching out to touch a sleeping tiger. What did the Yellow Guide Book tell you? Not to touch without rubber gloves. They had said that, too, about

AIDS—and had been wrong. *Don't touch. Don't move. Don't breathe.* They might as well have said: *be dead and be done with it.*

Well, Marlow thought, as he stepped away, *I am living in the real world, now.* There was Kurtz in the flesh, and the long confrontation with rumour was over. The man was dying. This was death. But the evil he had done would not die with him.

Marlow said to him: "I have come to tell you what I know about what you've done."

"You must let me explain," said Kurtz.

"You can never explain it to me," said Marlow. "My mind can't take it in. What were they to you, those children involved with the Club of Men? Lab victims?"

"It was not the children I was interested in," said Kurtz. "They were not my responsibility."

"Whose responsibility were they, then?"

"Their own, Marlow," Kurtz said. "They knew what they were doing."

"They didn't know what *you* were doing!" said Marlow, flaring. "Damn it—you didn't even give them a chance to say *no.*" He looked away. Whatever madness had possessed Kurtz, it had no scientific name of which Marlow was aware. Amorality. Absence of conscience. *Megalomania*—that came closest in the psychiatric lexicon. But megalomania alone could hardly explain the whole of Kurtz. Something else was needed that had not yet been defined.

"None of these children was forced," Kurtz said, staring up at the ceiling. "That was the beauty of it, Marlow. Every single one of them was persuaded from within."

"Taken over by drugs, no doubt."

"Taken over by greed, Marlow. If drugs were part of it, they craved them. But the drugs were the least of it. They craved their fathers, too. They craved their attention—their approval. I saw that with my own eyes."

"You watched?" said Marlow. Nothing in the files had told him this.

"Once, I watched. Yes. Only once. Otherwise I saw the photographs. They held no interest for me. The activity itself was puerile. My only interest lay in bringing two desiring factions together. I melded them. I made them one."

He might as well have said the plague and its victims had sought one another out.

"How was it made to happen? Tell me," said Marlow. "Don't lie. Stop lying. Tell me."

"Docility," said Kurtz. He was smiling. "Whatever cannot be enticed—whatever cannot be forced, Marlow, is locked behind a barrier of will. You know that. Sometimes, the will can be purchased—bought. Sometimes it can be bent by force. But when all else fails, the will must be broken. And drugs will break it." Kurtz took a painful breath. "Before you can give up caring what happens to your body, you must give up caring what happens to your mind—your spirit—your being. And I discovered—Shelley discovered—we each discovered that all these things can be eradicated by drugs. Once you accomplish this, the body follows..."

Marlow said: "these drugs—what were they? Nothing I've ever heard of will create that kind of zombie—unless it was something that backfired. But nothing deliberately manufactured." He was leading Kurtz, now. He wanted him to volunteer the information. He wanted him to say it without prompting. "What sort of drug was it? Where did it come from?"

"I got it by chance," said Kurtz. "It fell into my hands by chance..." He named the same pharmaceutical company already familiar to Marlow from his reading of the document. He told of how, in conversation with one of their biochemists, he had heard of an experiment in behalf of *pliancy*—a word that came close enough to *docility* to catch his interest. And then of how, some months later, the biochemist had come to Kurtz and offered him the drug, which then had not received human testing. The experiment, in the biochemist's words, was *controversial—iffy...* Kurtz had spoken to Shelley. Shelley had said *yes*. Stage one—stage two—stage three had been conducted under her guidance. And then...

There was the Club of Men—and their desires.

As Marlow listened, his anger rose to the point where he feared he would do Kurtz harm if he heard any more. But he had to hear it. He had to know. Not to know would be unforgivable.

And so it was that he walked away and turned his back so as not to see Kurtz tell the rest. About the first experience of administering the drug, which now had a *drawing-board name—a blueprint name,* as Kurtz explained. It was called *Obedion*—a name so crassly descriptive that Marlow almost laughed when he heard it. *Obedion*—a small yellow capsule. *Yellow.* What other colour might a person expect it to be, in this age of yellow D-Squads, yellow D-Spray and yellow tanker trucks? *Obedion 1. Obedion 2. Obedion 3.* All the way from: *do you want to take my picture* to *do you want to kill me now?*

"George? George Shapiro?"

"He died." Kurtz's voice had a drifting quality to it, now.

"No. He was slaughtered—sacrificed. Damn you," said Marlow.

"Don't damn me. Damn Robert Ireland. Damn Shapiro. It was their desire for George that killed him."

"But you unleashed them."

Kurtz was silent.

And then, as if nothing at all had been said of George, as if nothing at all had been said of slaughter, Kurtz said: "I had immense plans. I was on the threshold of great things..."

Marlow said: "were Eleanor Farjeon's children—her brood—were they the result of this scheme—this Obedion programme?"

"Eleanor Farjeon's children," Kurtz said dreamily—barely raising his voice, "were killed in an accident with their father..."

Marlow turned and stared at him.

What an apt description Kurtz had given of the brood. And the brood dismissed with a wave of Kurtz's speckled hand, even though they were clearly the progeny of Kurtz and Shelley's druggings. Of the drugs provided by a renegade pharmaceutical company anxious to jump the gun and gain the market. The brood had served a purpose—and now they were gone.

Kurtz's voice went on with its whispers—the voice itself an explorer lost in the wilderness to which its owner had led it, saying: *speak from here.* Out beyond the bounds of permitted aspirations. *Tell it from here.* Kurtz had cut himself loose from reality—from the strictures of reality. *That is where,* Marlow thought, *the absolute exercise of absolute power puts you.* Not beyond reality itself, but beyond the awareness of it. Even knowing it could not be so, Kurtz had played the government's hand in the sturnusemia scandal. Having rid the world of Smith Jones, he had played five aces and got away with it. Start a silence—end with one. Even if it kills you.

Now, as Kurtz continued to speak, Marlow wandered to the windows, which showed the city spread out before him in yellow light. What was the point, any more, of anger—of rage? The word *desolation* moved over him. What Kurtz was saying—his *apologia* for the darkness he had engendered—could not be accounted for within reason. Where had reason gone—and humankind—humanity? All Marlow felt was despair, augmented by the view before him—a set design for a nightmare. A dozen fires or more had been lit in the parks as dusk was falling—and the smoke that rose from them clouded the last of the faltering sunlight. Dead birds afire in great swept piles of fallen detritus, the way that leaves once burned. Filter down, go back into nature where you were. *All life,* Marlow thought, *now ends in fire.*

If life is what we have.

Kurtz was saying: "I will get well. There are ways of beating this..." He would recover. He would return to his work. He would give the future back to the present; it would be his gift to his society.

"I had other ideas," he said. "Other projects. Schemes. Doctor Shelley was already halfway there with one of them. My *Sleep Project.* New people rising from the old, Marlow. We were almost there!" Kurtz now tried to lift himself. "But we have to pay for it. Pay for it..." He attempted an expansive gesture. "It's a business proposition, Marlow," he said. "The future is a business proposition..."

Marlow turned away and looked at his feet.

A business proposition.

"I gave them what they wanted," said Kurtz. "I gave them permission."

Permission.

"That was the source of my power, you see. I went to them for money. They came to me for permission. We made a pact—a fair exchange. The Parkin got its new wing—I got my research funds—and they got..."

"Their children."

"They got what they wanted, Marlow. They got what they required."

It went on. He got up. He moved from sofa to chair. He spoke of the present as being a *long dead civilization*—the stuff of dreams for archaeologists to ponder. *It is all changed now,* he said. *There will be a new social contract,* he said. *All those fires beyond the windows...* he said. *There is nothing down there for us, Marlow. Not any longer. Go out and light more fires. If everyone did that, we would have the stuff of a new world ready for the making...*

Ashes.

Yes. He believed in ashes. He believed in burning down minds and memories—turning them into ash. *Out of ashes—miracles,* he said. He spoke of Maynard Berry and the reconstructed victims of fire. He reminded Marlow there was no such thing as a restored human being—*not in mind—not in body—there is no restoration, there is only renovation. Only something new.*

Marlow could not abide what Kurtz was saying—but equally, he recognized the futility of trying to make the man see what he had done. Kurtz could only see the gestures of it, now—the words that described it, but not the thing itself. All along, it now seemed, Kurtz had been standing in front of his beloved triptych, watching Slade's horror unfold in perfect order—the savage men—the feeding white dogs—the severed heads high up on their poles.

"Why?" Marlow said, at last. "Tell me why."

Kurtz had gone to stand in the doorway to his solarium. He was soaking wet—melting, so it seemed. He looked at the speckled backs of his hands.

"When I was a boy," he said, "at school..."

Nothing became of the sentence. It drifted into silence.

Marlow waited.

Kurtz said: "I wanted..."

Silence.

And then: "...I wanted not to be me."

Marlow bowed his head.

"Anyone but me," said Kurtz. "I wanted to be..."

After a moment more, he said: "...my father."

And then, turning back to gaze at the fading rooms behind him: "...and my intended, what of her?"

Silence.

The word *Fabiana* hovered and faded.

It was getting dark.

Marlow said: "let me help you lie down."

He drew Kurtz over to the sofa and lowered him onto the pillows. He drew the sheet there up to Kurtz's chin—Kurtz shivering—afraid to close his eyes. He stared up hard at the ceiling. Marlow waited, looking down.

"Don't malign me, Marlow." Kurtz said. "I'm a scientist. So are you. We should not malign one another. We should not distort one another's visions. I wanted something. It was within my grasp. Until Austin pulled the trigger, and it all began to unravel. Don't malign me, Marlow. Don't misinterpret me... Don't. I was not an evil man. Just lost."

Whether lost or found, Marlow wondered how it would be possible to misinterpret Kurtz.

"Goodbye," he said.

Kurtz did not answer.

"You want me to turn on some lights before I go?"

"No. Thank you. No..."

Kurtz was immobile. Marlow could just barely see him in the flickering lights of the yellow fires beyond the windows.

"Leave the door unlocked," said Kurtz. "I don't want it broken down when they come in the morning."

After a moment, he said: "are you there, Charlie?"

No. Marlow was on the other side of the door and moving towards the elevators.

In the morning, the D-Squad would come and find him. Marlow would send them. Kurtz would become the property of fire. This was how it always ended, now.

15

The Fabiana Gallery was closed. An exhibition was being mounted. Lillianne Tanaka was seated at her desk with a number of posters and flyers rolled up and stacked beside her. She had already spent two days on the telephone, encouraging patrons and cajoling the press to take an interest and pay attention.

Fabiana wore black trousers and a black silk shirt and had thrown a black shawl around her shoulders. She wore no make-up. Her skin was blue with fatigue. "This is my mourning, Charlie," she said. "My sign that he was here."

Marlow walked with her through the empty rooms. This was the afternoon of the day on which Kurtz had died—had been discovered dead in his apartment. The long oak planks of the floor creaked beneath them as they went from station to station of Fabiana's refusal to be still.

"You loved him?"

"Yes."

This answer was so simple—so direct—it seemed inadequate.

Someone had loved him.

Don't ask why.

"He offered me, once, the whole of his life," Fabiana said, as they moved towards the three tall windows that broached the street. Across the road, the Victorian mansions sat in the blinkered splendour of their canvas awnings. Nothing of the sun could reach their depths. Yet still it poured its light at Fabiana's feet. No awnings for her—or blinds or curtains. Not, at any rate, in the world through which her body moved. Marlow thought the truth must be otherwise in her mind, in her spirit. Something was hidden there—shaded by Kurtz's shadow—protected—not allowed the light of day.

"When was that?" Marlow asked. "The offer of his life."

"Before I married Jimmy Holbach." Fabiana paused to run her finger across the glass of the right-hand panel of the window-triptych. "When we were young."

"I must admit," Marlow said, "it is hard to imagine Kurtz as ever having been young."

Fabiana moved to the central window. Her hand fell back from the glass. "In a way," she said, "you are right. He never really was a boy—he never really seemed to be a young man. He was always striving to be other than he was—taller—thinner—darker. Older." She smiled. "He even wore suits when he attended university. Always, always grey..."

A large, dark car came along the street—turned at the end by the park and drove away again towards Avenue Road.

"No one ever believes it's a dead-end street," said Fabiana. "The signs all say so—but no one believes."

She moved to the final stand of glass. The windows were so tall they all but reached the ceiling—and the ceiling rose twelve feet above the floor.

"This was a whorehouse, once," Fabiana said. "A high-class bordello. What do you think of that, Charlie?"

"I think it has found a better profession. Vibrant still—but less demeaning."

Fabiana, at last, was still. Facing the window and away from Marlow, she said to him: "you were with him when he died?"

"No. He died in the night. I left him in the evening."

"I see." And then, as though to herself: "he died in the night, as befitted him."

"Possibly."

"Why did he go there, Charlie? Off into the dark. What was he doing in there?"

Marlow refrained from the absolute truth. That would have been too stark. Instead, he said: "I think he was lost."

Fabiana said: "You should have known him before all this—before the last ten years of his life. I remember a man caught up in the science of what he did—the adventure of science. I remember a vibrant man. A living man."

"But you turned him down."

"Yes. For Jimmy Holbach. Who also went away into the dark. I must be some kind of beacon to these people, Charlie. I mean, in the negative sense. A source of reflection—not of light."

"I doubt it."

"Rupert came to be monumentally unhappy. In time. Did you know his father?"

"No."

"His father watched his son from a distance. From a great way off, in the world of impossible demands. That, I think, is what set Rupert off on the wrong track. He wanted to please his father—not himself. He wanted to fulfil his father's dream—not his own. He wanted to best a man who could not be bested. Not because Kurtz-the-father was better, but because he could not bear his son's success. No success was going to outdo his own. *More, more,* he kept saying. *I want to see more. Run until you drop. Run until you die. I will not be bested.* His criterion, of course, was money—not achievement. In the end, he simply laughed at Rupert's efforts. Laughed at them, and died still laughing. Mocking. A multiple millionaire. All of it left, of course, to a mistress. None of it to his son."

Marlow wondered why anyone would love such a father. In a way, Fabiana answered him.

"You know," she said, "my father wanted nothing of me. Nothing *of* me—nothing *for* me. He simply stepped aside and let me through. I used to envy Rupert his father—his watchful, demanding father. I actually used to envy him that."

"Yes."

"May we step outside?" said Fabiana. "I need to be in the air."

"Of course."

They left the gallery and went down the steps and turned towards the park. They moved to its wrought iron fence and went through its gate. They walked on the path beneath the oak trees. For fifteen minutes, they did not speak.

Marlow noted the oversprayed, dying giants that spread their branches still above the grass and the benches there. It was such a little park—tiny, almost—perfect in its way. An absolute haven of peace and quiet.

On the grass, where there should have been birds, a Moonman had dropped his silver glove, which Marlow retrieved.

Fabiana sat on one of the benches. She gazed up into the sky beyond the thinning branches. *"Memento mori,"* she said. "Even the sky is dying."

Marlow sat beside her and looked at the glove, which he laid across his knee. "We are still here," he said.

Fabiana turned to look at him.

"Is it wrong that I loved him, Charlie?"

Marlow closed his eyes and looked away. It was unbearable.

"It is never wrong to love," he said. *So long as you know what love is*—which he did not say.

"Did he mention me, Charlie?"

Marlow looked down at the glove. Silver—left-handed. Sinister.

"Yes," he said. "He wanted me to tell you he was sorry."

"Thank you."

This way, he thought, *we write each other's lives—by means of fictions. Sustaining fictions. Uplifting fictions. Lies. This way, we lead one another toward survival. This way we point the way to darkness—saying:* come with me into the light.

Marlow placed the silver glove on his left hand.

We all could be Moonmen, he thought. *My hand in this glove—a perfect fit. Kurtz, too, in all of us. All of us in Kurtz.*

He removed the glove. *Not mine. Someone else's...*

He put it in his pocket. *There.*

Fabiana got up then, and began to move towards the gate. Marlow followed.

"I've been seeing more of Emma," Fabiana said. She took Marlow's arm. "You should, too."

One.

"Will you come and see me, Charlie? Often."

"Yes."

Two.

They stepped through the gate and closed it.

Fabiana took a deep breath—and exhaled it. Marlow could see the colour returning to her cheeks.

"Will you come back in?" she said, when they got to the steps.

Marlow said: *no.* He thanked her and began to walk towards his car. They had work to do: Fabiana, to unveil the talents of a prodigy—Marlow, to seek out Doctor Shelley and confront her and then, one by one, the members of the Club of Men.

Three.

Numbers may not be infinite. They do, however, he decided, have a way of proceeding in order—and of ending somewhere other than darkness.

16

Fagan had written. Lilah held the letter to her heart before she opened it.

Standing by her mother's bureau, she looked up into the mirror. There she was, with her butterfly's wing of a face all white—and there were Fagan's initials and her own cut into the glass.

> *Dear Miss Kemp,* he wrote, *I thought you might want the enclosed for your copy of Mister Conrad's book, remembering that you had pasted my earlier thoughts about it between the covers. What a great pleasure it was to see you again and to bask, if only briefly, in your affectionate regard. I trust this will find you thriving and emerging from your time of trouble.*
> *Yours most sincerely,*
> *Nicholas Fagan.*

Folded neatly into the letter was a printed passage cut from *Granta,* the magazine in which the passage had first appeared as part of an essay entitled *Conrad, Kurtz and Marlow: Journeymen in Darkness.*

Lilah went to Marlow's kitchen and stood in the sunlight. Marlow was sitting at the table, exhausted, drinking a glass of Ricard.

Lilah said: "Kurtz is dead."

Marlow said: "yes. I know."

For a moment, they were silent together—one seated, one standing. There was nothing more to say.

Lilah went back to her room and lifted *Heart of Darkness* from its shelf. She looked at page 92, then on to 93—and smiled.

Kurtz had gone back in.

She read through the words and saw Marlow finding him.

He rose, unsteady, long, pale, indistinct, like a vapour exhaled by the earth...

At last, she was ready to close the book. But before she did, she looked at what Fagan had sent her.

This is what it said—which Lilah heard as if Fagan spoke:

> Every Kurtz must have his Marlow—and Marlow will always come to take Kurtz home. It is a mark of our respect for those who lead us into darkness that we bring them back for burial, pay their debts and console their loved ones with lies. This process is played out over and over—and with every journey up the river, we discover that Kurtz has penetrated just a little farther than his counterparts before him. Poor old Marlow! Every time he heads upstream, he is obliged to a longer journey, through darker mysteries. Well, we might wonder, why does he always agree to go? For myself, I would guess it is because he is beholden to Kurtz for having provided him, after darkness, with a way to find new light.

Out in the passageway, Grendel barked at the cellar door. The beast down there was beginning to gain its identity—turning and rising in Lilah's direction. She held Peter Rabbit's shoes very tightly in her hand. Later on, she would fold them and roll them in their tissue paper. *Thank you.*

She looked askance at her vial of tablets. Infratil. *Time to go back to these. And to Modecate.*

She sat on her bed with *Heart of Darkness* beside her.

Who would believe it?

No one.

Not even Marlow, himself, out in his kitchen.

It's only a book, they would say. *That's all it is. A story. Just a story.*